THE SHE-KING: BOOK THREE

SOVEREIGN OF STARS

LIBBIE HAWKER

Cover design: Running Rabbit Press
Cover art: Joelle Douglas

Running Rabbit Press
Seattle, WA

ALSO BY THIS AUTHOR

THE SHE-KING SERIES
The Sekhmet Bed: Book One
The Crook and Flail: Book Two
The Bull of Min: Book Four

TIDEWATER
A Novel of Pocahontas and the Jamestown Colony

BAPTISM FOR THE DEAD

DAUGHTER OF SAND AND STONE
A Novel of Empress Zenobia
(Forthcoming, 2015)

CONTENTS

CHAPTER ONE.....13
CHAPTER TWO.....23
CHAPTER THREE.....29
CHAPTER FOUR.....39
CHAPTER FIVE.....49
CHAPTER SIX.....55
CHAPTER SEVEN.....61
CHAPTER EIGHT.....67
CHAPTER NINE.....75
CHAPTER TEN.....85
CHAPTER ELEVEN.....97
CHAPTER TWELVE.....105
CHAPTER THIRTEEN.....113
CHAPTER FOURTEEN.....123
CHAPTER FIFTEEN.....131
CHAPTER SIXTEEN.....139
CHAPTER SEVENTEEN.....151
CHAPTER EIGHTEEN.....163
CHAPTER NINETEEN.....173
CHAPTER TWENTY.....183
CHAPTER TWENTY-ONE.....195
CHAPTER TWENTY-TWO.....203
CHAPTER TWENTY-THREE.....211
CHAPTER TWENTY-FOUR.....225
CHAPTER TWENTY-FIVE.....237
CHAPTER TWENTY-SIX.....249
CHAPTER TWENTY-SEVEN.....259
CHAPTER TWENTY-EIGHT.....265
CHAPTER TWENTY-NINE.....275
CHAPTER THIRTY.....281
CHAPTER THIRTY-ONE.....289
CHAPTER THIRTY-TWO.....295
CHAPTER THIRTY-THREE.....301
CHAPTER THIRTY-FOUR.....307
CHAPTER THIRTY-FIVE.....313

Historical Notes.....319
Notes on the Language Used.....323
Glossary.....325
Acknowledgments.....327
About the Author.....329

THE SHE-KING: BOOK THREE

SOVEREIGN
OF STARS

Behold, Amun: I make offerings unto thee; I prostrate myself before thee; I bestow the Black Land and the Red Land upon my daughter, King of Upper and Lower Egypt, Maatkare, living eternally, as thou hast done for me. ... Thou hast transmitted the world into her power; thou hast chosen her as King.

-Inscription at Ipet-Isut by Thutmose the First, third king of the Eighteenth Dynasty.

PART ONE

THE GOD'S WRATH

1483 B.C.E.

CHAPTER ONE

SENENMUT WATCHED FROM THE SHADE of the royal canopy as the last known enemy of his king left Waset forever.

The fine ship cleared the calm waters of the harbor and rocked gently as it settled into the deep, confident current of the river Iteru. Broad across its beam, its hull painted the bright turquoise of a Shemu sky, its gilded rails glinting in the sun, the ship was as beautiful a vessel as any great lady could desire. But Mutnofret stood stiffly at the rail, ignoring the musicians who struck up a jaunty traveling tune, the servants who bowed at her elbow offering jars of cooled wine and beer. The ship pulled farther away and Mutnofret's stare vanished, the piercing, helpless ferocity of those tragic black eyes fading from view with the Amun-blessed distance, though the lady kept her face turned toward Waset – toward the king – for as long as Senenmut watched, until at last the boat grew too small and blurry for him to make out anything more than the sparkle of the sun on its rails.

He shifted the slight, dear weight of his burden: the king's infant daughter, Neferure, sleeping contentedly upon his shoulder. He had not realized the tension he had carried in his own body until now, when it drained away like water into thirsty sand. He sighed with the relief of it, and turned his eyes to the king.

Hatshepsut remained motionless, staring after the ship, her body rigid with the quivering wariness of a cobra poised to strike. Beside her the Great Lady Ahmose, King's Mother and one-time God's Wife of Amun, gazed unseeing into the yellow haze of the quayside, into the rising dust of dock-workers' feet, of children and dogs prowling between moorings for scraps of discarded fish and dropped crusts of bread. Her lined face wore an expression of tentative grief, a mild confusion of sorrow and solace. Beyond the King's Mother stood the ranks of guards in their short striped kilts, encircling the stone dais where the royal family now stood. The guards faced outward, alert and ready. They went everywhere now – everywhere the Pharaoh went.

An escort of guards was always a prudent measure beyond the palace walls, within the press and bustle of the city. The Pharaoh, after all, was nearly a living god, and one never knew when a crush of rekhet might surge toward her royal person, seeking to touch the hem of her kilt, her golden skin, seeking to take some small essence of her ka to their own hearts for the luck and prosperity it might bring them.

But so many soldiers were an excess. Hatshepsut had nothing to fear from the rekhet, Senenmut knew. The people still adored her, and would go on adoring her for as long as Senenmut could engineer it. Beer houses and rest houses continued to bubble with talk of the treasure the Good God herself had shared out amongst the people on the day of her coronation, two months past. Waset remained enamored enough with her generosity to overlook the fact that their Pharaoh was a woman. She had enriched them all, and so she was loved. For now, this was enough to hold her close to their hearts.

A crowd of sailors erupted into coarse shouts and Hatshepsut turned toward them with a twitch; the guards nearest the sailors clutched the hilts of their weapons. But in another moment it became clear the shouting was no more than an argument over some dockside matter – where to tie the lines, where to stack the cargo – and the royal contingent lapsed back into guarded peace.

Neferure made a noise at the interruption, a murmur of

sleepy complaint. Senenmut swayed unconsciously, soothing his charge. Of course, he thought, stroking the baby's back as one might calm a bristling cat, it was neither rekhet nor sailors the king feared. It was plotters, politicians, those who would take her power for their own. Those who would not balk at sending knives in the darkness, or poison in the wine. And he knew as he rocked the King's Daughter that Hatshepsut feared less for her own well-being than she did for those she loved. She would take any measure to ensure their safety. She would even banish her own kin.

"I did right," Hatshepsut said suddenly.

Ahmose turned a questioning look on the king.

"I did right by sending Mutnofret away." She said it as a declaration, as confident and regal as ever, though Senenmut saw the flicker of doubt in her eyes and knew she wanted reassurance. He was about to give it, but Ahmose laid a hand on her daughter's shoulder.

"You did," she said, a note of resignation in her voice.

"Will you miss her, Mother?"

Ahmose considered the question for a long while, weighing it, Senenmut thought, testing its heft and the heft of all its possible answers. At last she said quietly, "I have always missed my sister."

Young Thutmose, riding in his nurse's arms, began to writhe and squeal, pulling irritably at the blue wings of the small cloth Nemes crown tied about his head. It was midday and the little co-Pharaoh was hungry, no doubt, and had had all he could tolerate of this standing and gazing after ships. As the nurse struggled to soothe him, Neferure woke, stared a moment at her crying brother, and broke likewise into wails.

Hatshepsut laughed. It was the first merriment Senenmut had seen in her for days. The light of it shone in her eyes.

"My little ones say it is time to go."

She raised a hand, casually imperious, to signal for the royal litters.

In the king's apartments they sank onto couches opposite one another, the wide ebony supper table crouching between them on its carven lion's paws. Senenmut was weary. Caring for Neferure drained his energy and often left him dull-hearted with sluggish, sleepy thoughts. The baby never allowed him more than two or three hours' sleep at a stretch. She would wake squalling, and often even the breast of her wet nurse could not soothe her in the darkness. She would settle again only in the arms of her steward and guardian, the one the Good God had appointed to watch over her. He would hum to her, lullabies or tavern songs, anything that came to him in the daze of interrupted sleep. Sometimes he would simply talk, carrying on a one-sided conversation about any stray idea that wandered into his tired heart – the health of the temple's sacred cattle herd, the details of quarrying blocks for the new monuments – as though the tiny girl were a fellow steward or a wise and attentive priest. But the sound of his voice sent her back to sleep as nothing else did, and Senenmut always took a small and secret pride in that fact. Though his duty was taxing, he would not trade it for any other.

Hatshepsut's women brought in the supper trays. Batiret, a slim brown girl still some years away from womanhood, bowed and showed her palms to her mistress while the others set the fare upon the table.

"I did not leave the food for a moment, Great Lady," Batiret said. It was the same litany she recited at the presentation of every meal, and yet she said it with a crispness to her voice, as though her words were fresh. "I stood by and watched as the cook prepared each dish in turn. I tasted each with my own tongue and waited an hour, and have no complaints. I broke the seal on the wine jar with my own hands and allowed no other near it. It, too, is pure."

"Good. We will eat, then, and I thank you as always, Batiret."

When the servants were gone Senenmut ladled a little of each dish into Hatshepsut's wide, shallow bowl, then into his own. Peas cooked in duck fat and herbs, doubtless plump and juicy when they came from the cook's pot, were now withered and gray, and the fat had congealed into thick lumps. Medallions of gazelle meat, once tender, now stood drying and crusting around the edges above a puddle of unappetizing sauce. He lifted a pottery dome from a platter to reveal white fish steamed in grape leaves, after the northern fashion. The steam had gathered on the inside of the dome; at his disturbance it rained down upon the soggy fish and their sad shroud of limp greenery in fat, cold drops.

"A feast," he said sardonically.

"Safe," she replied, and tucked into her meal.

Senenmut picked at his meat. He had never been overly fond of gazelle. It was worse when it was cold. "Where did you send her?"

"Mutnofret? I found a fine estate for her near Ankh-Tawy. A farm with a great house as pretty as a palace, with its own private lake and an olive orchard. It is far enough from the city to afford her plenty of privacy."

"Far enough from the city that she will meet no noblemen with whom she might conspire."

"I do think Mutnofret's conspiring days are over." She paused in her attentions to the cold gazelle. A thoughtful stillness settled over her features. "There have been moments when I have thought myself cruel to send her away now. Thutmose has been in his grave hardly two months. Was it just to remove her from the vicinity of her last son's tomb? I look at my own children, and I do not know if I did right."

"You said at the waterfront..."

She waved her supper knife, dismissing his words. "Yes, yes. I know what I said. It was right, in the end – to send her away, I mean. I only question my timing. I have no desire to be cruel. Mutnofret is my own kin, after all: my mother's sister, the mother of my dead husband, grandmother to my son."

17

"Your stepson," Senenmut corrected gently, quietly. Before Neferure arrived, he had never objected to Hatshepsut's motherly tendencies toward the boy. Somehow things were different now. Neferure was the child of her very body, after all, while Thutmose was the get of her despised and mercifully departed husband, conceived on a harem girl. But it would never do to refer to Iset as a mere harem girl – not where the king could hear. She was something more to Hatshepsut. Senenmut knew that. And so he must accept that Iset's son was something more, too, no matter how it galled him.

Hatshepsut went on as though she had not heard his interjection. "But Mutnofret plotted against me. She has always plotted against me. I cannot forget the way she brought her influence to bear on Waset, how she took my throne right from under me."

"You ceded the throne," he reminded her, not knowing where his impertinence came from. Perhaps it was the disappointment of the peas and sodden fish.

"To save Egypt from destruction," she replied, narrowing her eyes. "You are most foul-tempered tonight. You are not getting enough sleep."

"The King's Daughter won't allow it." He smiled to appease her, though he did not truly feel like smiling.

"At any rate, she was the last known agitator in my city, and she is gone from Waset now like the rest of them."

The king had moved swiftly, sussing out those who opposed her and propelling them up or down the Iteru to comfortable but distant banishments. Only time would tell whether the measure had increased or diminished her security on the throne.

"With your enemies confirmed gone, perhaps we might get back to hot suppers."

"My taster must have time to do her job. If you are displeased by the rate at which peas cool, take it up with the gods, not with me."

Senenmut scowled. "That child is too young to be a taster. If you believe some enemy or other will try to poison you again, why risk an innocent girl to find out?"

Hatshepsut lowered her eyes. "I know. I feel the same. I tried to discourage her, but she insisted. She all but begged for the honor of the duty."

"You are the king."

"Batiret has proven herself unusually loyal. I would give her whatever she asks of me."

"Loyal?"

"She chose to keep a secret rather than take it to my husband, or to Mutnofret, and profit by it." She held his eyes for a moment, sober and pale, and he nodded, biting his lip. "Besides," Hatshepsut went on, "the girl is at least as smart as you are, and twice as observant. Nothing slips past her notice."

"If nothing slips past her notice, then why not allow her to supervise the cooks and leave off the tasting duties? You could eat your food at the proper temperature once more. After months of cold peas and sauces turned to jellies, a bowl of hot broth would be as good as a festival."

"I am surrounded by enemies."

"You are not, Hatet. You said as much yourself moments ago." He stared at her resolute face helplessly. A sudden burning in his chest caught at his ka, a relentless tenderness for her, a fierce desperation to comfort her, though she was as far beyond his comfort as the moon was beyond the reach of his hands.

"I have managed to rout only the enemies I knew from my city. It's the enemies I cannot identify that keep me awake in the night. They are like shadows in darkness. I cannot see them, but I feel their chill. I know they are there."

"By the gods! You cannot live like this indefinitely. You'll make yourself mad. You have Nehesi and his guardsmen. You have me, for whatever that is worth. You even have the hearts of the rekhet; they love you! What more do you want?"

She did not answer for a long moment, but stared cold-eyed into the king's chambers, past arrangements of ebony tables, black granite statues of gods, through walls painted with chariots in battle and papyrus in bloom. She saw nothing that Senenmut could see. Then without warning her lips trembled, and she raised her hands to her face, pressed the heels of her palms hard against her eyes. Senenmut was beside her in an instant, dodging around their supper table, pulling her into his arms, rocking her the way he rocked her child.

"I want peace," she said in a strangled, plaintive voice – a small voice, high and childish.

She is only seventeen, he reminded himself. *Seventeen, and a woman, and the king.*

Hatshepsut reined herself in, gathered herself up. Her hands fell away from her face and it was calm once more. The only evidence of her loss of control was the light tremor in her chest, and the single tear that crept down her cheek. The tear was black with kohl. Senenmut smoothed it quickly away with his thumb.

"All I want is peace – that is all. I want safety. I want to know that no man will ever take from me someone I love – anything I love, including my throne. Yet how can I have peace now, knowing as I do how many men wait to tear me from my birthright? Ankhhor was not the only one – I am not naïve enough to think that he was the only one."

"No," Senenmut said. "You are not."

"It is only a matter of time before some enemy emerges again. Where is he now? Is he in my city? In my palace's own walls?"

"You will make yourself mad..."

"Then I shall be mad!"

"It is no way to live."

"*This* is no way to live." She waved her fist at the king's chambers, an arc that took in the gilding and faience, the fine furniture, the gentle whisper of cool air through the high, ornate wind-catchers. "And yet I love it. It is what the very gods bred me for. I cannot turn my back on it, any more than I can allow another to wrest it from me."

Silence fell heavy between them.

Hatshepsut jabbed at her cold peas with the point of her knife. "I wish sometimes that I had been born a rekhet. Then I could live how I please, without the gods' yoke around my neck. I could love whom I please."

Senenmut looked away from her, blushing, though there were no servants here to see. He went reluctantly back to his own couch and drained his wine cup. "No rekhet lives as he pleases. They all wish to be nobles."

"Then I wish I had been born a noble, or a priest."

He laughed. "The nobles and priests all wish to be the Pharaoh."

She smiled in spite of herself, and in another moment, quick as a leaping fish, she had snatched a green fig from the bowl on the table. She threw it at him hard. It would have smarted, had it connected with his forehead, but he caught it and bit into it. The flesh was grainy and still just shy of sweet.

"You are trying to start a war," he said around his mouthful.

The smile dissipated from her face with a curious slowness, as a water-fog disperses from the city streets on a winter morning, receding by increments, quiet and inevitable. It was replaced by a look of deep contemplation, her brows drawn together, eyes distant once more, but lighting moment by moment with the glow of revelation.

Senenmut swallowed the fig with great difficulty.

Chapter Two

T HEY DRIFTED OUT ONTO THE king's private lake, the clear waters lapping and gurgling against the hull of Hatshepsut's boat. It was a small replica of the great pleasure barges which plied the Iteru in the cool of the evening, carrying the wealthy from estate to estate, from feast to fancy, their decks ringing with music and flashes of color as dancers twirled for the delight of noblemen and ladies. Hatshepsut's barge was as brightly painted as any of its larger cousins, but it fit only two passengers beneath the red linen sunshade raised on gilded posts. It was a craft meant to facilitate private conversation, for while the palace bustled with servants and politicians, ambassadors and guardsmen, in the center of the king's lake there was none to overhear but the fishes and the flies.

Hatshepsut's women stood gathered on the shore, awaiting their mistress's return, growing smaller and more distant as Senenmut poled the small barge toward the center of the still, warm lake. The king reclined on a pile of cushions, trailing one hand in the water, smiling whenever one of the tame yellow carp rose to nibble at her fingers. With the ever-present eyes of the palace receding on the shore, he stared openly at Hatshepsut. Her smiles were thin and rare these days. It was a treasure as good as gold, to see her lose herself in the pleasure of the moment – even if that moment was brief.

Too soon, they reached the middle of the lake and she

gestured for him to stop. He laid the quant in the hull and joined her beneath the canopy. The shade of it was soothing, cool even in the windless afternoon, drowsily red.

Several days had passed since they had seen Mutnofret off, and Senenmut had been too busy with his duties to the King's Daughter to inquire into Hatshepsut's thoughts. But the way her smile had faded at their supper had remained with him, gnawing into his heart with a faint, distant worry. When she summoned him for a private discussion – matters of state, her messenger had said – he attended with both relief and trepidation, for he sensed that this evening she would make her intentions clear.

"I know how I will keep my throne," she declared when Senenmut was settled upon his cushions.

Your throne is not in danger, he wanted to tell her. But her words at their cold supper had remained in his heart, taunting him. *Ankhhor was not the only one. I am not naïve enough to think....* He remained silent, waiting.

She held up one hand in the red light of the canopy, fingers spread. "Egypt is a chariot, and I must hold three reins to drive it. Here..." with her other hand she indicated one space between her spread fingers, "and here..." she touched the next space, "and here. I am a fist." And she closed hers, held it steady in the space between them. "So long as I hold all three reins in my fist, no man will be able to stand against me, for then he will stand against all of the Two Lands.

"The first rein is the Amun priesthood. Amun is the king of the gods, and all other gods and all other priesthoods bow before him and before his servants. I have that rein. His name is Hapuseneb."

Senenmut nodded. "He is loyal to you; I am sure of it."

And why not? Hapuseneb was her own blood, if distantly so – his mother had been a harem woman under the reign of Hatshepsut's father; the woman was a cousin of Ahmose, which made Hapuseneb a cousin of sorts to Hatshepsut. Senenmut furrowed his brow, trying to visualize the complex web of family relations between the king and her new High

Priest of Amun. But it was not their somewhat diluted blood ties that had inspired Hatshepsut to raise her distant cousin to his high station. He had been the first in the crowd to proclaim her on that golden morning when she had appeared before her people in the regalia of the king, and raised the crook and flail before her bared breasts. Hapuseneb had not hesitated, and the Pharaoh had not forgotten.

"He risked his reputation – his very place amongst Amun's servants – to support me. Through him I hold the Amun priests, and through the Amun priests I hold the priests of every other temple, every other god.

"The second rein is the civil service."

Again Senenmut nodded. The nobles who were the merchants and other great men of Egypt – the architects, the scribes, the artisans, the land-owners – employed the rekhet and kept them fed. "What is the name of this rein?"

"Ineni. He is growing old, I know, but he is still influential amongst them, and very clever. He is loyal to me because he loves my mother; for her sake, he will hold to me, and will do whatever is necessary to hold the nobles to me."

"Well enough; I can believe such a thing of Ineni. He is a man of great influence, and he knows into which ears he should speak. That much is true."

"The third rein is the army."

Senenmut glanced at her face. She watched him levelly, a half-wary, half-triumphant light shining in her eyes.

"Nehesi?" Senenmut guessed.

"Nehesi is my man unto death; I have no doubt of that. But he is no rein upon the army's bit. He has little influence outside of Waset, and Egypt's army has a greater reach than the walls of my city. Nor could I make him my rein if I wanted to. Soldiers are not like nobles or priests. I cannot force them to revere a man, no matter how many titles or honors I heap upon him."

"Who, then?"

She lifted her chin, a familiar gesture that meant she knew his complaints were forthcoming, and that she would not suffer to hear them. "I must be the rein in my own hand, and win over the army myself."

"What?"

"I am going to war, Senenmut. This time I shall not fight with figs, I promise you."

"Win over the army yourself? You cannot mean to..."

"Ah, I can. How else do I bring them to me? For I must have them, Senenmut – all of them, generals and soldiers, each one. Would any man of Ankhhor's sort dare to stand against the entire army of the Two Lands?"

"Great Lady," he said, hoping the title would ingratiate him, hoping she would listen, "you are young, and inexperienced in battle."

"I rode my brother's chariot to save his men from the Kushites. I trampled them beneath my heel."

"That was one battle, and you were not in the thick of it. You have no training in warfare, strategy, combat..."

She waved a hand. "I am the son of Amun."

"Gods!" He threw up his hands, his stomach roiling with desperation.

"They will attack anyhow," she said coolly, dipping her fingers once more into the lake's placid waters. "The Kushites, or the Hittites, or the Heqa-Khasewet. Some tribe or other raises banners against Egypt whenever a new king comes to the throne; you know this, Senenmut. They have no doubt heard by now that my brother is dead and a new Pharaoh has taken his place. They are due at my borders, and they will arrive, as surely as the flood comes each year. I only propose to give them what they seek."

"You told me you wanted peace."

She raised her eyes to his. They were as dark and fierce as a falcon's eyes, the skin around them tight with rage. He drew back a little under the force of her glare, burrowing his elbows into his cushions as if he might physically retreat from her ferocity – though Senenmut knew it was not he who incited that stark, wild anger.

"And I will have it. I will not lose another one I love to a poisoner, nor to a knife in the dark, nor to any vile scheme invented by some loathsome man who sees me as nothing more than a girlchild, weak and disposable. I will not lose Neferure, nor Thutmose, nor my mother, nor a single one of my servants. I will not lose you, Senenmut. I will have peace." She raised her fist again. "And this is how I will have it."

Senenmut lapsed into uneasy silence. He watched the anger writhe across her face – anger at her own helplessness, at the impotence of her sex, the precarious way her very femininity made her teeter on the seat of her own great power. *If she finds no outlet for this rage, it will consume her. It will destroy her.* He would not see her destroyed – and yet going to war may do just that: destroy her, either in body or in ka. *I can do nothing to stop her. She is my lady, and my king.*

Reluctantly, Senenmut rose to his knees, bowed at the waist until his forehead touched the deck of her pleasure barge. It rocked gently in the rising evening breeze.

"Then it will be as you say, Majesty."

Chapter Three

THE WAR FLEET OF THE Pharaoh put ashore at Behdet, sending the tjati who ruled the ancient city in the king's name into a panic, for Hatshepsut had sent no word up the Iteru ahead of her ship's prow. As she progressed southward to the Kushite front, word would fly before her – of that she had no doubt. She could not contrive to moderate the gossip of fishermen and merchants, and so she must resign herself to an ever-decreasing advantage of surprise. She could not keep the cities along the Iteru's length unaware for long, but she hoped she might at least win the race against rumor to Kush's shores.

Behdet was her first port of call. It lay a day and a half south by fast ship, and the Pharaoh's fleet was nothing if not fast. While her sailors worked in groups, securing the lines that held *Amun Strides from Darkness* to Behdet's worn stone quay, she gazed down from her ship's rail on the furious bustle of the waterfront streets. Fruit- and fish-sellers scattered, sending their children home to fetch their mothers. Seamstresses and beer-brewers emerged from their shops, staring slack-jawed at the spectacle of the Waset fleet pulling into their humble harbor, the ships dropping their bright-colored sails, the oarsmen straining to hold each craft steady in the current until it, too, might pull to the quay and land alongside the glimmering brilliance of the king's own warship.

Beyond the eruption of running feet and frantic arm-waving in Behdet's nearest streets, the city stretched away from the riverside, low and dusty, to the center of town where the walls of the Horus temple stood tall and bright in the mid-day sun. Hatshepsut raised her palms toward the god's home, and toward the red stone form of the ancient step pyramid rising from the fields and orchards well beyond the temple, hazy and indistinct with distance.

Behdet was small now, but long ago it had been great: the seat of power of Upper Egypt, when the Two Lands had been two lands in truth, separate kingdoms at odds with one another, before the first Pharaoh Narmer had risen to unite them into the greatest empire the world had ever known.

Her men ran out a plank ramp for her feet. Nehesi preceded her down the ramp to the quay, and when none dared approach her hulk of a guardsman, Hatshepsut descended.

The tjati arrived, looking harassed and strained, in a chariot. "Majesty," he cried, dropping from its platform to kneel in the dust. "You honor Behdet. I apologize most humbly; the royal messengers did not reach me in time, and I had no word of your coming."

"I sent no messengers," she said, struggling to recall the tjati's name. Surely she knew it; the throne had its share of dealings with Behdet. "Goodman Khutawy, get up out of the dust. I wish to see your city's garrison."

Word scattered ahead of her in the form of boys running barefoot along Behdet's old, deep-rutted roads. Their side-locks waved like small black pennants; their loincloths were stained with the ocher dust of the city. She laughed as they sprinted like colts, striving to be the first to reach the garrison with news of the coming of the king. Behdet had no fine litters to carry her, and so she rode in the tjati's own chariot with Nehesi for a driver. He drove the horses at a walk and her people thronged behind her, the sailors shouting their joy, accepting dippers of beer from the city women, the soldiers chanting their marching songs. And her women walked among them, dressed in traveling tunics, simple gowns that were yet brighter and finer than anything worn in humble Behdet now that old king Narmer was so long in his tomb.

The day before she sailed from Waset, Hatshepsut had feasted her harem women. It was the custom whenever a Pharaoh departed that he should pay respect to his women, who were, after all, from important and ancient bloodlines themselves, many of them even gifts of goodwill from the kings of other nations – daughters of royalty. She had done her duty, bidding her friends farewell, expecting the matter to end at that. But Tabiry, the leader of her brother's small traveling harem, had leapt at the chance to take to the Iteru once more, and Tabiry's usual friends had agreed. "But I will have no use for women while I am at war," she had protested, confused by their eagerness. And Tabiry had said, "You will, Great Lady. You shall see." In the end, more women joined up than had been customary under the rule of Thutmose the Second, and Hatshepsut had set her stewards to scrambling for an extra ship that was fast enough to keep up with her war fleet. All told, fourteen harem women accompanied her to war. They felt a sisterhood with her, Tabiry had explained; they wanted to see their Pharaoh's victory with their own eyes, and contribute to her might in whatever way women could.

Now, as her retinue poured from her ships and made for the garrison, the women showed their worth. They danced and sang as they went, clapping their hands, rattling sesheshet high above their heads, twirling the skirts of their bright-dyed linens. And soon enough the pretty young daughters of Behdet's nobles broke from the crowds to follow them, evading the clutching hands of their mothers and ignoring their fathers' scowls. It must feel glamorous, Hatshepsut thought, watching the girls of Behdet take up the song, to do as the fine ladies of Waset did – these princesses from far-off lands, the pampered pets of the Pharaoh. But it was not Behdet's daughters who interested her most. For each girl surely had a handful of suitors, and as the sons of Behdet watched their pretty young lovers join the Pharaoh's ranks their faces grew thoughtful.

The barefooted boys who had run before her did their work well. By the time Hatshepsut reached the garrison, a collection of long, low buildings ringed by a simple, bare wall, the soldiery stood at attention in orderly ranks outside the walls, hide shields buckled to their forearms and each with a hand on the hilt of his sword. The general showed his palms when Nehesi drew rein.

"Majesty. An inspection?"

"Of a sort, General."

"You will find nothing lacking. Behdet is small, but she breeds good men. Here are the best in all of Egypt."

She walked through the ranks with the general, observing the strength of his soldiers' arms, the steadiness of their stances, while he recited numbers of troops and horses, described in detail his drills and training. At last she returned to the head of the ranks and looked up into the general's face. It was a broad, bluff face, full of honesty and intelligence. She had no doubt he would obey her. She only wondered whether he would do so gladly or grudgingly.

"It is good that your men are well prepared. I commend you."

The general gave a tight smile, lowered his head abruptly in acknowledgment of her praise.

"Well-trained men are useful to me now. I will take nine-tenths of your men with me."

He glanced at her face in surprise, then away again in quick deferment. "If I may be so bold as to ask, Majesty – where?"

"To Kush," she replied casually.

"Raids so soon? I had not heard."

"I will not wait for raids, General. For too many generations have kings sat by waiting for this enemy or that to rise up and challenge the throne. We have a new Pharaoh now, and she does not wait for her enemies to strike first."

The general barked a quick laugh. It reminded her, with a flash of pain, of her father. He had been a general once, before the gods had called him to the throne. He had been the greatest general in all Egypt, and the greatest king, too.

She felt a thrumming power deep inside her, rumbling below her heart, as if her nine kas shouted in chorus. She felt an undeniable confidence, looking upon this general and his orderly troops. Rank by rank, they were hers. She commanded them. She was the daughter of Thutmose the First; she was the son of Amun himself, and she commanded them all.

"Make your men ready to sail by this time tomorrow."

Her servants erected her tents in the fields beyond Behdet, in the shadow of the red pyramid. It was early in the season of Peret, the Emergence; the earth was black and deep and rich, just beginning to sprout with a thready new growth of weeds. Soon the farmers of Behdet would till the weeds into the soil, further enriching what the Iteru had already gifted them, and these fields would fill with barley and emmer, with flax and onions and the stalks of sweet roots. For now, her soldiers trampled the earth beneath hundreds of feet, and the field lay flat and dark in the sinking sun. The unbleached walls of the encampment's tents shone very bright in the glow of approaching evening, standing as they did tall and proud against the expanse of black earth.

She left Nehesi at her tent's door while she allowed the harem women to tend her, washing the dirt and sweat of travel from her body with soft cloths soaked in basins of cool water, scraping her dry with curved copper blades. A late golden light filtered through the smoke-hole at the tent's peaked roof; she sat in its beam while Keminub shaved the stubble from her head and massaged her scalp with a bracing oil of mint and juniper that made her skin prickle. Tabiry had been right. The women were useful already. They dressed her in a soldier's short white kilt and laid a marvelous pectoral of vulture's wings across her chest. It was heavy, but she liked the way it glimmered in the beam of light. She turned this way and that, gazing down at it, admiring its sparkle, and slowly she grew aware of a rising din outside, somewhere beyond the encampment. She glanced up and met Tabiry's eyes. The Medjay woman arched her brows; she had caught the sound, too. It was something more than the usual noise of a camp.

Nehesi clapped his hands at the tent door. She went to him, ducked outside and stood blinking at the distant line of the river, sparkling in the setting sun. A crowd of men advanced toward the camp. She could see the stark upward slashes of spears bristling from the body of the crowd, and here and there the sun fell upon hilt or blade of bronze; it flashed dull red against the uniform color of tanned skin and dust-stained kilts. For one heartbeat she thought perhaps Behdet was attacking. Then she caught the rise and fall of song and the occasional shout of boys' laughter.

Nehesi smiled wryly. "It seems your troops increase, Great Lady."

"Give me your sword belt, Nehesi."

He frowned. "I cannot defend you without my blades. What good will they do either of us on your hips?"

She laughed at Nehesi. "I need no protection from these men."

What a curious lightening in her chest. Her heart seemed to float, buoyed on a raft of confidence. She realized with growing awe that for the first time since Iset's death she felt strong and secure. The feeling warmed her deep in her middle, made her limbs feel pleasantly loose and energetic.

When Nehesi handed her his sword belt with stiff reluctance, she swung it about her hips and cinched it tight. It was heavy; it pulled at the knot of her kilt and made her sway a little as she walked. But she clapped her hands briskly and made for the pyramid at the edge of her camp, with Nehesi dogging her heels and her women trailing behind.

The old monument had been raised by some long-dead Pharaoh or other – Huni, she thought his name was, the second or third Pharaoh to reign after Narmer. It was not nearly so great as the mighty tombs of Khufu and his kin, far to the north. She had seen those massive pyramids once as a child and again as the Great Royal Wife, observing them in silent reverence from the rails of ships as the Iteru carried her north. Those were monuments to make the gods weep. The massive bulk of them, the precision of their symmetry, made them seem as permanent and enduring as the sun itself, even from the middle of the river, and she recalled gaping at them, disbelieving that there had ever been a time when the pyramids had not stood. Huni's redstone monument was less than a dwarf by comparison, the height of a few men only. But it would serve her purpose well enough.

She clambered up the first of its several steps and stood gazing down on the fields of Behdet. The city's young men were greeted with cheers by her own soldiers as they came into the camp. They kept marching through, directly toward her as if her kas whispered, *Come to me. Come and find your king*, and the men obeyed.

At last they stood in a ragged assembly at her feet, staring up at her in the simple white war kilt, a heavy belt laden with blades slung about her hips, the golden vulture's wings spread across her heart. She could feel the ancient slope of red stone rising at her back, drawing their eyes ever upward, across her, through her, with her into the sky where Amun-Re ruled. They ceased their songs and jesting; an expectant hush settled over the camp.

"My good men," she said, and though her youth and her sex pitched her voice high, still her words rang out clear and strong. "Never has a new king come to the throne in peace. Always the strength of Egypt is tested, by Kush or by Hatti, or by the Heqa-Khasewet. When my brother reigned as Horus, Kush picked at our southern towns for two years, as cringing dogs pick at bones. I tell you Kush will rise to plague us again. They are flies on a horse's hide – no more than that. But they thirst for Egyptian blood."

Voices swelled at her feet. *Never! They are dogs! Cowards hiding amongst their rocks!*

"I say this: if the Kushites want our blood, let us bring it

35

to them! Let us bring it still in our veins, still in our strong Egyptian hearts! Let them see how hot our blood runs. Let them feel Egypt fall upon them as Horus falls upon his prey, swift and sharp-taloned!"

She drew Nehesi's sword from its sheath and held it high. The camp erupted into cheers; the crude hunting spears and bludgeons of Behdet's youth raised alongside the fine bronze blades of her Waset soldiers. The roar of the cheering crowd settled into a rhythmic chant: the name she had chosen on her ascension to the throne, the only name by which her subjects might address her. *Maatkare! Maatkare!*

Nehesi lifted her down from the pyramid's step, and made the way through the crowd back toward her tent. "The men of Behdet are welcome at every cook fire," she told the stewards of her camp, shouting the command so that all might hear. "They are mine now; all my soldiers are brothers. Bring casks of wine from my ships and share it amongst my brothers equally."

Inside her tent she relinquished the blades to Nehesi while her women fussed over her bed. Night was falling outside; Tabiry struck the tent's small braziers alight. The smell of sweet oil and dark smoke enveloped the king.

"A fine show," Nehesi admitted. "Brewers' boys and farmers' whelps are often eager to prove themselves in battle, but you brought them running like loosed horses toward the stables. I've never seen men so ready to be shot full of Kushite arrows."

"I suppose it was the procession this morning that did the trick."

"You made them feel welcomed," Tabiry said, "and fierce. The last king never did as much for his men."

"The last king was a fool."

"Ah, Majesty; you will hear no argument from me."

Hatshepsut dismissed Nehesi and, when she had finished her supper of boiled eggs, melons, and wine from a jar unsealed by her own hands, she summoned harps and flutes to play for her. She lay on her cot drifting in and out of a strange, exultant half-dream in which she flew up to the sun on falcon's wings and dove like an arrow to strike at a strange, shadowy enemy whose face she could not see. Now and then a shout of *Maatkare* drew her back to bleary consciousness as outside the men celebrated around their fires. She was only partially aware of Tabiry and Keminub dismissing the musicians, tamping out the flames in the braziers, straightening the fine, light sheet over her body.

"Iset," she murmured, but the only answer was the din of her camp, celebrating its victories long before they were won.

CHAPTER FOUR

HATSHEPSUT ARRIVED ONCE MORE AT Egypt's southernmost fortress, deep in the sepat of Ta-Seti, as she had done a year ago when she had carried the tiny spark of Neferure in her womb. This time when she passed the thunderous cataracts spilling white froth between dark claws of stone she was not afraid. A year ago the journey had filled her with anxiety. Now, the roar of the water seemed to swell a great surge of rage and power within her heart, raising and spreading it as the demon wind spreads walls of sand in the desert.

The trek south had taken three weeks – longer than usual, for she had stopped in every city along the way to raise her troops and to inspire the courage and loyalty of Egypt's young men. At first she had maneuvered the same as she had done in Behdet, parading to the garrison in a show of vitality and pomp, then camping just outside each city with wine flowing freely and every cook fire ringing with camaraderie for new recruits.

But after a handful of days, word raced ahead of her ships, as she knew it would, and soon it was she who was greeted with parades, with soldiers turned out in their finest and generals boasting of their swelled ranks, of the boys who clamored to conscript themselves to Egypt's cause. By the time she reached Ta-Seti her fleet had more than doubled, sailing on a current of masculine fervor, the rails of the boats ringing with warriors' calls and the clangor of bronze.

Amidst Waset's fine war ships sailed the boats of fishermen and merchants, laden with soldiers. Their encampment filled the plain below Ta-Seti's fortress from hill to hill.

Now she stood on the walls of the fortress – *her* fortress, the one she had restored with her own riches, her first achievement as Great Royal Wife. The general Ramose detailed his strategy while she and Nehesi observed the camp growing across the plain below. She had sent three small, fast messenger boats up the Iteru ahead of her war fleet, carrying words for Ramose's ears only. They had reached Ta-Seti days before the Pharaoh, and Ramose was well prepared.

"I have kept my men monitoring the ravines since I received word from Your Majesty," the general said. "A few Kushite scouts have come near, but none survived to carry word home again."

"Good."

The plain where the fortress stood was separated from the settlements of Kush by a half-circle of steep hills. Four or five ravines cut through these hills, ancient stream beds, now dry, that afforded stealthy access to Kushite raiders.

"Nevertheless, they will learn of your presence here. We will not hold the advantage of surprise for long."

"I agree. And I tasked you with putting that advantage to good use."

"Ah, Majesty; I believe I have."

Ramose turned his back on the plain, looking down instead to the interior of the fortress. Hatshepsut followed his gaze. In the pale stone courtyards between barracks and stables, dozens of men worked in the hot sun, readying chariots, backing horses into their traces, strapping hard leather armor to one another's chests and backs.

"We move today," Ramose said. "Within the hour. The northernmost ravine leads to a village beyond the hills."

"Within the hour?" Nehesi shook his head. "Her men cannot move so soon. They have been aboard ships for days. They need time to sort their gear, to ready themselves."

"My men need no such time. Leave yours to prepare their

encampment, Majesty. By moonrise my captains will take yours in squadrons into the ravines. With such great numbers we can hold all the passages into Kush easily; they will have no access to this plain, nor to any of Ta-Seti's villages or farms. And we shall move freely between here and there."

"I shall find my own captains, and tell them what we intend."

"No time. Let me send a man into camp to spread the word. We must move quickly if we are to maintain our advantage."

Hatshepsut's body had never been lithe and curved like Iset's or Tabiry's. She was almost as straight and blocky as a man, and so Nehesi had no trouble choosing armor that fit her well. In the shade of the barracks she stood and allowed him to wrap about her a thick vest of layered linen hardened with linseed oil; it crossed over her breasts and was immediately stifling in the daytime heat. A sheen of sweat broke out on her bare belly and in the hollow of her lower back. He tied hardened leather breast- and backplates to her, fore and aft, until she felt as stiff and solid as a dung beetle. The plates were thin but quite rigid, and scarred from use by many of the fortress's soldiers. The leather smelled powerfully of horses and of men's sweat. The scent drove home the immediacy of the moment. *I am going into battle. Here and now. Bless me, Amun; protect your son.*

Nehesi belted her with a wide, soft band of linen. It soaked the sweat from her skin. To this belt he fastened a groin shield, a dense inverted teardrop of thick-braided flax stems, dried hard and tough. It hung to her knees.

"I haven't got much there to protect," she said, trying to laugh away her sudden anxiety.

"Ah, Lady, you have." Nehesi tapped his own thigh, high up near the knot of his kilt. "This vein, here. One nick to it and you'll bleed out like a butchered goat."

"I see." She turned away, trembling under the unaccustomed weight of her armor.

Most of the chariots were ready now; their drivers walked their teams in tight circles or allowed the horses to dance forward and back in the sun and dust of the bare courtyard.

Nehesi bent near her ear. "You do not need to ride into battle yourself, Great Lady. Let Ramose take the lead. You can stay here in the fortress and allow him to pledge his victory to your name when he returns."

"No; it will not do. I have come all this way to bind Ramose and all his men – and all the generals and all the soldiers in the Two Lands – to me."

Nehesi's face softened with something approaching genuine worry. "You don't even know how to use a spear."

"It seems a fairly simple concept."

He rumbled a laugh. "Ah, I suppose it is."

A collection of spears stood leaning against the barracks wall, ready for the soldiers' hands to take them up and carry them into battle. Nehesi sorted through them, testing the length and heft of a few before he settled on one and carried it to her. He showed her how to balance it for a thrust, where to place her hand.

"Don't grip it so tightly. You'll fatigue your arm."

She loosened her hand, made a few experimental thrusts at her shadow on the barracks wall.

"I have it, I think."

"You don't," he said, not unkindly. "No amount of practice can prepare you for battle, what it's truly like to face your enemy and kill him if you can."

She knew she blanched as she looked up at him; she could feel the blood drain from her face.

"Come along," he said, glancing past her, his voice suddenly cheery. "Your chariot is ready, Great Lady."

Hatshepsut was certain as they left the fortress that none of her men gathered on the plain knew it was she who rode into battle. There was nothing to declare the Pharaoh's presence to the casual observer – no banners, no gilding on her chariot, not even the blue war crown of royal tradition. She looked like any other soldier, gripping her spear with one hand and the chariot's rail with the other, swaying beside her driver, her head and neck shielded from the sun by a simple white cloth. She prayed the men nearest her – the men she now led toward the hills and the dark cleft of the ravine – could not see how her spear hand shook. Only her inexperience set her apart, but by the gods, what a great difference it made.

Ramose's face was imperturbable as his cart glided beside her own. He held his weapon with an easy confidence she knew she would never attain. His body shifted this way and that in an unconscious dance, absorbing the jolts and sways of travel. Their horses moved at a brisk walk toward the hills, and Hatshepsut watched Ramose grimly, silently, until at last he ordered his driver to draw rein at the mouth of the ravine.

Hatshepsut glanced back over her shoulder. The ranks of chariots slowed and milled in the grassy flat behind her. Far beyond, the fortress was a bar of pale light against the slight haze that demarcated the presence of the Iteru. Her camp's tents were as small as pebbles from this distance.

"The ravines are dangerous to traverse," Ramose said.

Nehesi, clutching the reins of Hatshepsut's chariot, eyed the ravine's floor. It angled sharply between two yellow cliff faces, bending into deep blue shadows. "The floor seems sandy enough. The rocks don't look so terrible."

"Ah, it's not the horses' legs we fear for." Ramose jerked his chin upward to where the cliffs rose above them, jagged and streaked here and there with dark desert varnish. "Kushites hide up there. My men have held this ravine for days, Majesty, and I have had no word that any raiders have overtaken them. Still, one can never tell with Kushites. They are fierce as demons and far cleverer."

Hatshepsut swallowed a mouthful of saliva. "And so?"

"And so we go quickly through, and hope that the cliffs are not full of enemy bowmen."

"Ah."

Ramose shrugged. "I believe we would have had word if our sentries had been displaced."

"You believe?" Nehesi said.

"Most likely."

He nodded to his driver, and the man hissed to the horses. They sprang into a run, rattling Ramose behind them, raising a wake of yellow sand.

"Amun's eyes," Nehesi muttered, and shouted to their own beasts.

Hatshepsut clung to the chariot's rail. The walls of the ravine closed around her immediately; they seemed to lean over her, and she felt the prickle of eyes watching from above, though whether they were Egyptian eyes or Kushite – or only the eyes of the cliffs, stony and impassive – she could not tell. For one brief moment she allowed herself to feel relief – it was cool in the ravine, almost cold, and the respite from the heat of sun and armor was welcome. Then her chariot jolted across a rut, and she lurched against Nehesi, righted herself on wobbling legs. The ravine walls shouted back at her with the tumult of their passage, magnifying it. It was a terrifying sound, and it drowned out her other senses. She was vaguely aware that she must keep her eyes sharp, must be alert for the sight of Kushites – but all she could do was hold tight to her chariot's rail and fight against the roaring in her ears that threatened to sweep her away like an unmanned boat down the cataracts.

They sped through the ravine. She was dizzied by the nearness of the walls, their rapid flight; she hunched beside Nehesi, cringing from the frightening way this chariot or that would overtake them and then fall back, blurring in and out of the deep blue shadow of cold stone like demons flickering around a brazier's weak light.

You are the daughter of Thutmose the First. You are the son of Amun.

She gulped in a deep breath, then another; her chest pressed painfully against her armor. She forced herself to straighten, forced her legs to steady. Her men would see her stand proud and unafraid – they would, by all the gods. She raised her spear above her head, and when she heard the men behind her shout in response a frail wave of gratification battered against her fear. It nearly managed to break through.

The ravine twisted this way and that; her horses leaned together in their harness, and she and Nehesi leaned with them, tilting their chariot to keep it on course. At last the cliff walls began to lower. She caught a flash of bright blue sky above, felt one quick buffet of heat as they passed through a patch of sun breaking over the hills to fall into the stream bed, then back into the dense coolness of shadow. Their passage straightened. She could see the far mouth of the ravine yawning upon the open sky, the green flush of new grass on the Kushite plain.

In that gap of revealed horizon, growing nearer and more real by the moment, a smudge rose vertically into the sky. Cook fires – the ovens of some small village, busily baking loaves of bread or simmering grain slurry for beer.

Gods. It's a village like any other, like any in Egypt. A village full of women and children, grandfathers and craftsmen.

Her heart quailed. She would have drawn rein then if she could, would have turned her troops around and ridden back to her side of the hills, packed up her encampment and sailed back to Waset in disgrace. But a wave of Egyptian chariots rolled behind her. They could not be stopped. Not now.

A loud *thunk* sounded from the vicinity of her knees. She glanced down the side of her chariot, stared dumbly at the short, fire-blackened shaft of an arrow vibrating above the wheel. She peered up into the ravine walls in time to see the dark forms of Kushites dodge from a cleft in the rock, loose a barrage of arrows down upon the Egyptian force. Instinctively she ducked, though she was beyond the path of the arrows now. She looked back to see shafts bury themselves in the sandy floor of the ravine, or stick in chariots' sides. She watched as one sank itself into the chest of a spearman. He fell backward, his mouth open in a howl she could not hear. The horses of the cart behind him trampled over his body.

"Amun!" she cried, her voice high and shrieking.

Beside her, Nehesi grunted in response.

They were nearly free of the ravine now, nearly upon the relative safety of the open plain. Ahead two troops of Kushites rose from behind ragged boulders that perched on either side of the ravine's lip. They seemed to move as slowly as lazy fish under water, raising their bows and aiming down upon her – upon the men who trusted her enough to follow her into this mad battle. She felt a scream rise in her throat, but before she could let it loose a high-pitched whistling sounded, and in the very instant the sound reached her ears an explosion of pain beat at her chest. Her left hand loosed its hold on the chariot's rail; she rocked back on her heels.

I'm falling, she said to herself, quietly, sensibly. *I'll fall and be trampled like that spearman.*

But Nehesi's thick dark hand closed on her wrist, jerked her upright, and she lurched forward to hang panting on the chariot's rail.

The ravine walls vanished. Re's blessed heat smashed into her body, pummeled her, screamed along her limbs. Freed from the confining walls, her force fanned out across the plain, and the deafening rattle of horses in flight receded. She became aware of a nearer sound, rumbling like the wheels of her chariot.

Nehesi was laughing.

He pulled her to her feet, steadied her. "You didn't drop your spear," he said. His face was strangely flushed. *Battle heat,* said a distant voice in her heart. *He loves this madness.*

She groped at her chest with her spear hand, awkwardly; her fingers were locked stiffly around the shaft. She had to coax them to loosen enough that she might probe one or two into her wound. The arrow protruded from the center of her breastplate.

I've been shot in the chest, she told herself in that same too-calm, too-sensible voice. *And now I shall die.*

Without looking round from his horses, Nehesi grabbed the arrow in his fist. Hatshepsut wailed wordlessly at him, fearful of the pain, but he yanked and it came free of her armor easily. She stared in horror at the hole in her breastplate, expecting blood to gush like wine from a cask. But none came, and she prodded a finger in tentatively, felt only the sturdy padding of her vest.

"Hah!" Nehesi tossed the arrow over the chariot's rail.

"How did you know I wasn't wounded?"

"No blood in your mouth."

"Amun's eyes – this is madness!"

"I *know*," Nehesi roared gleefully.

"They shot me!"

The Medjay laughed again, rasping and breathless. He pointed the horses' heads toward Ramose's chariot. The Kushite village was resolving now into distinct buildings – huts plastered with hard mud, the rounded lumps of ovens. She saw dim shapes move frantically between the houses.

"These dogs would have killed the Pharaoh!" she shouted, and gritted her teeth.

They overtook Ramose's chariot. The general stared at her levelly. *Are you ready?* his eyes seemed to say.

In response she lifted her spear again. The plain came alive with the shouts of Egyptian soldiers. Hatshepsut fell upon Kush with her talons outstretched.

CHAPTER FIVE

THE LANES BETWEEN THE LOW, mud-plastered houses were narrower than the ravine. There was hardly enough room for a careening chariot. People scattered, screaming; mothers dodged into the darkness of houses with children in their arms. Hatshepsut jabbed her spear toward the men she saw, who lurched out of doorways with blades in their hands, hacking at her as she passed. Many times she felt the shiver of her chariot as the edges of Kushite blades crashed upon it, reaching for her flesh. But Amun was merciful, and she remained unharmed.

The lane opened suddenly on a great courtyard. At the center was a communal well; a few scraggly trees sprouted from the hard earth around its mudbrick walls. A group of Kushite men gathered here, short swords raised before them, as Egyptian chariots spilled into the commons. They made for the men clustered around the well. Hatshepsut watched, quietly disengaged, her kas far away, as Egyptian spears cut down the Kushites with the swiftness of striking snakes. Soon the ground around the well was dark with bodies and blood.

All at once, Nehesi gave a hoarse cry and one hand left the reins. A dark, thin, fast-moving blur bounced off the haunch of one of their horses. Hatshepsut seized the rein with her rail hand before it could slither over the rail and fall amid the horses' pounding hooves. She returned the rein to Nehesi; his upper arm streamed blood.

"An arrow."

"Who shot it?"

She turned, tried to pick out the archer, but as they circled the commons all she could see was the dark shade of narrow lanes alternating with the sun-struck flanks of the houses. A slim form dropped from the flat of a roof into the commons, then darted into the nearest lane. The short dark curve of a horn bow was clutched in the man's hand.

"There!"

They gave chase. The streets were deserted now; the people of the village cringed inside their homes, hoping they would not be found. Ahead of them the bowman dodged around corners and through alleys; he was fast, and Nehesi was obliged to work the reins as deftly as a fisherman works his nets in a fast current. The horses roared deep in their throats as they responded to Nehesi's commands. The grating of their hooves on the packed earthen lane made a terrible sound, a dangerous rasp like a whetstone against a blade.

At last the Kushite slid into an alleyway too narrow for the chariot to follow. Hatshepsut leaped from the platform and gave chase. She heard Nehesi bellowing for her to stop; she ignored him, slipped between the two houses with the sound of the fleeing man's feet ringing in her ears.

The alley gave way to a tiny courtyard between four or five mudbrick homes. The courtyard was shaded by a small, wiry olive tree and by bright cloth canopies erected on poles. The man sprinted across the courtyard toward the door of one home. Hatshepsut could only presume that he thought he had lost the chariot in the village's lanes. He had not reckoned on its spearman following him to his own house.

She pelted after him, her temples pounding with her fury. The man was tired; his feet were slow now. She shouted something at him, some curse, or nonsense – just a cry of vengeance, of rage at the arrow that had stuck in her own chest, at Nehesi's bloodied arm. The man spun to face her nearly in the dark, open doorway of one of the low-roofed homes.

He was young – in truth, not much older than she. His

eyes were wide with fright. He had no blade, only his bow; he raised it toward her, nocked an arrow, though surely he could see that Hatshepsut would be within the range of the spear she carried before he could fire. Her heart worked calmly, calculating the distance, her speed, registering the terror in the man's eyes. Somehow his fear seemed to fuel her, as a breeze enrages a fire. She looked on him and thought of Ankhhor, of Iset dead in her arms. *You will die, that I might protect the ones I love,* she told him silently, and, as he aimed his bow at her face, she thrust her spear hard into his gut.

A hot spray fell upon her face, her hands. The man screamed, a terrible, grating sound, as he pitched backward with the force of her thrust. His arrow loosed over her shoulder.

She followed her thrust with her shoulder and back, just as Nehesi had shown her, and stood over him to reclaim the spear from his body.

Hatshepsut never knew what caused her to glance up then, into the doorway of the man's home. Some cruel god, no doubt, looking down on the scene with a cold, still heart.

A woman stood trembling, a baby no older than Neferure clutched in her arms. Her mouth was open with an anguished scream, but Hatshepsut never heard it. She did not know whether the roaring in her ears drowned out the sound, or whether the woman was too choked with the force of her grief for her voice to raise beyond her own chest.

Hatshepsut stared into the woman's eyes for one startled, pained moment. Then a rough hand seized her arm and she spun, raising her spear.

"Hold!"

It was Ramose.

Hatshepsut let her spear arm fall. Her whole body shook violently; she wanted to tear the armor from her and throw herself to the ground. She was unspeakably thirsty; her tongue felt thick and useless in her mouth.

Ramose took in the sight of the blood spattering her, glanced toward the dead bowman on the ground.

The woman had vanished from the doorway. *Thank the gods*

she is gone.

"Your first kill," Ramose said. He sounded as proud as a father.

Bile rose to the back of Hatshepsut's throat. She blinked rapidly, turned away from him. Was this not why she had come? To win the loyalty of her own army? *If I had been born male, I would not have to do this. It would be enough for me to wait on my throne while my men killed in my name.*

"Take his hand," Hatshepsut commanded. She felt relief when her voice did not shake.

She left Ramose bending over the man's arm with his knife drawn as she stumbled back to her chariot.

They had lost few Egyptians. Hatshepsut knew she ought to be proud of that fact, but her heart seemed able to do nothing but brood. She saw again and again the face of the woman in the doorway, and the babe clutched to her thin breast.

I have done a great evil today. And yet what else could she do? Allow her own children to fall victim to the same type of beast who had taken Iset from her? *You cannot have done evil,* she reasoned with herself. *Amun would have stopped you. If this had not been the god's will, you would not have succeeded.*

The Egyptian chariots made for the ravine, carrying the small treasures of their raid: sacks of grain and roots, jars of the sour beer Kushites preferred, a few bright pieces of cloth torn from the sunshades of courtyards and doorways. This had been only a small farming village. The material gains were slight, but through her pensive mood Hatshepsut saw that she had, after all, accomplished her goal. As their chariots passed hers, men raised their swords in salute to their Pharaoh, and cheered when they looked upon her blood-spattered face.

At the mouth of the ravine they were greeted by white kilts and head-cloths amongst the rocks. Her own forces had taken the whole length of it, driving the Kushite sentries away. Nehesi, his arm bound tightly in linen, drove the horses at an easy walk. The poor, brave beasts' heads drooped with weariness. The coldness of evening shadow sank deep, making the skin beneath her armor clammy. She pulled the head-cloth from her brow and used it to scrub the sweat and blood of battle from her forehead, her burning cheeks.

"You did well," Nehesi murmured.

Hatshepsut did not reply.

As night fell they gained the Egyptian plain. Nehesi escorted her to her tent; she stood quietly while the women washed her, hurried the basins of water from her presence so she would not have to see how the water was tinged pink with the blood of the Kushite bowman. Hatshepsut refused her supper and crept into her bed, shivering and silent, while across the camp the sound of celebration rang beneath the stars.

Not long after she had retired, she heard her women whispering. Two bodies slid into her bed, warm and gentle; hands caressed her shoulders, her back, brushed the tears from her face.

"I miss the children," Hatshepsut confessed in a voice barely louder than a sigh. She could not banish the image of the baby in the doorway, or its mother, from her thoughts. "Neferure – Thutmose. I want them."

"I know." It was Tabiry. Her voice in the darkness was soothing as balm.

"And Senenmut." *And Iset.*

"Yes," Tabiry said.

The woman lying at Hatshepsut's back threw a soft arm around her, pulled her tight against a comforting chest. "Weep, Great Lady. You are safe with us." She recognized the voice of Keminub, the soft-eyed, silly-hearted woman who had sighed like a little girl when Hatshepsut had come south to bed her brother. Her voice and her smell were warm and spicy, comforting.

"I killed a man."

"Ah, Great Lady."

"I never had before. Nebseny was different; he killed Iset. But that man – the Kushite – he was only trying to defend his family, his woman and his child."

They went on holding her in silence. Nearby in the camp a group of men burst into drunken song.

When Sinuhe came home
To the fair and green Black Land
Oh, the Pharaoh bent his knee to him,
When Sinuhe came home!

Tabiry dabbed tears from Hatshepsut's face with a corner of the linen sheet.

"I did not need to kill him. I did not need to follow him. I chased him down like a leopard after a gazelle. He was only one man – just a young father. His only sin was firing an arrow."

"He would have killed you, if he could have done so."

"Can I ever be who I was before, now that I have killed?"

"This is what it means to be Pharaoh. Your brother never understood, but you see it plainly."

"I do not want to be Pharaoh. Not anymore."

Tabiry chuckled like a mawat at a child's foolish declarations. Hatshepsut felt warm lips press against her forehead. "You do not mean that. I know it."

Hatshepsut lapsed once again into silence. *She is right.* For she could still feel her kas burning with a rage that cut through her shock and horror and grief. *No one will take my throne from me. It is mine. Amun gave it to me.*

This is what it means to be Pharaoh – to be the son of the god.

Chapter Six

HATSHEPSUT'S CHARIOT SWUNG ONTO THE main avenue of the cowering city at an undaunted trot. Above the rhythm of her horses' hooves she could hear Egyptian voices raised in cheers. Beyond the flat roofs of the mud-washed homes, the spindly dark point of a pyramid rose into the air, and about its peak billowed a cloud of dust shining in the mid-day sun. It was from the pyramid's base that the cheering rose. Not a single man accosted Hatshepsut from the houses lining the broad street. The city was thoroughly conquered.

It was her fifth victory in the kingdom of Kush. Five days she had been in the southernmost reaches of her empire, and five settlements had fallen to her spear: the tiny farming village first, but each victory larger, until at last she had taken a city of at least five thousand. Each day she rose from her camp brimming with fire, stoking her wrath with the sharp pain of memory: Iset's face, her body, her voice raised in song. She thought of her children, the feel of them in her arms, and strapped her ferocity to defend them like armor to her chest. Each morning she set out with her men at her heels, prepared to fight and wound and kill if it meant the army would be hers, loyal and ready to do her bidding no matter what whispering dogs like Ankhhor might tell them, now or in years to come.

But each night when she returned she fell into her bed buffeted by grief. She wrestled with it deep in the innermost seclusion of her heart, that quiet, dark place where her kas lived. She fought to overcome a suffocating weight of horror, always the same weight, always the same horrors, each night as the camp grew more wild with celebration. For now she understood what it meant to rule a kingdom. Now she knew that the Pharaoh must wield not only wealth and fair judgment and cleverness, but terror as well, when the gods required it. Each was but a tool in her hand, to carve the kingdom into whatever design best pleased Amun. And she must raise and wield each tool with equal ease, and never let the weight of her burden show on her face.

This would be her duty and her privilege, until the gods called her to the Field of Reeds.

She found the certainty of her task exhausting, and yet somehow exhilarating, too.

Hatshepsut's horses broke from the rows of shops and homes into a wide common square. At its heart rose the pyramid. Quarried from black stone, far too narrow at its base, it rose to an eerily slender point in the burning mid-day sky. A short hall, roofed in black, protruded from its foot. The hall was flanked by two pylons not unlike those which guarded Egyptian temples, yet they were far too alien in their darkness. The deep, light-eating blackness of the monument seemed to spurn the very idea of Re.

The conquered men of the city crouched near the mouth of the pyramid, kneeling in the dust with their heads bowed. They numbered perhaps a hundred, all told.

Hatshepsut landed from her chariot and paced the line of Kushite men, gazing down upon their stooped shoulders and heaving chests. Ramose joined her. He squinted as he approached, for the sun glinted sharply off her long tunic of polished bronze scales and the shining pinnacle of her bright blue war crown. She had worn the ceremonial battle garb of the Pharaoh since her second conquest. It was heavier than she could believe, and the dragging weight of it surprised her each time she put it on. Yet once she was in the thick of battle she did not seem to notice its weight or heat.

"When they heard you had given word that their women and children were not be harmed, they fell back here, to defend their god," Ramose said.

"Dedwen."

When she said the god's name two or three of the nearest Kushites looked up in surprise. The glinting in their eyes quickly turned to anger. She could see it burning, this rage at hearing the name of their god on the tongue of the Egyptian king. And an uglier emotion dwelt in their hard stares: loathing for the fact – so obvious now, in the slenderness of her form, the lightness of her features, the pitch of her voice – that the new Pharaoh was a woman.

"I know of Dedwen." She emphasized the name, glaring into the face of one of her captives. He and his brothers dropped their eyes again.

Hatshepsut clasped her hands behind her back, turned to survey the square. Bodies lay scattered about – the still forms of Kushites in their strangely fashioned, bright-colored kilts, and here and there the white kilt of an Egyptian spotted with blood. Her men worked to remove their fallen brothers from the square, lifting bodies by arms and legs as if they were goats being carried from a butcher. She swallowed hard. The wreckage of a chariot lay nearby, splintered; one of its horses was splayed before it, the poor creature's neck resting at an unnatural angle to its body. A wide, dark pool spread from its throat – cut by its driver, no doubt, to spare its suffering.

She rounded again on the captives.

"And what am I to do with these?" She said the words in the Kushites' own harsh language.

Ramose answered in kind, a wry smile tightening his face. "I suppose you could take their hands, O Good God, but do it while they still live. Take their manhood, too."

One of the men whimpered, then stifled himself when his brother shot him a hateful look.

Hatshepsut lapsed back into Egyptian. "I would see this god of theirs for myself. Nehesi?"

Both her guard and the general accompanied her between

the strange dark pylons, into the mouth of Dedwen's temple.

The interior was very dim, and cold as moving water. Hatshepsut found it a pleasant relief from the beating sun outside. She pulled the war helmet from her head, tucked it under her arm, swiped at her sweaty brow with her dusty forearm. The scent of incense was so thick here that she nearly choked on it. A thin stream of light fell in from between the pylons; in its bronze-colored cast she could just make out carvings on the walls. They were depictions of Dedwen striding to face his enemies, of Kushite kings making offerings to this, the greatest of their gods. The style of the carvings was not as foreign as she had expected. But for the unfamiliar faces and trappings, the scenes might have been at home on the walls of an Egyptian temple.

Deeper within, at the pyramid's dark heart, the figure of Dedwen himself sat upon a black stone pedestal. He was carved from a lighter rock, so he stood out amidst the dense blackness of the pyramid's interior with disturbing vividness. Hatshepsut gazed up at him. A wide, unkempt beard fanned out above his chest, dense and curly. His hands rested in fists upon his knees. His face, with the broad nose and mouth of a Kushite and hard, staring eyes, seemed to promise her a wealth of unpleasantness.

"I do not want to do this again," she said quietly.

"Great Lady?" Nehesi was at her side, as ever.

"I must find a way to keep Kush subdued now and for all time."

"Kush, subdued for all time?" Ramose shook his head. "An impossible task, Majesty. Subjugation is not in the nature of such a people."

"And yet I must find a way. I must force a peace, and it must hold at least as long as I live."

"There are not only Kushites in the world," Nehesi said, his voice low and amused. "What of the Heqa-Khasewet? What of Mitanni, and Hatti, and the Greeks?"

"I will have peace from them all."

"You will have war. It is the lot of a king."

"You presume to tell me what is the lot of a king?"

In the darkness she felt Nehesi's familiar, care-nothing shrug.

Hatshepsut returned her eyes to Dedwen's menacing stare. "I have no stomach for war."

Nehesi chuckled. "You have made me a fool, then. I've never seen such confidence on the field. The way you lead the men..."

"Ah, Majesty," Ramose interjected. "You are the very image of your father. The men say you are possessed by the spirit of Sekhmet."

"Do they?"

"They call you seshep."

Seshep. The name did not displease her. The mythical beast embodied the warrior's power: a crouching lion with the head of a man. She tried to imagine herself with a lion's body. The image made her smile.

"All the same," she said, somewhat cheered, "if this is the last I ever see of war, I shall die a happy Pharaoh."

She returned the war helmet to her head, spun on her heel, and led them back out into the painful glare of the commons. "You," she called, gesturing to the nearest Egyptian soldier. "Bring me the reins from that dead horse's bridle."

When she had the reins in hand, she summoned more men, and led them, whispering and looking about them in apprehension, into the black pyramid. The men hung well back from Dedwen's stone feet. Soldiers were ever superstitious.

"Nehesi, Dedwen wants a garland about his neck." She tossed the reins into her guard's hands. He moved quickly, lofting them up to fall across the god's shoulders. They landed against his divine body with a soft slap.

"Bring him down," she ordered her men, and stood watching impassively as they hauled on the reins, rocking Dedwen upon his base until he tipped up on the edge of his carven throne, hung balanced for one breathless heartbeat, then crashed to the floor of the temple.

They dragged the god into the stark light of his courtyard.

The Kushites crouching in the dust seemed to moan as one, burying their eyes against bloodied shoulders, rocking in dread.

Her Egyptians raised their spears and their voices, hailing her.

Seshep! Seshep! Seshep!

Hatshepsut remained still as they chanted. A small, quivering uneasiness gripped her stomach, threaded its way into her heart. This thing she did – it was blasphemy. She had never blasphemed. *But after all, who is Dedwen beside Amun? He is not even an Egyptian god. And I am Amun's own representative on the earth. It is given to me, to lead the Two Lands, the greatest kingdom in all the world. It is given to me, to make it known that Amun rules all the sun touches. Even the land of Kush.*

From the roofs of the city, the piercing cries of women rose into the sky with the commons' dust and the groaning of the men. The sound clambered above the chant – *Seshep! Seshep!*

Peace – for Iset. For my little ones.

Hatshepsut lifted her foot. The scales of her armor clattered like Amun's holy rattles. She drew in one long breath that tasted of hot earth and blood, then brought her heel down on the side of Dedwen's face.

CHAPTER SEVEN

*A*MUN *STRIDES FROM DARKNESS* ROCKED as Hatshepsut's personal guardsmen boarded, followed by Tabiry and Keminub, who had agreed to tend the king on her own ship for the long trek back to Waset. Seven days had come and gone since she had taken her first village, and each day brought another settlement conquered.

In truth, for her final two victories Egypt had barely to lift a single spear, for the people of those cities had heard already of the woman Pharaoh who pulled Dedwen from his temple and trampled the god into the dust. Each was quick enough to surrender whatever goods they could offer as a hasty and desperate tribute, that their own temples might remain undisturbed. There was no telling what wrath an offended deity might bring upon his own people if they allowed him to be so debased.

They presented her with gold and turquoise, and with incense in great overflowing sacks. They even made to offer a portion of their grain supplies, but she waved it away and told the city-kings in their own tongue, "Egypt does not take from the mouths of children."

The city-kings of both settlements made pledges of fealty to the Pharaoh. Hatshepsut knew those pledges would be broken, but not, she hoped, too soon or so egregiously that she would be compelled to return in person and mete out a fitting punishment.

Along the length of the rough quay, soldiers trooped up

61

LIBBIE HAWKER

planks to the decks of ships. More than half were returning home. The rest would remain in the south, billeted at her fortress under Ramose's supervision, until she could send another wave of men to refresh them. Kush would be sore, she knew. They would come looking for vengeance soon or late. She wanted the plain on the Egyptian side of the hills to bristle with ready spears when they did.

The final man boarded her ship; the oarsmen skillfully slid the plank onto the deck while men still ashore cast off the lines. Nehesi appeared at her side, arms crossed over his broad chest, following her gaze out across the tents and cook fires of the plain.

"A good campaign," he said.

"Ah."

"You seem distracted."

"I only hope it will be enough."

"The men you leave behind?"

"That, and what we did here."

"You pulled a god down – *a god!* Yes, Great Lady, it will be enough."

"For how long?"

Nehesi shrugged. "Peace never lasts long. It will be whatever the gods decree. Weren't you a priestess of sorts once? You should know these things."

She scoffed at him. "*Of sorts?*"

The captain shouted for oars. They slid from the ship's sides, splashed into the water, nudged the hull from the quay. Hatshepsut watched the quay's stone wall slide smoothly from her. Then an abrupt movement on the waterfront caught her eye; she glanced up and checked at the sight of four young boys playing at the landing. The larger boys carried the smaller upon their shoulders, and they laughed and called insults to one another as their riders tossed a leather ball back and forth. The mounts dodged, hooting, around barrels and bundles of linen and long bare poles which had until recently held soldiers' tents.

"Nehesi! Whose boys are those?"

"Uh? I do not know, Great Lady."

"They are so young."

"Probably discontented apprentices – ran off to join the army, I'd wager, when you came through their towns."

"They are far too young for a war camp." Then a queasy thought occurred to her. "Oh, gods – they didn't go into battle, did they?"

He chuckled, laid a hand on her shoulder. "I should think not, Great Lady. War camps always have their share of sneak-away boys. Soldiering is a far better life than leading their fathers' cattle to the river or being beaten by an ill-tempered trade master. The older men always keep the boys too busy with camp chores for them to get into much danger."

"But still, a war camp is no place for children. Gods, what will their mothers think of me?"

Nehesi roared with laughter. "They will think you are the king! What else are they to think?"

The boys disappeared into the crowd milling about the waterfront, taking their ball and their happy shouts with them. A quiet melancholy welled up in her heart when they vanished. Nehesi, too, went still and pensive. Did the sight of children playing make him feel wistful, as well? Or was he only reliving his exhilaration on the battlefield? Was she painting her own feelings onto Nehesi's stony wall?

"I want my own children to play that way," she said, "to be young and carefree for as long as they can."

Nehesi turned to look at her, and his eyes were uncommonly solemn. "They are the children of the Pharaoh. One is a Pharaoh himself. Is it reasonable, Great Lady, to expect them to ever be young and carefree? Even as babes, they have their roles to play."

The fortress grew smaller by the moment as *Amun Strides from Darkness* slipped into the swift northward current. The waterfront was a jumble of men blurred by distance, but Hatshepsut knew the boys still played somewhere within that crowd.

"Perhaps not, Nehesi. But I will try all the same – I will try to make it so."

Tabiry bowed at Hatshepsut's elbow. "Great Lady, shall I prepare your meal?"

"Good," Hatshepsut said.

"Boiled eggs and uncut melons, I presume." Tabiry waited, patient expectation on her face.

Hatshepsut took one final look at the shoreline. Above the scrape of oars running out to meet the river, above the call and response of the rowing song, she heard a man's voice shout a single word, joyous and full of triumph, from the quay. *Seshep!*

"No, Tabiry. Tell the captain's cook to roast me a fat fish. And it has been a very long time since I've tasted fresh bread. Tell him to make me a honey cake, cooked over the brazier's coals. I want it so hot it burns my fingers and my tongue."

Tabiry tilted her head, disbelieving.

"Is there any wine?"

"Ah, but only the great jar in the captain's store. Its seal has already been broken."

"Bring me a cup. I am thirsty."

Tabiry turned to do the Pharaoh's bidding with a bubble of laughter. Ta-Seti fell away behind the stern of Hatshepsut's warship. The northern horizon glowed beneath the high sun. Beneath that sun, in the quiet peace of her palace garden, Senenmut waited, and her children, too. When the current caught the ship and pulled it insistently toward Waset, Hatshepsut smiled.

PART TWO

ADORATION OF THE GOD

1476 B.C.E.

Chapter Eight

THE AIR WAS ALMOST COOL on the rooftop of Waset's great palace, high above the stink and closeness of the city. A fitful breeze moved in from the river, lifting and dropping the colorful cloth canopies of the sunshades with lazy movements, with a thrumming, flapping sound like the wing-beats of a great, careless bird. Ladies in their best finery stood clustered beneath the canopies – ladies of the noble houses and of the harem – while men of rank ambled from one group to the next in long formal kilts, raising their wine cups in praise of the women's beauty. Servants made their way unobtrusively through the gathering, offering platters of spiced dates or lettuce-boats filled with minced beef, bearing jars of cooled beer and wine, and water sweetly scented with flower petals.

Hatshepsut watched the children, who in turn watched the long straight line of the eastern canal, stretching their necks to peer over the low wall of the rooftop. Their feet fidgeted constantly. Thutmose could not seem to stop himself kicking at the wall, no matter how many times his nurse scolded him for scuffing the toes of his golden sandals. And Neferure danced forward and back between the wall and the royal sunshade as if gripped by some childish anxiety.

The girl's eyes were large and sober, as serious as Senenmut's, though it was the only resemblance she bore him. She had not come to resemble Hatshepsut as she grew, either. Her features were far finer than her mother's, lacking all of the

Thutmoside harshness and, thank the gods, the familial toothiness. In fact, Neferure was positively beautiful, even as a small thing, still wearing the side-lock of childhood. It was something Hatshepsut never heard said about herself as a young girl – not in honesty, at any rate. She was glad for her daughter. Neferure would grow into an enchanting woman.

At the rooftop's far corner, the musicians changed from a low, sweet, soothing tune to a livelier one, and a few of the harem women danced. Neferure sucked a forefinger as she watched the show, as she observed the men watching. Hatshepsut had the uneasy feeling, as she often did in her daughter's presence, that the girl understood far more of the adult world than any seven-year-old child ought. Neferure seemed neither delighted by the bright dresses and rollicking music nor disgusted by the somewhat wanton display. She merely watched, intensely observant as always.

"I see them!"

When the dance had nearly concluded, Thutmose's squeal of excitement broke Neferure's unsettling concentration, and she turned to regard her brother with a dark, thoughtful stare.

Senenmut clapped his hands; the gathering drifted toward the eastern wall, buzzing with excitement.

The usual gray waterside haze of dust and moisture hung thickly at the point where the canal vanished among the low, dry hills beyond Waset. But a blocky shape condensed slowly from that haze, and little Thutmose pointed, quivering with excitement.

The crowd seemed to hold its breath; Hatshepsut's heart pounded in her chest.

The massive shape broke free of the haze and resolved into a clear image of the Pharaoh's twin obelisks moving ponderously down the canal. The crowd of nobles exhaled as one, a sigh of awe and admiration.

"...they are laid, you see, on a barge that is near as wide as the canal itself."

Hatshepsut allowed herself a tiny smile at the sound of

Senenmut murmuring to four or five nobles. The men nodded and hummed at his every word.

"The barge is sunk down with rocks for weights, and the obelisks pushed across the breadth of the canal, side by side, just so. When the rocks are pulled free, the barge rises, and lifts the obelisks off the ground."

"It's a wonder any barge can carry such a weight!"

"Egypt's engineers are the finest in all the world," Senenmut said, as proud as if he himself were an engineer.

"Look, Mawat, look!" Thutmose tugged at Hatshepsut's hand. Laughing, she followed him to the wall.

"Those are my obelisks," she told him, lifting him to her hip so he might see more clearly. "And one day, when you are grown, you will have obelisks of your own."

"Oh – see all the men!"

The two massive stones, cut entire from pale quarry rock, lay prone over their barge, close as lovers in a bed. Each hung over the stone lip of the canal by several feet on either side. A deep blue shadow crept along beneath them; the visual effect of shadow, of ponderous movement, and the great height of Hatshepsut's viewpoint made the monuments seem to separate from the dun landscape with a kind of supernatural force, as though they drifted on the palm of a god's hand and not a mortal barge. Dozens of men crept in the shadow of the conveyance, holding tight to the ropes that lashed the spires together, straining to keep the barge moving straight between the canal's sides. The load was so great it required at least fifty to each side, perhaps more. A handful of men rode atop the rough stone itself, scuttling from one side to the next. Their arms waved like the slender, mobile horns of beetles, gesturing wildly to the men hauling at the ropes.

It was a sight to make Amun proud. When the barge reached the confluence with the temple road, the obelisks would be unloaded and rolled atop fire-hardened logs to Ipet-Isut, where they would rest on their sides while Hatshepsut's artists embellished them with scenes of the king's glory. Then each would receive a crown of gold, so the light of her strength would reflect far out onto the Iteru; all who approached Waset would be dazzled by the greatness of the Pharaoh, and the greatness of Waset's god.

Neferure stepped to Hatshepsut's side. Her small, fine hands reached up to pull her frail little body onto its toes. She peered over the wall, her brow furrowed as if she were trying to solve one of Senenmut's clever riddles. "Mother, where will the new obelisks stand?"

Hatshepsut allowed Thutmose to slide back onto his own feet. He hopped in place, unable to contain his glee.

"They will stand where the blank pylons stood, outside the Temple of Amun."

Neferure stared up at her, still gripping the wall with white-knuckled fingers. "*Stand.*"

Hatshepsut watched her daughter's face, suddenly reluctant to say any more.

"The blank pylons are still there. They *stand.*"

"Yes," Hatshepsut said, angrily aware that she sounded foolish.

"You will tear down the pylons?"

"There is nothing on them." Thutmose the Second had never had a chance to carve the pylons with his own great deeds. Indeed, he had never committed any deeds to speak of; any carvings he might have made would have been fantasies – lies.

Neferure lowered herself onto her heels, stepped back to regard her mother in reproachful silence.

Hatshepsut called over her shoulder for Senenmut. "Take the King's Daughter to the garden. It is shady there; I believe the sun here on the roof is too much for her."

"It is not," Neferure said coolly.

"You will go."

She turned away from the child, back to the sight of her monuments making their way down the canal. *I will not let her strangeness best me. Not today.*

"A great accomplishment, Majesty – the finest monuments Waset has ever seen!" A man in the crowd raised his cup above his head, saluting Hatshepsut.

Grateful for the distraction, she raised her own cup in reply, grinning, and called for more music and dance. She sank down on the small throne beneath her sunshade, pulled Thutmose onto her knee, hugged him close to her chest while he giggled and squirmed and declared that one day he would have obelisks taller than the Great Pyramids.

"You are exactly as a child should be," she told him, and laughed at the face he made, innocent and puzzled.

She turned the boy loose to watch the obelisks once more.

Just after sunset, when the party had dispersed, she found them in the palace's great garden. Senenmut was making little boats from leaves and setting them adrift on the smooth, dark surface of the lake, while Neferure plucked petals from a bundle of flowers that lay on the lake's wall, and laid the petals carefully inside Senenmut's tiny green barques.

"May I come to your quay?" Hatshepsut called softly.

Senenmut glanced up at her and smiled, but Neferure pulled the thick black braid of her side-lock across her own eyes, hiding her mother from view.

Hatshepsut sat on the lake's low wall. "My sweet girl, you nearly scolded me in front of all our fine guests. You must not do such a thing. I am the Pharaoh."

Neferure turned away. "So is Thutmose. I can scold him."

"You should not."

"He is just a boy."

"He is the king. We all must show him respect."

"Even you?"

"Of course; even I."

"Then should you not show respect to dead kings?"

Hatshepsut glanced at Senenmut, thinking to give him a look full of reprimand for putting such ideas into his charge's heart. But he looked so genuinely startled, his brows arching

71

sharply beneath the fringe of his wig, that Hatshepsut could only turn her eyes back to her daughter in helpless silence.

At last she managed, "Are you troubled by the question of respect? It is only natural. Yes, Thutmose is just a boy, and perhaps it angers you that we must show him the respect due a king. Perhaps it is time for you to hold the respect of the court, too."

Neferure glanced up from her petals, eyes suddenly keen with interest.

"Yes?" Hatshepsut felt a sudden wash of relief at the girl's approval. "Would you like that? There is a special place for you at court, Neferure. A very sacred place."

"Sacred?"

Hatshepsut nodded. She caught Neferure's beautiful face in her hands and said, "How would you like to be God's Wife of Amun?"

Neferure frowned.

Hatshepsut's hands fell. "Will it not make you happy?"

The girl shrugged. "I am honored."

Senenmut grimaced, twirling a leaf in his fingers.

"I thought you would be thrilled," Hatshepsut said. "You are so keen on religion." Neferure said nothing, and Hatshepsut sighed. "What is this, child? What gnaws at you?" She bent over Neferure and said playfully, "I think you have little mice in your heart, gnawing and gnawing!" Hatshepsut tickled the girl's chest, but Neferure did not smile. She only flinched away.

Senenmut spoke up softly. "It is the pylons, is it not?"

Neferure nodded.

"Oh, dear girl. You cannot let such things trouble you."

"You should not tear them down." Tears came to Neferure's eyes. Hatshepsut drew back a little, startled; she had seldom seen her daughter cry, since she was old enough to speak.

"The pylons are blank. They were never carved."

"*You* should carve them."

Hatshepsut ignored the suggestion. "We build these monuments to the gods, Neferure. The gods deserve beautiful things, do they not?"

"Those obelisks are not for the gods. They are for you."

Heat flushed into Hatshepsut's face. Senenmut caught her eye and gave a tight half-shake of his head. *Calm*, his eyes cautioned.

"The gods...the gods will be angry." Neferure tripped over her own tongue, and flushed like her mother, frustrated by her own inability to explain. "And *I* will be angry."

"Why will you be angry?" Senenmut asked gently, taking Neferure's hand.

The tears spilled over her cheeks. She turned from Hatshepsut and threw herself into Senenmut's arms, her face pressed against his shoulder. "Because he was my father," she wailed.

Senenmut looked up at Hatshepsut over Neferure's frail little body, heaving with her sobs. The pain in his eyes stabbed deep into Hatshepsut's heart.

CHAPTER NINE

AHMOSE CAME TO THE PHARAOH'S chambers within minutes of Hatshepsut's summons.

"You are still living in the palace," Hatshepsut said, startled, taking her mother's hands in her own. "Wouldn't you prefer an estate in the hills, with breezes coming off the river, and good smells from your fields? Waset reeks like a midden heap half the time and like a whore's neck the other half."

"Who taught you such coarse language, Majesty? Never your mother."

Hatshepsut kissed her cheek. The lines of old worries had settled deep into Ahmose's face. The skin on her hands and had begun to slacken ever so slightly. Hatshepsut recalled her mother when she was a young regent, ruling Egypt in the name of Thutmose the Second, her face hardly touched by the cares of such an impossible task. She was over forty years now, well on her way to old age. Somewhere between then and now, the past had imprinted itself indelibly on the former Great Royal Wife.

"No, I do not wish to live outside the palace again. It has been my only true home since I became a woman. The years I spent living elsewhere were a mistake. I've no doubt an estate would be quieter – and yes, sweeter smelling than the city. But I would never know what to do with myself in the hills. Can you imagine me farming? Crops don't obey a command to grow. I know how to do nothing but give commands. Once a Great Royal Wife, always a Great Royal Wife, I suppose."

Hatshepsut led her across the bright tiles of the anteroom floor, past couches and tables of precious wood upholstered in eastern silk and fine Retjenu wool, past the alcove where her musicians' many instruments stood on polished stands, waiting the king's pleasure. She had had the walls painted and carved afresh when she had taken her throne, undoing the damage Thutmose the Second had caused, restoring what she could remember of her father's murals and the works of Pharaohs before him.

Ahmose hesitated before Hatshepsut could lead her through the doorway to the private chambers. She brushed with her fingertips the face of the first Thutmose, her long-dead husband, the father whose face and ways Hatshepsut could barely recall.

"I miss him," Ahmose said. Her voice did not rise above a murmur. She sounded like a woman talking in her sleep. "For all the difficulties between us, I loved him – my Tut."

Hatshepsut took her elbow. "I did not intend to wound you by summoning you here. These were his apartments, too, and you and he..."

"It is no matter. I am growing old, and old women are sentimental."

Ahmose allowed herself to be guided through the private chambers and out into the garden, where Hatshepsut's women were finishing their tasks, spreading a light supper on a table in the early evening shade. Where light lanced through the branches of broad-leafed trees, families of gnats spun in shimmering, wavering funnels above the grass. A hesitant evening wind shook the trees, disturbing the gnats. Ita and Tem had tied gleaming strands of copper plate in the branches, and they chimed with a musical patter like water pouring from a jar. Ahmose paused at the sound, smiled a little sadly. She was often melancholy now, in the years since Hatshepsut had sent Mutnofret away. The question of whether Hatshepsut had been cruel to exile her aunt had plagued the king often over the past seven years. Little Tut – Pharaoh Thutmose, Hatshepsut reminded herself; the boy

76

balled his fists and scowled whenever she called him Little Tut – was Mutnofret's grandson, and she had not seen the boy since he was a baby. *Perhaps there is little difference between cruelty and justice,* she thought as she led Ahmose to her place at the table.

"You brought me here for a reason," Ahmose said, lifting a pretty enameled bowl full of fine, light beer to her lips. "It was not to feast my excellency."

"You are quite excellent enough for any king to feast."

"A Pharaoh has no need to flatter her subjects."

"You enjoyed it, all the same."

Ahmose smiled. "Why did you summon me, Hatet?"

Hatshepsut drew a deep breath. "Neferure. I am concerned about her."

Ita presented a steaming roast duck on a platter carved with papyrus fronds. It smelled rich and earthy, filled as its cavity was with a bundle of herbs singed black at their ends from the roasting fire, but Ahmose did not touch the portion that was placed in her supper bowl.

"What concerns you? Is she ill?"

"I do not know, in truth. Something plagues her – has always plagued her. She is so solemn, one might almost call her grim. And she seems to understand things no child can understand."

Ahmose chuckled to herself, and sliced a bit of her duck. "Is that all?"

"She is upset over my obelisks. She knows I plan to tear down my brother's gateway and raise them in its place. It's put her into a sulk the likes of which I have never seen. I cannot get through to her."

"She will learn to accept it."

"She is too quiet."

"Most mothers would bless the gods for sending them a quiet child."

"There is a strangeness in her quiet. It is not...not maat."

Hatshepsut gazed into the dense shadows of the garden. The trees moved again in the breeze, and the copper bangles sounded somehow menacing, alien and knowing. "I fear Neferure may have a demon in her heart."

To Hatshepsut's surprise, Ahmose burst into laughter, full and loud. When she narrowed her eyes at her mother, Ahmose composed herself with an obvious effort, the fingers of one hand pressed to her mouth. "I am sorry, Majesty. Forgive me."

"Why do you laugh?"

"Oh, Hatet. Neferure is not demon-ridden. Don't you see? She is god-chosen."

Hatshepsut rocked back in the seat of her stool, relief warring in her heart with a new, nagging suspicion. "God-chosen? Are you certain?"

"Did I not tell you as much that night I found you in the garden, when Mut showed me what you intended to do and sent me to stop you?"

"You did not say..."

"Daughters never listen to their mothers."

Hatshepsut's mouth twisted wryly. "Ah, and that is the gods' own truth." She took a much-needed draft of her beer, for her mouth had gone quite dry.

"When Neferure seems quiet and strange, she is only listening to the voices of the gods."

A bristling intensity crept beneath Hatshepsut's skin. She stared blankly at her portion of duck, examining the sensation, prodding at it with her heart until at last its meaning became suddenly, shockingly clear. She was *jealous*. She envied the girl this connection to the gods. Indeed, it seemed more than a bit unfair, that Neferure should hear their voices speaking within her. She was but a child, and Hatshepsut was the king, and son of Amun, after all! Hatshepsut had never heard Amun's voice – not with any certainty, at any rate – not in the way the god-chosen reputedly heard. She tried to silence the voice of envy, but it only wailed the louder. Yes, and Neferure had so much more of Senenmut's heart than she, tied up as Hatshepsut always was with the demands of the throne. Ah, she and Senenmut saw one another often enough, worked together – but they had had no time of late to love one another.

You are being ridiculous, she told herself firmly. *The Pharaoh will not be consumed with envy over a seven-year-old girl. Do try to recall that you are the Lord of the Two Lands and not a shrieking fishwife.*

When she had stifled the flush of envy, a more sinister chill gripped her. She remembered too vividly the terrible night she had spent watching the bats flit over the palace lake, the reflection of the hanging star burning in the water, the cramping in her womb.

"I wonder whether she is god-chosen after all, or whether it was something I did that made her so strange. The potion..."

"It is not the potion, nor a demon. Neferure will come to understand what it means to be god-chosen as she grows. She will open to it like a flower in the sun. That is the way it happens for those who are chosen. It's how it happened for me."

"Will you tutor her for me?"

"She has her tutor, I think."

Hatshepsut smiled a little sadly. "Senenmut can teach her many things, but not this. She needs you to guide her."

Ahmose lowered her eyes, a show of obedience – but Hatshepsut could see the spark of joy that shone behind her downcast lashes.

"I offered Neferure the station of God's Wife recently, you know. She did not seem pleased."

"How could she be? She is far too young. You were twice her age when you took the station."

"She is not too young to begin learning. Just simple tasks – the temple songs, how to burn incense..."

"Ah, such tasks may be within her reach, but pushing her too far and too fast would be a grievous mistake. A woman – or a girl – should come to Amun's service willingly, ready to give her heart in full to the god." A muscle in Ahmose's jaw pulsed faintly; it seemed to Hatshepsut that her mother dragged these words from her throat. And well Hatshepsut knew why: Ahmose had not come to the station with a pure heart, but with selfish motives, and she had suffered for her folly.

"I fear what it could mean to Egypt, if I were to leave the station unfilled much longer. I cannot take it up myself; I am Pharaoh. I cannot perform the ceremonies of both a man and a woman. I already tread a careful road as it is. I would not risk the gods' wrath with hubris."

"I agree that Amun needs a wife, and sooner rather than later."

Hatshepsut eyed her mother, making no effort to disguise the scrutiny in her gaze. She would not re-appoint her mother to the position. Though it would pain her to deny Ahmose, she could not risk the gods' displeasure by reinstating a disgraced God's Wife of Amun to the temple. But in another moment Ahmose went on speaking, and Hatshepsut released the breath she had not known she held.

"Why not appoint a woman from the harem? They are all from good families, loyal to the throne. It would be a great honor, and doing honor to a powerful house has stood many a Pharaoh in good stead."

"I have my fears where that is concerned. If I extend such an honor to one house, would I not slight a dozen more? And well do I know that not all the women of the harem are from loyal houses. If I gave the title to some woman or other, must I not then strip her of her honors in order to set Neferure in her place, once she comes of age? It would only breed ill will toward the throne."

"Perhaps you are right."

"Nor will I see Neferure without some prominence at court."

"She is King's Daughter. What more prominence can any girl have?"

Suddenly uncertain, Hatshepsut swallowed a long draft of her beer.

Ahmose's mouth tightened, but her look was speculative, not disapproving. "You would make her your heir."

Hatshepsut pressed her hands to her face, rubbed hard

at her cheeks, her forehead, as if she could scrub away the buzzing ache, the tension that seemed to fill her body and kas whenever she turned her thoughts to Neferure. "The throne does need an heir."

"Whose throne? Yours or Thutmose's?"

"Our thrones are one and the same."

"You know they are not. He is eight years old."

"One day he will be a man."

"Until then, you are the sole power of Pharaoh. All of Egypt knows this is true."

"Very well. She will be my heir alone, if you like. My brother died young; I suppose the same fate could befall me. Though Mut knows I don't intend to go facing any captives unarmed."

"And you will not marry, to produce a royal son."

It was not a question, and Hatshepsut knew Ahmose expected no reply. What possible station could a wedded husband hold? Such a presence at court would only underscore the strangeness of Hatshepsut on the throne and undermine her power. Dissolution of maat would quickly follow. And because she could not marry, she could not birth an heir.

Ahmose fiddled with her supper knife, moving her portion of duck about her bowl. "I suppose it is to be expected, a female king with a female heir. And what of Thutmose?"

"He will sire his own heir one day."

"Two heirs to the throne, each the child of a ruling Pharaoh? Hatshepsut, you know this folly. This would endanger the peace of Egypt."

"And yet Thutmose is already a king. He cannot be my heir; he rules already, in whatever small capacity a child may rule."

"This skein has grown rather tangled."

Hatshepsut sighed. "What choices do I have?"

"Take no heir. Leave the throne entirely to Thutmose, and his own heir, when you go to the Field of Reeds."

"Perhaps."

"Perhaps? Any other decision would endanger the peace

81

you fought for in Kush. Would you pit your own children against one another? Your grandchildren? Would you tear Egypt apart with civil war to satisfy your own pride?"

"Pride?" Hatshepsut returned, wounded.

"What else shall I call it?"

"Maat," Hatshepsut insisted. "Amun came to you, Mother, to beget a king. The god did not appear to Mutnofret, nor to Iset. I love Little Tut, but it is I whom the gods have chosen. It is my blood that must continue on the throne."

"Then marry Neferure to Thutmose. Let an heir of your own blood come about through marriage. Let it be your grandchild – a son or a daughter, if you like, but do not pit your children against one another."

"Amun would not allow me to choose wrongly."

"Is that what you believe?" Ahmose laughed, a bitter sound. "If only the gods were so decisive. If only they spoke to us so clearly. Even the god-chosen cannot afford such reckless certainty, Hatshepsut."

They fell silent. The copper chimed in the trees, a small and forlorn sound.

At last Hatshepsut said, "There is no pressing need to name an heir yet. Perhaps you are right. Perhaps I am. Amun will reveal his truth in due time."

Ahmose nodded her acquiescence.

"But Neferure must be the God's Wife," Hatshepsut went on emphatically. "She will take simple tasks, to start. Egypt must have a living consort to Amun as soon as possible, for the sake of maat; on that, you and I can agree. I will begin teaching her the temple songs, the easiest dances, the prayers. And I hope it will be enough to appease the gods."

With effort, they changed the subject, and progressed their way through the final courses of their supper. The pleasant coolness of evening settled across the garden. Servants moved through the stillness, setting lamps upon bronze tripods along the paths. Moths, attracted to the lights, fluttered here and there. The shadows of their great, soft wings fell across Ahmose's face as mother and daughter conversed over a sweet course of figs stewed in milk. At last, pulling her shawl close about her shoulders, Ahmose rose from her seat.

"I must be on my way, Majesty. I am no longer a priestess, but still the gods expect my prayers before the night grows too late. The duties of the god-chosen are never done."

Hatshepsut embraced her. Ahmose's shoulders were thin beneath her hands. "It was good to see you, Mother."

As Ahmose led her women from the Pharaoh's garden, Hatshepsut listened to the chimes in the trees. They spoke soft and insistent as the voice inside her own heart. *Amun will not allow me to fail. If he wills it, it will come to pass. My mother and my daughter both may be god-chosen, but I am the son of the god.*

CHAPTER TEN

H EBENU. YES, THAT WILL BE *the next.*
Neferure sat motionless on her minor throne, back
straight and eyes forward, gazing down upon the great hall
with a serene face as a good King's Daughter ought, but the
thoughts of her heart were many days' journey away. For the
past year, ever since her appointment as God's Wife of Amun,
she had been absorbed with the restoration of her temples.
She often thought of them that way – *her* temples – though
of course they belonged to the gods, and Neferure was but
their loving servant.

Now and then she would wake in the night to the sound
of an indistinct whisper and would lie in her bed straining to
hear more. At such times she would think about her temples,
and wonder why she felt no fear at calling them hers. A wise
girl would be fearful. One did not stake a claim on that which
belonged by rights to the gods. But Neferure had never feared
the gods.

Oh, she was certain the gods could be wrathful when they
were displeased. The histories Senenmut taught her were full
of tales of angry gods. If they were angry with men, then the
river failed to rise, and people starved by the thousands. Or
illnesses swept through the Two Lands. Or one god or another
would lend his strength to enemies – or deny his strength
to Egypt; Neferure was never sure which – and Egypt would
be invaded. So many terrible things could happen if the Holy
Ones were not properly appeased. But this small thing –

Neferure and her temples – did not displease them. She was certain of it.

Hebenu. Pakhet's temple there has been in ruins for generations. Senenmut said so.

On the great Pharaoh's throne, Hatshepsut gave some command or other, and the stewards scurried about the hall like scarabs in the sun, blundering and worried and frantic, the way stewards always were. Neferure tried not to sigh at the monotony of court. She clung doggedly to her thoughts of Pakhet and her long-wrecked temple.

What did Senenmut tell me of the place? Hebenu is far to the south, and Pakhet guards the great ravine that is... she struggled to recall the words of her tutor's lesson. *...that is scoured by the flash floods.* In her imagination it seemed a dangerous, wild place, just steps away from the heat and dry desolation of the Red Land. A fitting locale for Pakhet, She Who Scratches, the lioness who was so like the fierce warrior-goddess Sekhmet. *She is a sister to Sekhmet. If I restore her temple and make it beautiful again, not only Pakhet will be pleased, but Sekhmet, too.* The thought was accompanied by a deep, pulsing thrill inside her belly, below the place where her heart beat. Her grandmother Ahmose had been teaching her near as much as Senenmut. Neferure knew enough by now to recognize the assurance that only the god-chosen can feel. *It is right – it is maat. My heart tells me so. Pakhet's temple at Hebenu will be next, and Sekhmet's wrath will be stilled.*

She would give the order to Senenmut as soon as court was finished.

A year ago, shortly after she had tried to make her mother see the folly of tearing down the former king's uncarved gateway, Senenmut had arranged for Neferure to turn her energies to the restoration of the many old, ruined temples throughout the Two Lands. It was a sop to her disappointment and helplessness at being cornered into the station of God's Wife of Amun. She knew that, and at first she had tried to be displeased with her tutor for thinking he could soothe her so easily. But the truth was, she did feel gladdened. She and Senenmut often sat together in the evenings when her supper was finished, he reading descriptions of the ruins, she dictating which were the next to be rebuilt, and how. She even decreed which scenes were to be painted on the walls. Senenmut wrote her words down in his careful, neat hand, and a few days afterward a crew of builders would be dispatched to one of Neferure's temples to make her word into deed. It was a heady thing, and it gave her purpose. It distracted her from the confinement she felt serving Amun. For though Amun was a god, to be sure, he ignored Neferure, never entering her heart the way her secret god did, the one who whispered to her, faceless and mysterious, in the night.

The double doors at the end of the long hall opened, and the Steward of Audiences approached the royal dais, bowing. "Majesties, Good Gods of the Two Lands, I present the families whom you summoned."

Neferure watched with growing curiosity as a crowd came hesitantly into the great hall. There were men and women dressed in the quality clothing and bright colors of nobles, and each pair ushered a girl near Neferure's own age of eight. She glanced across Hatshepsut's throne to Thutmose's on the other side of the dais, hoping to catch her brother's eye, but the young Pharaoh sat regally still as he had been taught, his arms lying on the golden rests of his own kingly chair, his feet propped on a small ebony footstool studded with turquoise so that he would not forget himself and swing his legs in an undignified manner. He wore a child-sized replica of Hatshepsut's own crown, the tall, tiered structure of red and white that represented the unity of Upper and Lower Egypt.

The families made their way down the length of the chamber, gawking about them at the massive pillars that lined the hall, at the vivid paint and gilding depicting generations of kings and their mighty deeds, depicting the gods who moved them. Stewards flanked the group like shepherds driving their flock to water. Neferure almost giggled at the thought, but chased the smile from her lips as they drew up near the foot of the dais. She was not just King's Daughter now, but God's Wife of Amun. It would not be maat to giggle in the presence of Egypt's subjects.

"Welcome," Hatshepsut said.

The families bowed low, showing the palms of their hands to the royal family in a display of obedience.

When they straightened, Neferure passed her gaze swiftly across the faces of the girls. There were perhaps a dozen of them, none quite old enough to have bled. All wore the side-slicked hair, the braid over one ear, of girls still dwelling in the realm of childhood. Neferure wore the braid, too, but she did not feel any kinship with these girls. She was not a child, whatever her years might suggest. She was the God's Wife, and god-chosen, as Lady Ahmose had declared. Did these geese trembling at the foot of the throne look upon the King's Daughter and think, *Look, there is a girl just our age, a girl like we...?* If they did, then they were fools.

"Do not be frightened, dear girls – my flowers of Egypt." Hatshepsut was speaking again in her throne voice, richer and deeper, more carrying than the voice she used in her chambers, which was, Neferure thought, rather shrill. "We have brought you here to honor you. Yes, you, and not your fathers and mothers, though they are also worthy of honor."

At the word *we* the elder girls flicked quick glances toward Thutmose. One or two blushed and made cow eyes at him. Neferure's eyelids grew heavy at their displays of silliness, though it was the only disdain she allowed her face to show. For his part, Thutmose remained regally uncaring on his throne, oblivious to the girls' discomposure.

"You know, girls, how important is the happiness of our gods. We must always give them the best we have, the very best that we can offer, for this is maat. We have identified each of you as the very best. You come from good families, noble and loyal to the gods and to your kings. And you yourselves are good girls, obedient and quick to learn, strong and healthy in body, pleasing to your mothers and fathers. You stand before your Pharaohs so that we might invite you to be the very best of offerings. Would you go to Iunet, to the Temple of Hathor, and learn to serve the Lady of the West?"

Suddenly a great, painful lump rose up in Neferure's throat, choking her. She swallowed hard. Her ribs seemed too small for her heart, squeezing it like a fist.

The girls, startled out of propriety, looked at one another in shock or seized their mothers' hands. Some of them looked decidedly frightened, on the verge of tears – though a few appeared to grasp at once what an honor, what a glory it would be to become a priestess of Hathor. Those stood a little taller, while Neferure sank into her throne.

Hatshepsut rushed to soothe the fear of the more timid children. "You will not be required to go, nor will your families make the decision for you. It is each girl's choice, for Hathor wants her priestesses to come to her willingly, and to devote their whole hearts to her service.

"She is a mighty goddess, you know, one of great power and mystery. She once ruled the west bank of the river herself. She wears seven guises, and brings joy to our hearts and children to women's wombs. And she is the fiercest warrior, the face of Sekhmet, who protects our lands from enemies."

Neferure's heart beat so hard she thought her whole body must shake with its rhythm. But the eyes of all – the nobles and their daughters, the stewards and servants of the great hall, even Thutmose – were on the Pharaoh, not on her daughter. She felt a pulling sensation deep in the seat of her ka, a longing she could not name, a whispering she could not hear.

"You have two weeks to choose. But it must be your own choice, and no other's. Those of you who do wish to serve the goddess shall be provided with all you need by your Pharaohs, and given gifts of gratitude, and sent to Iunet like the worthy tributes you are."

Neferure saw the consideration in the eyes of the noblemen and their wives, saw the excitement grow on the faces of the girls clustered about them. She wanted to leap from her throne and join them, stand before her mother's throne and declare that she was the flower of Egypt, the daughter of the king, the worthiest tribute of them all. She would go to Iunet, not these mortal-bred children, and Hathor would rejoice in her presence as Amun never had.

But Senenmut and the king had too often filled her heart with the tenets of maat. Neferure had no more courage than did a mouse, no will to defy her training. She sat still on her throne as the noble families were ushered out of the royal presence, her back straight, her face serene, her eyes betraying nothing, the very picture of a good King's Daughter.

That evening Neferure's ka would not settle. It moved uncomfortably between a curdled, shivering weakness and a boiling rage that made her feel as though her skin might burst, as though her body would split in two and her angry spirit swell to engulf her whole room – the whole of the House of Women, in fact – with the force of her fury.

She ignored her supper and would not even touch the sweetened cow's milk her former wet-nurse Takhat offered, but told the silly-hearted woman that she wanted strong red wine. Takhat only laughed, which made Neferure all the angrier. She stalked about her chamber, throwing cushions against the walls and stomping her feet until Takhat's composure finally broke. The nurse unbent from her sewing and drove Neferure out into the twilit garden with shrieks of "Out, out from under my wig, you nasty little lioness!"

But the garden provided no relief to Neferure's ka. She tried to sit still on the bench beneath the sycamore, tried to open her heart to the gods as Ahmose had taught her. She tucked her legs up beneath her skirt, clasped her hands lightly and rested them on the tight linen bridge her dress made between her knees. The garden whispered in deep blue shadow, and bats made their miniscule chirps among the sycamore leaves, but the gods said nothing to Neferure, and her fury only grew.

It's not fair. It's not maat!

"I want to be a Hathor priestess," she said aloud. Her voice stumbled somewhere between plaintive and commanding. The only reply was the small, flitting song of the bats in the gathering darkness.

At last, when she knew that peace would evade her until she had set the world's greatest injustice to rights, Neferure went back through her lamp-lit doorway to her small chamber in the House of Women. Takhat looked up warily from her needlework.

"I want to go to my mother."

The wet-nurse sighed.

"I want to go to my mother *now*."

"This is behavior unbecoming the King's Daughter."

"Don't talk like a noble lady to me. You're just a rekhet."

"I am the wet-nurse to the King's Daughter, and that puts me a good deal higher than any fancy lady covered in gold and gems."

"Well, it doesn't put you higher than me."

Takhat rolled her eyes. "That long-faced nurse of yours... *tutor*...whatever he calls himself now – *Senenmut* should have thrashed you more often when you were a little thing. Maybe then you would know the proper way to treat your servants."

"Don't you talk of Senenmut that way. He knows better than to thrash me."

But the mention of his name sparked an idea in Neferure's heart. It caught alight, flaming hot.

Where was Senenmut tonight? Typically he would take supper with Neferure, and they would go over plans for the temples, and he would listen to all her cares and concerns and smooth them away with a gentle hand on her brow and a soft, loving smile. Surely his absence was a part of what unsettled her ka, but it was the injustice she had been made to suffer through in the great hall that truly vexed her.

Even Takhat did not know where Senenmut was. Neferure could see that at once; she felt the assurance of it deep in that place Ahmose had spoken of, where her ka quivered and raged. And without Senenmut close to hand....

"Take me to my mother or I'll scream and cry!"

"Oh, stop this at once! It's been six years since you last nursed at my breast. You are not a baby any longer."

Neferure sucked in a breath, held it a moment, held Takhat's eye. The challenge crackled in the air between them, but Neferure knew she had already won. She unleashed a high-pitched scream that rebounded off her chamber walls.

"Set take you!" Takhat threw her sewing onto the couch beside her and clapped her hands over her ears, glowering, thinking to outlast Neferure's tantrum.

But she screamed again and again, and pitched herself onto the floor, kicked her heels against the tiles, beat her fists until Takhat stormed from the room calling Senenmut's name. Neferure kept up her shrieking, though her throat felt raw. It almost felt good to scream, to give some voice to her ka's great anger. And she knew Takhat would not find Senenmut in his apartment at the outer wall of the House of Women, where he was supposed to be conveniently located to see to the needs of the King's Daughter. If he had been nearby at all, he would have come to Neferure's chamber with her supper tray.

She let her tantrum go on until at last Takhat returned to the room, scowling her defeat, and said, "Get up, you beast. The guards are fetching a litter to take you to the palace."

Neferure ceased her screaming and climbed to her feet. She tugged her dress straight, smoothed the locks of hair that had pulled free of her braid, and walked sedately from her chamber with Takhat trailing behind, muttering in impotent wrath.

The guards on Hatshepsut's door clapped and called out Neferure's presence, but it was a long time before the door opened.

To Neferure's uneasy surprise, it was Senenmut who opened the door. He gazed down at his pupil slack-jawed, in a state of dumbfoundedness totally unfamiliar to the girl. She narrowed her eyes at him. His only duty was not to Neferure, she knew. He was still the king's chief steward, and had many other titles besides. There were a dozen reasons why he might be in the king's personal chambers so long into the evening, but it rankled her all the same.

"I want to see my mother."

Senenmut glanced over his shoulder, into the dim depths of the king's anteroom. It was poorly lit – too dark for reading off tallies or drafting plans for more obelisks or...or whatever Senenmut's duties to Hatshepsut may be.

The sound of a far door swinging reached her, and the light scuff of slippers on faience tile. Senenmut pulled the door wider, stood back for Neferure to enter. Takhat refused to come; she lurked in the hall with the guardsmen, her hard stare full of unpleasant promise. Neferure shrugged at her wet-nurse and escorted herself into the king's presence.

Hatshepsut made her way from the door to her private chamber, wrapped in an informal light robe instead of the gown or kilt Neferure had expected. Had she been sleeping, then?

"Light a few more lamps, Senenmut. Neferure, what is the meaning of this?" Her voice held an unmistakable impatience. Hatshepsut was often awkward in her attempts to be motherly, but she seldom lost her patience.

Courage flooded Neferure's limbs; it replaced the former quivering in her ka with a welcome rush. "I want to be a Hathor priestess. I want to go to Iunet and pledge myself to the goddess, like those other girls." She felt grown-up and powerful, standing in the king's chambers without her wet-nurse, speaking the true words of her heart.

Hatshepsut frowned. "You cannot. Your duties lie in Waset, with Amun. You know that."

Somehow she had not expected such a flat denial, though

flat denials were Hatshepsut's most oft-traded ware. "But why? You told the girls in the throne room today that they were the best in all of Egypt. I am the King's Daughter. I am descended from a god! Am I not better than they? Will I not please Hathor more?"

Senenmut had finished with the lamps; he sank onto the edge of the couch where Hatshepsut sat and clasped his hands on his rather rumpled kilt. "You are the very best girl in all of Egypt, Neferure."

"And that is why you are reserved for Amun," Hatshepsut added.

"I am not even God's Wife! Amun will never miss me."

"You are God's Wife; don't say such things."

"I am not!"

"You hold the title, and you are learning the duties, little by little, as is maat for a girl your age. One day you will take on the role fully and serve Amun as I did, and as your grandmother did, and her grandmother before her. You will be his adoratrix. That is your duty: the adoration of Amun. It is a light duty, to love a god. Would you rather grind wheat? Tend cattle and step in their dung? Get blisters on your fingers from spinning and weaving?"

"I am not his wife. He spurns me!"

"What makes you say that?"

"He never speaks to me. Lady Ahmose said I could hear the gods speak, but I...I..." Bereft of words, she could only pound her fist against her chest, helpless to articulate the way she burned there, the way some unknown god always whispered there, too distant to hear, too unknowable to draw near. She craved that nearness, yearned to feel enlightened, understood in the way only a god could understand. And she would be understood, and enlightened, and known if she could but let that quiet god in. She was sure of it, *sure* of it.

Senenmut's eyes filled with sympathy, but something else, too. Resignation. Even he knew it was useless to make such demands of Hatshepsut. She was the Lord of the Two Lands, and Neferure was, in spite of the vast potential she felt coiling far deep inside her like a seed in the black soil, nothing but a little girl.

Briefly she considered another tantrum, but her mother's eyes were dark and hard and impatient, her mouth tight with disapproval, and Neferure's throat was too raw and constricted to scream.

All at once her vision blurred. Hot tears slid down her cheeks, tickled alongside her nose. She wiped at them, angry to have lost composure before the king.

Senenmut came to her. He sank to his knees so that she might weep on his shoulder. But Hatshepsut rose and returned to her private chambers, a coldness in her silence that both frightened Neferure and made her feel faintly, quietly triumphant. But far larger and darker than her triumph, she felt a weight of sorrow dragging at her heart. It was a desperation she could not explain, even within her own thoughts. She only knew that inside she was like a chasm in the hills, a dark cleft in stone that echoed with a terrible emptiness Amun could not fill.

Chapter Eleven

THE GRAIN STOOD WAIST HIGH. It tickled Thutmose's forearms and the small of his back, but he did not flinch. He tried to stretch himself taller, to rise out of the emmer field as regally as Hatshepsut, who stood proud and unmoving like a statue beside him, gazing toward the procession that made its slow way from the Temple of Min.

The two Pharaohs were dressed in identical finery: long formal kilts, white-pleated below the embroidered and beaded aprons which hung to their knees. The aprons depicted the Two Ladies who protected the double land, Nekhbet of the south and Wadjet of the north, the vulture and the cobra everlasting. Woman and boy wore broad golden collars adorned with long cabochons of turquoise, lapis, and carnelian; they glowed in the mid-day sun.

The collar was heavy; Thutmose shrugged his shoulders, slowly and carefully, to ease its weight. He hoped none of the festival-goers would notice his discomfort. Hatshepsut made no concessions to the weight of her ceremonial garb, and Thutmose was determined to follow her lead as best he could. Sweat had begun to collect beneath his stiff artificial beard. It was made of braided flax stems wound about with golden bands, and it was unwieldy and itchy at the best of times. He was afraid it would become a torment in the heat of the day, but he would not poke his fingers beneath the straps to rub the irritation away. Not unless Hatshepsut did first. The only kindness of ceremony was the high spire of his white crown. In spite of its height it was ingeniously made, light and hollow. It protected his head from the sun and kept him cooler than any wig would have done. The Pharaoh's crown was one small mercy.

Yet for all their matching garb, Thutmose felt conspicuously inferior beside his co-regent. It was not only that she was taller – though in truth, she was by no means a statuesque woman. Hatshepsut exuded a compelling force of absolute confidence, a natural power which Thutmose despaired of ever developing himself. He loved and admired her, for she was the only mother he had ever known. And he envied her with the casually entitled envy only a boy-king can feel. Why should she not have such a force of presence? She was the offspring of Amun himself, while Thutmose was the son of a Pharaoh, ah – but a Pharaoh bred of distinctly mortal flesh.

"You remember what is required of you," Hatshepsut said quietly as the approaching procession drew nearer the edge of the field.

It was not a question, and Thutmose had no need of questioning. In his drive to become as much a Pharaoh as she, he had immersed himself in his studies, surpassing the expectations of his tutors, even of Hatshepsut herself. He remembered the required steps of the Min ceremony. Of course. They were in his blood now, so thoroughly had he pored over the scrolls and practiced the movements, the words, even rehearsing alone in his chambers when his tutors had left him. He nodded without looking up at her.

The procession came singing, acrobats with long-braided, unshorn hair flipping hand over foot along the broad, dusty road, priests and priestesses waving papyrus-frond banners on painted poles high above their heads. Thutmose caught a flash of gold from the midst of the parade. It flashed again, and he heard a bellow. *The white bull.* The representation of Min in the flesh, who would oversee the opening of the harvest and impose his mighty fertility upon the Two Lands – and upon the Pharaohs – for another year.

Beyond the bull, the statue of Min bobbed above the crowd,

held aloft on a broad wooden shield borne by a cadre of priests. The nobility of Waset thronged behind, clapping and singing, some of them already well and truly drunk, to judge by the stumbling and laughter. Let them be merry: the fields had been remarkably fertile this year, and it was only the first of three or perhaps four reapings. This harvest would be one to celebrate.

When the priests of Min reached the edge of the field, they used staffs and switches to maneuver the white bull into position so that he faced from the east, from Min's direction, with the red desert at his scornful back and the black soil before his approving gaze. Thutmose watched the beast warily. It was huge – much larger than he had expected, its shoulders high and rounded with tense, quivering muscle. The priests had pampered it and fattened it on sweet grains and beer; its body trembled with weight and power when it stamped a gilded hoof. A burnished sun-disc was tied between the bull's upright horns, and when it tossed its great, stern head amongst a cloud of black flies the disc shivered and swung and threw bright light into Thutmose's eyes.

The shield that bore Min's statue sank to the ground so the god might watch the proceedings. When the priests backed away, there was Neferure, slim as a reed, frail-looking, with her large, haunting eyes peering solemnly out from the cascade of ribbons adorning her God's Wife crown. She stepped upon the shield with tiny silver sandals and laid one hand on Min's shoulder. She was only a little girl, but already she was beautiful, with delicate features and luminous skin, and a quiet, obedient, thoughtful nature. More than once, Thutmose had wondered why Hatshepsut had made no move to betroth her daughter to him. He had overheard enough talk amongst soldiers and guards and drunken men at feasts to know that grown men were especially happy when they could marry beautiful women, and Neferure would grow up to be the most beautiful woman in the world. Gazing at his sister now, at the brightness of her crown and the elegance of her small hands, Thutmose wished jealously for her, but she remained as distant and aloof as a star.

When the nobility had drawn up in a wide arc and some semblance of quiet fell over the crowd, Hatshepsut raised her palms toward the statue of Min. Thutmose did the same.

"A blessing to you, Min, who fertilizes the Mother. Deep is the secret of what you did to her in the dark."

The High Priest of Min stepped forward, bearing the ceremonial hoe. Its handle was carved at each end with lotus blooms, and it was painted in bands of red and blue – too ornate an instrument for any rekhet farmer to use. Thutmose had his doubts about its ability to break the soil. But he stepped forward to receive it, proud that his movements were sure and direct. He drove its tip into the earth, pulled with all his strength; the roots of grasses and weeds made a tearing sound as the deep black earth revealed itself, full of the rich scents of growth and renewal.

The High Priest appeared again, and passed a golden vessel of river water into Thutmose's hands. The vessel was heavy; he took an unsteady step, clutching it to his chest, his heart lurching in a moment of terrible panic. Water sloshed onto his shoulder, and his face went hot with humiliation. But he righted himself, and with great solemnity he poured the water into the trench he had opened.

"The earth is renewed," the priest intoned. "Thanks be to Min."

Hatshepsut came forward from the emmer field to stand at his side. The priestesses sang their hymns to the god while the sun grew ever hotter. Thutmose willed himself to remain immobile, staring over the heads of the gathered crowd with what he hoped was a mysteriously distant expression, silently cursing the flies that landed on his legs and arms to drink his sweat with their prickling tongues.

Over the harmonies of the hymn, the white bull's tail sliced repeatedly through the air with a sharp whistle like a goose's wing. Thutmose heard the best grunt and stamp. Suddenly he gasped in pain – one of the flies had bitten him on the back of his knee. He could not stop himself slapping at it, shaking his leg to ease the sting.

Mercifully, the hymn came to a close and Neferure presented the double crowns, red and white, to the two Pharaohs. The opportunity to bow his head to the God's Wife and receive the new crown was welcome; with his face ducked and Neferure's slight body blocking the eyes of the crowd, he could flick the sweat from his eyes.

"Thank you, sister," he murmured.

Neferure made no reply.

Thutmose was still too small to draw the ceremonial bow, and so he retreated gratefully to the emmer, where the flies were less thick, as Hatshepsut stepped forward. A priest had planted four different-colored arrows point down in the soil.

"In the name of myself, Maatkare Khnemet-Amun Hatshepsut, and in the name of Menkheperre Thutmose, the third of his name, the Good Gods, I fire these arrows to the four winds."

She drew the bow so effortlessly, looked so strong and divine as she held herself poised for a moment, the fletchings against her cheek, her eyes keen and far-seeing beneath the double crown. When she loosed, each arrow passed above the crowd faster than a falcon diving.

It was Thutmose's turn to resume the ceremony. He reached both hands into the small wooden cage the High Priest proffered. The black gebgeb birds inside scolded and snapped at his fingers, but he caught one and drew it forth. It glared at him with a spiteful yellow eye.

"For the son of Horus, Imsety," he announced, and tossed the gebgeb into the air.

It fluttered, faltered, caught itself on indignant black wings, and sailed into the field of emmer.

Thutmose drew out another.

"For the son of Horus, Hapi."

The second gebgeb flew in the opposite direction to its brother. It was a good sign.

"For the son of Horus, Duamutef."

This bird soared over the heads of the noble ladies gathered in a knot to Thutmose's left. They shrieked good-naturedly, and the bull snorted. The deep animal sound made Thutmose uneasy.

He reached into the cage for the final bird, but it evaded him, rattling between its wooden bars, screaming. At last he caught it and winced; its strong bill closed over the skin of one knuckle and twisted viciously, but Thutmose would not let it go.

"For the son of Horus, Qebesenuef."

He tossed the gebgeb into the air. It scolded as it righted itself against the hot blue sky, then sailed directly toward the white bull of Min.

He heard the women scream before his eyes registered the danger. The bull, already tormented beyond its patience by the flies, raised its head to roar at the black bird. The motion jerked the restraining ropes free from the priests' hands, and in a heartbeat the bull was charging straight toward Thutmose. He was aware of the High Priest leaping out of the way, but could not seem to make his own legs move. The bull bore down upon him, and his eyes filled with the image of the sun disc swinging wildly between the sharp horns, blinding him with its brilliant and terrible light.

A hand hard as bronze caught his upper arm, yanked him backward into the wheat. He had a brief glimpse of a canopy of green-and-gold emmer heads nodding above him, shielding him from the bull's view, as he fell hard onto his backside. Thutmose scrambled up at once. Hatshepsut was beside him, her hand still clutching him, her eyes wide with shock.

The awful, roaring weight of the bull thundered past, scattering nobles into the field and back toward the temple road. But rather than give chase, it turned, flipping its head this way and that in a fury. The sun disc spun madly on its ties. Thutmose could smell the bull – a sharp, bestial odor of sweat and power, of a god's rage. He watched, helpless, as its eye fell upon little Neferure standing still beside the statue of Min.

The bull bellowed, and Thutmose screamed, "No!"

He could do nothing to stop it. It lowered its horns and charged.

Thutmose heard a strange, sudden sound, high and wailing and helpless. In an agony of disbelief, he realized Hatshepsut was crying out for her daughter, all her regal composure gone, her voice womanish and afraid.

There was an explosion of dust and a terrifying thunder like two great blocks of stone scraping. Thutmose could not see; all was too-bright dust glimmering in the sun, obscuring everything, everything but the sounds of panic.

But in another moment the dust settled, dissipated on a river breeze. The bull stood quivering in its tracks, its legs still rigid from the abruptness of its stop.

Neferure stood on her toes at the edge of Min's shield, face to face with the white bull. She reached a small, pale hand up and allowed it to smell her skin. It blew out fiercely. Then it lowered its head, nodded, bowed. Neferure caressed the broad white forehead, the tense, mobile ears, the triumphant, shining horns.

She peered up from amidst the ribbons of her crown, caught Thutmose's eye. The piercing force of her look stole his breath away, and he knew all at once that the girl held within her ka a power as great as Hatshepsut's. Perhaps greater.

For the first time in his life, the young Pharaoh feared his sister.

CHAPTER TWELVE

NEFERURE HAD BEEN BACK IN her small private apartment only a handful of minutes before the summons came. She heard a clap at her door, followed by Takhat's muttering as she scrambled to answer it, dumping the load of linens she had been sorting for washing and pleating onto Neferure's fine red couch. Neferure, reaching up to place her God's Wife crown upon its shelf, froze and held her breath, listening.

"To the palace?" Takhat said. "But we must prepare for the feast! If we go to the palace now, there will be no time..."

The messenger said a few words Neferure could not catch, and Takhat hastened to reassure him. "No, of course not. The God's Wife is always the humble servant of the Horus Throne. Did you bring a litter for the Great Lady? Good. You may go; we will be along shortly."

Takhat scowled as she shut the door – nearly slammed it, in truth. Neferure finished securing her crown and turned to face her servant, waiting.

"Well, is that not the way of things! You are wanted at the palace, *immediately*, to hear that puffed-up fancy of a man tell it. *Immediately*, said he! As if I haven't enough to do already, preparing you for the Feast of Min. Pah!" She fairly spat at the pile of linens. "By all the gods, I work harder every year, and who sees it? Not the Pharaohs, oh, no! No, not even you, Lady! You see only yourself in the mirror, or your little statues of Hathor."

Neferure frowned at her, trying for a stern look, although in truth her heart was leaping. She had known her mother would send for her – *known* it, and it had come to pass. *It must have been a god who told me. How else could I have known?*

Takhat clutched frantically at this bit of linen and that necklace, wedged a small cosmetics box beneath her bony arm, and bundled Neferure from the apartment, still sighing and groaning over her sad lot in life. The brightness of the sun in the harem courtyard made Neferure blink; it blazed off the gilt sides and canopy of an ornate litter. Ringed about it were eight men with the sun-darkened skins and flat, muscular shoulders of bearers, and a contingent of palace guards, too, standing at attention in kilts striped blue and white. It gladdened Neferure to see that the golden uprights which held the litter's curtains were carved with Hathor's smiling face.

Neferure clutched her hands to her pounding heart as she boarded the litter and sank onto its cushioned chair. Takhat drew the curtains to shut out the dust, and one of the guards barked an order. The litter lifted onto the shoulders of the bearers, and Neferure's heart lifted, exulting, into the sky.

She was admitted at once into the king's chamber, as she knew she would be. She entered with her chin raised, flush with a new confidence she had never before felt in the presence of her mother. She felt the power of the gods beating within her, throbbing with the strong, steady pulse of her heart.

When the guard on the door announced the God's Wife, Hatshepsut sprang from her couch and came to meet her, pulled her into an embrace that lasted a moment too long. Neferure squirmed away, took a step back to regain her regal composure.

"Gods, but I feared when I saw the bull.... Neferure, my daughter. If I'd lost you, I would have gone mad."

"Lost me?" Neferure wanted to tell her mother not to be foolish; the bull had been in her command all along. Was the beast not the embodiment of a god, and did the gods not love her? But a familiar voice shouted from the rear of the chambers, a wordless cry of relief, and Senenmut rushed to her side. He gathered her into his arms, kissing her cheeks and giving vent to a sound that was nearly a wail. She laughed at his silliness and wrapped her arms around his neck, kissing him in return, until Hatshepsut spoke again. Neferure recalled herself and stepped away from her tutor, resumed her tilted chin and her air of confidence.

"Yes, lost you," said Hatshepsut. "You are lucky to be in one piece. Perhaps you are too young for this God's Wife business after all. I was hasty…"

"No," she said quickly. "It suits me."

Hatshepsut sighed. "A year ago you were demanding that I make you a Hathor priestess. You said Amun spurned you. Has the god changed his heart, then?"

Neferure's chin and ka fell a little. "No," she admitted. "But at least the work keeps me near the gods."

Hatshepsut tilted her head to one side. Her eyes were very dark in their cage of black kohl, and stern as Thutmose's gebgeb birds. They lingered on Neferure's face a long while. She held her mother's gaze with great effort, but she was proud that her legs did not shake.

At last Hatshepsut said, "You have been…different of late, child."

"Different, Mother?"

"Settled. Dare I tempt the gods to make me a fool by saying it aloud? Yes, *settled*."

Neferure's hand flexed at her side. She could still feel the dryness of the bull's dusty coat, the intensity of holy life quivering within his great, blowing, roaring body. She felt still the connection that had thrilled from his forehead where she had stroked him, into her palm, up her arm, into her heart. It sped its beat again as she recalled that she had touched a god. Neferure felt anything but settled. She felt like a chariot horse when the reins are loosed.

She held her tongue, waiting.

"Maat," the king said, as if to herself. "I am the Pharaoh; I should see clearly what is maat."

"Do you not see clearly?" Neferure's voice was high and shaky. A curious energy flowed through her; her blood was all waves and whitecaps.

"What if, child. What if I sent you to Iunet, only part of the time?" Hatshepsut at once turned away, paced the floor of her great, richly decorated chamber. She picked up some small silver bauble from a waist-high table and turned it over in her palm, watching it intently as though its rotations might reveal some great mystery. Neferure squinted at the bauble; it was the figure of a bull.

"It could be useful, after all, to have my...to have the God's Wife trained in the ways of the Lady of Seven."

Hatshepsut glanced up, looked to Senenmut. The steward frowned in mild confusion and said nothing. Hatshepsut replaced the silver bull on its table and turned back to face Neferure.

"I shall think on it, child. Continue your work, and let me pray, and consider all the consequences. If it is maat – if Amun wills it – you may have your time with your goddess yet."

Neferure clapped her hands together; she bit back the squeal that fought to spring from her throat. Squealing would be most undignified. But she beamed at her mother, and at her tutor, overcome with joy and the heat of triumph.

Hatshepsut laid a hand on her shoulder. "Nothing is certain yet. Much depends on the High Priest, and on the god."

"Do not allow your hopes to run way from your good sense," Senenmut added quietly. But his voice was warm, and carried in it a note of the same happiness Neferure felt filling her heart, spilling over like a vessel overwhelmed by sweet, cool wine.

"I will not; I swear it."

Hatshepsut smiled, shook her head. "It is good to see you so pleased, Neferure. If ever I knew what maat looked like, I could swear your happiness is its very image. Now run along; Takhat is waiting. You have a feast to prepare for, God's Wife of Amun."

"Thank you, Mother. Oh – thank you, thank you!"

That evening when the court gathered for the Feast of Min, filling the great hall with the colors and songs of celebration, all the talk was of Neferure. Hatshepsut suspected it would be. She gave the invocation in a loud, clear voice that commanded attention, yet so sensational were the rumors that half the guests could not keep their eyes on their Pharaoh. They eyed the King's Daughter instead, and whispered with heads together when Hatshepsut had finished her speech. She could read Neferure's name on their lips.

It troubled her in ka and in heart, to know that such a young girl should be the center of these wild stories. But Neferure seemed oblivious to the attention. She sat serenely at her small table to the left of the Pharaohs' thrones, eyes humbly downcast, attending to her supper with courtesy and grace. She even seemed to be engaging politely with Takhat for once.

A great side of roasted beef entered the hall, garlanded with long loops of braided herbs. Three strong men carried it fore and aft on a stout pole. It dripped red juices down among the bearers' feet. The scent of smoke and spices trailed it like a banner. The people cheered to see it, raising their beer bowls high as the beef paraded down the length of the throne to the foot of the dais, where Hatshepsut approved it with a nod and a smile and commanded the cooks to cut a portion for each guest in attendance.

With the crowd distracted by the spectacle, she eyed this face and that warily, searching for some sign that the rumors might be multiplying and flying. The tales were already lively enough. Neferure had kissed the bull, they said, and the bull knelt to her. Or she had ridden on its back. Or she had slain it with a touch of her hand, then raised it back to life with a word.

The truth of the matter was hardly supernatural. The bull had been raised in the presence of people since it was a calf. Once its rage at the flies had passed, why should it not calmly accept the attentions of a child? All bulls enjoyed a scratch between the horns – even the newest acolytes to Min's priesthood knew as much.

The kitchen staff bore in more courses: trays heaped with sticky honey cakes, melon balls wrapped in flower petals, waterfowl and game birds roasted or stewed, sweet or savory. Between each course the entertainers moved about the tables, women in bright-banded wigs singing sweetly with their harpers in tow, drifting from one great man to another, laying a hand on a shoulder, proffering a lotus blossom to a lady of the court. Acrobats wheeled and tumbled, their bodies glistening with paint, their brief loincloths flitting like sun-beetles on the wing. At a particularly daring tumble, the court would raise its cups and bowls high, cheering, and Thutmose would reach for the tray of trinkets his servant held. He scattered handfuls of jewelry, rings of gold and silver, chains bearing lapis and turquoise pendants, and tossed larger handfuls as the court increased its acclaim. When an especially light and pliant young girl flipped toward a table of drunken nobles, lifted herself to a hand-stand upon the merchant Ranefer's unsteady shoulders, then vaulted clear over his companion's heads, Thutmose nearly shouted himself, so thrilled was he with the girl's performance. He lifted a double fistful of baubles and let them fly through the air, and the girl gathered up the best of them in her hands as she tumbled past the dais, then bowed low in thanks.

As course followed course and singer followed acrobat, Hatshepsut found herself bracing for the aftermath of the Min incident. She watched her children attend to the feast, Thutmose with cheer and enthusiasm, Neferure with quiet dignity, while a creeping sense of foolishness plagued her thoughts. Neferure had not intentionally upstaged the

Pharaohs at the Min Festival, yet she had stolen their majesty all the same. Hatshepsut picked at her dish of duck breast stewed in pomegranate seeds, wondering what her subjects thought of her now. The Good God Maatkare leapt from the path of a charging bull, but an eight-year-old girl had seemingly tamed it with a touch of her hand.

Will they think my authority is diminished?

She allowed her eyes to wander down the length of the hall, scrutinizing each conversation from the lonely pinnacle of the throne. Ladies in beaded gowns tipped their heads together to mutter close to one another's ears, the cones of perfumed wax adorning their wigs coming together in a conspiratorial manner. Noblemen nodded over their beer with intense murmurs.

At a nearby table, where the women of the harem sat passing bowls of sweets and laughing, the tjati of a local district knelt to make conversation with Opet, Hatshepsut's half-sister. She watched as the man spoke near Opet's ear, smiling; Opet glanced up toward the dais, her eyes wide and startled.

He is plotting, was Hatshepsut's immediate and forceful thought. *He knows she and I share a father, that marriage to Opet could place him on the throne. He thinks me weak, frightened, powerless.*

She resisted the urge to clutch Thutmose to her protectively. Instead, she looked round for Senenmut.

"That man down there – the tjati of Herui. What is he doing?"

Senenmut smirked down at the women's tables. "Looking for a little favor with a pretty lady, I assume."

"He is plotting something."

He stifled a sigh – she could see him struggle to stifle it. "Great Lady, I advise you against..."

"We must find out what they are planning."

"They are planning nothing." Senenmut's voice dropped low so that none, not even Thutmose who sat swinging his legs in anticipation of the next performer, might overhear how he argued with the king. "I would advise you against allowing old fears to overtake you."

"Are they so very old? I saw the way Opet looked up at me when he whispered to her. She looked startled, and...and speculative."

"They were probably looking at Neferure. Everyone else is."

Hatshepsut drew a deep breath, held it until it pushed painfully against her chest. Senenmut was right. She must not allow fear to rule her. The old fears were gone now, she reminded herself. She had driven them away on the battlefield in Kush.

When she exhaled, the tension drained from her, and only a calm cunning remained in her heart. "How is Ineni managing?"

"Managing, Great Lady?"

"His influence amongst the nobles."

"As well as ever, as far as I can see."

And how long would be go on managing? His mind was still sharp, but he was older than Ahmose, and the gods never gave years back to any man. It was but a matter of time before Ineni left for the Field of Reeds, and when he did, who would be her rein on the nobles' bits?

She searched the hall again until she found him. Ineni sat in the midst of a circle of great men, merchants and governors, judges and architects. His mouth moved in careful speech; his head tilted in that thoughtful way he had, mild and yet so impossibly clever. The men leaned toward him eagerly, like children seeking sweets from their nurse. Even at this distance she could see the age on his face, the slight stoop of his shoulders.

"Go to Ineni, Senenmut. Give him a summons to my chamber, tomorrow at mid-day."

Senenmut bowed again and turned to descend the steps of the dais. She caught his hand. He smiled down at her, briefly, covertly.

"And the High Priest of Amun, too."

Chapter Thirteen

SENENMUT ARRIVED OUTSIDE HATSHEPSUT'S QUARTERS before mid-day, just as Nehesi rounded a pillar and stepped into the king's outer hall. The Medjay moved with the same bullish stride and imposing power he had always shown – a marvel, for Nehesi was older than Senenmut, and at thirty-three years, by the grace of the gods, Senenmut was no longer a fresh colt. Of late he had noted a persistent ache in his right knee, and his shoulders did not want to ride as squarely as they once had. They drooped some, if he did not pay them heed. The effect made his chest and stomach seem rather rounder and softer than they were. True, Nehesi was an active soldier. The profession tended to weed out those who could not meet the physical demands of the work early on. Only men lucky in breeding and extensive in blessings could keep up with such a career.

Senenmut's work had its own demands. In addition to managing his estates, he oversaw – in an official if not a practical capacity – dozens of the king's interests, including the granaries, the treasury, and the sacred cattle of Amun. And the King's Daughter – never forget her. Most of his work, excepting that which involved Neferure, was conducted by scroll and scribe, with Senenmut seated at a table, running figures and tallies, issuing orders for the dispensation or acquisition of this or that or another. Small wonder a man such as Nehesi, who hurled spears and rode the chariot day in and day out, should still have the physique of a young soldier.

Of course, knowing the reason for their discrepancies did not cause them to sting any less. *The gods can be monstrous cruel sometimes*, Senenmut mused, jerking his body upright and setting his shoulders well back.

"The King's Great Steward has eaten a sour fig," Nehesi said when he noticed Senenmut's scowl.

Senenmut was about to rejoin, but one of the ornate double doors to the Pharaoh's chamber gave a small, high-pitched creak as it opened abruptly. The fan-bearer Batiret peered out at them, frowning.

"Maatkare is not within."

Nehesi grinned at the woman as he leaned one massive shoulder against the closed door. "I know, sweet lady. I am her chief guard, after all."

"Then why are you not guarding her?"

A tiny laugh escaped through Senenmut's nose. Batiret had been in Hatshepsut's service for nearly ten years now. In these very chambers she had grown from a skinny, wide-eyed girl to a woman of simple yet frank beauty, with an open, questioning stare and a serious angle to her dark brows that other men seemed to find enchanting. She was impertinent, but with good reason. Was she not the handmaid of the king? Had she not earned the Pharaoh's most intimate trust, risking her own life to taste food and wine in those dark, early days?

Batiret made a shooing motion with small, golden-brown hands. "Off the Good God's door. You will get nothing from me. It takes more than ox muscles to impress this lady."

"Oh-ho! Senenmut, our little cat likes to hiss."

"She is not my little cat, Nehesi. You are welcome to get yourself clawed and bitten; leave me out of it. And leave off her. The poor lady is only doing her work."

"As you should be, Chief Guardsman," Batiret said. "Shall I tell my lady you could not attend her because you were too busy looking for a flower to sniff?"

The heat rose to Senenmut's face.

"By Set!" Nehesi roared in appreciation. "She has a tongue

like a dock worker! As it happens, Lady Batiret, the Good God is right behind me. I left her with a contingent of my best men. They accompany her and the High Priest of Amun. She summoned all of us."

A soft yet masculine voice called from somewhere inside the king's chamber. "She did."

"You've got a lover in there," Nehesi said. He clutched at his heart, feigning grave injury.

"I have no such thing. If I had, I wouldn't be dull enough to bring him to my lady's chambers for a tryst. What kind of a fool do you take me for, Nehesi?"

Batiret stepped back, let the door swing wide to admit them. She jerked back against it abruptly to prevent Nehesi brushing her skin as he entered.

Ineni sat upon one long couch in the middle of Hatshepsut's chamber. Its legs and back were aged ebony, black as a starless sky, carved with lines of lotus and papyrus blossoms. He did not lounge against that ornate backrest, nor lean one elbow on the silk cushions, but held himself straight and alert. In his eyes, keen and penetrating for all the lines surrounding them, Senenmut saw a glimmer of amusement at Nehesi's and Batiret's exchange.

"Lord Ineni." Senenmut clasped his forearm warmly. "It has been too long."

"You are a busy man these days, Senenmut."

"I do the tasks the Good God sets me, as do we all."

Batiret fetched a painted clay jug from the blue-shadowed shaft beneath a windcatcher. When she poured, the wine was so cool Senenmut could smell its inviting crispness. He raised his bowl to his lips gratefully; the day was hot, even in the king's chambers.

"And what task has the Good God set us today, I wonder," Ineni said, tasting his own wine.

Senenmut recalled Hatshepsut's growing agitation at last night's feast, the dark slits of her eyes as she watched the tjati whispering into Opet's ear. He could not say, *The king is frightened again.* Not even to Ineni. It was disloyal, but more:

Senenmut was not at all certain Hatshepsut had no reason to fear. The harem was fairly brimming with women who might conceivably provide an ambitious noble a path to the throne. Nine years had passed since Iset's death – ah, and Nebseny's, and Ankhhor's. Hatshepsut's wrath had been swift and efficient, but men's memories seldom lasted nine years. Not when Egypt's throne hung before them, a prize they might yet win.

Senenmut had puzzled it all out last night, remaining awake nearly until dawn, staring into the darkness of the unlit chamber while Hatshepsut turned in restless sleep beside him. The harem was full of royal and semi-royal women; Hatshepsut could not banish them as she had Mutnofret. To do so would only bring about the wrath of near-countless great houses, and foreign kings besides. Hatshepsut may feast the harem and keep the treasury of the House of Women overfull, may send them musicians and sweets and Egypt's finest seamstresses, but there was one thing she could not provide her women. They had no chance now to bear the Pharaoh's children, and thus to further their families' various glories. No chance until young Thutmose came of age, and that was still some four or five years away, at least. Many of them would be too old for children by Thutmose's majority, and those who were still fertile may be too aged to spark the typically fickle interest of a very young man. In the House of Women, Hatshepsut had a pot over a high blaze, and it was a breath away from boiling over. How long before they began petitioning for release – for marriage to powerful houses? How long before great men began to woo them in earnest, to use the women's royal blood and their children as claims to the throne?

And however will I stop them?

Batiret saved Senenmut the trouble of trying to formulate a reply to Ineni's question. She hastened to set her jug on the floor and made her way toward the doors well before Senenmut caught the sound of Hatshepsut and her guards returning. The fan-bearer swung both doors wide to welcome the king.

Hatshepsut wore a man's kilt in the day's excessive heat. The floor-length, bright white linen was overlaid with a long beaded apron. The vibrant blue-and-green polished stone feathers of a vulture spread its wings across her chest. The pectoral was large enough to cover her breasts completely, offset by a counterweight that swung by a thick gold chain down the length of her short but elegant back. The double crown of the Two Lands, white and red and spired like an obelisk, rose from her brow.

Batiret clapped loudly to summon the king's body-maids; they emerged from the bedchamber in a rustle of airy gowns, took the crown from her, loosed the pectoral's chain and caught it as it slipped from Hatshepsut's body.

"The apron, too – here. And my wig."

"Your wig, Majesty? With these men here to see you, and..."

"It's hotter than beneath a spice-seller's kilt."

Hatshepsut pulled the wig from her own brow and tossed it at one of her women. The wig's hundred tiny braids separated as it flew, spread in the stifling air like the arms of startled women. The body-maid let loose a small squeal of dismay as she snatched it to her breast.

"My apologies to the High Priest of Amun. My old nurse was never able to beat the coarse language from my tongue. The gods know she tried."

Hapuseneb the High Priest bowed. A vast collection of medallions swung from a tangle of cords round his neck: protections and beseechings of all kinds, all to channel the power of Amun. "Majesty, with the offering you just made at Amun's temple I am prepared to forgive your tongue and your nurse most anything."

"I take it you know Lord Ineni, High Priest?"

"Ah, an accomplished architect and tomb-builder, if I am not mistaken. Amun smiles on you."

"Hapuseneb." Ineni inclined his head.

Hatshepsut took a bowl of wine from Batiret, then dropped peremptorily onto one of the couches. "It is too hot to play-act as coy politicians today. Let us be forthright, shall we? Ineni is a good influence amongst the nobles, but as my reign goes on, everlasting if it be the gods' will, men will find their own ambitions too great a temptation to ignore. I already faced that trouble once, and I will not face it again. How, then, do we curb Egypt's nobles?"

At such a frank question, the men were momentarily speechless, grasping for some solution to Hatshepsut's problem. But as the cool wine flowed more freely, so did their words, their ideas, until the king's chamber grew lively with their voices and the emphatic gestures of their hands, even in the stifling heat.

"I know noble men," Nehesi said. "They respect great wealth more than anything else – more even than kings, or gods, with apologies to you, Majesty, and to you, High Priest."

"Maatkare has made Egypt wealthier than any king before her," Hapuseneb pointed out. "But this wealth takes the form of cattle and cloth, trade goods and increased yields of crops. It is real, ah, as real as any gold bauble. Yet men like Ankhhor do not see such wealth, I think. They see only the glint of gems, or the fineness of a gown's weave. It's treasure they must see in order to recognize – and fear – your power."

Hatshepsut leaned back against a cushion. Her breasts heaved with her sigh. "And how do I convert Egypt's trade wealth into trinkets shiny enough to impress a lot of fat old men?"

"Hiring craftsmen to make wagons full of jewelry and fine cloth, just for the fun of the thing?" Nehesi shook his head. "It would be too ostentatious, even for a king. They would see at once that you were trying very hard to prove something. Any advantage you might gain from the wealth would be lost in appearing less than confident before them. No – what you need is another campaign. Into a rich land, this time – richer than Kush. You need to capture treasure, bring it back in triumph."

The men went very still at his words. Ineni swirled the wine in his bowl, his eyes thoughtful, considering. Senenmut glanced at Hatshepsut; her face had blanched.

"He may be right," Hapuseneb admitted. "Kush seemed to fortify you, not only in the eyes of the army, but, if you will forgive my presumption, Majesty, in your own eyes. Another campaign – north this time, perhaps..."

"No." She turned her face to Senenmut, held his eyes with her own dark stare. He recalled how, years ago, she returned with her fleet in triumph and paraded through Waset's streets at the head of her army. That night he had clutched her to his chest in the pale gray twilight, out in the garden beneath the forgiving coolness of the sycamore, while she sobbed out the story of the man she had killed – the man, his woman, his child. It was all she could talk about, all she could think about, for weeks afterward.

"Great Lady," Nehesi said, "a campaign can do much for your ends. Hatti has always been rich in copper, and..."

Batiret bent close to Senenmut's ear. "Lord Steward, your man is here. He begs your attention."

"My man?" Senenmut looked around. The slant of light falling in through the wind-catcher's bars angled more acutely than he'd thought to see. It was a darker golden hue, too. Far more time had passed than he had realized. He was expected to meet with his scribe Kynebu nearly an hour ago. Senenmut made his excuses to the circle, now coming very near to squabbling with their king, and allowed Batiret to accompany him to the chamber doors.

Kynebu, a smart lad of sixteen years with a fine, steady hand and a good head for numbers, stood in the king's hall tapping a fat scroll against his palm. "Master Senenmut. You forgot our appointment, I think."

"The Pharaoh's work has kept me. Still keeps me, I'm afraid."

The boy smiled in his usual good cheer, held out the scroll. "No matter; I've finished the work for you."

"There's a good man. Remind me to double your wages."

"Triple them, I think. I made an extra copy of the plans in case you should find it useful, and recopied your notes so they are more legible."

Senenmut frowned. "I am accounted a more than fair scribe, Kynebu."

"No doubt, Master!"

"One does not rise to my position with a sloppy hand."

Kynebu winked, and drew from his sash a small bundle wrapped in stiff, greasy papyrus of a coarse, common make. He tossed it to his master. When Senenmut opened it, the aroma of nuts spiced in honey rose up to meet him.

"The Great Scribe's favorite sweet, because he is a good and worthy master."

"Bribery does not become a man of your station," Senenmut said. But he tipped a few of the nuts from the papyrus into his mouth. The sweetness invigorated him at once. "Ah. I could face a dozen more hot afternoons doing the Pharaoh's work now."

"So, triple my wages, then?"

"Get on, you. I will send you more work tomorrow."

Senenmut quickly emptied the package of the remaining spiced nuts, chewing carefully as Batiret closed the door firmly on the praises Kynebu sang to her. The thick scroll crinkled where he'd tucked it under his arm. He pulled it free and shook it in the air to dissipate the moisture of his own sweat from the papyrus.

"What are you waving about there?" Hatshepsut called. "A sword for the campaign these three would have me undertake?"

Senenmut stopped chewing. His hand tightened on the scroll. He swallowed reflexively, astonished at his own inspiration, and winced as sharp bits of spiced nut scraped down his throat.

At last he managed, "A sword? A campaign? Ah, perhaps it is, at that."

Hatshepsut summoned her maids to clear away the food and wine; Senenmut unrolled his scroll atop the king's table, weighted its corners with their silver drinking bowls. The king leaned toward the table, humming her interest. Even

Batiret, waiting some distance apart with her lady's great fan of white plumes, craned her neck to see. Their interest was gratifying, but it was Hatshepsut's reaction Senenmut cherished. Her face grew very still, eyes widening, mouth compressing into a tight, pale line. He watched the pulse over her collarbone speed.

"It's beautiful," she whispered.

"What is it, by Amun?" Hapuseneb's hand trembled as it clutched the strands of his amulets.

Senenmut allowed himself a thrill of pride – a rare pleasure, for he tried to remain humble. It was not always easily done. Hatshepsut had made him a great lord, and to retain proper humility sometimes felt as much a chore as any of his other duties. "Plans," he said, pleased that his voice did not carry too sharp a note of pride, "for the mortuary temple of Maatkare Hatshepsut, the Good God."

Kynebu had done his work well. Senenmut was an excellent hand when it came to writing, but he had only ever possessed average skill at drawing. The boy had taken Senenmut's detailed notes and calculations, turned them into a stunning depiction of the temple that would soon stand tall above the great, dry valley folded within the yellow cliffs on the west bank of the Iteru. Senenmut recognized it at once, the dimensions, the lines, the terraces rising one above the other, the porticoes both welcoming and enigmatic, intoxicating and inscrutable, like the face of the woman he loved. He recognized it, and yet Kynebu's sketch was more beautiful than Senenmut had imagined the temple to be. He flushed, looking down on the symmetry of it, its boldness and pomp. Its ramps rose like two crescendos from the harmony of pillar and courtyard, lifting the eye and the ka to the sanctuary that rested at the temple's crown. Senenmut knew, with a hot wash of justifiable pride, that Egypt had never seen its like before. A fitting tribute to the woman who was king.

"It's like a song," Hatshepsut said, tracing the course of the upper ramp with a finger. "It sings." She stared up at him, and her eyes were wide with gratitude and wonder.

"It is beautiful," Ineni said. "The pyramids in the north stand higher, but are not half so artful or entrancing. My congratulations to the architect."

Senenmut bowed in thanks.

"This could do it, all right," Hatshepsut said. "Here is a treasure even a man as snake-hearted as Ankhhor will understand."

"Then my king instructs me to build it?"

She raised her eyes to his, and they were bright with gratitude, with love. "Build it, Senenmut. Your king commands."

CHAPTER FOURTEEN

T HE MEN ROSE TO RETURN to their various duties. Amidst the farewell bowing and murmuring of her praises, Hatshepsut laid a hand on Senenmut's forearm as he rolled up his miraculous scroll. Their eyes met; he gave a minute nod, and she watched with quiet approval as he found enough small, insignificant tasks to occupy him about her chambers until the men depated and she and her steward were left alone with Batiret. At length the fan-bearer withdrew as well, taking the emptied wine jugs with her. They clattered as she gathered them up and shoved aside the door to the servants' quarters with her hip. Then the door closed, and Hatshepsut was alone with the Great Steward.

She sighed and pressed herself against Senenmut, fitting her forehead against his neck, her palms against his back. Her hands knew just where to go. The territory of his flesh was so familiar to her now, the borders of his ribs and shoulders, the valley of his spine, the well-trammeled front of him, soft and warm, where she pressed herself as she had uncountable times before. He was her home, as the palace, as these very chambers, never could be.

"And so Her Majesty approves of her temple?"

"You know I do. How not?"

"Pharaohs are often fickle."

She drew away from him, laughing. Beads of sweat cooled on her skin where it had touched his. "It is a house fit for a god. Egypt has never seen its like before."

123

"So you were wise to send me packing off to Ankh-Tawy all those years ago, to learn architecture. I have become the greatest builder in the land – is that the way of it?"

"Your pride is appalling." She kissed his cheek, and felt him smile beneath her lips. "One would almost believe you the Pharaoh, and I your servant. The temple still must be built. Now it is only a few pretty lines of ink on papyrus."

"Only?" He clutched at his heart. "My lady wounds my very ka."

"Perhaps it will not stand. Perhaps the walls will fall over. I shall call you the greatest in the land only when I see it standing."

He pulled her onto the couch; she tumbled down beside him eagerly, stretching her body along the length of his own, buoyed by the twin pleasures of the temple and Senenmut's hands. She could have purred, had she been a cat. She raised up to kiss him, but worry tightened his face, and she froze, staring.

"What is it?"

"The temple, Hatshepsut. It will do only half the work of keeping the noble houses in your hand."

A groan rose up in her throat, but it escaped as nothing but a quiet breath, as if even her body had grown too weary of politicking. "Half the work?"

"Your harem."

Her brows lifted.

"It is full of well-bred women: your cousins; your half-sisters, like Opet. Women who carry the blood of kings in their veins."

"I care for them well. I treat them as sisters. Some have even gone to war with me; they are loyal to their Pharaoh."

"That is as may be, and yet they are women like all others. They crave the touch of a man now and then, and why not? The gods made us all alike." His hands roamed down her spine, over her hip, as if to illustrate his point. "A woman in the Pharaoh's harem craves more than that, too. She is there for a reason: to give the king a child, if she can, and secure her own fortune, and the fortune of her family. You cannot give any of your women a child. Why should they remain in your House of Women, serving you, if all their service is for naught?"

"Because I am their king," Hatshepsut replied. To her dismay she fairly sputtered, so great was her distress at Senenmut's words.

"By rights, that should be reason enough. And yet it is not. Most women desire children; you know this is true. The women of the harem may desire children more than most, for a harem woman's child is a token of power."

"I have no wish to mistrust my own cousins and sisters. And yet..."

"It is not so much the women I mistrust – not yet, though it is not reasonable to expect them to remain childless and loyal forever. It is the men of powerful houses who deserve your suspicion."

She caught that fish at once. Indeed, it had been thrashing in her net ever since the Feast of Min. "Such men will court my women. You are right – I know you are."

"Ah. And without any reason to stay in your harem – without the hope for children who may secure them far better standing than any nobleman may provide – they will petition you for release, so that they may be free to marry."

"Then I must allow them to marry. I will not keep women against their will."

"And once they marry, and breed a few sons with men already rich and influential, sons with Pharaohs' blood...?"

"Yes. I see the trouble."

Loosing her women back into Egyptian society could reap a harvest of challengers to her throne – would almost certainly do so. By the time her cousins' sons came of age, she would be an old woman, easily displaced, and Thutmose may lack sons of his own to secure their family's legacy. Hatshepsut's own grandfather had managed to produce only royal daughters, after all. No, until Thutmose was married and had a son or two of his own, the women must remain.

"How, then, do we solve this? How do we make them choose to remain in the House of Women of their own will?"

Senenmut furrowed his brow, deep in thought. But after a long moment he said nothing, and in despair Hatshepsut sagged down upon his chest. Tears burned her eyes; she blinked rapidly, furiously, and they vanished without falling. How had she inherited such an impossible tangle? Was there any way to put it to rights without cutting threads?

Amun, there must be.

She bolted upright, elbowing Senenmut in the stomach; he let out a grunt and clutched himself.

"Amun," Hatshepsut blurted. "The god is our solution."

"The god?"

"No, not the god. The God's Wife."

"Neferure?" A defensive edge rose up in Senenmut's voice.

"I will not send her to Iunet after all. She must remain in the House of Women. She is god-chosen; we will have her read dreams for the harem, as my mother once did. She will be a constant presence there. You know how pious she is, how she talks endlessly of the gods."

"Hatshepsut..."

"With Neferure always in their midst, preaching to them as she does, the women will be reminded of my own divinity, and none will dare to marry away. Is not the favor of a god's daughter worth much more than a fat old man in a fine kilt?"

"You cannot do this to her."

"*Do?* What do I do that is so terrible? She will be given the best rooms – no; build her a little palace adjacent; her own complex. Yes, that is fitting."

"She wanted so badly to go to Iunet, to become a Hathor priestess."

"We can build Neferure her own Hathor temple if she wishes it, right there on the grounds of the House of Women."

"It is not the same."

"You said yourself she shouldn't allow her hopes to run away with her heart. I made her no vows. I said it depended on the gods."

"This is your will, not a god's."

"I am the Pharaoh. Amun himself sired me. He will not allow me to choose wrongly. He would stop me, if he did not approve. The girl will do as I say."

Senenmut held himself perfectly still, his eyes and mouth betraying nothing. Hatshepsut knew that blank look, the silence. He would agree to do her bidding because it was his duty, but not because he believed she was right. Anger boiled up inside her; she drew well away from him, sat rigidly apart on the couch.

He sat, too, his shoulders stooping. "It will be..." Senenmut began, but she cut him off, rounding on him.

"As the Great Lady commands? Of course it will be. I am your king; I know what is best."

Senenmut's eyes were dark, shadowed by sorrow.

"What?" She almost shouted the word.

"It burns me, to think what this will do to Neferure. She is so young, Hatshepsut. She understands little of politics. She is just a girl, with a girl's heart."

"She is the King's Daughter, and God's Wife of Amun. She has her roles, her duties."

"She understands little of those, too."

"You are her tutor; make her understand."

He huffed, looked away from her sharply, as if he could not bear to meet her eyes.

"Can you think of any other way? What other means do I have? Only give me another option, Senenmut – one that will work half as well – and I will take it. I birthed the girl, and the women of the harem know that I am more than any Pharaoh before me: I am the son of Amun. Neferure will be my presence when I cannot be present. Short of moving into the harem myself, what better choice have we until Thutmose comes of age and sires his own sons?"

Senenmut hung his head, pressed and smoothed his wig with trembling hands. At last he raised his eyes to hers, and the look he gave her was so forceful, so direct, that she drew back in shock. No one had *glared* at her since Thutmose the

Second was living.

"She is your daughter," he said, his voice ringing with a sternness she had never before heard, not even as a child, as his student. "You are her *mother*. She must be more to you than a pawn on a senet board. You must be more to one another." Suddenly he softened, nearly pleading. "You said yourself, Hatet, that her joy is maat. I feel that, too. You know I do. I only want her happiness; her smile makes me live. Why does that girl's heart matter so little to you?"

Tears shone in his eyes, and blurred her own, too. She wanted to fall into his arms and weep for his forgiveness, wanted to retreat to the sanctuary of his body, her home – but she was surrounded by the king's chambers, by the histories of all the kings who had come before, graven into the very walls. Their faces stared down at her with expectation. She could not retreat from her own duty and rank. Neither, she knew, could her daughter.

"Senenmut, you are cruel."

"I mean no cruelty. But I cannot be disloyal to her. She is my...." He choked off the word. It hung in the air between them, as forceful in the silence as if he had shouted it.

"When I left Kush," Hatshepsut said quietly, her voice barely more than a whisper, "I stood at the rail of my ship with Nehesi, and watched a group of boys sporting on the riverbank. They were so young, Senenmut, and yet they had come all the long way from their homes like soldiers, lived amongst the army, seen the hands of our dead enemies piled up and rotting in the sun. They were just lads. I remember how they played. I remember what I told Nehesi: that I wanted my own children to be so carefree, to play and be... be *children*."

Senenmut reached for her hand, squeezed it gently. She laced her fingers with his. Her hand was so cold that her skin burned against his warmth.

"Do you know what he told me? He said, 'They are the Pharaoh's children. Can you ever expect them to be carefree?' He was right, Senenmut. Neferure's blood is royal. Hers is the blood of a god. Her smile is maat to me – hers and Thutmose's, too. And yet even I am not free to protect their happiness."

"You are the Pharaoh. Your word is the command of all the people."

Hatshepsut rose, turned away from him so he would not see the tears break from their dam, streak down her cheeks to stain her face with kohl.

"Do you truly believe that? Is the greatest architect in the land such a fool? Tell it to the man who whispered in Opet's ear. Tell it to Nebseny's ka. Tell it to Ankhhor's tomb."

Senenmut said nothing. Hatshepsut wiped the kohl from her face with the hem of her kilt, and turned back to face her steward. "There is only one way more to secure my bloodline against the ambition of my subjects. And that is to make Neferure my heir."

Senenmut's hands fell limp onto the couch. "Your heir?"

"Why not? She is my first-born child."

"But she is not..." Senenmut smiled ruefully, despite his distress, and Hatshepsut knew what words had died on his tongue. *Not a son.*

"Can you think of a more powerful token to secure my position? Our position, Senenmut, for if I fall, so will you. Blood of a god, god-chosen, and heir to the throne, living amongst my women, ministering to them as a priestess. What greater security have we than Neferure?"

His eyes left hers, wandered forlornly about the room, as if he searched for an alternate path – any path that would spare his charge a career of politicking and grant her the life she yearned for. But at last he met her eyes again, and said reluctantly, "None."

Chapter Fifteen

EVEN WITH THE CURTAINS OF the litter drawn, the day was unbearably hot. Neferure reached from her chair to flick one length of cloth open, hoping she might allow a breeze inside. But the heat was intense, demanding in its stillness. There was not a breath of air in all of Egypt. Had there been, the gods surely would have sent it to cool their favorite daughter's skin.

"That is the fifth time you've opened the curtains since we left the ship," Thutmose said. He waved a stiff fan of crimped and painted papyrus before his face. Sweat glistened along his upper lip. "It doesn't make us any cooler. All you do is allow dust inside."

With a disgusted grunt, Neferure let the curtain fall. The half-sheer weave of linen did little to block the white intensity of the midday sun, but Thutmose was right, after all. The stifling interior of the litter was at least less dusty with the curtains drawn.

What madness was this, to travel across the river and into the bleak, dry valley on the western bank during the hottest part of the day? Neferure missed the comfort of her little palace, the house of a dozen small but beautiful rooms Senenmut had built for her on the grounds of the Pharaoh's harem. Her rooms were full of rich, dark ebony furnishings, soft couches upholstered with cool silk, hundreds of bright linen cloths painted with goddesses, with scenes of priestesses in worship. Senenmut had been wise in designing the wind-catchers, and in positioning them, too. They cupped the smallest breeze from the river in clever hands, and poured the coolness and perfume of moving water down upon Neferure and her servants.

Her home was the best and most comfortable in all the harem, and never lacked for visitors because of it. When she returned from her morning duties at the Temple of Amun, she settled into the business of reading dreams for the Pharaoh's women – or trying to, at any rate. It was often a frustrating proposition. The meaning of a dream never seemed quite clear to Neferure, and more often than not, she was left wondering whether the interpretations she offered the women were from the gods, or from her own hazy and bewildered heart. She reasoned her doubts away by reminding herself that the gods would not allow her to speak an interpretation they did not approve. Such thoughts were good enough for her, and, it seemed, good enough for the women.

When evening fell, she would retreat to her rooftop. There stood her own shrine to Hathor, roofless so that she might sit in the midst of her seven statues of the goddess and watch as the stars emerged. It was only by their soft silvery light that she felt at peace. As the spray of Hathor's nurturing milk spilled across the dense black sky, twinkling like the rattle of sesheshet, singing to her heart, Neferure could forget the heat and heaviness of her days, the weight of duty and expectation.

She could even forget that Senenmut's pretty little palace was nothing but a cage, commissioned by her mother the king as a sop for taking Hathor away from her. It had been two long years since Hatshepsut had rescinded her promise to send Neferure to Iunet. The palace was a sop, and the title, too. They called her now not only God's Wife, but Divine Adoratrix, as if to emphasize her love for the gods. A cruel thing, for the only god she was allowed to adore was Amun, and he cared little for her. Sense told Neferure that time would lessen the sting of that loss, and the shame of Amun's denial. But two years had only caused her heart's wound to fester.

What festered more was the other title – the one she tried never to think on. *Heir.* It was a sacrilege, she knew without know how she knew it. Something about the arrangement was not maat, but it frightened her to think on it, frightened her to acknowledge it. And so she let it alone, and let the title wash over her indifferent shoulders whenever the heralds cried it, whenever her mother demanded it.

Thutmose jerked forward in his chair, causing the litter bearers to sway and mutter. He dropped his fan atop his sandals in his excitement. "Look, sister! There it is!"

This time he did not object when Neferure parted the curtains to clear their view. Ahead, Hatshepsut's own solitary litter progressed down a barren flatness the color of old, brittle papyrus. The white broken bones of long-dead myrrh trees stood at regular intervals, demarcating the remains of an ancient road. Beyond the king's litter, the face of a great cliff, yellow as burnished gold, rose high into the glaring sky. At its base stood the pale new facade of Hatshepsut's mortuary temple, and the wall that surrounded it.

Despite her resolve to be unmoved by the latest of her mother's several ostentatious monuments, Neferure could not suppress a tremble of admiration. They passed beneath the pylon of the outer wall, and she saw that the temple's base was wide and sturdy, sprawling along the base of the cliff. Dozens of new-quarried pillars glimmered in the sun, the shadows between a violet-black so intense that they burned their image upon Neferure's eyes. As she took in the sight, the number of pillars seemed to multiply, to dance before her eyes, to expand the already considerable dimensions of the temple. A shining ramp lifted from the road to a broad terrace high above, and beyond, another ramp rose above yet another row of pillars to the uppermost shrine. Higher still, the yellow rock of the cliff face gathered itself into an imposing natural spire, tall and bright as a beam of Re's holy light. Neferure had the immediate impression of looking upon a body in the throes of worship, arms wide-spread below a face up-tilted, a face raised in awe to take in the blessings of the gods.

"By Amun," Thutmose said, nearly laughing.

She gave him a sharp look to quell his unseemly enthusiasm. He was twelve years old now, and preoccupied, as were all boys of his age, with tall monuments and other such displays of royal power.

Their litter drew closer to the temple's first ramp. As it grew in her sight, slow and inevitable as the Iteru's flood, Neferure's awe gave way to unease. She let the curtain fall.

"I want to see it," Thutmose protested.

But Neferure did not respond; she sat back in her gilded chair, watching through the weave of the linen as the dark slashes of shadow between pillars lengthened and towered overhead.

At last their guard called out a halt. The litter sank to the dry, bare earth. Thutmose could restrain himself no more; he sprang from his seat, his arms tangling in the curtains as he staggered out into the dust. Neferure followed more sedately, taking care with her gown's pleats, stepping from the litter with quiet dignity.

Hatshepsut, too, rose calmly from her litter and stood gazing up at her monument. The fan-bearer Batiret emerged from nowhere Neferure could discern, carrying, as ever, her great half-circle of ostrich plumes on its familiar long pole. The shade closed over the king's face just as she turned to smile in Neferure's direction. The sudden sight of Hatshepsut's bared teeth in the deep darkness of shadow made her shiver. Then her own fan-bearer appeared, and the relief of shade was so sudden, so protective, that Neferure nearly gasped.

"What do you think?" Hatshepsut said, turning away again to stare up the great, bright length of the walls.

Thutmose answered. "Astounding!"

"Both Pharaohs approve," said Senenmut quietly. He stepped beneath Neferure's fan, and she slipped her hand into his, grateful for his presence. "But I would know what the God's Wife thinks."

"Does it matter what the God's Wife thinks?"

"It matters very much to me."

In spite of the heat and the strange unrest tingling along her skin, she smiled at Senenmut's words. "It is beautiful," she said, because she knew his heart longed to hear it.

"Shall we go inside?"

Hatshepsut led them up the ramp. Neferure's vision swam from the height. By the time they gained the first terrace, a broad expanse of perfectly smooth stone, laid so well the eye could hardly pick out the joins between blocks, the guardsmen and their litters looked like a child's discarded toys in the valley below. She noted two small pools in the courtyard. The spikes of new papyrus shoots cast deep blue shadows upon the water.

The straight line of the ramp continued across the width of the terrace via two rows of seshep. They crouched in pairs, staring challenge into one another's eyes, so proud and fierce she thought she might hear the scratch of their claws digging into their granite plinths. Each lion's body wore the head of Hatshepsut, and each head wore a different head-dress, though all wore identical, knowing, almost mocking smiles.

The second ramp took them still higher. The air was hotter here, for the sun reflected off the cliff's face and struck mercilessly at Neferure's skin if she allowed herself to out-stride her fan-bearer. They reached the upper row of pillars, stepped through a pair of doorways, and the blessed coolness of shade closed like healing water over their heads. Before them lay a final courtyard, small and intimate, ringed by a depth of pillars yet to be painted and carved. Across the courtyard, the door of a sanctuary for Amun's holy person stood closed so that the darkness the god favored would not be disturbed. Neferure's stomach quivered at the sight of the sanctuary. She felt at the same time attracted and repelled, and, unsure whether to approach or flee, she stood rooted near a pillar while her family and their servants moved across the courtyard, inspecting, chattering, Hatshepsut and Senenmut pointing out this feature or that to Thutmose, who ran here and there like a child hunting frogs in the reeds.

At length they retreated down the highest ramp, and Hatshepsut led them into another hall where artisans had already set to work. A depiction of Hatshepsut's campaign into Kush, enacted when Neferure was a suckling babe, spread over the nearest wall. The carvings were fine and sharp, beautifully detailed. Fine grit from the artists' labors lay heaped where the walls met the floor. A set of chisels and picks had been left behind. Thutmose inspected them, then lifted one and mimed carving until Hatshepsut chased him away.

"Don't dare ruin it! If you do, I'll have to march on Kush all over again."

"It was a mighty war," Thutmose recited, his eyes gleaming in their black rings of kohl. "The Good God Maatkare swept through the ravines and into Kush's weak and trembling territory..."

"And took them unaware, falling upon them from her chariot," Hatshepsut finished, crowing.

Neferure sighed. She and Thutmose had heard the tale of the conquest of Kush uncountable times from their nurses and tutors. Thutmose never tired of it, while Neferure would be well pleased if she never had to suffer through its recitation again. She paced the length of the carved wall. The too-familiar tale unfolded before her. Hatshepsut led her men into battle; Hatshepsut brought the Kushites low; Hatshepsut accepted their surrender, the bound captives in rows, trembling and bowing before the Pharaoh's majesty.

The final panel of the carving caught Neferure up short. It depicted a portion of the tale she had never heard before. Hatshepsut, wearing the kilt of a man and the Pharaoh's high, rounded war crown, strode across the face of a *god*, treading him into the earth. Neferure gaped at the scene, at the sorrowing, helpless face of Dedwen, god of the Kushites, and the fearsome straightness of her mother's body, the triumph of her dark eyes.

Senenmut's hand came down softly upon her shoulder, but she could not tear her eyes from the image.

"Did it truly happen?"

"Truly," he said.

She conquered a god. She trampled a god *into the dust.*

Neferure tore her eyes from the face of conquered Dedwen, peered over her shoulder at her mother. Hatshepsut smiled broadly as she spoke to Thutmose, gesturing at the wall opposite, describing the scenes she would commission there. Her face was so plain, for all her divine origin, the bigness of her teeth and the roundness of her chin so unassuming, so mortal. There were lines around her eyes when she laughed at something Thutmose said. *This king – this woman – destroyed a god.* True, Dedwen was a god of Kush, and so by definition inferior to even the humblest household god of Egypt. But still, Hatshepsut had defeated him.

What other gods might she bring low? There could be no doubt that Hatshepsut was the offspring of Amun. Not that Neferure had ever doubted it.

She returned her gaze to the temple wall, though now she saw none of it. Her eyes seemed to look beyond the stone into a black distance pricked by the light of thousands and thousands of stars.

I, too, have the blood of Amun in my body. Do I have the power to trample gods? Or the power to raise them up?

With a bitter pang, she recalled the white bull of Min, the feel of its hide beneath her fingers. She remembered the whispers that ran through Hatshepsut's court, circulated amongst the palace servants. Oh, yes, she had heard them – heard all the rumors. Why should they not be true? *Neferure tamed the white bull. Neferure is favored by the gods. Neferure's very name is holy. She tamed the bull. There is nothing the King's Daughter cannot do.*

She reached out a trembling hand, laid her fingers on Dedwen's cheek. She willed him to live again, to rise up and roar like a bull in the emptiness of her mother's bare hall. She opened herself, reached her heart out to the divine, offered it like a piece of myrrh on the sacred fire.

Live, she commanded the god.

But the wall remained flat and cold, and Dedwen only stared back at her with empty, defeated eyes.

CHAPTER SIXTEEN

BY NIGHT, THE VALLEY LIVED.

By day it was a flat, dry expanse, as blank and unused as the untouched clay shard of a lazy schoolboy. After sunset, the floor of the sacred ravine turned from dry yellow to a mysterious blue-black as deep and dark as ink, and the vertical rock walls faded into blackness. Lights bloomed in the dark: scores upon scores of torches flaring, moving, swaying forward and back like a garden in wind. Revelers carried their torches and lamps from the valley floor up secret, hidden trails that climbed into the rocks, where they found the tombs of ancestors a hundred years gone. Lines of light flickered as they ascended, draped like golden chains across shoulders of night-blue stone. The living once more carried bread and beer, honey and wine to the homes of the dead, too long forgotten. The night rang with songs of celebration, cries of drunkenness, of fear, of passion. Fires blazed along the length of the newly built canal, and reflected in a double row that wavered and shimmered, that bent with the water's movement like a snake dancing in the grass. The movement of light was as the movement of the Iteru, constant, vital, an unceasing mystery. For the first time in generations, Egypt celebrated the Beautiful Feast of the Valley, resurrected from obscurity by the majesty of the king's new temple.

Hatshepsut leaned alone on the low wall surrounding the highest terrace of her temple. The wine bowl beside her was empty. She closed her eyes, feeling the touch of the valley's brisk wind on her eyelids. Her wig's many braids shifted when the wind touched them; the feel of it set her to swaying. She rocked high above the deep blue valley, the wine a warm pulse in her blood, listening to the rising and falling of song, the calling of the kas of the dead amongst the rocks.

West, she thought. *Here I am as far west as I may go, unless I were to dwell in the Red Land.*

She had built her temple in the west, the place where the god died each night in the form of Atum-Re, the sun who set in all the colors of blood – the bright, the deep, the fiery. The place where the god entered the underworld, where he would strive each hour to return to the sky. The west was the place of the mysterious Lady, Hathor, She of Seven Faces, who welcomed all into the underworld.

I built my temple in the west. I dedicated a beautiful sanctuary to her, in this very spot. What more does Hathor want?

Hatshepsut had increased the numbers of girls she dedicated to the Lady's service at Iunet. Each year she sent more than the last, until she was hard-pressed to find suitable candidates near Waset, and was obliged to send her stewards and priests to search farther afield. She had given a larger portion of the treasury to restoring temples up and down the Iteru, joining her own plans to Neferure's, ensuring the disused shrines to Hathor – or any ancient aspect of the Lady's being – were renewed prior to any other god's.

And yet the dreams had not ceased. With cruel reliability, her sleep was haunted every handful of nights by the image of the goddess who strode into a circle of light and changed her face from gentle smile to lioness's leer. And each time, no matter how Hatshepsut pleaded, no matter how she ran, no matter how bravely she stood and challenged the goddess, the fangs sank deep into her neck, and ripped and ravened, and her blood flowed like hot, choking wine. Sometimes the goddess had eyes of two colors, and white braids in her hair. Sometimes she had Ahmose's eyes, or Senenmut's, Iset's, Hatshepsut's own.

This year will be different. I have revived the Lady's own celebration.

I have rededicated the Beautiful Feast of the Valley to her, and she will be appeased. She will go quietly into the west, and let me be.

Hatshepsut opened her eyes. Her vision swam, seemed to lift a chain of lights making its way up the most distant cliff face high into the stars, so that some stars burned a steady silver-white, and some flickered golden. She rubbed her eyes with the heels of her hands, then cursed at the smear of kohl and malachite powder on her palms. At the sound of her voice Nehesi glanced up from where he stood below, guarding the base of the ramp, defending her loneliness. The ululating wail of drunken song lifted from somewhere deep in the valley. It pierced her heart and left her gasping. Then it faded away again, and Hatshepsut shivered.

She groped for the wine jar and found nothing.

"Batiret!"

Her woman appeared – the only attendant she would keep tonight, high and solitary at the apex of her great temple. Tonight Hatshepsut would remain alone with the god.

Batiret appraised her mistress with the usual no-nonsense flick of her eyes. "Water, I think," she said.

"More wine."

"The Great Lady will have a terrible headache in the morning."

"The Great Lady does not care. The Pharaoh must be drunk! It is the way of the festival!" Her words ran together.

"The Great Lady will vomit."

"Let her!"

"And I shall have to clean it up."

Hatshepsut draped an arm across Batiret's shoulders. "You are beautiful."

The woman bore it patiently. "Most definitely water for you."

"Kiss me!"

Batiret leveled a dry look at Hatshepsut. "You do not desire me. I am not Iset."

The name jarred her. She inhaled sharply, the scent of fine wine and myrrh from the braziers in Amun's sanctuary, the fainter overtones of acrid dung-smoke and sweet wheat cakes baking over open fires far in the valley below. She smelled water from the canal. That canal had taken a year to construct, so that Amun's barge might be floated the length of the valley to her temple's forecourt. All to revive the festival. All to appease Hathor. All to protect the ones she loved. Like Iset.

"She wants Neferure," Hatshepsut muttered.

"Great Lady?"

"But she cannot have her. I pledged her to Amun. Neferure is God's Wife. She is Divine Adoratrix. She is my heir! That is maat."

Batiret's arm went around Hatshepsut's waist; the woman tugged at her until she took a few stumbling steps toward the private courtyard at the temple's crown.

"Maat is all," Hatshepsut said in a booming voice that sounded comical even to her own ears.

Batiret giggled behind her free hand.

"My father used to say it. Hatet, maat is all!"

In the center of the courtyard, Batiret lifted her face to gaze up at the stars. Hatshepsut imitated her, but the stars lurched and rotated like an unmoored boat in a fast current. She clutched at Batiret's shoulders. "What is maat, anyway? Do you know? I surely do not. Every time I think I've served maat, I discover I've done it all wrong. What is it, then, Batiret? Tell me."

"For you, maat is water," she said, and disentangled herself from Hatshepsut's arms.

Hatshepsut swayed, swam in a pool of starlight. The shimmer of it on the stones of her temple's floor seemed to take the shape of faces. She stared at them, trying to identify them, trying to discern who stared back, who stared at the Pharaoh with such impunity. But the eyes kept blinking, the mouths kept twisting; she could make nothing of them.

Batiret set a pottery jar on the floor. The circle of water visible at its lip reflected the points of a hundred stars, stretching and breaking as the vibration of the jar's movement ran in rings across its surface, expanding and contracting.

Batiret lifted a dripping cup to Hatshepsut's lips. "Drink."

When her belly was full, Hatshepsut staggered past the pillars to the wall of her temple. In the dimness she traced the shape of a body with her fingers, carved into the smooth stone. Artisans had worked a full year to adorn the temple with the images she had commanded, and now she could not remember whose image dwelt on this wall, rendered eternal by chisel and pick.

A sudden weariness gripped her. She pressed her palms, her cheek, against the unseen figure in the stone.

"Leave me, Batiret. Join Nehesi. Keep everyone away. I must be alone. Alone with the god."

Hatshepsut was aware of the gentle scrape of stone against her knees, aware of a sinking sensation, aware of her knees buckling slowly, so slowly, as if all happened in reverse. She heard herself snore as she surrendered to sleep.

When she rose up, her legs were steady. The walls of the temple pulsed with a faint light: green, the color of resurrection.

She gazed up at the wall where she had crumpled – hours before? Days before? She could not tell how long she had slept. A bead of green fire ran along the edge of a carving, tracing the form of a striding king. Wherever the fire traveled, it left a line of its own substance glowing, until it traced the king's arm, his shoulder, his face, the great arcing reach of his proud crown. The fire met its own tail and the king stood outlined in eerie light.

Hatshepsut stared, wondering. Was it an image of her own self, or of her father? She could not discern the king's face. She stepped nearer, cautious of the fire, hugging her body with trembling arms.

Hatshepsut.

She had not heard her father's voice since she was a small child. But she recognized it at once, the deep, mellow softness,

143

so incongruous a voice for a king or a soldier.

"Father."

You must remember, Hatet. Maat is all.

"But what *is* it? You must tell me."

I did not listen. I did not serve. And all my sons died – all but you.

"Only tell me how to serve, and I will do it."

Thutmose the First laughed, a loud percussive sound, drums in a temple, a jackal in the night. The memory of his laugh beat painfully at Hatshepsut's heart. She remembered his smile close to her own, his voice whispering legends in her ear as he held her to stand on a ship's rail so she might watch the great pyramids, black against a setting sun, slip past their boat. She did not fear standing on the rail. She did not fear the river below, though it was full of crocodiles and weeds to tangle her. She could never fall. Her father held her tightly.

Who is the son who loves Aakheperkare, the king, Thutmose, he who has gone to live forever with the gods?

It was part of the litany of the Opening of the Mouth, the rite a new Pharaoh performed when his predecessor died. It was the rite that sent the old king to the Field of Reeds, granted him eternal life, and passed kingship of the Two Lands from the deceased body to the living body. Hatshepsut had never been granted the privilege of performing the rite for her own father. Ahmose had spoken the words on behalf of Thutmose the Second, whose regent she was, and Hatshepst herself had spoken the words on behalf of her own Little Tut over his father's gilded coffin. But she had never given the gift of the afterlife to her father, nor received the kingship from his arms into her own.

She stepped toward the fiery outline of Thutmose the First until she stood eye to eye with him, until she felt his gaze look into her own kas, filling her with a throbbing green light. She did not have the netjerwy, the sacred metal rod that opened the mouths of kings. She laid her bare fingers on the stone lips of her father, and felt him breathe in.

"I am the son who loves Aakheperkare, the king, Thutmose."

When she stepped away from him, his face had changed. The mouth was twisted with disgust, the eyes burning with hateful light.

Hatshepsut cried out in shock. Her ka crumpled as if dealt a blow; she quailed on the floor of her temple.

And then she recognized the face. It was her brother's.

Hatshepsut. He spat her name as though the taste of it was foul on his tongue.

She made herself stand up, made herself face him. "Thutmose."

Where is my kingdom? Where is my throne?

She narrowed her eyes at him, and he glared back at her, his pupils sparking, flaring.

You took it from me. You took it all; even my son.

"They were never yours, brother. Egypt was never meant for you."

Do you not see? This is not maat. You are not maat. You will walk in darkness forever, because you are not maat.

Against her will, she took one small step backward, retreating from his words, from his hate-filled grimace.

My kingdom, wailed Thutmose the Second. His voice rose and wavered like the cries of the revelers in the valley. *It is a terrible thing you do, Hatshepsut, Hatshepsut!*

She threw her arms up to shield her face, crossed them before her eyes, trying without success to block out the rage and misery roiling in Thutmose's resurrection fire. The heat of him beat at her body, and she stumbled backward, afraid she would burn.

It is a terrible thing I do.

The voice whispered now, and was low and rich, laden with despair. Hatshepsut uncovered her face, peered cautiously at the king. She did not recognize him, and yet she did. The jaw was strong, the prominence of the Thutmoside teeth softened by the influence of some great beauty that refined the king's features, enriched the familial roughness, turned and smoothed the face like a clay pot in an artisan's hands. The eyes were closed in grief, but when they opened, Hatshepsut knew them well. They were Iset's eyes.

"Little Tut."

He was a grown man now, wearing all the trappings of a king, with the mantle of pain and weariness a king must wear, too. She came toward him, holding her arms wide for the little boy, the child of her heart and Iset's beloved body. But he was not a little boy any longer. He did not see her.

It is a terrible thing I do. And yet, can I do any differently?

Thutmose the Third paused, as if listening to the counsel of another voice. Hatshepsut strained to hear it, but heard only silence. At last the king hung his head in defeat.

Hatshepsut, forgive me. She must forgive me. She must understand.

And he raised a chisel in one hand, a mallet in the other. They lifted slowly, their weight great in his reluctant hands, and hung poised in the air before Hatshepsut's eyes. The sharpness of the chisel flooded her with terror. She cried out to him, begged him to stop. But he did not hear.

When the mallet fell against the chisel, the crack of stone split her ears. The pain of nothingness split her heart.

Hatshepsut fell to her knees, screaming.

A sharp crack across her face woke her. She lurched to her feet, and immediately fell again, her head pounding.

"Oh," she groaned, clutching her stinging cheek. Her gut clenched; she levered herself carefully onto hands and knees and retched again and again. Nothing came up but a thin stream of saliva, which dangled from her lips until a gentle hand wiped it away with a soft square of linen.

"There, child. There."

"Sitre-In."

The presence of her old nurse was an unspeakable comfort. The woman knelt on a mat beside Hatshepsut, her lap as welcoming as it had ever been. Hatshepsut crept to her and sank onto the mat, her throbbing head on Sitre-In's bony old thighs. Sitre-In rubbed her fingertips in small circles across Hatshepsut's forehead, her temples, the back of her neck. Hatshepsut sighed in relief.

"Batiret sent for me," the nurse murmured. "That servant of yours is as wise as a goddess."

"Where were you? I have not seen you in so many years, not since you took to your estates."

"I was down in the valley, of course, celebrating the Feast."

Hatshepsut smiled at the thought of Sitre-In getting riotously drunk and carrying a torch with the other revelers, up into the tombs cut into the high cliffs. "You were not truly celebrating."

"Not all of us celebrate by ducking our heads into a wine cask," Sitre-In said drily. "You did not have enough water. Shame on you."

"Batiret tried her best."

"You'll have more water now. And some herbs for your head."

"Good."

Sitre-In rolled Hatshepsut over, onto her own mat. A few cushions and a sheet of soft linen lay upon the mat, crumpled by Hatshepsut's dream. The bedding had not been there when she had fallen asleep; she was sure of it. Batiret had thought of everything. She pressed her face gratefully into a silk cushion, moaning. A green light flared and dimmed behind her closed eyelids, pulsing with the beat of her heart.

"Here, Great Lady. Drink."

Batiret sank onto the mat beside her. Hatshepsut lifted onto one elbow to accept the cup of cool water. It tasted of some woody, sharp herb. She drank it all.

"You slapped me," she said, rubbing her hot cheek.

"Not I; it was your nurse. You were screaming, and we could not wake you."

Hatshepsut remembered the mallet in Thutmose's hand, the grief in her grown son's eyes, and shivered. She took several more cups of the infusion, and when the pounding in her head receded, she ventured to stand. Her senses were still somewhat furry from the wine, but she was sobering, and her stomach and head had settled.

She made her way out onto the highest terrace with her women following close behind. The night had turned the corner, as the rekhet said; the warmth of a summer night had passed into the refreshing chill of the few hours preceding dawn. Many of the stars had faded. The torches in the valley were mostly extinguished, the revelers having retreated to tents or tombs to sleep off their wine. Along the dim length of the canal, the fires had died to heaps of embers. No more songs rang from the cliffs. The night murmured with the metallic, nasal call of insects. Hatshepsut felt the need to shake off the strangeness of the night. The green fire of her dream still haunted her. She laid a hand on Sitre-In's shoulder.

"I am going to walk alone. Just below, on the next terrace. I think the movement and the air will do me good."

"Let Batiret go with you."

Hatshepsut shook her head. "Nehesi is down there. He stayed awake all night, didn't he?"

Reluctantly, Sitre-In nodded.

"I will be well. Nehesi will watch me. I need to be alone with the god's presence."

She made her way down the ramp to the terrace. The line of seshep stood like blue sentinels before her. *My soldiers called me seshep once.* She did not feel like a lioness tonight. She turned her back on them and retreated to the portico, drifting from one pillar to the next, tracing with her fingers the images of her works and her glories. They all seemed as nothing to her, naught but paint on stone, as though they had never happened – as though she herself had never been.

The scuff of running footsteps roused her from her dark thoughts. She ducked behind a pillar, and as she did so caught sight of Nehesi across the terrace, his body taking form out of the shadows of night. He came to alertness, stared with hawk-like intensity toward the sound of running – and then subsided, relaxing, his hand leaving the hilt of his blade.

Hatshepsut moved around the pillar until she too could see

the runner. It was Neferure, the hem of her gown dark with water or mud, its pleats crumpled and ruined. She staggered into the shadow of the nearest seshep and fell against its plinth, her body shaking with sobs. She looked the picture of perfect grief, limp and helpless, her head bowed and arms draped across the lioness's paws.

Is she that drunk? She should not have had so much wine. I shall speak to Senenmut about it; he must watch her more closely.

Hatshepsut pushed herself from the pillar, ready to approach Neferure, to guide her to Sitre-In for care. But she saw a figure rise from the far ramp – head, shoulders, the swaying hips of a woman – to step up onto the terrace. The woman was dressed in a white gown that glowed faintly in the remnants of starlight. Silver at her wrists and ankles gleamed now and then as she moved. As she drew nearer, pacing between the seshep, Hatshepsut could see the locks of her black wig swaying around her face – a face incised with the lines of age and cares innumerable.

"Ahmose," Hatshepsut murmured. She sank back against her pillar and willed herself to stone-stillness.

When Ahmose reached Neferure, the girl crumpled to the foot of the plinth, balling herself up like a bit of discarded cloth. Ahmose sank more gracefully to sit beside her.

"It's not fair, Grandmother!" Neferure wailed into the darkness. "I hear the Lady calling me, and yet I cannot answer!"

"You are so full of fire, Neferure. Still it – control it."

"I try."

"Try again. Take a deep breath; stop your crying. Take this cloth and dry your eyes. There. Now breathe. Allow your breath to come how it will. If it would be slow, let it be slow. If it would be harsh, let it be harsh."

Neferure sat up straight, closed her eyes, and breathed. Hatshepsut watched her daughter's chest rise and fall several times, slowly, her small, new-formed breasts stirring against her gown.

"Let your ka fall open," Ahmose said, "like the petals of a

flower."

Neferure remained still and silent for a few more breaths, then struck her knees with her palms. "It's no *use!*"

"You give up too soon. It is never easy to touch the gods, child."

"Why do they not touch me? Why am I barred from them? I am the Divine Adoratrix! It is given to me to worship them, to love them! And yet they hold me away. Why? I, who tamed the white bull!"

"Be sensible. Did you tame the bull in truth, or are you confusing rumor with reality?"

Neferure lifted her chin, looked sharply away from Ahmose in that petulant way she had. "Of course I tamed it. You were not there; you did not see."

Ahmose shook her head, but subsided.

"Grandmother, there must be some sin in me, some stain that taints me in the gods' eyes. What else could it be? I have devoted my service to Amun; I have restored their temples since I was a small child. I make offerings every day. I live my life in goodness and maat. I do everything my mother asks of me." Neferure buried her face in her hands, and her cry of despair echoed amongst the pillars. "Oh, what is it in me that turns their faces away? I only want to adore them. They will not dwell inside my heart. What about me displeases them so?"

Ahmose did not answer. She lifted her face to stare into the shadows between the pillars. Her eyes found the place where Hatshepsut stood, pressed breathless against the stone.

She cannot see me. I stand in blackness.

But Ahmose did see her; Hatshepsut was sure of it. And the directness of her mother's gaze frightened her more than had any vision in that terrible dream. More than her brother's hatred, more than the chisel in Thutmose's hand.

"I do not know," she heard Ahmose say to the weeping child.

But she did know. Hatshepsut was sure of it.

CHAPTER SEVENTEEN

T HE MOOD IN THE HOUSE of Women seemed light
enough, though the night air was dry and smelled of dust
when it should have hung rich with the clean, loamy odors
of the flood. In the third year after Hatshepsut dedicated her
great temple to Amun, the river failed to rise more than a
handful of spans. The fields nearest the banks were covered
by no more than a few fingers' breadth of water, and it was
poor in silt. The fields beyond the roads and causeways,
nearer the hills, remained cracked and dry. There would be
no planting and no harvest this year.

Hatshepsut maintained calm throughout the Two Lands
by distributing from her ample stores of grain. In prior years
the gods had been more than generous; often the stores were
filled to capacity and the throne was obliged to ship great
surpluses of emmer and barley to other lands, lest the excess
spoil. There was no threat of famine. Every belly in the Two
Lands would remain full, even should the flood fail for two
or three years more. Senenmut and Hapuseneb did their best
to assure the king that such an occurrence was unlikely.

She strolled the great communal garden of the House of
Women arm in arm with Opet, patting her half-sister's hand
as she listened to the harem gossip, able to lend barely half
her heart to the conversation. Her thoughts strayed again and
again to the river. The Iteru was sluggish and dim, and stank of
decay. Crocodiles and water-horses grew bolder, encroaching
on fields and quays where they never dared go when the

currents ran high. Though she smiled and laughed at Opet's tales, and tossed her head as though she had not a care in her heart, the implications of the failed flood consumed her.

There is plenty of wheat and barley, she told herself firmly, accepting a bowl of beer from the serving woman who met them at the lake's shore. The lake was low, too, of course. The raised retaining wall showed a dark ring even in the moonlight, and the leaves of lotuses drooped, wan and rotting, across its surface.

"...and oh, wasn't Djefatsen sore when she saw Iy wearing that turquoise necklace! I warned her she was too fond of wagering, and she'd regret it one day! Iy won't part with the necklace now. Not for ten of Djefatsen's best silver bracelets, or her malachite earrings. Well, that is what comes of wagering.

"I was not the only one who warned her, either. Hetepti dragged Djefatsen off to see the God's Wife in her little palace, and Lady Neferure burned some incense and prayed and gave Djefatsen a terrible future, but said she could avoid it if she would give up dicing with the guardsmen. The Holy Lady told her she would wager away her firstborn child one day, but if she made offerings to Hathor daily for ten days, the goddess would break her habit."

"And has it worked?"

"I do not know, Great Lady. Djefatsen is too afraid of Hathor to go into the Holy Lady's shrine."

"Afraid?"

"Ah. Hetepti told me that when the Holy Lady was praying her eyes rolled back into her head, and she made a terrible croaking sound like a great frog in the reeds, and Djefatsen decided the goddess had entered your daughter's body. Hetepti said Djefatsen was near to weeping, she was so frightened by the sound. She won't even look at a carving of Hathor now."

So Neferure was using her status in the harem to terrify the Pharaoh's women. Hatshepsut clenched her hands into fists. "Croaking like a frog. It seems Neferure has kept herself well occupied. How else does she spend her time?"

Opet peered at Hatshepsut from the corner of her well-painted eye. "Do you not know?"

"I have been preoccupied of late," Hatshepsut said drily. "I've had little time for keeping up with the Holy Lady."

"Well..." Opet's voice went limp with reluctance, as weak as the lotus leaves in the shrinking pool. "She has put it about that the...the river, Great Lady...is..."

"Yes?"

"...that the river is the work of Hathor."

"Hathor. Of course."

"She says that Hathor is angry with you, Great Lady."

Hatshepsut held her tongue and her composure with difficulty. She eyed the outline of Neferure's small palace, dim across the span of the garden. A single lamp burned in one of its windows, flickering and low. There was no sign of movement within.

More men than ever before had engaged her harem women in polite conversation at festivals and feasts. How much longer would it be before the women returned their affections, and petitioned her for release? And once she granted them the freedom to marry and become mothers, they would spill Neferure's tales directly into the ears of Egypt's noble men. *The Sovereign of Stars is angry with the Pharaoh. The king has lost all favor with the Mistress of the West. The goddess caused the flood to fail, because Hatshepsut displeases her.*

"What exactly does my daughter say?"

Opet ducked her head in apology. "In truth I know very little about it. I am repeating only the murmurs of the other women, you see. The Holy Lady is careful never to speak against you where I might hear it directly. She knows how close you and I are."

Hatshepsut rode back to the palace wearing pensive silence like a winter shawl, drawn tight all about her. Nehesi accompanied her back to her own chambers, and there she fell upon her bed, wracked with superstitious dread. She kicked her feet against her sheets and fine cushions, unable to find any comfort. *Was* Hathor angry with her, after all? Were Neferure's whispers true? The girl was god-chosen;

Ahmose was still certain of it, though for all her mystical airs, Neferure had shown precious little talent that Hatshepsut could see. She had been certain, ever since the Feast of the Valley, that Hathor wanted Neferure. Yet as much as she feared Hathor, she feared Amun more. He was the patron of Waset, the king of the gods, and her own sire. Amun required a God's Wife, and Hatshepsut would not offend him by taking Neferure, gifting her to Hathor like a basket of pomegranates. To say nothing of the vital part the girl now played as Hatshepsut's heir, a charm to protect the line of succession against scheming men until Thutmose came of age and sired an heir of his own.

Unless the High Priest or Ahmose told her otherwise, Hatshepsut would retain the girl for Amun's service. She had committed Neferure, and her word before the god would remain unbroken.

No, she told herself, trying to sound sensible within her own troubled heart, *it is not Hathor who's stayed the flood. It cannot be.*

Which god, then?

A spasm of fear seized her belly and ran cold up her spine. *Amun?* Was the king of the gods himself displeased with his begotten daughter?

If he is angry with me, it can only be over Senenmut.

She would marry him. Yes – take him to her bed as a husband, not as a lover, and the holy trinity would be complete in the mortal world as it was in the world of the divine: mother, father, and child.

But in another heartbeat she rejected that idea, too. A man who would be Pharaoh might marry into the blood royal, as her own father did. There was no shame in raising up the low. But for a Pharaoh to marry a commoner – and not only as a concubine, but as Great Royal Consort...? As much as she loved Senenmut, she saw at once that such an action would not raise him up, but would degrade her own position. Were the Pharaoh to give in to her emotions so completely, so publicly, she would only seem too mortal, not the slightest bit divine. *It would only speed them taking my throne from me. No – I can never marry the brother of my heart.*

She fought to clear herself of all thoughts, to sweep herself clean so she might at last sleep. From the direction of her servants' quarters, she heard a rustling, the sound of a woman shifting heavily in her sleep. Weariness dragged at her, a desire for peace. She cast her heart back to the days when Iset still lived, recalled with a tender pang the night she had convinced the girl to lie with her brother and conceive their Little Tut. What a good mother Iset would have made, had she lived. She would have known how to handle Neferure, how to appease the gods. She would have danced, and sung in her sweet, lilting voice, and told Amun tales of the deby in the northern marshes, and he would forget his wrath, and let Hatshepsut sleep.

Senenmut was a clumsy hunter at best. At worst, he was a humiliation to men everywhere.

As a youth his friends had goaded him into fowling one day when the afternoon had grown too hot to continue their lessons at the Temple of Amun. They had begged a little reed-cutting skiff from the priest whose duty it was to keep the temple's canal clear of weeds, and paddled it out into a thick stand of papyrus. Meryre, one of his friends, had a fine horn bow, a gift from his father. They had taken turns firing rather cheap, disposable arrows into the green density of the riverbank until at last a flock of geese rose, honking indignantly at being roused from their afternoon nap. By then it was Senenmut's turn with the bow and he could not even pull it; his chest was too weak. All the geese got away. The boys watched the flock glide across the expanse of the river and settle, a line of black dots, onto the far bank.

His skill with a spear was nearly as lamentable. The skiff nosed through a wall of reeds to reveal the haul-out of six or seven crocodiles. They lay half concealed in mud, their malevolent pale mouths open as if they might speak. One rolled a strangely keen, golden eye toward the boat and slid into the water. The boys screamed, paddling frantically to make their escape. The crocodile kept coming, though, and Senenmut was obliged to pick up the hunting party's lone spear in defense. He jabbed it at the crocodile, striking its face twice, and the beast fled with a great thrashing of its tail. The other boys hailed Senenmut as a hero all the way back to the Temple of Amun, but even now, standing on the deck of the Pharaoh's hunting boat with her servants in a bustle around her, he recalled the weakness of his blows, the ineffectual way the spear's point had bounced off the crocodile's snout. He certainly had not killed it; he had not even drawn blood. For all he knew, it was the stink of his terrified sweat that had driven the crocodile away, and not his spear.

In spite of his unimpressive record as a huntsman, Senenmut felt a certain gladness to be underway. Hatshepsut, driven to distraction by her worries over the harem, had thrown up her hands two days ago when court duties were done, and declared that she would hunt lions, though Senenmut was certain she had not hunted since her youth. Now here they were, rocking together on the deck of her swift hunting boat, watching as a singing band of sailors scurried from rail to rail, preparing to land the boat deep in the valley opposite Waset.

Hatshepsut, clutching the rail at the ship's sharp-pointed nose, breathed deep as the canal narrowed. Before their prow, the broad face of the temple stretched along the base of the cliffs, dominating the valley. Djeser-Djeseru, Hatshepsut had named it: The Holiest of the Holy. It was a good name. The avenue of seshep paralleled the canal. Each face that rose above each lion's body was a match for Hatshepsut's own, rounded and firm, the eyes insistent, the mouths barely curved in knowing smiles of complete self-assurance. Even without celebrants to tread from the quayside to the temple for a festival, the whole valley felt stately, holy. Perhaps the only feature that marred the effect was the bleached skeletons of the long-dead myrrh trees, strange white slashes like scratching nails against the golden landscape.

They landed at the clean new stone of the festival quay. Senenmut escorted Hatshepsut ashore, where they stood in the welcome coolness of a hastily erected cloth sunshade, watching while a veritable army of servants and soldiers unloaded their boats. The cloth and poles of tents came ashore on the shoulders of strong young men. The more adventuresome women from the palace's cadre of servants bore baskets of fruit and sacks of flour, which they would make into fresh cakes around nightly campfires. Soldiers led teams of skittish horses down the ramps, and staked them out with piles of hay on the bare ground between seshep. The horses' tails made sounds like whip-lashes as they swatted at flies. Men lowered sections of chariots from the boats' rails. Here a platform, there a pair of wheels, here an axle and tongue came together with pegs and mallets until the Pharaoh's small fleet of hunting carts gleamed in the mid-day sun. Men sang as they worked; women danced the rustic steps of servants, shouting and clapping their hands. A hunt, it seemed, was nearly as good as a festival.

Hatshepsut seemed to have caught the mood, and Senenmut quietly rejoiced to see the old worries fall from her face, even for one day. She cheered the women's dances, and chattered with Nehesi about the horses, finally instructing him to set aside for her own use the team of dark brown mares with blazes of white up their faces. She encouraged two soldiers to wrestle to settle their good-natured argument over who should be first to kiss a pretty serving girl, and when Nehesi kicked the winner's feet out from beneath him and planted a long kiss of his own on the girl's lips, Hatshepsut roared with laughter.

"Gods, but it is good to see you this way," he said close to her hear. "It has been long since I've heard you laugh. It's better than music to me."

"I laugh like a braying ass. Don't argue; I've always known

it to be true."

No one was near, and Senenmut could not resist catching her hand in his own. He held it just for a moment before she tugged it away, smiling.

"Your laugh is a tribute to Amun," he murmured.

"I can see that the prospect of hunting inflames you. I never knew you were so blood-thirsty."

"You know I'm not. I live to see your smile; that is all."

She did smile up at him then, full and joyous. The sight of it caught at his heart. There were lines around her eyes now, fine when she was still, but definite when she smiled. He loved the lines as he loved all her features, the sharp curve of her nose, the roundness of her face, the ostentatious teeth. She was imperfect, and unspeakably holy.

My djeser-djeseru, he said silently.

A commotion rose up from the quayside. They looked round in time to see Hatshepsut's team of brown mares backing frantically as four soldiers struggled to harness them. Nehesi shouted and dashed forward to seize their reins, but not before the hindquarters of one careened into the body of a chariot. The cart lurched backward and smashed into the trunk of a dead myrrh tree.

Hatshepsut strode to Nehesi's side, stroked the mare's neck until she was calm and blowing.

"Has the chariot been much damaged?"

"Just a bit of a wound to the platform, Great Lady. It is still sound enough to drive."

Senenmut followed Hatshepsut as she inspected the cart, shaking its platform side to side, assessing the creaking of its springs, the stability of its wheels. The rearmost portion of the platform was dented and splintered, but only a hand's width of wood was damaged.

"It seems sound enough," Nehesi said, then cursed as a great white claw dropped onto his face, scratched his shoulder. It bounced from Nehesi's body and fell onto the chariot's platform: an old, twisted branch of myrrh.

Hatshepsut scrambled into the cart. She laughed as she

raised the branch, held it aloft like a war banner. "Nehesi, beware! These trees were sacred to Amun once. Has the god cursed you?"

"Amun's eyes!" Nehesi swiped at the scratches on his skin. Senenmut could see that he was not bleeding.

Hatshepsut dropped the branch and grimaced; she spread her fingers wide, then flexed them, spread them again.

"Is something wrong, Great Lady?" Senenmut said.

"Sap; it's only sap."

"I am impressed that trees so long dead can still have sap in them."

"Not much," Nehesi said. He scored the trunk of the myrrh tree with his knife, rather viciously, taking vengeance for the tree's attack. Only one small bead of sap appeared, hardly as large as a pomegranate seed. "These trees are so dry, it's no wonder the god throws their branches at innocent men. He must be furious."

Hatshepsut raised her palm to her nose, closed her eyes as she inhaled. "Gods, but it smells glorious. Even better than it smells when it's burning on the temple fires."

When she opened her eyes again, she looked down at Senenmut with a wide-mouthed grin of triumph. She stretched her palm down to him, and because he could not resist the opportunity to touch her skin, he took her hand in his own and breathed in the scent of the sap. It was warm with spice, sweet as fresh wine, and beneath the odor of the myrrh tree was the odor of her skin, golden and dusty, sharp with sweat. He breathed it in again, deeply.

"Do you know what it smells like to me, Senenmut?"

Reluctantly, he let her hand fall from his and gazed up at his king. A halo of light surrounded her face, and the shadow of the myrrh branches fell across her chest like the intricate lace of a fisherman's net.

"It smells like an answer to my riddle. It smells like our salvation."

The soldiers backed her horses into their traces, fastened their harness, brought the reins up to the Pharaoh's hands.

She took them up with a confidence she should not by rights have possessed, having been nowhere near a chariot team for years. She laughed at the way the sap stuck the rein to her palm.

"Come," she shouted. "There are lions in the hills, and my spear is impatient!"

She hissed, and her horses sprang away, galloping across the avenue of seshep and out into the barren gold of the valley. Senenmut gestured for his own chariot, but no matter how he drove his team, he could not catch his king. She thundered before him, her short kilt flying in the wind of her passage, her laughter coming to him now and then, faint and sparse, like the memory of myrrh sap in his nostrils.

"Djeser-djeseru," he called after her, and urged his horses to run faster.

PART THREE

THE GOD'S LAND

1467 B.C.E.

CHAPTER EIGHTEEN

HATSHEPSUT ALLOWED THUTMOSE TO DISMISS the evening's final courtier. The boy performed the gesture smoothly, pointing out across the great audience hall; the massive gilded double doors swung open at his indication as quickly as if the movement of his hand had physically thrown them wide, and not the scrambling of the attentive door guards. The courtier, one Penhat, a merchant of great wealth and greater complaints, was quick to bow his gratitude to the two Pharaohs and make his exit. When he receded across the length of the hall, his fast-moving sandals slapping against their own reflections in the floor of well-polished malachite slabs, Hatshepsut permitted herself a small smile. Thutmose had handled Penhat well, deflecting the man's customary gripes with an unyielding yet gracious confidence.

He is not a boy any longer, Hatshepsut reminded herself, eying him, seeing as if for the first time the strength of his jaw, the height of his brow, the stern angle of his nose. His sudden maturity always startled her anew, no matter how many times she saw him in a day. Somehow, in an eyeblink, the softness of those fat baby limbs had turned to muscle, just beginning to find its definition through near-constant work with spear and chariot and bow. The protruding belly she had tickled and kissed so many times until he giggled had changed to the lean, straight body of a soldier. Even his smell had altered itself from the sweetness of childhood, a scent like honey and cut grass, to the sharp, acrid stink of a man's sweat. She had employed several servants whose sole purpose it was to urge the young Pharaoh into his bath between drilling with the soldiers and courtly duties. She had admonished them to keep the king's armpits well perfumed.

All my years are gone, she thought, staring at Thutmose's new manly bearing with a morose pang. Then she chided herself for a fool.

"Your servant missed a patch shaving," she told him, and tapped her own jaw near her ear to show where.

Thutmose blushed. "I did it myself. I told them to leave off; I wanted to try it."

"No matter. It takes practice, or so I have heard."

"Are you ready for supper? I am famished. I'll dismiss the whole lot of stewards and guards if it be your will. Or you can dismiss them," he said, his brow pinching in the way it had when he was just a small thing, his peculiar means of looking both certain and uncertain at once. "I don't wish to take all the work for myself."

Hatshepsut turned to the Steward of Audiences, opened her mouth to speak the closing of the court. But the doors at the far end of the hall opened again, their twin scarab carvings winking in the bright lamp light as they swung to face one another. Hatshepsut and Thutmose held one another's eye, the boy quizzical, she with pursed lips and a growing sense of irritation.

It was Senenmut who entered; even with the distance of the great hall separating them, Hatshepsut recognized him. She would have picked out his posture, his quiet stance and his deliberate gait from a crowd of a hundred men. But he did not make his way to the foot of the throne, as supplicants did. He moved a few paces into the hall, then stepped to one side and called out in a clear voice, "The lady Opet of the King's House."

The breath caught in Hatshepsut's throat.

Opet wore a flowing gown of pale red linen, an open weave that clung to her skin. Her upper arms were bound in gold and silver torques, her throat adorned with the large, shining body and spread wings of a turquoise scarab in flight. A somewhat old-fashioned wig of long, braided locks framed her shoulders and face, which was demurely downcast. As she drew nearer the foot of the throne, her steps grew hesitant and her face blanched beneath its artful paints.

Opet bowed very low and presented her palms to the Pharaohs. Hatshepsut, sensing already what was to come, peevishly let the woman hold the position until she saw Opet's back begin to tremble. Then she scolded herself once more.

"Lady Opet, rise."

Opet did so, straightening and clasping her hands at her waist, though her eyes remained on the floor.

"What brings you to court?"

"I have...I have come to petition the Good Gods for release from the harem." At last her eyes lifted, met Hatshepsut's own. They were full of apology and fear...and pleading.

"Does it not please you to live as a king's woman?" Hatshepsut struggled to keep bitterness from her voice. *Senenmut told you this day would come. You have expected it.* But not from Opet – not from her own half-sister, with whom she had so often walked arm-in-arm through the harem gardens at night.

"It has pleased me for a long while, Majesty. But I have seen more than thirty-five years, and I have no children."

She spread her hands before her body, as if to emphasize the point. Through the loose linen of Opet's gown, Hatshepsut noted the girlish firmness of her breasts, the tightness of her belly. It was a body that had never known motherhood, and yet a body that was still surely capable of bearing...for a few more years. Sympathy for her sister overtook Hatshepsut's bitterness. Opet had always been kind, a friend and ally. She would not deny a child to such a loyal servant of the throne, even had she the strength of will to do so.

She glanced at Thutmose. The young king was subtle and observant enough to grasp that there was more at stake here than the simple petition it seemed. He leaned forward slightly in his seat, his mouth firm and pale, as he took in the scene. And yet Thutmose could know nothing of the closeness between Hatshepsut and Opet, could know nothing of the stinging in her heart. Far more important than her stinging heart, she suspected her co-regent grasped little of the political implications, bright as he was. His blindness was not his fault. It was an artifact of age. A boy whose primary preoccupations were his bow and his team of horses would have had little reason to turn his thoughts to what it could mean for a lesser daughter of a long-dead Pharaoh to conceive a son with some tjati or some general.

Hatshepsut wondered whether she might convince Thutmose privately to sire a child on Opet. Straight away she dismissed the idea. He was a fifteen-year-old boy – a young man in truth, and by the gods, *young* was the meat of it. Beautiful though Opet may be, she was more than twice Thutmose's own age. He was not likely to turn his attentions to her – not over a bit of politicking he could scarcely grasp.

There was nothing for it. Opet must be granted her release, to go forth and breed with some scheming noble. Hatshepsut could not countenance keeping any woman confined against her will, but particularly not Opet. She of all women deserved to know that peculiar, painful joy of watching a sweet baby grow into a man like Thutmose.

She rose from her throne abruptly, made her way down the steps to take Opet's hands in her own.

"Sister, I wish you happiness, and a house full of children. Is there some man already?"

"No, Great Lady," Opet said, her eyes flooding with tears of gratitude. "I thought to set myself up in a small house with a staff of a few servants, and to enter Waset society with the next festival. I may be able to find a suitable husband before it is too late for me. The kings I have served have been good to me; I have some small store of my own things – jewelry, fine linens, some furniture. I can sell them and buy a little home of my own in the city."

The news that no ambitious man had yet attached himself

to Opet gave Hatshepsut some small measure of relief. "Senenmut will see to you; he will give you enough goods and silver and gold to establish yourself well."

To Hatshepsut's surprise, Thutmose also descended from the dais, and took Opet's hand in his own. "Lady, I regret that we had no opportunity to become well acquainted. But the throne makes its demands on me, and I have less time than I wish for my women."

"Thank you, Majesties."

"Senenmut, see her out, and arrange a gift suiting her years of service."

"Well," Hatshepsut said, lifting her cup of wine toward the Great Steward, raising one black-painted brow in a half-resigned, half-angry arch. "You spoke the words, and like a slighted god's curse, they have come to be."

Thutmose exchanged a rueful glance with Senenmut. The young Pharaoh liked his step-mother's steward. Senenmut was thoughtful and sensible, quick with a solution to near any problem, and deeply loyal to Neferure, whom Thutmose thought of often. The steward was a good sort, as Nehesi would say.

Senenmut drew in a deep, long breath before he replied. "It's not as though you failed to see this coming yourself, Great Lady."

Hatshepsut grunted in disgust, set her cup rather heavily on the table. "I know. I *know*. And yet what else could I have done with Opet, but let her go?"

The supper Thutmose had been so eager for lay barely touched on his co-Pharaoh's table. When the great hall's doors had closed behind Lady Opet's retreating back, Hatshepsut had all but dragged Thutmose to her apartments for a rather rushed and sober meal. He could sense the tension crackling in the air about Hatshepsut's body, and by the time their food and Senenmut arrived, both Pharaohs had gone off their appetites. Stewed greens went cold and rumpled in their onion sauce; fish roasted in their scales stared up, their flesh still untasted, from their beds of spiced lentils. Somebody – Thutmose was not sure who – had torn a leg off the well-browned goose, then let it fall back onto the platter uneaten.

"You could have done nothing, Great Lady, and that is the gods' own truth. Unless you would have her killed."

"Of course not."

"Then it does you no good to brood over the thing. It has happened. Opet will not be the last to leave the harem. Rather than fret over it, best to plan now how you will cope."

"I know how. I have been planning it for more than a year. And yet...." Her voice grew small and quiet. Such gravity was so unlike Hatshepsut; it made Thutmose feel quite uneasy. He picked at the goose leg while she spoke, glad for the distraction. "With the flood's failure last year, how much more disruption can I face? How much time do I have? Will there be enough time, to get there and back before my enemies can move?"

Thutmose blinked several times. *Get where? What enemies?*

"You recovered from the bad flood well enough."

"Only just. It was touch and go."

"Your building projects were a wise move in dealing with the flood. A public display of piety went far in reassuring the people that you still have the favor of the gods. And when we return from Punt laden with treasure, with myrrh trees to restore Amun's full glory, none will find doubt in his heart. Not even your enemies."

Punt. Thutmose knew the name well. The land was far-off, across the waterless heat of the Red Land to the east, and further still. Some said it required ships to get there – ships worthy of waters far rougher than the Iteru in full flood. It was reputed to be the original home of Amun, his favored land where the myrrh trees he loved grew in profusion, where magic fell from the sky as rain. Some said Punt was naught but a myth, but Thutmose had read scrolls written by men who had been there, who had seen its strange people, its unique animals, its wealth of exotic treasures.

"The only question that remains, I think," said Hatshepsut, "is how much longer I can retain the women still in my harem. Oh, the daughters and sisters of merchants, or architects, or various high priests can leave at any time. I shall not worry over their departure. It's my cousins and half-sisters I must keep, at least until our plans are final. At least until we return."

"They will become pawns on the nobles' senet board," the Great Steward said. The words were an agreement with Hatshepsut, but as he spoke he looked levelly at Thutmose. *Do you understand what is going on here?* his eyes said. *Do you grasp the danger? Do you see our need?*

And at once, Hatshepsut's dilemma struck Thutmose with full force. *This is about the succession. It is about an heir – my heir.*

Ah, he understood the complexity of the problem now. This was not about Hatshepsut's half-sister yearning for a child. It was about the blood Lady Opet carried within her – the same blood Thutmose himself carried: the blood of Thutmose the First. How many other relations dwelt in the harem, ready to bear children – impatient to bear children? Poised to leave, to lend their royal blood to some other great house, to pave a way – witting or no – to Thutmose's throne?

But I am the king, he wanted to shout, right there in Hatshepsut's fine chambers, as though the men of those shadowy great houses might hear him. He clenched his fists, dismissed the childish urge.

"Oh, Amun," Hatshepsut sighed. She lifted herself from her couch, made her way to one soaring, painted wall. Her footsteps dragged with weariness. "If only I could clear my thoughts. If only I could *think*. My heart is all a-scatter; I will not sleep a moment tonight, I promise you."

She stood for some long time, her back to Thutmose and the steward, studying the images on her wall. In bright reds and golden ochers, in lapis-blue, some old king Thutmose could not identify lifted a bow to a flock of birds in flight.

No doubt he could have brought down a whole brace with a single shaft. Kings in paintings had no cares at all, and their arrows always flew true.

"You must move in this," Senenmut said, "and the sooner the better. Allow me to announce your expedition to the court. We need no more preparation; we can have all the supplies we need within two weeks or less. The season is right for the journey. If you wait longer, you must wait an entire year before the Red Land is cool enough once more to traverse."

Hatshepsut turned. Her face was solemn with thought. "You are right," she said. "The time is now."

"Trust that it will work. Have any of my plans failed you yet?"

"This was my plan," she said peevishly, though a glint of good humor sparkled in her eyes. She sank onto the couch beside Thutmose, laid one hand gravely on his shoulder. "I will be gone for many months, Thutmose. It is necessary. The throne will be yours alone while I am away."

He nodded, striving to quell the sudden nausea of excitement and fear that rose in his belly.

"I will leave you with advisors, of course, but you are old enough now to rule wisely." She hesitated, then added, "I trust you."

"Thank you, Mother." His voice was hoarse and quiet. He drank a draft of his beer to wet his throat, not tasting its pleasant bitterness. "I will rule well."

He thought of heirs, of successions. There were many lovely girls in his harem, and he visited them as often as time allowed, though none, so far as he yet knew, were with child. He should take one as his chief wife, he knew. A child from the body of a Great Royal Wife would be most definite in the line of succession; no man could dare to raise his eyes to the throne if Thutmose had a wife, and his wife had a boy. He considered the harem women one by one, pondering which would be the best choice, whose lineage was purest and closest to the throne.

"I know you will rule well." Hatshepsut gazed at him levelly, and he returned his bowl of beer to the table before she could see the tremor in his hands. "Your word will be command, Thutmose, and so you must think carefully before you speak. What a Pharaoh says to his subjects cannot be unsaid."

Thutmose nodded.

"It is settled, then." Hatshepsut stood briskly, stretched with her hands in the small of her back, suddenly as carefree as a girl. "Make the announcement in the morning, Senenmut. In two weeks we leave for the god's land."

CHAPTER NINETEEN

THE COURT IN ALL ITS fulsome splendor turned out on Waset's whitestone quay to witness the departure of the king. Beyond the protective rank of soldiers that were the hallmark of Hatshepsut's reign, Ahmose watched the press of the crowd move this way and that like a school of lazy fish, arms and throats banded in gold, the hems of bright-dyed gowns and kilts rippling. Women displayed the latest fashion, the short-cropped, round silhouette of the Nubian wig, which left necks temptingly bare, shimmering with dampness in the humidity of the crowed riverside. The ladies of the great houses waved fans before their faces, leaning to whisper behind their plumes. Men eyed Hatshepsut's war ship, *Amun Strides from Darkness*, with a speculative air as it bobbed against its lines, rocking to the rhythm of the final lading. When the last man scrambled aboard, a large clay jar of provisions perched atop his shoulder like one of the chattering pet birds so popular with the harem girls, Hatshepsut emerged from her ship's cabin. Expectant silence spread through the crowd.

The Pharaoh made her way to the ship's gilded rail. Since the day of her coronation, Ahmose could recall few occasions when Hatshepsut had presented herself to such a large crowd in a man's clothing. Yet now she was dressed simply and distinctly as a male, with a plain white kilt falling to her knee and the simple cloth crown of Nemes flaring about her face like a lapis cobra's hood, rippling lightly in the wind. The golden visages of vulture and cobra reared above her brow, the king's simplest circlet decrying her power in frank and forceful terms.

"In the name of the god," Hatshepsut said, her voice rich and low, a voice meant to carry to every ear in the crowd, "I travel to Punt, the legendary place, to bring back gifts for Amun. Your king Menkheperre shall rule in my absence, wisely and well."

Ahmose glanced across the small bare patch of whitestone to young Thutmose. Menkheperre himself stood with arms folded across his well-muscled chest, watching his co-king's departure with an air of perfect confidence, the two-tiered Double Crown rising tall upon his head. His poor dead mother's beauty had refined the stamp of Thutmose the First, Ahmose's own departed husband, but the resemblance was there, for those who had eyes to see it. The young Pharaoh was not as tall as most men, yet the breadth of his shoulders promised a burgeoning strength at least as great as his grandfather's. His nose had grown out of its childish snub and was beginning to take on something of his ancestor's hawk's-beak. And the way his jaw set firmly, the way his eyes remained steady and calm on Hatshepsut, pained Ahmose's heart with remembrance.

Hatshepsut spoke on, and the crowd beyond the ring of soldiers cheered. Neferure, reed-slim and swaying lightly in the morning heat, twitched at the sudden sound, lifted her eyes from the paving stones to gaze about her for a moment, her expression vague, a woman coming out of a dream. Neferure's quiet obedience in the face of her mother's stirred Ahmose's pity, as it so often did. The girl had always served loyally, had always been mindful of maat, and yet she was so sad, so unfulfilled.

I was that way once, Ahmose mused, lifting her hand in farewell as the sailors cast off the lines and the royal musicians raised a triumphant song. *Young and earnest and confused, wanting to serve maat and never knowing what maat was.*

Amun Strides from Darkness pulled from the quay, drifted westward to meet the remainder of Hatshepsut's expedition fleet where it held mid-river. Neferure trembled amidst the cheering, and Thutmose glanced at his sister from the tail of his kohl-rimmed eye. The look he gave her brimmed with an intensity that made Ahmose wonder. Was it desire in the young Pharaoh's gaze, or...fear? Thutmose offered his arm to Neferure, who took it with wordless complacency. He steered her across the paving stones to where Ahmose stood in the mercy of her sunshade.

"Grandmother," said Thutmose, by way of greeting.

She was not his grandmother, of course. The young man did not know his true grandmother; she had been banished to some lonesome estate when the king was but an infant. *I suppose I am the closest he has to a grandmother. How Mutnofret would hate me afresh, if she knew.*

She bowed to him. "Majesty."

"It will be a fine expedition." Thutmose patted the back of Neferure's hand absently, gingerly, as one pets a skittish cat.

"Ah, I expect it will."

"Will you...will you come to me at supper time, Grandmother? I would enjoy your company."

He wants my counsel. She saw it at once in the slight tension around his eyes. *And he is too clever to admit even the smallest misgiving where his courtiers and soldiers might hear.*

Ahmose turned her head casually, feigning to glance toward the jar of wine her women poured for the king. But she raised her eyes past her servants, past the backs of the soldiers, to the press of the crowd. Here and there a pair of noble's eyes made contact with her own, then blinked and slid away again with a palpable air of nonchalance – and here and there one lady swayed close to another, her mouth tight-pursed. *Ah, there will be eyes and ears on you, young Menkheperre. There will be lions waiting to close for the kill, with your mawat gone from the throne.* At least, thank the gods, the boy was wise enough to know it.

"I would be honored, Majesty. I shall come to you at the customary hour."

"Good." Thutmose took the offered cup of wine, drained it

in a single long draft while the horns keened their marching tune and the rattles chimed. When he returned the cup to Ahmose's servant with a nod of his head, his hand did not shake.

Ahmose was admitted into the presence of Menkheperre Thutmose, the Third of His Name, by a strange, wispy fidget of a man, lanky and wiry with a mouth that was too soft and too wide. Hesyre was Ahmose's own age, if not older, but the lines of his face had more to do with particulars and details, fusses and primps, than with the cares of governing a kingdom. She raised her brows at him, assessing as he bowed and stood aside to admit her. She was amused to note that his brows raised in return, tenting the loose skin of his eyelids, weighing Ahmose fearlessly in his turn, and measure for measure.

"Hesyre." Thutmose's voice called from the depths of his apartments. "Is it my grandmother?"

"Ah, Majesty," Hesyre responded in a voice of carefully modulated respect. "The Great Lady Ahmose of the house of Waser Thutmose the First, may he live; the dowager regent."

Thutmose laughed, a sound full of his youthful exuberance. "I know who she is."

"Ah, Majesty."

Hesyre gestured, and Ahmose fell into step behind him.

There had never been any dispute that Hatshepsut was the more senior of the two kings, and so the original Pharaoh's apartments – the rooms ready-built for the king by the palace's architect – had gone to her. But she had gifted her co-regent the next-finest rooms since his infancy – a complex that had originally been built to house high-ranking dignitaries from foreign lands, to impress them with the splendor and wealth of Egypt. Thutmose's chambers lacked for no luxury. Angular arches spaced at regular intervals near the ceiling held well-placed windcatchers, which filtered a sweet-smelling breeze from the adjacent garden and cooled the interior of the apartments. The anteroom was wide and well-lit by ranks of bronze lamps with electrum reflecting-discs. The flickering light of the many braziers illuminated a ring of fine couches, their legs carved of ebony and marble, upholstered in the priceless silks of the far north, brightly dyed in an array of colors. The silks could only be obtained through costly trade of gold and turquoise. That Thutmose owned many lengths of the precious fabric, and had used it for the express purpose of sitting upon, spoke of the young man's subtlety. He was savvy enough to obtain such goods in quantity, and clever enough to display them in such a carefree manner. Only a man thoroughly secure in his own power would upholster his couches in silk. *Of course*, Ahmose mused, *it may have been Hesyre's idea.* Beyond the couches, a brilliant and thorough mural of Egypt evicting the Heqa-Khasewet from the Two Lands wrapped the antechamber on three of its walls. Ahmose recalled it from her early days in the palace, when she was the Great Royal Wife, younger than Thutmose himself. She gazed about her, allowing her eyes to roam over the scenes of conquest and victory, wondering that Thutmose hadn't ordered the murals painted over with fresher, more modern scenes.

As she stood inspecting the walls, one of several cedar doors banded in bronze and gold swung wide, and Thutmose emerged. The scent of fine oils – a masculine perfume of galbanum and the blood-red resin of Kush – followed him into the antechamber.

"Grandmother. It is good of you to come to me."

Ahmose smiled. "You are the Pharaoh. Should any lady of the court disobey a summons from her king?" Thutmose waved her to the silk couches, and she sank onto one the color of emeralds, the deep, rich green of the season of growth, when the Two Lands came to glorious life and the river banks and fields teemed with new leaves and the rich scent of foliage. Surreptitiously, she allowed her hand to smooth across the surface. It was cool beneath her fingers. Ahmose could never resist the lure of silk.

Thutmose seated himself with an easy confidence and clapped for his servants. Their supper shortly arrived, but Ahmose left her bowl empty, waiting for the young Pharaoh to fill her ears instead. When the meal had been laid out to his satisfaction, he dismissed his servants and sat listening, his head tilted almost imperceptibly, until the door to their quarters down the hall closed with a muffled bump.

"And how can I serve His Majesty?" Ahmose said softly.

Thutmose narrowed his eyes. "Was it so obvious, that I need your advice? Already, when Hatshepsut has been gone from the palace only a few hours?"

"Not as obvious as you fear. I have learned a certain degree of observation and inference, you see, serving the throne as long as I have." She smiled wryly, and he relaxed.

"You know why Hatshepsut undertook this journey to Punt, I assume."

"My daughter has always enjoyed adventure."

"This is no mere adventure. She went because she had to."

"Had to?"

"She has built more monuments than any Pharaoh before her, I think, but has had fewer military campaigns. Her temples and obelisks are for the gods, yes, but more so for the people. To prove to them – to make a point, you see – that she has the gods' favors, and therefore cannot be lightly displaced."

"She fears displacement?" It was not a surprise. Secret bids for Egypt's throne began nearly fifteen years ago, when Iset was killed by poisoned wine meant for Hatshepsut's lips. Of course the senior Pharaoh feared displacement.

"What she needs," Thutmose said, his voice hesitant with care, "what *we* need as the Great House of Thutmose the First, is an heir."

"She made Neferure heir." Despite her resolve to remain neutral before the king, Ahmose's mouth tightened.

Thutmose raised his brows when he noted her expression. "Neferure is a woman, and I wonder whether a woman as heir might stretch the bounds of what Egypt is willing to accept. I do not speak of disinheriting Neferure – there is no need, and I will not see my sister ill-treated. But surely by all the gods' laws a male heir would come before a female."

Ahmose sat forward on the silk couch. "You would marry, then, and get a son. Yes – that would do the trick. Neferure could remain heir until you have your son. Then she would not be disinherited – only superseded, as the law of the gods would decree." Ahmose had never approved of Hatshepsut's decision to proclaim Neferure heir, but as she had fought tirelessly to place her own daughter on the throne so many years ago, she could not in good conscience gainsay Hatshepsut's decision. If Thutmose had a legitimate heir by a Great Royal Wife, the priests of Amun would indeed uphold a son's claim over a daughter's. Ahmose felt sure of it.

"It may be our only means of keeping the nobles in their place – of giving Hatshepsut enough reassurance that she rests easily at night, and Egypt continues its business uninhibited."

Ahmose lifted her chin in admiration for the young man's quick and thorough thinking. It seemed impossible that such a bright and earnest king could descend from Mutnofret's insecurity and the pig-headed selfishness of the second Thutmose. And yet here he was, as worthy a descendant as Ahmose's dead husband could have wished for. She felt one brief stab of envy that the boy did not come from her own blood, then pushed the unbecoming emotion away firmly. *I am the one he calls Grandmother, after all.*

"Your insight is to be commended, Majesty. I believe you are right."

"You do?" Thutmose squared his shoulders, and Ahmose stifled a fond chuckle at his sudden boyishness.

"I told Hatshepsut as much, years ago, well before she proclaimed Neferure her heir. I warned her against it. I feared it would pit you and Neferure against one another someday – or at least, would set Neferure at odds against your future sons. But I don't think it would trouble her, to know that you had an heir of your own. I don't believe the girl cares for the title at all."

Thutmose squinted at the beer in his drinking bowl. "It is difficult to know what Neferure cares for. Hathor – I know she cares for Hathor. Whenever I visit the harem, I hope to see her among the other women. But she is always in her little palace, apart from them. And it seems there is a constant stream of smoke rising from the rooftop, where her Hathor shrine stands. Beyond the goddess, though..." He shrugged.

"Well," Ahmose said, setting aside the familiar pang of sadness at the thought of Neferure, "I suppose we must choose a Great Royal Wife, then."

A flush crept into Thutmose's cheeks. "I don't know how to choose."

"And so you have turned to your old grandmother." Ahmose waved away his embarrassment. "It is only natural. I am honored to be of service, Majesty."

Thutmose put forth the names of several young women from the harem, each of them worthy candidates who could trace their lineage easily to the throne. He had put as much careful consideration into this matter as any other, and Ahmose felt a glow of pride at the young Pharaoh's competence. They debated the women in turn, examining the benefits each might bring to Thutmose's court with a detachment that left an uncomfortable pinch in Ahmose's belly. *This was how my mother and my own grandmother discussed their choice – Mutnofret or me for Great Royal Wife.* It sickened her, to realize she examined so many young women as if they were objects, baubles to set upon a bedside table to beautify a room. And yet what else could she do? The wrong choice could incite political disaster. Egypt was at stake. *Mother, at last I understand you.* Ahmose pressed her hands to her stomach to soothe away her guilt and regret, and the conversation went on.

Thutmose summoned his servants to replenish their food and fetch wine. They had debated the women for hours, and at last had settled upon three, all of them girls with royal blood whose families had so far shown no alarming signs of overt ambition. A platter of figs and cheese arrived, and Thutmose stared at it morosely, all the talk drained out of him.

Ahmose leaned back into the luxury of the green couch, eying Thutmose's weary expression. There was a becoming melancholy about him. It charmed her when she recognized its source, and she laughed lightly. "All three of these girls are good choices, yet you do not love them."

He shook his head. "Love doesn't enter into it, Grandmother. My duty is to get a legitimate heir, to protect the throne."

She recalled the look Thutmose had given Neferure that morning on the quay, the sidelong glance full of some potent, un-nameable emotion. "We have overlooked one candidate for Great Royal Wife, I think."

He sighed. "And who is she?"

"Neferure." When she said the name, the prickle of the gods' touch ran along Ahmose's skin. *Yes*, her heart whispered. Ahmose breathed deep, accepting the certainty, the inevitability.

Suddenly animated, Thutmose stared at her, a tension of longing brightening his eyes. "But she is Hatshepsut's heir."

"A position she does not want. I think her heart craves something else. Consider her: she is dutiful to a fault, dedicated to maat. She is god-chosen." *And well do I know how that qualifies a woman to be a Pharaoh's wife.* "And she is lovely." She added this last offhandedly, but allowed a small smile when she saw how Thutmose flushed. "If you married her," Ahmose added, "and she bore you a son, the child would be unassailable as heir. You and Neferure are both the children of Pharaohs – she is the child of two Pharaohs, in fact." After fourteen years of keeping up the deception, the lie of Neferure's parentage slipped easily from Ahmose's lips, without a single hesitation. "You are a Pharaoh yourself. Can an heir have a stronger claim? How could any noble hope that his fellows might proclaim his son king, if the best he could offer Egypt was the child of a Pharaoh's cousin? Your son with Neferure will be four times royalty, and through her, descended directly from Amun."

"Yes," Thutmose said. "She is the ideal match. But Hatshepsut has already proclaimed her. What a Pharaoh says cannot be unsaid."

Ahmose tasted the wine in her cup. Its initial sweetness was undercut by a powerful bitter, musky note, not at all unpleasant. But the echo of it on her tongue slowed her reply, and she had to swallow several times before the words would come. "Perhaps the only person who can unsay a king's words is another king."

"Perhaps," said Thutmose. His fingers twisted into a knot in his lap.

CHAPTER TWENTY

I T TOOK ALL OF NEFERURE'S considerable discipline to remain still and silent in her litter. Her heart leapt and sang within her breast, straining against her flesh and bones, striving to fly free, a bird on a joyous wind. The city of Iunet was alive with the din of merchants crying their wares, of women gossiping at wells, of children laughing as they dashed across the road, crossing the path of Neferure's litter-bearers. She watched the city through the gauze of her curtains, beaming at the people she passed, although they could not see her face.

Thutmose had sent her to Iunet – Thutmose and Ahmose. A few days after Hatshepsut set out on her great expedition, the Pharaoh and Lady Ahmose had come to Neferure's palace, and with a knowing smile Thutmose had instructed her to take a great offering of gifts to the Lady of the West, beloved Hathor, the goddess who was all goddesses in one. She would spend two weeks in Iunet, he had explained, measuring out the wealth he had designated for the Hathor temple and its staff, acting in the name of the Pharaoh, as he was too busy himself to attend in person. Neferure had been hard-pressed to keep herself from squealing like a girl. She embraced her brother, clung tightly around his neck until he was obliged to disentangle her arms with a timid smile.

From the moment she boarded her ship at Waset's quay, Neferure had felt the swell of triumph rising in her ka. Iunet lay nearly a day's sail upriver, and the closer she drew to its shore the more rapturous she became. She would spend two weeks with Hathor – two precious weeks in the glow of the goddess's love. Neferure could not recall a time when she had been so filled with joy. She trembled with it, and the smile never left her face.

The procession of treasure wound its way through Iunet's dusty streets, with Neferure, the best and brightest gem of Thutmose's offering, at its head. Beyond the final homes and store-houses of the city, the road, raised on an earthen causeway, cut across a field knee-high with emmer. Through her curtains, she could see how the late afternoon light danced on the backs of the small birds that dove down among the wheat heads to snap up their supper of flies and gnats. The emmer itself glowed, each seed-bearing tuft of each plant alight with the sun's warmth. The goddess had set the world to sparkling, just for Neferure.

At last they reached the temple itself. Perched on its small hill, it rose above the fields with a stately grace, backlit by the vermillion glow of the setting sun. Neferure's throat let out a tiny squeak of anticipation as her litter sank to the ground. She controlled herself, closed her eyes, breathed in the deep, calming breaths Senenmut had taught her, and when her ka was as still as it ever would be, she parted her curtains and stepped from the litter with precise dignity. The afternoon was cool, and the sun well on its way to its nightly journey through the underworld. No sun-shade was needed, but her women appeared quickly with their white-plumed fans to stir the gnats away from Neferure's skin. Takhat appeared at her elbow, bowing slightly. "Are you ready, mistress?"

For answer, Neferure strode up the stone ramp toward the temple at the hill's crown.

She paused at the ramp's apex, overcome with the force of the goddess's presence. A forest of pillars greeted her, arranged in neat ranks to either side of an avenue worn smooth by generations of priestesses and worshippers. Where the avenue ran, the temple remained unroofed, open to the blood-red sky. As Neferure gazed up through the pillars, a flight of geese traversed the narrow patch of sky, sudden and black, their wings speaking loud in the still air. The speed of their movement set her vision to spinning. She reached out to steady herself with one hand against a pillar, and when her flesh touched the sacred stone a fierce warmth flowed into her, as startling as the passage of the geese.

"Welcome, God's Wife."

Neferure looked round. Two women approached down the avenue, moving with the quiet pride of priestesses. She felt the sudden urge to bow to them, to prostrate herself on the stone floor like a slave. But she recalled her position, and with an effort she stood firm.

When the women halted in front of her, it was they who bowed, proffering their palms the way courtiers and rekhet bowed to the two Pharaohs. Neferure dropped her eyes so they could not read her startlement.

"We have waited long for you," said one priestess. "Longer than was maat."

"I have also waited long," Neferure said. Her voice seemed to murmur back at her from amidst the pillars.

"No matter, Great Lady. The Pharaoh has sent the promised gift. We will not dwell on its delay. Come."

They led her through a set of pylons, across a courtyard, dimmed by the encroaching twilight. The door to the temple itself stood before her, suffused with a steadily growing light as inside, amidst the soft chanting of many voices, lamps kindled to life. The warmth of the temple tugged at Neferure; she forgot herself and her steps quickened, carried her past the priestesses who guided her. She heard one of them laugh with pleasure and satisfaction as she brushed past.

Inside, a melody of color met her eyes. The righteousness of Hathor so overflowed that it spilled down the walls in the form of bright paint, of images of the goddess in all her several forms, intense and vibrant, leaping from the stone walls into bright and present life. Neferure spun in a circle, her feet dancing over the great red sun-disk set into the floor, and the colors whirled. Song rose up to soar amidst the smoke of incense and lamp-oil high above her head.

> *O Mistress of jubilation,*
> *Lady of the dance,*
> *Mistress of music,*
> *Lady of the harp,*
> *Lady of song,*
> *Lady of the wreaths,*
> *O Mistress of joy*
> *Without end!*

"Mistress of joy without end," Neferure whispered.

"The goddess delights in you, as you delight in her."

The two priestesses were at her side now. Full of gratitude, Neferure looked upon their faces for the first time. The one who spoke was thin and wiry, and had the confident posture of one who had been appealingly slender and womanish in her youth. She was a youth no longer, though; her face had begun to show its years, the pale brow crossed with fine lines, and deeper lines edged her nose and mouth. But she was as full of confidence as she must have been in her younger days. She smiled benevolently at Neferure, and Neferure could not help grinning back.

The other was more arresting. Shorter and broader than her companion, her face was curiously broad, the eyes wide-spaced, and while one was as black as any Egyptian's, the other glimmered a sharp, intense blue. The braids surrounding her face were no wig, but the woman's natural hair, and at her brow the braids glowed bone-white in the lamplight. Her appearance was so startling that Neferure nearly took a step backward. If not for the open delight of the other priestess, Neferure may have fled from the strangeness of her companion.

The odd-eyed priestess gestured elegantly, and the other spoke. "Do not be afraid. She is Imer, chosen of the Mistress. The goddess has brought you here, Lady Neferure, most fortunate and blessed of women."

Imer moved her hands again, and again her companion's voice filled the silence. Neferure realized that Imer could not speak with her tongue; her fellow priestess understood her signs and spoke in her place. "The goddess has a great work for you. Open your heart and receive her."

"I try," Neferure said. To her horror, tears stung her eyes. *Weeping, in the very seat of the Mistress of Joy. It's shameful.* But she could not stop herself. Tears broke to spill down her cheeks. She wiped frantically at her kohl with her fingers. "I try, but the Mistress never enters my heart. Not she, nor any other god."

Imer smiled broadly, and pulled from her red sash a square of linen. She dabbed at Neferure's cheeks with the gentleness of a nurse.

"It is no matter," said the thin priestess. "Imer will teach you."

The days bled one into another with the sweet, lazy slowness of honey dripping from a knife. Neferure meted out Thutmose's treasure as he had instructed, but that task cost her hardly a day. For the first time in her life she was freed from duty, imbued with a sense of liberation that tingled along her spine. Never before had she chosen for herself how she would spend her time. And she knew that if she had been fortunate enough to have been born something lesser than a King's Daughter, she would have chosen no other life than this.

Each morning she rose early to the high-pitched song of an apprentice, no doubt one of the many girls Hatshepsut had conscripted into Hathor's service. The girl stood on a stone platform in the center of a small, sparsely planted courtyard behind the temple itself, her voice rising and falling as the sun made its way inevitably up the great blue vault of the sky. Her hymn was sweet. Neferure never tired of hearing it, though it brought her out of too few hours' sleep on a rather hard and unfriendly bed.

With the other apprentices, Neferure tended the shrines, parceling out the offerings that best pleased each of Hathor's faces: sweet cakes to the face of love; plain, honest wheat bread to the face of judgment. Strong beer to the Mistress of Dance, she who loved inebriation; milk to the mother; blood to grinning lion-face of She Who Scratches.

She joined in the dances, giving her ka over to the trance of movement, until, spinning and stamping, she was transported into another realm, where her thoughts swam dizzily and her breathing grew sluggish on the thickness of incense.

By night, she joined Imer on the rooftop sanctuary. They sat deep in conversation, bathed in silver starlight, discussing each facet of Hathor's sevenfold self for hours. These were the best times. The sounds of night insects drifted up from the fields surrounding the temple, an endless chant to the goddess's greatness. At first, Neferure had needed the assistance of Imer's thin companion to understand the great priestess's words. But with diligent practice, she came to grasp most of Imer's signs for herself, and could even respond with her own clumsy form of the gestures. Imer's wisdom was boundless. She unlocked mysteries like long-forgotten chests, and the gems contained within dazzled Neferure's ka.

It was nearly her final night at the Temple of Hathor. Neferure's feet dragged with the knowledge that she must soon return to Waset and the roles fate had laid out for her, but she climbed the stairway to the rooftop sanctuary in spite of the cold fist of sorrow clutching her heart. The stars were especially bright tonight, each one shining with such an individual intensity that she thought she might reach out and pluck a handful from the black sky. If they had been discs of electrum strung on a belt, they would have chimed in the gentle night wind.

Imer sat in her accustomed place, her back against one of the many pillars that stood on the rooftop, holding up nothing but the vibrant night sky. Her little reed mat was below her as always, and some servant had laid out a clay platter of melon slices and a jug of water. Neferure approached, full of melancholy. When Imer saw her, she bowed low over her own lap, as an apprentice bows to a High Priestess.

"Sit," Imer said with her hands, her gestures clear in the ample glow of starlight. She offered Neferure a little mat of her own; Neferure took it with a nod of thanks.

"You are sad tonight," Imer signed.

"I will miss the temple, and the Mistress."

"You can let her inside now."

Neferure hoped it was true. Certainly, under Imer's tutelage she had allowed some presence into her heart more fully than ever before. Her face warmed to recall it, the insistent throbbing that filled her middle, the hot thrumming along her limbs. She assumed the presence to be Hathor. Who else could it have been, here in this place? She demurred with a gesture, and Imer went on:

"Something else troubles you."

"Many things."

"Tell me."

Neferure sighed. Her hands failed her; she could not seem to recall all the signs she needed to express herself, and at any rate, mere hand-signs seemed insufficient to express the weight of duty that dragged at her, pulling at her ka as a crocodile pulls at its prey.

"Speak, if you will not sign. I will watch." Imer tapped her own lips.

She drew a deep breath, and the scroll of her sorrows unrolled. She spoke of the way Amun spurned her, turned his back on her entirely, so that in his presence she felt only a great, uncaring distance, a coldness of abandonment, though she danced for him as passionately as she danced for Hathor, and burned myrrh until the smell of it singed her nostrils, and poured oil over his visage until the floor of his dark sanctuary was slick with it. She spoke of the way all gods drew back from her, retreating from her worship, though there was no one in the Two Lands as devoted or as earnest as she. She spoke the word *heir* with loathing, said it was not maat, not her fate, but she was chained to it like a bull is chained to a temple wall.

"What can I do, Imer? I am god-chosen – everyone says it, and I can feel the gods so close to me. Yet they do not come in. Why? All I wish is to be here, in Hathor's temple, serving the Mistress of the West. Oh, can't I stay? Can't you find some way to make my mother release me from my duties?"

Imer sat unmoving for a long while, her blue eye gleaming in the starlight. Neferure grew uncomfortable under her scrutiny. She fidgeted on her mat, embarrassed of the way she had poured out her fears and insecurities. Finally, though, Imer lifted her hands.

"You must return to Waset."

Neferure's ka fell.

"You have duties yet to be done, child."

Always duties. Always more to be done. Neferure felt tears rising, but squeezed her eyes tightly shut to drive them away. *I will not weep again in the House of Joy. I will not so offend the goddess.*

She steadied herself, then said with her hands, "Very well. What duties?"

"You will learn that for yourself."

Neferure sucked at her lower lip, waiting for the priestess to say more.

"The goddess will make it plain. Sit in the shrine of your choice from starlight to starlight. Take only one jar of water, but no food. The goddess will fill you, child, I swear it."

Neferure had her doubts, but she also had her instructions. Ever obedient, she rolled her mat and bowed to Imer. She turned her back on the blessing of starlight and descended the stairs into the heart of Hathor's temple.

With her belly clutched by fear and the anticipation of failure, Neferure did not pause to consider which shrine she entered. She staggered through the darkness of the unlit temple, one hand on the wall so she would not lose her way entirely. Her sandals slid easily along the slick faience floor-tiles. Beneath her blind fingers, she felt the carven scenes of Hathor's presence flicker and shift about her. At last her hands found a door, and she pushed it open, stepped into a darkness that was denser still.

"Lady," she whispered in the cool blackness of the shrine, "have mercy on me at last, and fill me."

Neferure sank to the floor, folded her legs beneath her, and waited.

She waited for hours, until her legs seared with cramps. She stretched them out on the floor and shook them, but she did not rise. She waited until the thin sound of the morning song came through the shrine's walls as pale and distant as a waning moon. Morning had come, but the shrine she had chosen remained closed, and she remained enveloped in darkness. She waited as hunger seized her belly, an insistent gnawing at first, then, as the darkness whirled through her senses, intensifying with a ferocity that rent her from within.

"Neferure." The voice was sharp, shrill. Her mother's voice. It rebounded off the unseen stone walls, echoing, reversing upon itself as a ring of ripples rebounds when a stone is dropped into a pool. "Neferure, Neferure, Neferure, Neferurerurerurerure."

The voice quieted, became melodic and soft. "Neferure."

She felt an unseen presence bend over her, a warmth tipping across her body, the warmth of a nurse raising her from a cradle and holding her close against a bare, male chest.

"Who is there?" she said, and her words came out slowly. Her tongue, addled by hunger, did not know how to speak.

"Mistress of jubilation," said the soft voice, "Lady of the dance."

"Lady?" Neferure turned her head, quivering with eagerness. She tried to do as Imer had taught her, as Ahmose had taught her, letting her ka fall open like a blossom in the sun.

"Mistress of the harp, Lady of joy without end."

"Yes," Neferure sobbed. The blackness drew in close about her, touched her with eager, rough hands, and she fell open, a blossom wilting in the sun. "Lady, come in!"

There was a pressure against her chest, a rushing sensation as a chariot in the wind, a gasp, a chill rising through her body, a warmth pulsing deep inside. *O, gods*, her ka cried, overwhelmed at their sudden presence, the undeniable force of them, all clamoring at once within her heart. She would burst – she could not contain them all.

And then she saw, with pale, trembling disbelief, that she did not need to contain them. She was becoming them, becoming one of them, by the grace of Hathor, whom she had served selflessly for so many years as she had served the thronw, patiently awaiting her reward.

"How?" she cried out, reaching for the divinity that was her birthright, not knowing how to grasp it.

She stretched her hand into the darkness, and beneath her fingers she felt once more the dry, dusty hair of the bull of Min, its hot, trembling strength beneath her fingers, its breath on her thighs. She had looked up from the bull, gazed through the settling dust, and it was Thutmose she saw, staring back at her, his eyes full of fear, of awe, of worship.

It is my birthright, her ka insisted. *But how?*

Thutmose and the bull merged into one form, and it was her brother she felt now beneath her grasping hand, his breath blowing like a bellows, his body roaring with a god's might.

"You begged for a god to fill you," the soft voice whispered, "and so he shall."

"Yes," Neferure said again, but this time she did not weep. At the sound of her voice, a hinge sang behind her. Someone was pushing the door to the shrine open. Lamplight fell across the floor, crept toward Neferure where she crouched on the cold floor, pained by her cramps and by hunger. The light crossed her face. She squinted, eyes streaming with tears.

"Great Lady," said a young apprentice, "Imer told me to

bring you water."

There was the thump of a jug settling onto the floor beside her. Neferure thrust her hands into its mouth, sucked greedily at tepid water cupped in her palms.

"What is the hour?" she croaked.

"First starlight, Great Lady."

"Help me up."

The girl obliged, pulling Neferure to her feet, then sliding one thin shoulder beneath Neferure's arm to support her. A wise decision; Neferure's legs shook, weakened by her long ordeal. With the apprentice's help, she staggered toward the door. When she reached it, she clutched at the stone, sagging against the doorway. She could not move another step.

"Bring me food – bread and beer. Meat, if there is any."

The girl ran to do her bidding. Neferure listened to the sound of her retreating footsteps, and when silence filled the temple again, she shut her eyes to remember the vision.

A god will fill me in truth, she said within the quiet of her heart, and the joy of the knowledge weakened her legs anew.

She turned to offer her thanks to the aspect of Hathor that had guided her. The light streaming through the open door penetrated the shrine with a shaft of brilliant gold. It fell upon the painting of the goddess on the shrine's far wall: the lion-headed one, grinning her feral smile, teeth flashing like daggers as she strode through a river of blood.

Chapter Twenty-One

THE DAWN CAME RED, A rising swell on the eastern horizon. Hatshepsut stood in the door of her tent and watched morning break. The living sun cast a ruddy mantle on the world below. The line of cliffs to the north, the rank of rocky hills to the south, and beyond them, in the cruxes of their hunched shoulders, an endless expanse of dunes – all were like carnelian stone, luminescent and burnished in the blood-red light. Her bare feet sank into sand. It, too, was red, a powder so fine it worked its way into the cracks of her skin, dried her out, roughened all she touched with the faint trace of desert dust.

It is no wonder the gods have named this place the Red Land, she mused, brushing her hands together to clear them of the powdery sand. Her efforts made no difference. In moments her hands would be coated again. *Everything is the color of blood.*

As the sun shrugged itself free of the horizon, Hatshepsut became aware of a deep violet haze hanging below the dawn's glow. *The sea.* They would reach it by evening – at last, after a week of trudging through the Red Land. She had sailed her fleet upriver one day's journey from Waset to the place where the river bends. There she moored and met with a fleet of a different sort: an overland one, made of donkeys and men in vast numbers, strong men with broad backs to tote the light poles and linens that would become her tents, to carry uncountable skins full of tepid water, to carry great woven baskets upon their shoulders bearing to Punt vast measures of Kushite gold and Egyptian turquoise, and which would, she hoped, fill with the exotic treasures of Punt for the trek back to Waset. They had set out eastward, at first following the flat plane of an ancient trade route, a depression through the desert sands barely visible to the untrained eye. Ineni had hired the best and most experienced desert navigators the king's wealth could buy; within hours of walking the faint track, it led them between two low lines of hills, ridges of deep red rock against which the sand lay in great soft heaps. The hills turned to cliffs, and the track became a broad, long-dry wash, not unlike the one she had ridden between Ta-Seti and Kush, years before when her blood had been as hot and fierce as the desert itself. The wash went on for spans uncountable, for days, and Hatshepsut's expedition followed it under the guidance of Ineni's navigators.

Nehesi had taken a great liking to those navigators, learning the secrets of desert travel from them and chattering back what he'd learned to Hatshepsut, secrets of finding the rare seeps that held water far below the sand, clever ways to trace the flight of birds to rare patches of greenery where leaves and roots could be chewed and sucked for moisture. Nehesi seemed to thrive on desert travel; in no time at all, he had grown to love the long mornings of trudging through deep sand, the afternoons crouched and dozing beneath dust-stained linen shades through the worst of the daytime heat. He loved the evenings, too, when the expedition would strike its temporary encampments, roll the linens and poles onto the bearers' backs, dole out a few mouthfuls of water to each man and each beast, and head into the gathering night to walk until the moon was setting.

Nehesi loved it, but Hatshepsut despised it. Late mornings were a torment, an unbearable slog with sweat coursing down her back, running into her eyes and stinging until her vision clouded with tears. She would force herself onward until she could tolerate the heat no more, and then would call a halt and fall, grateful but uncomfortable, into the wan shade of her makeshift tent. At least the night walks were cooler, but the hours allotted for sleep were too few, and she was soon plagued by headaches and the shakiness of exhaustion.

We will reach the sea tonight, thanks be to Amun. She could press on for one more day.

Senenmut emerged from his tent, separated from Hatshepsut for propriety's sake but pitched nearby in case his lady should call on her steward. Her lips cracked as she smiled at him, aware it was the first she had smiled at anyone in days of trekking. The violet horizon cheered her. Her goal was within sight. Senenmut ambled over, kicking his feet in the sand, and bowed to her.

"Great Lady."

"Do you see it, Senenmut?" She pointed eastward.

"Ah! It is the sea, unless it's another cruel illusion made by the gods."

Those illusions had tormented Hatshepsut at first, those green shimmers in the near distance, a wavering in the air as of the humidity above a fresh, cool garden. Ineni's navigators had warned her that the gardens were but a trick of the eyes, and soon Hatshepsut had taken to cursing their sight as she sucked her spare mouthfuls of musty water from her drinking-skin.

"It's not an illusion. Oh, Senenmut, won't it be wonderful to see the water again? I miss the Iteru."

"I miss it all – the Iteru, cold water, fresh food. Our wheat cakes have gone stale, and I have never liked the taste of dried fish."

"I would wrestle a man for a fresh melon."

"Had I any melons hiding under my wig, I'd take you up on that."

Hatshepsut laughed. She pulled her own wig from her head and ran her hand over her hair. Natural hair, unshaven – something she hadn't experienced since she still wore the side-lock of childhood. The growth was not much more than stubble, but still she had forgotten how it felt, tickling against her scalp, the nape of her neck.

"Leave it on," Senenmut warned. "The sun will be well up

soon, and without something on your head you'll catch heat-sickness."

"Yes, Mawat." She replaced the wig while Senenmut affected a scowl.

Ineni approached from the direction of his tent. Hatshepsut had worried about the old steward, thinking the journey too trying for a man of his years. The week in the desert had thinned him, so that the skin hung more loosely from his deep-lined face, but he had held his own admirably, often striding alongside Nehesi, engrossed in conversation.

"Great Lady," Ineni said, bowing. "Are you ready to strike camp? The navigators estimate that we will reach the port of Tjau by early evening."

"I am more than ready," she said.

From somewhere in the encampment a donkey brayed, its grating voice sounding clear and close in the dry dawn air. The murmur of men's voices came to her, the clack of poles being bundled together.

Hatshepsut clapped her hands, and raised her voice to the morning. "Break camp, men! Tonight we meet the sea!"

The expedition marched into the port town of Tjau to the cheers and acclaim of its meager population. Tjau was a distant outpost in the vast Egyptian territory, and had little care for proper Egyptian culture. Rather than kilts and linen gowns, men and women alike wore simple tunics of coarse wool, and kept their heads unshaven and unwigged, though close-cropped. Their deep, rich complexions and broad faces indicated their Puntite heritage; these people were descended from the god's land. The fact of it buoyed Hatshepsut's kas. It seemed a good omen.

Tjau, being remote and far removed from the Pharaoh's benevolence, was a poor holding. Its governor had little, and so Hatshepsut did not require a feast, but accepted his obeisance with good grace and his offerings of fresh meat and fruit with eagerness. She took the small tribute of Tjau to her encampment at the edge of the town, and sat in the confines of her tent reveling in the taste of melon juice on her tongue. The water in her cup was cold and fresh and tasted lightly of a mineral saltiness. She drank it greedily until her belly protested.

When she felt rested, she emerged into her night camp, happy at the sound of men laughing. The air was dense with humidity, a familiar feeling reminiscent of home. It lifted the spirits of her men. She breathed deep; the smell of the sea clutched at her senses with a compelling force, an odor of clean air and faint decay, of sharp salt and the pale skin of fishes. Its movement made a continual susurrus in the night-time, a soothing sound.

She found Ineni passing through the crowd, a skewer of goat's meat in his hand, and called to him.

"Great Lady. Try the meat; it is well spiced."

"Thank you, no. I had my fill in my tent. Walk with me; I would see the water."

She summoned Nehesi, and Senenmut came along with her guardsman, for they had been engaged in a game of dice and an earnest discussion of the problems of desert warfare. They walked together through the camp, past the place where the donkeys stood tethered in rows, switching their tails against the small, persistent flies of the seaside, their shaggy heads buried happily in heaps of cut grass and scatters of grain. A rocky strand led out to the hard-packed sand of the shore. South of where they stood, the poor buildings of Tjau flickered with torch fires and rare spots of lamp light, burning in the high, narrow windows of the mudbrick houses.

A cluster of torches bobbed near the shoreline like a flock of waterfowl on the Iteru. Ineni pointed toward them. "The men I hired, Great Lady. They are making ready to assemble the ships in the morning."

He had told her of the process before they'd even set out from Waset. The port of Tjau was full of clever ship-builders, who could piece together great boats as a child assembles a wooden puzzle. Hatshepsut's gut quivered with worry. Ships were solid, enduring things. She had been uncertain in her throne room, when Ineni had delineated his plans, that piecemeal boats could carry her safely to Punt and back. Now, as she stood listening to the sea move restlessly in the night, her uncertainty tipped closer to fear.

The calm, cool air of the seaside was a relief from the ferocious heat of the Red Land – ah, no mistake in that. But the sea itself turned out to be a beast just as fearsome as the desert. She had envisioned another Iteru: wider and deeper, to be sure, but with gentle, lapping waves, the kind children may swim in on a Shemu day. The reality was sobering. It pitched constantly in the starlight, each wave a sharp tooth in a black mouth, tipped by a cold white glow. Nearer, where the water met the shore, it curled in cascades that chased one another down the strand, and the violence of its movement set froth to churning, leaving webs of white behind that dissipated from the surface of the gravel.

"Can their boats truly carry us all that way, Ineni?"

"It has been done before, Great Lady."

"Not for many generations."

Nehesi slapped his hands against his broad hard stomach, as if preparing for a much-anticipated feast. "Have you lost your taste for adventure, Great Lady? Why, I recall a girl of seventeen years who kicked the Pharaoh out the back of a chariot and raced against the Kushites. Surely that girl is not so far away."

Hatshepsut squinted at him. The starlight limned his features, the bull-strength of him, the eager gleam in his eye. "Perhaps I should give this expedition over to you," she said. "You are so hungry for adventure, after all."

"Ah!" He laughed. "You could make me a chancellor. I like the sound of that."

"Very well," Hatshepsut said, grasping at the suggestion, absurdly grateful for the distraction from her growing fears. "You are my chancellor, and if you keep our toy boats together, and bring me to Punt and back still in my own skin, the gods will never forget your great deed."

"*Chancellor* Nehesi. Do you hear that, Senenmut?" He pounded Senenmut on the shoulder, and the steward winced. "Watch yourself, or you may find yourself deposed. *Great Steward* Nehesi has an even prettier ring to it."

"Remember," Hatshepsut said, "you still must keep me alive until we return to Waset."

"An easy thing."

"We should rest, Great Lady." Senenmut bobbed his head at her elbow, and she recognized her own anxiety in the tightness of his voice. "Ineni tells me that the boats will be sea-worthy by tomorrow afternoon. We must set out then. It has been a long walk across the desert. We all need a good night's rest."

Sea-worthy. She gazed out at the waves for another long moment. Their incessant clamor, their sharpness and single-mindedness, brought to her heart the image of a lioness clawing doggedly at a small creature's rocky den. *Have I overstepped myself? Have I reached too far in my desperation to retain my throne?*

But no. No – Punt was Amun's own land, full of all the sweet perfumes and beauties that appeased the god. He would not allow her to reach too far. He – and Nehesi – would see her home safe again.

Chapter Twenty-Two

THUTMOSE COUNSELED HIMSELF TO LAY back calmly on his cushions as Neferure approached the palace lake. He lay in his two-person replica of the great pleasure barges, reclining against his rich silks as he watched her come, making her quiet, careful way down the garden path. Her entourage of women trailed her, four of them holding aloft a bright red sun-shade. In its warm shadow her face was demurely downturned, her eyes shyly on the gravel of the path. Fan-bearers flanked her, stirring the air, and a harpist trailed the lot, plucking a sweet and soothing melody. Even gazing at her feet, she was fine as an artist's carving, smooth-polished and delicate. Her two weeks in Iunet seemed to have lent a glow to her cheeks, a secret, confident happiness that Thutmose had never seen in his sister before.

She arrived at the raised stone lip of the lake and paused, waiting for her servant to offer a hand. Neferure stepped lightly onto the stone. Her sandals were polished silver, chased across the upturned toe, and a collection of bracelets at her ankle chimed gently, a coy counterpoint to the slap of water against the boat's hull. She lowered herself carefully into the boat, sinking with her customary light, natural grace to the cushions. Thutmose's man on the shore cast off the line, and the boat drifted toward the center of the lake, carrying the two into privacy.

Neither spoke. Neferure watched Thutmose with shy, dark eyes, painted with the alluring, metallic shimmer of the crushed carapaces of sacred beetles. The light danced around her eyes, which said all that her lips did not. He took in her fragile beauty, her retiring gentleness, in contented silence. *I could look at you for hours and never mind the passage of time*, he wanted to say. But he did not wish to break the beguiling silence.

When the boat found the center of the lake and rotated idly in a chance breeze, Thutmose recalled the work at hand. He cleared his throat, and Neferure looked away, her lashes lowering like a modest fan obscuring a court woman's face.

"You enjoyed your time in Iunet, I trust."

A smile lit her face, so sudden it made the breath catch in his chest. "Oh, yes, Majesty. I will be forever grateful for your gift." Then the smile faded, and a queer intensity flooded her face, an expression tense with the weight of momentous expectation.

Thutmose's thoughts fumbled about inside his heart. He recalled the mystery of her face as she gazed up at him from the side of the white bull, recalled the ribbons of the God's Wife crown dancing about her shoulders. Here were those same shoulders before him now, bared to the sun, adorned by red ribbons that held up a strange white gown. It covered the swell of her small breasts against all dictates of current fashion, and was closer in style to a priestess's robe than a great lady's sheath. The fabric of it was enticingly sheer, so that he could see the color of her skin beneath it, but no detail of her body.

"Well," Thutmose said, flustered. "Well. I have brought you here to ask...to tell you..." Inwardly, he cursed himself for a fool. In the three weeks since Hatshepsut had been gone from Waset, he had accounted himself well, handling the court and the throne with an alacrity that at first surprised him, then seemed only natural, only maat. Was he not the Pharaoh, after all? But here, before the shy gaze of his sister, his confidence and his words failed him. He drew a steadying breath and tried again. "I would make you," he said in a voice that sounded far more confident than he felt, "my Great

Royal Wife."

Neferure stared at him, her expression unreadable.

"If you would have it," he added weakly.

"Great Royal Wife," she repeated, her voice faint, considering. Then her eyes sharpened, and she leaned toward him on her cushions, as hawkish as her mother ever was in negotiation with ambassadors or nobles. "But the Pharaoh has already made me heir. The other Pharaoh, I mean – Maatkare. A Pharaoh's proclamation cannot be undone, brother."

Thutmose sat up straight. A sudden quiver of excitement came to life in his belly, a trembling of power he had not felt before on his throne, at the reins of his chariot, training with his soldiers. "It can be undone by me. I am a Pharaoh – as much as Pharaoh as she."

"My mother will be angry." The prospect did not seem to displease her.

"Only at first. When she sees the reason of it she will understand."

"The reason of it?"

"There is no woman in the Two Lands as fit to bear an heir as you, Neferure. Both your mother and your father have ruled from the Horus Throne, and your mother was sired by Amun himself."

"Yes," Neferure said quietly, that curious intensity lighting her face once more.

"What is more maat – that a woman such as you, with your breeding, your blood, *be* the heir, or *bear* the heir? Our child," he said, low and urgent, "will have more royalty and more divinity than any man who has ever lived. The gods mean this, Neferure. Look into your heart – you will see it."

She breathed deeply; her eyes fluttered closed, sparkling in the sunlight reflected from the surface of the lake. A rising joy seemed to suffuse her, coursing along her skin until she visibly trembled.

She sees it, Thutmose thought, half frantic, half afraid, entirely eager.

"I will," she said at last. "It is maat. At last, maat will be served."

And before he could speak another word, Neferure reached up to the red ribbons at her shoulders, loosed the ties. Her gown fell to her waist, exposing in one rapid, ragged heartbeat the smoothness of her chest, the slimness of her body, the dark shadow of her navel, the sweet, ripe fruit of her breasts. *Stop; go slowly*, a voice cautioned in Thutmose's heart, but he was already moving toward her. His hands found her, reached to trail along the hollow of her back until she arched, gasping. He bent his head to take her breast into his mouth, and her cry of pleasure was filled with a wild ecstasy.

Thutmose had never seen such eagerness in a woman before, not in any of his harem concubines, though they never failed to please him. Neferure was something different altogether. She fumbled at her gown, tore it from her hips, then went for his kilt with her nails flashing. Thutmose shied back, undid the knot himself. When he stretched her along the cushions, down in the warm hull of the boat, she clawed at his shoulders, pulled him to her body, raised to meet him, her legs locking around his hips with a force he never dreamed the small, delicate girl could command.

When he entered her, whimpering, yoked and trembling under the power of her passion, she whispered a word in his ear. Her breath was hot with the sound of it.

Maat.

The king and the King's Daughter summoned Ahmose two days after their union. She was not surprised. In fact, she expected the summons sooner; gossip concerning the event on the palace lake reached her well before Thutmose's brief letter informing her that Neferure had accepted his offer and would soon be declared Great Royal Wife. She sat limp in the shade of a sycamore, Thutmose's papyrus curling on her lap. She watched the gardeners go about their business of weeding and watering with unseeing eyes, puzzling at her sudden despondency.

I have done wrong, somehow, somewhere. Yet the gods would not elaborate, and Ahmose still felt a thrill of certainty that this marriage was right. She had told Hatshepsut once that even the god-chosen could not always be sure of divine will. Hatshepsut had countered that Amun would not allow her to choose wrongly. *And what of me? Would Amun allow* me *to choose wrongly? He has before now. Oh, Mut, bless your foolish daughter. Guide me.*

She waited a long time, while the gardeners moved from row to row, and finally worked their way out of sight, their bent backs disappearing beyond the dark line of a hedgerow. Mut stayed silent. Ahmose shook her head, rose briskly from her bench, braced herself against the dizziness that accompanied such movements of late.

I am growing old. Gods, so many years have passed me, and what wisdom did I glean from them?

She recalled Mutnofret in her youth, splendid and arrogant, swaying through the House of Women as bright and arresting as a beam of light through a temple door. A sudden yearning to see her sister again seized her, so sharp it pierced her heart and would have made her cry out, had its force not stolen her voice away. Did Mutnofret still live? Ahmose did not know.

"Lady?" One of her servants left her spinning lying on the grass and stepped quickly to Ahmose's side, steadying her sway with a strong young arm around her shoulders. "Are you well?"

"Yes, yes, Tenetsai. It is only the heat."

"I'll fetch you some cold beer, Lady."

Ahmose stepped away from her on steadier legs. "Very good. And lay out a better gown than this one, if you would be so kind. The king has summoned me, and I must go to him."

An hour later she was admitted again to the king's fine chambers, and swept inside on a tide of firm self-admonishments that she was god-chosen, she had been a

Great Royal Wife once herself, consort to a god, and was surely no fool, no matter how adamantly her beating heart said otherwise. Thutmose and Neferure rose to receive her, then settled again onto one of the fine couches, huddled close as only two children in love may do. Neferure held tight to Thutmose's hand, a soft, dreamy glow pinking her skin. Thutmose looked at Ahmose with a somewhat bewildered gaze.

"I was pleased to hear your news, Majesty."

"Yes. It is a great thing."

"And Neferure – you are amenable to this?"

"Amenable, Grandmother?" Neferure laughed sweetly. "Of course."

"It is nothing to be undertaken lightly. The mantle of Great Royal Wife is a heavy one."

"I know it. I supposed as much. But it is an opportunity, too – one I cannot pass by."

"An opportunity?"

"I learned so many things in Iunet, Grandmother – so many wonderful things. If I am Great Royal Wife, I will have the freedom to restore Hathor to her former glory: all her temples, all her rites. I will spread the love of Hathor throughout the Two Lands, and it will be as it was long ago."

Many people, even in the royal family, had their particular preferences among the gods. There was nothing unusual about a woman devoting herself wholeheartedly to Hathor, who was, after all, the paramount of women. But the fervency of Neferure's devotion stirred Ahmose's vague sense of uneasiness.

"You will still be God's Wife of Amun. On that we are agreed." She looked to Thutmose for confirmation, and he nodded. "You will not neglect your duties to Amun in favor of Hathor."

"No." Neferure spoke the word solemnly, and turned an intense gaze, full of palpable longing, upon Thutmose. "I will not neglect any of my duties to Amun."

Ahmose stood, went to them, took their hands in her own.

"Then I give you my blessing, Majesty, God's Wife. Not that you require it – but it is yours."

They passed an hour in conversation, planning the marriage rites, which were, at Thutmose's insistence, to be announced and enacted in all haste. Ahmose suspected that he hoped to have a little heir already growing in Neferure's womb by the time Hatshepsut returned. *That might stay her anger, some,* Ahmose thought.

When the king dismissed her, Ahmose walked slowly back to her own apartments. Night was gathering above Waset's palace, filling the courtyards with the softness of violet shadows. From the direction of the ambassadors' wing, the sound of foreign music lifted and moved gently through the night-darkened pillars. The tune was both bright and melancholic, soft and benign. Yet somehow the sound of the reedy flute filled her with guilt, with horror. She stopped at the edge of a courtyard, looked about her with wide eyes. A breeze ruffled the leaves of a climbing vine winding its way across the porch of an apartment with a tight-shut door. A cat trotted across the smooth paving stones, slender tail erect. Ahmose's women drew up around her, glancing curiously about, looking for the threat that had stopped their mistress in her tracks. But only shadows moved in the courtyard, only late-roosting birds moved in the dusky sky.

"Lady?" Tenetsai said softly.

"Nothing – it is nothing at all," she said, and led her women on.

I have stayed too long in Waset, Ahmose said sensibly to herself, passing from the courtyard and back into the deep blue shadow of a pillared hall. *Perhaps I should take to one of my estates in the country, after all.*

Hatshepsut's wrath would be terrible when she returned from Punt to find her careful plans undone, no matter that a Pharaoh was the one who undid them. Ahmose had played a part, and she would be blamed.

CHAPTER TWENTY-THREE

FIVE BOATS SET OUT FROM Tjau. They were made from planks of a lightweight wood, well lacquered with wax and oil, lashed one to the other by ropes of some rough, pale fiber. Lengths of rope mortared the cracks between planks, too. Ineni had explained to Hatshepsut how the fibers would swell in the sea water, packing the space between the planks until the hull became watertight. Hatshepsut did not quite trust the engineering, and yet the boats did float. They floated perhaps too well, yielding to any small movement, rolling violently on their bowl-shaped bellies with the passing of each wave. And thousands upon thousands of waves came and went, came and went, as the little fleet made its rocking way along the red coastline south from the isolated port. No ship on the Iteru ever sailed so roughly – not even in the cataracts. Hatshepsut braced herself against the nausea of the motion. Most days she was able to keep her water and dried fish in her stomach.

They put ashore each evening at sunset, camping gratefully on solid land that still seemed to pitch with the fearsome memory of the angry sea. The shore was a wilderness, showing no signs of human use. Her expedition raised tents whose linen walls felt entirely too thin against the vastness of the untamed land. Every night she brought into her tent a certain gift from the governor of Tjau: Bita-Bita, a young woman of the port town whose mother had come originally from Punt. Bita-Bita did have the dark skin the people of the

211

fabled god's land were reputed to have; Hatshepsut had no cause to doubt that the girl was authentic. Bita-Bita's now-dead mother had taught the girl the Puntite tongue from the cradle, and she still spoke it passably well, as far as she could tell, having never ventured outside of Tjau. It would suffice. It must suffice; Bita-Bita was the only Puntite speaker that could be located, even by Ineni, though he had assured her that trade could still be accomplished using nothing but hand-signs, if necessary.

On nights when her stomach was not too tender from the disorienting motion of her boat, Hatshepsut joined the men in hunting. It was a welcome distraction from the strain of long travel, and for the most part, the creatures of this land were the same as the creatures of the Iteru's green valley: waterfowl and brush birds, pigeons in the stands of trees, dark-colored gazelle that sprinted along the crests of grass-fringed dunes. When they were a week outside of Tjau, Hatshepsut even managed to bring down a gazelle with a shot through the heart – a shot which was more luck than skill. That night she tried to focus on Bita-Bita's lesson in rudimentary Puntite, listening from the solitude of her tent as her sailors and basket-bearers sang around their fires, roasting bits of gazelle meat on twig skewers. Senenmut brought a haunch dripping with savory juices, dismissed Bita-Bita from her duties, and shared the meat with Hatshepsut, wiping the fat from her chin, kissing the sheen of it from her lips there in the lamplit glow of the king's tent, where no one else could see.

Senenmut had grown foreign to her, as foreign as the shores where her encampments rose at night, but as exotic and enticing. There was no room on their Set-cursed boats for luxuries, and neither time nor still mooring to attend to one's appearance. Razors and cosmetics were left behind, save for the kohl that protected the eyes from the sun, so even the king went as plain-faced as a rekhet. Senenmut's hair, like hers, grew, and stood out in tufts beneath the foremost fringe of his wig. It was shot with silvery grey, an intrigue she found most appealing. His cheeks and chin roughened with a sparse growth of hair, and a trail of black fluff crept from the belt of his kilt, up his rather soft belly like a climbing vine. His legs and underarms darkened. He was a wild thing, as was she, stripped of civilization, pure as Atum's first creations. She loved him anew, seeing him so untamed.

In another week more the shores turned from dry grassland to scrub, with pockets of trees holding fast in the stream-carved depressions of the hillsides. In the evenings when they landed Hatshepsut could see the dense dark greenery looming to the south, where the land sloped steadily from waterline to a wall of hills so large and steep she could sense their monumental weight even from a great distance. "Forest," Ineni had said, nodding to the wash of deep emerald along the southern horizon. Hatshepsut tried to imagine what a forest was like. She pictured a garden, well-trimmed and planted in organized beds and rows, and knew in her kas that it could not be so.

At mid-day, when the sun was high and merciless on the restless, gray-green surface of the sea, the expedition of Maatkare, the Good God, arrived in Punt. "Thank Amun," Hatshepsut whispered fervently as her boat rolled toward the shallows. She peered anxiously over the dipping and rising rail. A crowd of people had gathered on the sand, waving their arms. Most of them were rather short of stature, with the cool-hued, deep brown skin of southerners. Men and women alike wore brief aprons about their waists, made from some rather sheer cloth; yet she could tell even from the rail of her ship that it was not fine enough to be called linen. Their chests were bare, and she could see ornaments of gold and polished stone glinting at the women's breasts, pierced through their nipples.

Beyond the strand where the waves made fall in long, frothy arcs, a line of short dunes stood sentinel amongst tufts of salt grass – the kind with leaves as sharp and strong as blades, as they had seen on Tjau's shoreline. Beyond still, the deep green-black density of forest reared toward the sky, a profusion of heavy, damp trunks, cold shadow, and the incessant, mindless, sinister waving of the leafy canopy.

The boat ran aground with a loud scrape. Nehesi was the first over the rail, and he reached up to assist first Hatshepsut onto land, then her servant Bita-Bita. Hatshepsut's feet hit the cold water with a splash; the feel of the waves surging about her calves, seething up to soak the hem of her kilt, filled her with excitement. She strode toward the Puntites with Nehesi and Bita-Bita in tow, heedless of any danger. In spite of the dark menace of their environment, there was nothing to fear from the people themselves. Of that she was certain. They welcomed the Egyptian fleet with eager gestures, with broad smiles, and she smiled back at them, throwing her arms wide.

Bita-Bita took to her work at once. She raised her girlish voice above the cheering crowd, speaking her mother's native tongue. When she fell silent, the Puntites looked at one another in confusion. Hatshepsut waited.

"I told them you are the king of Egypt, Great Lady," said Bita-Bita apologetically.

A man's voice burst into laughter amidst the Puntites. Nehesi took a menacing step toward the crowd, one hand on his hilt.

Before the chancellor could do more, though, a stir of activity rose. Bita-Bita craned her neck to see, and said in hasty Egyptian, "Many of them are speaking two names, Great Lady. Parahu, and Ati."

"Important folk," Ineni suggested.

"King," Hatshepsut said. "I heard the word *king*, did I not, Bita-Bita? And queen."

As a child's sand-palace crumbles at the touch of water, so the crowd of Puntites fell, dropping to their knees on the sandy expanse of the beach, heads bowed and hands outstretched. As they lowered, Hatshepsut could see into the crowd's depths. It parted before the progress of a man, wizened, small in stature, his close-cropped, tightly curled hair showing beneath a red cloth cap. His beard was likewise shot with white, and curved upward at its point, like the beards of many of the Puntite men in the crowd. The well-stretched lobes of his ears swung with golden bangles; about his shoulders he wore a wide collar, similar in style to those of fashionable Egyptian courtiers. But where an Egyptian collar was made of gold and precious stone, or electrum foil shaped into dozens of tiny flowers, the man's was made of feathers – hundreds of iridescent feathers, catching the light in ripples of blue, violet, green. The cloth wound about his waist was white, embroidered brightly at its hem with images of running animals whose forms Hatshepsut did not quite recognize. Each stride jangled, for one leg was bound with hundreds of metal rings – copper, silver, gold, above the knee and below it. He carried a staff as he walked, ebony worn smooth and shiny from many years of handling. He did not seem to need the thing for support, and Hatshepsut understood that the staff carried ceremony, reverence – as her own crook and flail carried reverence. The man cried out as he went, his voice nasal and high, brandishing his black staff, shouting words Bita-Bita struggled to interpret: admonishments to be wary of him, for he carried great magic in his bones.

Behind the man, a tiny white donkey moved with mincing steps, its neck thrown back with the strain of carrying its burden through the sand. For on its back rode the largest and strangest woman Hatshepsut had ever seen. Her shoulders were round and broad, slick and shining with some aromatic oil that caused her skin to glow like polished wood. Her breasts, exposed, hung pendulous against her body, each one fleshy and wide, the large nipples bearing gleaming golden studs. Her abdomen sat upon itself in neat stacks of flesh. When the king in his feather collar halted, so did the struggling white donkey, and, with an air of immense dignity, its rider dismounted. Standing, the woman's hips and thighs were especially large; they soared from her body, clearly visible beneath the sheer weave of her bright yellow kilt, the flesh dented and pocked as the sand was marked from the activity of so many feet. The woman slapped her thighs, drawing all eyes to her body; she turned slightly, as if giving Hatshepsut a better view of her full majesty. Her buttocks jutted well out from her back, and gleamed in the sun beneath the kilt. When the woman looked frankly up and down the length of Hatshepsut's frame, her keen, wide-set eyes darkened with something close to mockery, and the full lips twisted into an appraising sneer. Hatshepsut was not accounted the slenderest woman in Egypt, but beside this woman's size and forcefully female shape, the Pharaoh felt positively puny.

"He is Parahu, king of Punt," Bita-Bita said, crouching beside Hatshepsut in a half-bow. "And she," the girl indicated the great, strutting woman with a quick shift of her eyes, "is Ati, his queen."

Decades had passed since Punt had enjoyed major trade with Egypt. Parahu was eager for the gifts Hatshepsut bore. Once her mission had been made plain – to give Kushite gold, and a goodly sum of it, in exchange for the wealth of Punt – its fine woods, its animals for Egypt's menageries, and most of all the resins, incense, and myrrh trees so beloved by Amun – the people on the strand set up a great cheer, some of them breaking out into a lively, hopping dance right there on the sand. Hatshepsut's men caught the festive mood, and when the ships had been made secure the whole gathering, Egyptian and Puntite, went clapping and singing songs by turn, each people doing their best to pick up the words and the tunes of the others' music, all encompassed by a feeling of brotherhood and, for the Egyptians who would not be required to return to their boats for several days, relief.

They were led through the grassy dunes to the edge of the forest, where the village of Parahu resolved out of the gloom like a vision in a Shemu heat-dream. Naked children swung from the branches of trees, dropped down to dodge between great trunks that stood in groups of four, stripped of bark, stoic and still like the legs of oxen waiting at the plow. It took Hatshepsut some time to realize that the trunks held aloft platforms, and on the platforms, half-concealed by the lower reaches of the forest's canopy, stood strange houses made of mud. They were heaped and rounded like bee hives, each one with a little door covered by a cloth. Thin wisps of smoke rose from some houses to dissipate among the treetops. Near each home's base-poles stood smaller mud hives; a girl bent over one, feeding sticks into its depths, and a shower of sparks rose up from the oven to dance about her face.

They gained an open clearing, ringed all about by the elevated houses and the dark sentinel trees. In the midst of the clearing stood a fire-ring as wide as a man was tall, lined with large white stones and heaped inside with piles of ash. The ground around the ring was well trampled, worn featureless by generations of feet. Hatshepsut was reminded of the courtyard in Kush where she had conquered Dedwen. This, then, was the communal meeting-place of Parahu's village. The king of Punt circled the unlit fire-ring, his arms thrown wide, his black stick waving. He cried out in his strange, high voice. Bita-Bita leaned close to offer her translation. There was to be a celebration, it seemed, to welcome the She-King of Egypt to Punt's glorious shores. The people cheered, the women trilling a piercing, wordless song of joy. Hatshepsut grinned.

A retinue of young women led her along a dark forest path wet with dew and rich with the scent of loam. They came upon the four posts of a Puntite house, and indicated with gestures that Hatshepsut should climb up into it via a crude ladder made of lashed wood. She stared up at the platform, which seemed to stretch above her, tripling its height.

"Nehesi, you will go up first."

"And leave you here with these strangers?"

"I'll be all right. The sharpest weapon any of them has is a feather fan. An anyhow, I have Ineni and Senenmut here."

"Stewards! What good are stewards?"

"What good is a chancellor? Climb."

Grumbling, Nehesi tested the ladder with his hands and the toes of his sandals, bounced against it to be sure of its solidity, then climbed gingerly up to the platform. He crawled through the rounded door of the mud hut. Hatshepsut waited until his head and shoulders reappeared; he motioned to her, and she made her way up the ladder, cringing at the way it wobbled faintly beneath her. Arms and legs trembled from the effort by the time she gained the platform. It was made of split logs laid side by side, lashed together by some tough, fibrous vine. The platform created a small porch before the door of the mud hut. Nehesi was holding aside the door-cloth, which was, she could now see, made of thick wool colored a deep purple-blue. Hatshepsut crawled inside.

The interior was not at all unpleasant, for all the humbleness of its outer walls. The mud was thick and dry, quite pleasantly cool. It trapped the ample shade up among the leaves of the nearby trees, and the sweet smell of the treetops, too – exceptionally fragrant growth, as pleased the god Amun. Even Nehesi could stand to his full height inside. Many soft mats, covered in woven wool bright with unfamiliar patterns, lay along the walls. The inner walls themselves were painted with bold shapes, some of them recognizable as dancing women, men wielding spears and short bows, gods in postures of supernatural power. Other shapes were painted only, it seemed, for the harmony of their proportions: rows of circles, squares within squares, a line of triangles dancing now on their bases, now on their tips, like pyramids frolicking in a child's dream. At the door's threshold an intricate white line writhed in a circle, twined back upon itself. Bita-Bita whispered that it was a charm to keep tree-snakes away. In the center of the floor, below the highest point of the humped roof, sat a low table of ebony wood and several three-legged stools. The table was piled with fruits Hatshepsut did not recognize, jars of sweet-smelling liquid, tiny eggs with pale blue shells in bowls made of slick-polished wood.

Bita-Bita ducked into the house and gazed about, smiling.

She was followed by a Puntite girl of a similar age, who immediately prostrated herself full length across the log floor, her fingers outstretched toward Hatshepsut. The girl murmured a few words, and Bita-Bita said, "She has been given to you as your servant for the days you will spend in Punt, Great Lady. And this house – this house is very fine, and belongs to Queen Ati, who has loaned it to your pleasure, although you are quite small for a woman, even a king-woman."

Hatshepsut grinned wryly. "The Queen is too kind, and very stately. I am humbled before her obvious majesty. What is the girl's name?"

"Kani," said Bita-Bita, and soon Hatshepsut set Kani about the task of making her own majesty more obvious, in accordance with Puntite custom.

By the time bells rang near the whitestone firepit – an announcement of sunset and the feast to come, Kani said – Hatshepsut looked as close to the Puntite conception of royalty as she could manage. She wore a knee-length kilt of red wool, undeniably itchy compared to the fine linens of Egypt, and two cuffs of iridescent feathers around her wrists. She would not allow Kani to pierce her nipples with her long, translucent fishbone needle; instead, she had Senenmut fetch from their own trade goods several lengths of golden chain. Draped round her neck, the chains did the trick of adorning her breasts with the requisite gold, and spared her the pain of diplomacy. Baubles of glimmering white shell were tied to the braids of her wig, and at last Kani painted her face, rubbing an intense red stain into her cheeks and onto her lips. It had a bitter taste that made her mouth tingle; when Bita-Bita explained that it was made by crushing up the bodies of certain insects, Hatshepsut restrained herself from shoving away the little pot of dye in Kani's hands. Brushing powder of scarabs' wings onto her eyelids was one thing. Smearing crushed grubs across her lips was quite another.

"You look breathtaking, Great Lady," Senenmut said, his voice dancing with laughter.

Parahu's men kindled a great fire in the central pit. Hatshepsut was ushered to a low-backed ebony throne beside Queen Ati's own. The Queen was adorned simply by Egyptian standards, with a necklace of golden discs and the bright yellow cloth she seemed to prefer, a skirt of open weave loosely draped across the thighs of which she was so proud. A yellow ribbon lay flat across her lined forehead, holding back hundreds of thin black braids. Close to the woman now, Hatshepsut was startled to note that two blue-green lines had been permanently tattooed around Ati's mouth, accentuating the woman's natural, stern frown. Ati needed no ostentatious finery to prove her power. She wore it in her very flesh, in the broadness of her face, the forceful jut of her chin.

Course after course was brought before the royal thrones, proffered up on great platters held by pretty girls with wide, laughing smiles. The deep ruddy glow of the firelight, its constant movement, had a soothing, intoxicating effect. Despite the foreignness of the feast, Hatshepsut found each dish more delicious than the last. She sampled round-bodied fish with intensely salty flesh, charred in their own crisp skins; gamey bits of meat on skewers, the name of which Bita-Bita translated rather hesitantly as "tree rat". A dish of some hard, green fruit with grainy flesh pleased her, for it was drizzled in honey and sprinkled with the spicy petals of an unknown flower. There was gazelle meat cooked with the pods of red peppers, fiery on her tongue; bread made from the tubers of a woodland plant; songbirds stewed until even their bones were tender, and hardly crunched in her teeth. A girl unfolded shiny, broad leaves of a tree, fire-singed. The opened packet set free a gout of steam, exposing the delights inside: several fat white grubs as large as Hatshepsut's thumb. Feeling brave, she popped one into her mouth and was surprised that it tasted creamy and mild, and was not unlike the fine cones of cheese she favored at her own feasts. She turned nothing away, but partook openly, expressing her approval to the Queen in ever more earnest gestures and the few Puntite words she had.

Even more than the food, the entertainment entranced her. Punt had no lack of fine performers. Troupes of adolescent boys danced, stomping, their bodies trembling with dramatic tension as they enacted a tale of bravery with well-rehearsed coordination. A chorus of girls sang in the firelight, whirling and clapping, their colorful skirts flying, their voices high and sweet. Tumblers broke from the great ring of feasters who gathered just beyond the reach of the light, springing hand and foot across the courtyard, leaping and twisting in the air, and the flicker of the fire seemed to still them against the night sky so they hung in lively tableaus like scenes on a temple wall. With each new performance, Hatshepsut cheered her approval. And Ati, her imposing body overfilling the throne beside her, softened her aloof arrogance, eying Hatshepsut with reluctant approval.

Between a course of sweet nut milk drunk from salty shells and a trio of women playing on reed flutes, Hatshepsut ventured to look Queen Ati full in the face. The woman returned the stare, unblinking and direct. Her eyes, wide and dark as the mouths of tombs, reflected back at Hatshepsut the hypnotic dancing of the firelight. Ati's red-stained lips tightened in slow deliberation, darkening the lines around her mouth with shadow. She leaned toward Hatshepsut as if drawn suddenly toward an irresistible prize.

Hatshepsut, forgetting her careful diplomacy, shrank back on her ebony throne, momentarily seized by terror. In another moment the tumblers began their performance again, and she forced her eyes away from Ati's face, fixed a smile onto her lips with effort. She could still feel the Queen's stare prickling along her skin.

The days that followed were rapid and wild with activity. At the base of an especially large and well-tended hut, in the growing humid heat of the Puntite afternoon, Hatshepsut presented her full array of Egyptian treasure. Parahu and Ati sat once more on their ebony thrones, which had been carried and placed here, before the stateliest of their royal dwellings, by two strong young men with the upcurved beards characteristic of their land – sons of the Queen, Bita-Bita said. In a grove beyond the great house's pilings, the little white donkey grazed in the undergrowth, tethered to a tree.

Ineni directed the laying out of Kushite gold in all its forms for Parahu's inspection, while Hatshepsut stood by unmoving, her arms folded beneath her breasts, supervising the offering. Ineni presented plates and cups, bracelets and chains, figurines of animals and lesser gods. There was gold in flat discs to be used by smiths as raw material; gold tainted by copper so it shone with a pinkish hue; gold in thick nodules, pulled straight from the earth. And he offered, too, several large baskets of turquoise, unworked and ready for a craftsman's touch. Ineni licked one raw stone and held it out in the sun, so Parahu could see the rich quality of its color.

The king of Punt seemed beyond pleased. He held himself in regal stillness, nodding lightly at the offering, his metal leg-rings chiming softly whenever he shifted this way or that to gain a better view. But Hatshepsut did not miss the glimmer in Parahu's eye, and indicated to Senenmut with the raising of her brows that they ought to bargain well. In the end, Parahu agreed to a healthy quantity of incense – resins of three types – along with a brace of baboons trained to the leash, twenty cords of precious ebony wood and twenty-three of cedar, several tusks of elephant ivory, and a selection of precious oils in well-made clay jars. Best of all, though, were the trees. Ineni and Senenmut secured the king's permission to transport enough living myrrh trees to line the avenue leading to Djeser-Djeseru. Amun's walkway would bloom again with fragrant, green life.

Nehesi set about organizing squadrons of men to measure out their share of Parahu's stores of resin and fashion secure cages for the baboons. Day by day Hatshepsut oversaw the preparations and the collection of her goods, busying herself with the work. It seemed no matter where her work took her, moving from this group of men to that, approving the packing and loading of the fragrant myrrh into bundles and baskets, Queen Ati lurked somewhere nearby, perched on the back of her sweating donkey, watching Hatshepsut's movements with quiet intensity in those dark, deep-set eyes.

Soon messenger girls began arriving at Hatshepsut's hut, begging the She-King's pardon for their intrusion, but wouldn't she please come share her supper with Queen Ati? Hatshepsut scuffled her feet against the snake-charm set in the floor and told Kani to refuse the invitation with regrets. For she could not forget the way Ati had lurched toward her suddenly at the feast, her eyes alight with an unsettling greed. Hatshepsut was all too aware that she was in the god's land, and the divine drew as close in this place as in a temple. Ati was a force Hatshepsut could not quite bring herself to face.

One night when a messenger lobbed some insult at Kani and the two fell to pulling each other's hair, screeching like cats, Hatshepsut realized she could push propriety no further. Ati was growing impatient, and her brusqueness was rubbing off on her servant girls. The following day Hatshepsut's men would depart for the deep woodlands with their shovels and coarse linen slings, to dig up and bind the precious myrrh trees, roots, soil, and all. Hatshepsut would not accompany them, as such work was unfit for a king's hands. She was as sensitive to image as always, and knew she could not twist her way into accompanying them into the forest – not without making herself seem even more peculiar than she was already. There could be no more avoiding the Queen of Punt, or her hungry, black stare.

Hatshepsut shook the two girls apart and said to the messenger, "Tell your mistress that I will come at sunset tomorrow."

The look of keen, almost mocking gratification in the girl's eyes was nearly masked by her quick bow, and then she was down the ladder as fast and lithe as a tree-snake.

The encroaching dusk swallowed up her form as she ran through the shadows of the forest to the place where Queen Ati waited.

Chapter Twenty-Four

HESYRE WAS QUICK WITH HIS copper scrapers. In moments Thutmose's skin was dry, pleasantly throbbing from the passage of the curved blades. The freshness of his skin seemed to pass into all his senses, until his entire being, even his ka, trembled with wild anticipation. Water from this bath puddled about his feet. It was scented with mint and honey, and a drizzle of the musky, bitter oil of the mandrake root – a thoughtful touch, added by Hesyre when the master of the Pharaoh's bath thought himself unobserved.

The man lifted a hand mirror of polished electrum. Twin carvings of Hathor, the lady of love, adorned its edges. The goddess arched her graceful body to cradle the mirror's disc, and Thutmose found the sight of her round breasts and hips so distracting, he could scarcely inspect his face to ensure his shave was smooth and complete. At last he stepped back, nodded to Hesyre, and allowed the man to wind a fresh white kilt about his hips. With a few quick motions of his experienced hands, the ends of the linen were tied in an elaborate knot, tailed by a fall of fine white cloth to Thutmose's knees.

"Well," Thutmose said when he was dressed. Silence descended into the bathing room, so he whirled and fled from it, out into the anteroom of his chambers, where the women who cleaned the rooms and pressed his kilts were setting his lamps aglow. Their forms made him faintly uneasy, the sway of their hips, the slenderness of their arms and ankles.

225

He dismissed them, and with the tickling rustle of women's skirts, they vanished from his apartments.

"My lord is unsettled, I think." Hesyre stood beside the bath's door with head deferentially bowed, but Thutmose did not miss the note of amusement in his body servant's voice. He knew, however, that Hesyre held a great affection for him, and so he issued no reprimands.

Instead, he laughed. The sound surprised him. "Is it so obvious?"

"If my lord should need any...advice..."

Thutmose stared at Hesyre. The man was not ancient, but the lines on his face and the way he favored one knee attested to advancing age. He was also pinched and fussy, and somewhat effeminate. Thutmose found it rather difficult to believe Hesyre could serve as a font of advice. Perhaps on the best oils to use in a bath, or the way to polish the straps of one's sandals, but not in this matter. He wished frantically that Ahmose had not moved to one of her southern estates. Her advice had always been reliable, and, though she was a woman, it had never filled Thutmose with the embarrassed panic of Hesyre's wisdom.

The man evidently took Thutmose's astonished silence for permission to speak on. "My lord has no doubt visited the harem several times."

"Ah," Thutmose said impatiently, feeling the heat rise to his cheeks.

He had, in fact, visited the harem several times – as often as he could manage, between drilling with the soldiers and hearing the endless stultifying complaints of courtiers in the great hall. He never knew how he found the courage to enter the first time, though he'd repeated to himself again and again as he rode from the palace to the harem in a closed litter, *You are the Pharaoh. The women are yours.* Still, his legs had shaken violently as he allowed his guards to lead him into the intoxicating cool shade of the harem garden. And when he greeted the surprised and enthusiastic women, his voice had cracked like a worthless boy's.

But they had been good to him. A few in particular, young and gently spoken with smooth faces and soft breasts, had led him into the great inner chamber of the House of Women. Servants had gone before them, scattering flower petals and singing, and the women's hands had been both coaxing and instructive. He passed nearly a whole day there, and when he returned two days later his legs did not quiver so badly. In two days more, he strode into the chamber on his own, and called his favorite women by name.

This business, though – Neferure – this was a different matter. How could he explain to Hesyre the strange potency that pulsed within his frail, pretty wife? How could he admit that lust for her and fear of her unknown power pulled at him equally, drawing him like a beast to water, so that he could not turn away from her, even if he had wished to?

"I would implore my lord to recall that the Great Royal Wife is very young, and lacks the experience of the women of the harem. It would be wise to treat her gently."

Thutmose snorted. "Hesyre, how little you know her."

"My lord, you are pale. Please, sit. I will fetch wine."

"I don't need any wine," Thutmose said, but he sank onto his couch all the same.

How many years had passed since Thutmose had seen his sister tame the bull of Min? He counted backward. Five, it must be. Five years, and all that time he found himself unable to look upon her without a tremble of awe, a shiver of foreboding. Even these past months since Hatshepsut had been away, each night when he held Neferure locked in his arms, their bodies moving in concert, somewhere through the fog of lust his ka quailed at her nearness. At festivals he watched her make offerings to Amun, her eyes burning with an intensity he could not understand, and he remembered the white bull. At court he watched her sit still as a seshep upon her small golden throne, the vulture crown of the Great Royal Wife gleaming on her brow, her mouth and hands revealing none of her thoughts. He remembered the white bull.

He remembered the thunder of its passing, the rage in its breath. And the slender paleness of Neferure halting that terrible beast in its tracks, taming its wild heart with the touch of her hand. Never could he forget the way she had looked up at him as she stroked the bull between its horns. Her eyes were like offering fires.

For all the power he wielded, for all the divine might his seat granted him, Thutmose knew he could not understand the haunting combination of darkness and light that moved in Neferure's ka. He could only sense that it was a power all its own – a power of a sort he could never grasp. Its starkness and strangeness filled him with fear.

And yet her body filled him with desire. She was undeniably beautiful. Her solemn face was as finely made as the greatest artist's carving, with full lips and dark eyes that seemed to place her very ka on delicate display. Her body now had the shape of a woman, with high breasts unmarked by the smallest freckle, with a backside as round and swaying as any harem girl's. Recollecting the way she moved when she walked, his mouth went dry. He wished suddenly for Hesyre's wine.

A clap sounded outside his door. Thutmose leapt to his feet.

Hesyre opened the door a crack, peered into the darkness of the hall.

"The Great Royal Wife," said a familiar voice: Takhat, Neferure's peevish old wet-nurse.

Hesyre raised his meticulously painted brows, waiting.

"Let her come in," Thutmose said. "Hesyre, accompany the lady Takhat to the garden until I send for you."

Neferure appeared in his chamber with a supernatural speed. It seemed he blinked, and she materialized like a goddess stepping from the river mist. More likely, his agitated nerves altered his perception of time, so he did not see her stepping across the threshold in her tiny golden sandals, did not hear her words as she dismissed Takhat. But she was suddenly there, standing in the center of a fine carpet of felted wool, pulsing with a radiance he could scarce look upon, and could scarce look away from. Thutmose did not know whether the glow about Neferure's face was from the lamplight or from her own being, but with wonder and trepidation, he saw that she was in fact glowing. A palpable longing seemed to travel down her skin, from her bare shoulders over her thin arms to her clasped hands. It was a desire more akin to religious rapture than physical longing.

She shivered.

"Are you cold?" Thutmose asked foolishly.

"No." Her voice was high and bright, a chime in a temple.

"Please, sit with me."

As if his invitation had snapped some tethering cord, Neferure swept to the couch, nearly running. She settled upon a silk cushion and stared at him, the usual wild expectation evident in the blackness of her eyes. Thutmose's heart told him desperately that he did not know how to meet her tacit demand. But his body said otherwise, and as always, he responded to her presence, and the mist of his desire for her enveloped him, silencing the worries of his heart.

He kissed her neck below her ear, and felt a hot thrill run through him when she arched her back, encouraging him with a moan. He liked to draw her out, to push her longing further until she was frantic for him, and fell upon him scratching like Pakhet, and so he fondled her breast for a time until she was panting, clutching his shoulders. Then he made himself pull away.

"Are you hungry? Would you like beer, or melon water?"

She steadied herself with a few breaths, warming to his game as she always did. "Melon water," she said.

"I will have beer, myself."

He realized with a sudden clutch of embarrassment that he had sent all his servants away. There was no one to pour. He wondered, was it more seemly for a Pharaoh to serve the God's Wife of Amun, or for the wife to serve the king? In his indecision he stared helplessly at the jugs on his table, then, unnerved by his own stillness, lurched forward and seized the jug of melon water. It sloshed over the rim and splashed on the table, but he managed to offer Neferure her bowl at last.

She took one small sip and set it aside. As he raised his bowl to his lips, she lowered it for him with a hand on his wrist. Her fingers were cool; a shiver traveled up his skin from the place where she touched him.

"I come to you eagerly," she said.

"I can see that."

"I am ready."

Thutmose gaped at her. She was always ready, it seemed, always desperate for him – a fact that flattered him as much as it frightened him. But she did not speak now of merely lying together. He caught in the dark fire of her eyes some deeper meaning.

"I have waited, Lord. I have opened myself to you, so many times. I have lain before you as a holy offering."

Thutmose drained his bowl of beer in one long draft. When he returned it to the table, Neferure was suddenly upon him, pressing herself against his chest, her back arching, her mouth tickling the sensitive skin of his neck with a soft moan.

"Oh!" said Thutmose. He could think of no other response for his mouth to make, though his body had no such trouble. He tore fiercely at her gown, seeking to raise it to her waist, to take her now, there on the supper couch, and to Set with drawing her out. He hurt everywhere from the need to be inside her, *now*, to hear her cries, to feel her hot breath on his neck, to spend himself within. But her gown had twisted about her legs, and he only succeeded in tangling it more. He stroked her shoulders, which were as smooth as new leaves, trying to calm her enough that he might sort out her linen. Neferure's breath hissed, a sound that lit all his veins afire. Even the soles of his feet throbbed with the feel of her, and he kicked his legs helplessly. The movement shook her, for she was half in his lap, and she dropped one hand to steady herself. It landed on Thutmose's thigh beside his aching manhood.

Neferure sat back suddenly, staring at where her hand lay, at the shape of Thutmose's member beneath his kilt. In an instant her eyes raised to his, and it was as though a different girl sat in her place, as though a different ka inhabited her body. She looked at her brother with mild confusion. A slow frown creased her brow, pinched her features. It was a look of disappointment.

"I...I..." Thutmose squirmed away from her, tripping over his tongue.

They drew apart, sat for some long time in heavy silence while Neferure jerked at the accursed skirt of her gown. Neither dared to look at the other. The despondent fizzling of a lamp's wick burning out echoed in the vastness of Thutmose's chamber. It made a sound far too large for itself. At last, Neferure turned to face him.

"Well, after all, I am the Great Royal Wife," she said.

Thutmose could not discern her meaning. He thought it wisest to make no reply.

"Do you wish to use me for your pleasure? Very well."

"I...what?"

"It is my duty."

"After so many times, after the way you've behaved toward me, I should think, Neferure, that it is more than duty to you." The sudden shift in her demeanor stung him, and he scowled at her, offended.

"I make no complaints."

"You come to me wet as an eel every night, and yet you sit there and say 'I make no complaints!'"

"Is my lord angry?"

"No. Yes! I don't understand this. I don't understand you!"

Neferure shrugged.

"You came into my chambers looking like you greeted a god."

She flinched, looked quickly away from his face.

"And now you talk of duty, and look on me with...with disappointment. No, with *disdain*. What is happening, Neferure? Was your ka somewhere else?"

She drew a shaky breath, held it a moment, then said, "Perhaps. When Takhat brought me your summons, I was praying in my temple."

Of course.

After their marriage, Neferure had refused to move from her little palace in the gardens of the House of Women. Ahmose, before she had fled for her estates, had advised him to let the matter lie, to allow Neferure her private residence so long as she maintained her duties. It seemed the Great Royal Wife spent all her free time in the Hathor shrine on the palace's roof-top, praying. Nearly every evening that Thutmose had visited the harem, he had seen the orange glow of an offering brazier moving fitfully between the pillars of Neferure's temple. Its light cast a feeling of eerie unwelcome to the night-time garden.

Against his better judgment, Thutmose said slowly, "What did you pray for?"

"The same thing I pray for every night: for the god to fill me."

"Which god?"

"Amun. Or any god. Each day, each night, I make the same prayers. And why not? It is my birthright, to be the consort of a god, to be the beloved of a god, as Ahmose was. To bear a son who is half-god himself, as my mother is. I prayed tonight, as every night, that the gods would fill me at last. That they would be unambiguous, that I would know their hearts, and they would know mine. That I would come into my own powers as a god-chosen woman. That I would be god-chosen in truth, and consort to divinity."

These were things Thutmose truly could not grasp. Hatshepsut had long said that Neferure was god-chosen, as had Ahmose. He knew being god-chosen must have something to do with her strange, compelling force, even with the white bull of Min. But he did not care to understand the matter further. It made him feel weak and frightened, as though in this realm he had no say, no control, Pharaoh or not.

"I thought," Neferure said, "that when I came to you

tonight we would join as Nut and Geb are joined, the earth with the sky, and at last the gods would fill me. It was my vision in Iunet, you see."

She gazed at him expectantly, but Thutmose was forced to shake his head. *Vision in Iunet?*

"When you said you would take me as Great Royal Wife, I saw my way clear. You have seen the carving on the wall of Djeser-Djeseru, the story of Hatshepsut's birth. Don't you see, Thutmose? Amun came to our grandmother because she was Great Royal Wife, and worthy to love Amun." She panted with exasperation, her brows pinching at the confusion on his face. "As I am your Great Royal Wife, I, too, am worthy! Amun is supposed to come to me through your body! I will join with you, but it will not be you – it will be Amun!"

In spite of her strange words and the angry fire in her face, Thutmose's own body still throbbed with its untended wants. "We can still join," he offered sheepishly.

"No! Don't you see?" Neferure scrambled to her feet, trembling. "I was wrong, this whole time, the whole time we've been married. And I only see the truth now. It's like I've wakened from a dream. I was not meant for Amun, Thutmose. He does not love me."

"...Amun?"

"I serve him, as I serve all the gods. I do my duty to him, and to the throne, because is Maat herself not a goddess? How can I serve all the gods, even Maat, if I do not *serve maat*? If I do not do my duties – all of them?"

Thutmose was well and truly lost now. He sank against the backrest of his couch and watched as his wife paced the length of his felted carpet with clenched fists, words spilling from her mouth faster than Thutmose's ears could catch them.

"I was pledged to Amun from my childhood, and yet he wants nothing of me! It's another god who longs for me, but I am kept from her side by maat. Hathor calls to me, Thutmose – Hathor desires me, for her own purpose. I am hers, her vessel, her tool – and yet because I am the King's Daughter, and the God's Wife of Amun, and the Great Royal Wife, I can *never* be hers! I must serve *Amun*, a god who is cold, who cares nothing for me and spurns even my body. Why does he turn his back to me? Why? I have done all my duties, fulfilled all the commands. I have done as my kings have commanded – the Pharaoh is the body of the gods on the earth, even of Amun! Especially of Amun! And yet Amun will not love me!" She stared at him. Her eyes traveled down his body to his lap, and he folded his arms protectively there, shielding his vulnerable parts from the fury of her gaze. "You have a man's body, and always have. I see that now. You are not a god."

Tears coursed down her cheeks; her nose ran, but she did not wipe the mess away. Thutmose found a square of linen in the box beside his couch and went to her, offered it, but she continued pacing as if she did not see him.

"Amun, why can you not love me as Hathor loves me? Don't you see how it pains me, that you spurn me so? Oh, what have I done to deserve your scorn? How am I unclean?"

She fell to her knees, wailing. Thutmose gathered her in his arms and rocked her, his heart pounding wildly in his chest.

"There, sister. There. Amun doesn't hate you. You are his wife – my wife. You are the most blessed of ladies in the Two Lands."

"I am not," she insisted, her tears hot and wet on his shoulder. "Amun wants nothing of me. And I can never be with the goddess who loves me."

"I'll send you to serve Hathor permanently, if it will make you happy."

She pushed him away. "You cannot. Don't you see? Mother is right, though it's bitter on my tongue to say it. I am needed here, in Waset, at Amun's temple, to perform all the rites of my offices. It is maat, and without maat, Egypt will die. Oh, unhappy me! I am cursed to misery forever!"

Thutmose took her hands, coaxed her to her feet. "I don't like to see you so distraught."

She took the square of linen from his hands, wiped her

face clean. "It is my duty as Great Royal Wife to lie with you," she said calmly, "and I will do it. I am nothing if not dutiful."

"I can see that you are," Thutmose said dryly. "We do need to get an heir, Neferure. It's of the utmost importance, now that I have removed you from your heirship and made you my wife. Without an heir, the throne is in danger."

She nodded, took a step toward the couch. He stayed her with a hand on her arm.

"The way you looked at me...earlier, when we stopped. I may not be a god, Neferure. I may have only the body of a man. But I am still a Pharaoh."

He had meant it lightly, but she did not smile. "Ahmose is god-chosen, and she lay with a god. I am destined for the same. You may be a Pharaoh, but a Pharaoh is not a god until he is dead and resurrected. Now you are only a man, made of mortal flesh. I deserve no lesser a consort than a god."

Thutmose's heart chilled. *What kind of a woman disdains even the love of a Pharaoh?*

And at last he knew where his dread of Neferure came from. Now he understood the fear he'd felt when she tamed the bull. There was something dangerous in the way she understood herself – in her very will. Something inhabited her heart that did not dwell within normal women, nor within men. Not even Pharaohs thought so highly of themselves. At least, Thutmose did not. There was danger in such self-assurance. He could not quite grasp the danger – could not discern its exact shape, or know its boundaries. He only knew it was danger.

Thutmose let his hand fall from her arm. He made his way to his door, summoned his guard, and asked the man to send for Hesyre and Takhat. When the wet-nurse arrived, she looked expectantly at her charge, but at the sight of Neferure's tear-stained face and still-clothed body, Takhat's face fell into a deep, worried frown.

"The Great Royal Wife is too tired for company tonight," Thutmose said. "Take her back to her Hathor shrine and let her pray before she sleeps."

When they had gone, Hesyre turned to Thutmose, dry-washing his hands. "Lord..."

"I'll have that wine, Hesyre. Bring it to me in my garden. I need fresh air."

He walked the paths alone until Hesyre found him and pressed a large cup of deep, blood-red wine into his hands. Thutmose drank of it, nearly gagging on its bitter potency. It was a strong vintage. But he drank it all, and as it settled into his blood, he moved from the protective shelter of hedges and broad-leafed trees into the open glare of starlight. His head swimming with the wine, he tilted his face up, staring undaunted into the night sky, until his wig slid from his scalp and landed with a thump in the grass.

"I am the Pharaoh," he said to the stars, emboldened by the wine. "One day I will be as much a god as you."

Hathor did not answer. Her stars shone down indifferently, white and cold.

"She has duties to Amun, duties to the throne. Release her; I command it."

Still the goddess made no reply. Abashed, Thutmose retrieved his wig from the grass. He crept back into his chambers and fell into his bed, pulled the linens up to cover his face. He did not want to see the patches of starlight that played across the bars of his wind-catcher. He did not want the starlight to see him.

Chapter Twenty-Five

"W OMAN-KING."
Hatshepsut blinked in the smoky dimness of the
queen's great house. The door-cloth swung closed, falling into
place with a sound like linen dropping on a stone floor. The
arching walls reached above her, around her, a net drawing
tight.

Ati lay in all her vast, arrogant glory on a pile of cushions,
leaning her impressive bulk on one deeply dimpled elbow.
Her thighs and hips spread around her, shining with the
remnants of some fine, spicy-scented oil in the light of a
great brazier which burned on a pad of red wool in the center
of the floor. A girl with a regal bearing nearly as great as
Ati's own bent over the brazier, tossed a handful of resin on
the glowing coals, and a cloud of incense smoke billowed
about her face, dissipated in the shadows hanging in the peak
of the roof. The girl was clad in the same brilliant yellow
skirt that Ati wore, her forehead similarly adorned with the
simple yellow band. And though she was young, her body
was beginning to show the same fatness of which Ati was so
proud, the thighs heavy and thick, the hips wide and pocked
here and there with dimples. Hatshepsut guessed the girl to
be the Queen's daughter.

"Sit with us, King of Egypt."

Ati's voice was as deep and lustrous as long-worked wood,
resonant with a low, rich tone that was almost masculine.
The barest hint of amusement was in it, too, and Hatshepsut

raised her chin imperiously. She was a visitor in Punt, but she was still a king, still the son of the very god who called this strange land his home. She made her way across the split and bound logs of the floor, uncomfortably aware that empty space yawned below, a drop the length of three tall men from the platform to the hard ground outside. Perhaps because it supported the great weight of Queen Ati, the floor seemed to quiver lightly with her step, seemed to bounce faintly – a feeling not unlike walking across the deck of a ship in its moorings.

Bita-Bita and Kani trailed her, and, when they saw that Hatshepsut was seated comfortably on her own cushions, the two girls prostrated themselves before Queen Ati and her royal daughter in the Puntite fashion, full length along the floor with hands reaching. Ati acknowledged them; the girls retreated behind Hatshepsut; she could feel them there in the shadows, tense in their attentiveness.

At a signal, Ati's daughter approached with a grace that was incongruous to her large form, offering a bowl of palm wine. Hatshepsut took it with a nod of thanks, surprised that a royal daughter was expected to play the role of servant. The wine was pungent and faintly bitter, with a curiously green aftertaste that made Hatshepsut long for the coolness and kind perfumes of her palace gardens.

"You have been avoiding me," Ati said.

Her directness took Hatshepsut aback. "Certainly not," she replied after a moment. "There is much to be done, and I have been regrettably delayed by my work."

Ati's red-painted lips pursed in wry amusement. "As you wish. Abaty, bring the meat."

The daughter produced, from its unseen resting place in the shadows, a platter laden with raw meat on skewers. Hatshepsut was not fond of uncooked meats, and she worried that she would be made to choke the meal down for the sake of Puntite propriety. But Ati took a skewer delicately between her fingers and laid it directly on the coals and resins burning in the brazier. Hatshepsut did the same; the hut filled with the enticing odor of charred meat.

"You traveled long to reach us," Ati said, turning her skewer, not deigning to look at Hatshepsut's face. As fat fell from the meat, flames licked up, and the queen's face leaped out of the dimness with startling brilliance, the deep blue lines tattooed around her mouth as dark as plow lines in silt.

"The riches of Punt are famed all over the world," Hatshepsut said. "My god greatly desires them, and I serve my god faithfully and well."

They pulled their meal from the coals. The meat carried the rich, somewhat floral taste of the incense – a flavor that was not unpleasant on Hatshepsut's tongue. Ati considered Hatshepsut as she nibbled at her meat. At last she said, "The god desires my riches, or you desire them?"

Hatshepsut smiled a small, acquiescent smile, bowed her head slightly, and made no reply. Her skill with the Puntite tongue was not nearly strong enough to rejoin, and in any case, she would not make excuses for her motives. Hadn't the throne been given to her? Hadn't she every right to maintain her hold on it, using any means at her disposal? She would not stammer and apologize before this arrogant river-horse of a woman.

"I, too, am a loyal servant of the gods, she-king."

Ati added something else in the same amused tone – something Hatshepsut could not quite catch. She called quietly over her shoulder, "Bita-Bita."

"The Queen says," Bita-Bita supplied, her voice scarcely louder than a whisper, "that the gods of Punt are not so different from the gods of Egypt."

"Gods all want the same," Ati went on. "Power, and acknowledgment of that power. Worship. Obedience from their servants. And all people are servants to the gods, would you not agree, King?"

"I do agree."

The Queen's daughter offered more courses, bearing her trays of fruits and breads and sweet cakes with silent dignity while Ati and Hatshepsut (often with Bita-Bita's aid) talked of small, incidental things. The differences in the seasons, and how Punt and Egypt marked the change of months. The music each enjoyed; a comparison of musical instruments and the skills of singers. The habits of their men, who seemed to have more similarities, in their need to swagger and boast, than differences. Hatshepsut relaxed into the conversation, and Ati, too, seemed to drop her cold formality, warming to Hatshepsut's company. The Queen even laughed now and then, a loud peal like temple bells, trailing to a crackling wheeze deep in the woman's chest.

The coals in the brazier burned low, dimming the glimmer on Ati's well-oiled skin. Her face sank into half-shadow. The silent daughter knelt at Hatshepsut's side, bearing one final tray. A single bowl sat in the center of it, filled to the rim with some dark liquid. Hatshepsut lifted it carefully.

"What is it?"

"A message from the gods."

Hatshepsut said nothing, watching Ati carefully across the rim of the bowl, raised halfway to her lips. The queen stared back with that familiar, hungry intensity on her dark features.

"What message?" Hatshepsut said at last.

"Would you hear it, truly? Or would you disregard it, yet again?"

"I don't understand."

Ati sat up, reached across the brazier with both hands. The light played across her flesh, moving in golden ripples like a school of shy fish. Hatshepsut placed the bowl in Ati's palms. A bit of the liquid escaped the rim, spilled over Ati's knuckles. It fell viscous and red into the coals, and Hatshepsut choked on the familiar smell of blood.

Amun's eyes – I nearly drank it!

Ati turned her face down to gaze at the bowl, blew on its surface, watched the ripples with pinched and furrowed brows. She tilted the dish this way and that, until the blood rolled around the rim, coming close to spilling over, and Abaty, the silent daughter, suddenly raised her voice in a loud chant. The sound made Hatshepsut gasp. Although she understood none of the words, their forceful cadence beat under her skin like a hot pulse. As the chant rose to a climax, Ati gave the bowl one final tilt, and blood splashed over her hands, falling into the brazier, splashing onto the floor. Kani and Bita-Bita moaned softly in terror.

Ati raised one blood-covered hand stiffly. Her daughter fell silent. For many long, trembling heartbeats, the only sound was Hatshepsut's own ragged breath in her ears, and the crackling of the coals in the brazier.

Then Ati spoke. "Even here, we know of the Mistress of Stars, the goddess who wears many faces."

"Hathor?"

"She has many names – all names known to women. Lover and virgin, mother and crone, queen and warrior. Dancer, singer, hunter, maker."

Hatshepsut clutched her own hands, determined to show no fear. But she remembered how Hathor had pulled at her years ago during that dark night, the Beautiful Feast of the Valley, the cliffs echoing with the cries of her people, the night shimmering with torchlight.

"You have spurned her," Ati said. "And she is not pleased."

"I never spurned her. I have restored her temples, raised her up. I have increased her priesthood with the best girls in Egypt."

"And yet you have withheld what was promised, the tribute she demanded."

"The goddess cannot have Neferure. She is my heir, my hold on the throne."

"So flat a refusal. The she-king is indeed an arrogant one, so puffed with her own power she would naysay even a goddess."

Hatshepsut bit her tongue, fought back a bitter laugh. To be called arrogant by this great hummock of a woman...! *Puffed, indeed.*

Ati rumbled out a few more words, and Hatshepsut, distracted by the offense, shook her head, turning to Bita-

Bita, who sat quivering with tears standing in her eyes.

"She says..." Bita-Bita faltered. "She says that even kings are not as great as the stars."

"What does she mean by that?"

"I don't know, Great Lady."

Hatshepsut forced away her anger, made herself concentrate on Ati's words.

"You came here to my land seeking a gift to please your god," Ati said, her voice drawling now, slow with amused contempt, the twist of her mouth speaking plainly of the mistrust she had of Hatshepsut's motives. "And yet you withhold from your gods. What am I to make of it? What is the Mistress of Starlight to make of it?"

"You forget," Hatshepsut said, making as if to rise, "that I am a king, and not subject to your insults, Ati of Punt. I will gladly take my gold and turquoise and leave your land empty-handed, rather than suffer your disdain."

"It is not I who disdains you. Look to the goddess to see true wrath." The odor of burning blood seemed to steal the air from the dark hut. Hatshepsut clenched her fists.

"But there is yet time to amend your wrongs."

"Oh?" Disbelief at the woman's audacity pitched her voice high, and she bit her lip at the childlike sound of it.

"If the tribute comes to the goddess from your own hand, woman-king, then you will be spared. If not..."

"Spared! Indeed!"

"If not, death in this life will be the end for you. A true death. A final death."

Bita-Bita gasped. Hatshepsut held her body very still, while inside her chest her heart fluttered wildly.

"No afterlife," Ati said. "The goddess will see to it."

In the call of crickets in the forest canopy, Hatshepsut could hear the cold ring of a chisel on stone.

Senenmut heard the murmur of Hatshepsut's voice, talking to her servant girls in low, urgent tones, long before he saw her come through the forest gloom. From where he crouched on his heels, sipping palm wine on the platform outside Hatshepsut's borrowed hut, he saw the golden necklaces around her neck first, pinpoint gleams of starlight reflected in their finely worked chains. The shape of her body followed, the tension of her shoulders evident in the darkness, the stiff carriage of her neck. She fairly stamped her feet as she walked the forest path, making the rough fabric of her Puntite skirt swing from side to side. He rose smoothly when she reached her ladder, so his presence would not startle her, distracted as she was.

"Great Lady. How was supper with the Queen?"

Hatshepsut stalled on the ladder's lowest rung. "Senenmut." She said his name with a note of deep relief, and, sensing her need, he climbed down to her side.

"Leave us," she said to her girls, and they scampered up the ladder, disappearing into the quiet hut as though they feared she might recall them.

"Something is wrong," he said.

"The Queen of Punt," Hatshepsut growled, "is a foul-tempered, unpleasant, vile sorceress of a woman, with a black, hopeless ka."

"So it did not go well," he guessed.

To his surprise, she covered her face with trembling hands and sniffled, holding back tears.

"Now, now," Senenmut murmured. "Don't fret. Tell me."

"Not here. My girls – anybody may hear."

And so they took the path deeper into the forest, following its dark breadth with hesitant feet, their hands clasped together so they could not lose one another in the gloom. The leaves moved constantly above them, a sound almost like falling water, but not nearly so soothing. There was an undeniable menace to the forest, a pale, unseen threat hanging all about the god's land. Senenmut had felt it, an itch on his skin, all that day while he and Ineni and Nehesi led the men into this very wood to procure the saplings of myrrh. They would sail soon for Tjau, and Senenmut would be glad to see the tiny, stinking port town. When they reached Tjau, they would be that much closer to Egypt, and a more benevolent environment with kinder, more sensible gods.

Their path gave way to a wide clearing, a swath of grass and weeds close-cropped by animals. Senenmut suspected it was a favored pasture for the little donkeys the Puntites rode. The ever-present, ever-whispering canopy drew back, and the silver of moonlight fell bright and clear into the grass, turning all it touched to colorless uniformity, dreamy but clearly seen, nothing hidden. Hatshepsut let his hand fall and stepped out into the pale light, turned her face up toward the moon. Tears slid from the corners of her eyes.

Senenmut sank onto his heels again, for he was tired from the day's long work. The grass was soft and welcoming. He sank back further, lay along it with his head propped on one arm.

"Tell me," he said again, and watched her as she simply stood, calm at last, bathing in the light.

"Khonsu," Hatshepsut muttered. "The moon god. Here he is, even in Punt, shining as he always does."

"Of course."

"Do you think it's true, Senenmut, that the gods of this place are no different from the gods of our land?"

Senenmut considered the question. "Well, after all, this is Amun's homeland."

The answer seemed to displease her. She turned away.

"You were hoping I would deny it."

"No – yes. I don't know."

"What troubles you, Hatet?" There was no one to hear him use the pet name, the name she had been called from the time she was a child, learning at Senenmut's knee. No one to hear his outrageous disrespect, the unseemly familiarity of a simple scribe for Maatkare, the Good God.

"I am afraid," she said, and her voice broke with the strain of keeping her tears in check. He stretched his arms toward her, and she crumpled onto the grass, pressed her face against his chest. Her body shook with sobs.

"What? What do you fear?"

But she would not answer. She only wept.

Far in the forest, echoing amongst the trees, a coughing call sounded, then a yowl. The men had heard something similar in daylight while they dug the myrrh saplings. Their Puntite guides had identified the caller as a cat: one of the cats that stalked the woodlands – small, but known now and then to attack a man when easier prey was scarce. Never had two people been easier prey, lying prone in the grass, one of them weeping like a lost ka in a tomb. And yet Senenmut was not afraid. Was she not the Pharaoh? Did the gods not watch her and protect her? He pulled her tighter against his body, his shield against the terrors of the night.

Hatshepsut mumbled something against his chest. He drew back, looked with concern at her deep-shadowed face.

"What is it, Great Lady?"

"I do not want to be forgotten."

He laughed, the way he had often laughed at Neferure's small fears when she was just a little thing. "You can never be. Look at your temple, your monuments! Look at your works! Your name is carved on every beautiful thing in the Two Lands – every obelisk, every mural, every palace wall. The gods will always know you – ah, and men, too. You will not be forgotten."

She drew away from him, sat up, rubbed the heels of her hands into her eyes. "Yes. Yes, my monuments. My temple. My name." She pulled her knees to her chest and hugged them, lost in her own thoughts, and Senenmut studied her face in the moonlight. She had grown thinner under the strain of their journey, the long trek across the dry Red Land, the lean provisions, the heaving and dullness of appetite on the sea. The shape of her face stood out sharper and starker than ever before, and he was struck by how like a falcon she was, the sharp curve of her nose, the piercing darkness of her eyes. And how frail she seemed, holding herself, pensive and quiet. This was a Hatshepsut he seldom saw, and though her strange, dark mood disturbed him, still he reveled in their solitude, in the chance to drink the sight of her as a parched soldier drinks at an outpost well.

"Will you tell me why you are so upset?" he said, hesitantly, reluctant to break this rare spell.

She shook her head.

"Then let me cheer you, at least."

"You cannot cheer me."

"Oh, can I not?" He stroked her shoulders, let his fingers run slowly down the curve of her spine, the skin smooth and supple and scented with the lush oils of Punt.

"*No*, you cannot. I am in no mood for lovemaking tonight."

"When will we have another opportunity?" Likely not until they were back in Waset, and even then it would be days before they settled into the court routine, before chance was kind enough to lend them a few precious moments of solitude and they could touch each other's skin, taste each other's bodies. Senenmut was parched for her, starved of her. He brushed the strands of her wig aside and took her ear in his teeth gently, and heard her quiet gasp of pleasure. It was her secret place – the one way he could always turn the current of her moods to his favor, turn her refusals into acquiescence.

"That's not fair," she said, shrugging her shoulder to push him away. But then she was in his arms, pressing her mouth to his, slipping her tongue past his teeth. Her breath was faintly perfumed with incense.

Senenmut pulled her to her feet, the better to undress her, and stood back to take in the sight of her as the skirt fell from her hips, as she pulled the wig from her brow and shook out her natural hair. It was grown to a hand's width now, dense and tightly curled, black as onyx. It framed her eyes with a dark halo. Her unpainted face was as colorless as silver in the moonlight, but still its tones darkened with a flush that filled him with impatience. Yet he made himself wait, made his body yield to his eyes, allowed his eyes the rarity of the sight of her unclothed. Beneath her wreath of golden necklaces, her collarbone moved delicately with her breathing, and her breasts, flattened only slightly by motherhood and the intervening years, stirred too. Below the shadow of her navel, below the few pale tracks in her skin bearing witness to her long-ago pregnancy, a thick thatch of unfamiliar hair darkened the unplucked crux of her thighs. A jagged line cut through it, the scar – the wound she had inflicted upon her own flesh to win over the men of Egypt's court. Senenmut recalled, with a force of memory that startled him, the weight of Hatshepsut falling into his arms, fainting away from the pain and the loss of blood. He recalled how light she had been. He had lifted her, cradled her, shouted for a chariot – and known in that moment that she carried his helpless heart, held it as tightly as he held her body.

He fell to his knees before her, pressed his face against the scar. The black hair of her groin trapped the smell of her, intensified it, and his senses were flooded with her scent, flooded like a field yielding to the rising river, encompassed entirely by her.

The cat in the woodlands coughed again. He tugged at her until she, too, fell to her knees, and put her arms about his shoulders, covering him with the shield of her power. He kissed the tears from her cheeks, from her eyelids. He tasted her salt.

"Senenmut," she whispered, and his name on her lips was deep with the sound of relief.

"Maatkare," he replied, invoking her divinity, pulling her protection like a cloak around their two hearts.

CHAPTER TWENTY-SIX

IT WAS NOT SUCH AN unusual thing, Neferure told herself, scowling, to see the Great Royal Wife in Waset's palace. So why, then, did the people who filled it glance at her wide-eyed and startled before they dropped into their requisite bows? Indeed, Neferure spent much time alone in her small private palace, sequestered with her own thoughts, her prayers, her worship, her endless longing. But she made her appearance at court daily as duty dictated. She presented herself to Thutmose whenever he summoned her – though he had summoned her again only twice since that disastrous time when the magic of her own expectations, the anticipation of her great and beautiful fate, had fallen from her eyes. Now when she went to her husband, she lay back as servile as a captured slave and allowed him to rut upon her, tainting her with his mortal flesh.

True, she was not yet the consort of a god, and so her own flesh was still mortal. But this unfortunate circumstance was only temporary. She would discern her sin – whatever unknown flaw in her person blocked her divine lover from coming to her bed. She would make the proper amends, debase herself before the proper altar, grovel, sacrifice. And then she would be elevated.

Neferure paced from the doorway of the audience hall through a long colonnade where pale light alternated with the shadows of the great pillars. The sun was high and hot, the season of Shemu nearing its close. The light in the palace's halls was bright and blue. All about her, servants moved with lagging feet, their linens damp with sweat, their minds dully on their small and meaningless tasks until they caught sight of the Great Royal Wife moving among them, a shaft of sunlight in cloud, and staggered into their bows. Neferure ignored them. The impudence of their behavior infuriated her – the implied insult, that they should be startled by her presence in the palace.

She left the colonnade and made her way through the long eastern garden. A god's-kiss bush held the last of its pink blooms up to the sun; small birds dived among its branches, feasting on the insects attracted to the sweet smell of the flowers. Neferure stood and watched a moment, soothed by the simple beauty of the scene, encouraged by it. She plucked the freshest blossom she could find and tucked it into the strands of her wig so that she might enjoy the perfume of the god's-kiss all afternoon while she searched.

For it was a search, a restless roaming, chasing her thoughts down the airy corridors of Waset's great palace, circling her own footsteps past store-rooms, treasuries, ambassadors' quarters and servants' rooms. Any place in the palace might hold the answer to the mystery of her sin. Once her mother returned from Punt, Neferure's various duties to the throne and the Temple of Amun would redouble, and she would no longer be free to search. Hatshepsut had been gone over a month already. Time was growing short, and Neferure had found nothing to enlighten her in all her many days of searching.

As she stood gazing into the surface of the palace lake, watching the ripples of rising fish distort her dark reflection with its one bright pink bloom, she realized with sudden certainty where the answer to her quandary was surely hidden – the one place she had not yet thought to search, had not even dared to consider. She paused, listening to the whisper in her heart, half-unheard as it always was. She felt the faint wobbling in her middle that indicated the words of a god.

"Mistress," she whispered. "Lady of Delights."

Hathor struggled to respond through the dense cloud of Neferure's unatoned sin.

I will clear your way, goddess. I will.

It had been many years since Neferure had visited the Pharaoh's apartments – the other Pharaoh, the chiefest of the two. Her mother, Maatkare. Many years, yet still Neferure's feet knew the correct path. She allowed her own ka to lead her, obedient to the strength of her own assurance. Soon enough she reached the two great doors, carved with twin scarabs raising sun-disks above their backs, gilded and painted in lapis-blue. With the Pharaoh away on her expedition, there was only one guard on the door, and he stepped aside with a bow when Neferure smiled at him, sweetly, benignly. What harm was there in the Great Royal Wife, the king's own daughter, entering the royal chamber?

Her mother's fan-bearer looked up sharply, an angry remark ready to spit from her lips. When the woman saw who approached her, she dropped into a hasty bow.

"Great Lady," she said smoothly.

"Rise."

She did. The fan-bearer's face was calm, but Neferure did not miss the light of suspicion flaring in her eyes.

"Your name?"

"Batiret, Great Lady."

"You have served my mother long."

"Ah; I have served her since before you were born, Great Lady."

"That is a long time indeed." Neferure gazed around Hatshepsut's anteroom, outwardly airy, even lazy in the late Shemu heat. Her eyes, though, swept keenly over the rich hangings, the fine furniture, the very tiles of the floor she stood upon. She searched the scenes depicted on the walls, the various kings of the past striding and fighting, hunting, conquering, worshipping. They were all as alike as lentils in a pot, all of them mortal. And none of them yielded up her answer.

She made toward the first of several doors set along the nearest wall. Batiret scampered after her, fussing with the length of linen she had been folding when Neferure arrived.

"Great Lady, is there aught I might do for you?"

How to search the apartment thoroughly without this pest of a woman buzzing around her? Neferure turned to look Batiret full in the face – and stopped, seized with revelation.

"You have ever been loyal to my mother."

"Of course, Great Lady. Always." The gruffness of simple pride was in Batiret's answer.

Neferure considered the woman, her frank, honest face, her open and fearless nature, evident in the way she stood square and unafraid under the Great Royal Wife's scrutiny.

"I would reward you for your good service to my mother, and to Egypt."

"Reward me, Great Lady?" Suspicion crept into Batiret's voice, and she tried to temper it with a half-bow.

"I would have you come to supper tonight in my own palace."

Batiret straightened. She was silent for as long as propriety would allow, and in that brief moment Neferure saw the doubt and worry clouding in her face. But no one could refuse an invitation from the Great Royal Wife.

Batiret had no choice but to bow her acceptance. "As you wish, Great Lady, though I am unworthy of the honor."

Neferure took the flower from her wig, breathed in its sweet smell once more. Then she tucked it into Batiret's own hair, smiling, and left the Pharaoh's rooms.

Thutmose sighed as his guards closed the doorway to the House of Women behind him, shutting out the distant sounds of Waset – the merchants crying in the great central marketplace, the blows of carvers' hammers ringing like bird cries in the marsh. The doors shut out the smell of Waset, too, the fishy odor of the quayside, the acridity of pitch coating boats' hulls, sewage draining down the sides of the streets, the faint sweetness of bread baking, beer brewing, meat roasting. The young king did not know whether his sigh was one of relief or despair. For as the pleasant perfumes and soft music of feminine laughter washed over him, he felt the weight of duty settle over his shoulders, cold and stiff as a jeweled collar against his skin.

Neferure had grown cold and unresponsive in his bed, and his confidence in his ability to please her – as a husband or as a king – was badly shaken. He had turned to his harem nightly, taking two or three women into his bed, rising to the charms of each one until, by the end of the night, he had to be carried in a litter back to the great palace, too weak and sleepy to drive his chariot at the head of his guards. The women laughed with delight and made bawdy jokes about the greedy desires of their handsome young king. The men of his guard – those he was close to – advised him with knowing winks to enjoy his stamina while he could, for when his youth left him he would not manage to throw his spear so many times in a single evening. Hesyre wordlessly prepared salves for Thutmose's overworked flesh, raising his fussy brows in the bath while he bent over his work. But no matter how pained he became, no matter how he longed for a night of simple sleep, Thutmose returned to his women.

Part of it was the pleasure. Ah, as Neferure was quick to remind him, he was only a man, and what man could resist so many willing women in his bed, such an endless parade of beauty and variety? Ankhesebet with her squirming and her squeals, Nedjmet with her lithe dancing and her eager mouth, Sheshti's translucent white skin, always under veils to protect it from the harsh sun, Khuit with her skin as black and sweet as ripe figs. Bebi and Benerib, who would happily tangle the sheets together. Ankhesiref who liked it on her back. Meritamun who straddled him. Henuttawy with her firm, round buttocks and her preference for it on her knees, face pressed into the mattress, her yowls stifled by a silk cushion – no, he would be no man at all if the lure of so many singular pleasures did not draw him back night after night.

But more than the pleasure, it was the pressing need of his house. Neferure wanted nothing of him. That was now plain, and he would not force her. And so he told himself that even a son conceived on a harem girl would be better than no son at all, would hold the throne securely enough. Was he himself not the son of a harem girl? That was the thought that pushed him onward, to take another woman into his bed, and another, long after the lamps had burned low.

No woman had yet announced a pregnancy, though, and Thutmose felt his ka tremble under the weight of his unfulfilled duty even as he fell atop another willing woman.

It was Henuttawy who was the first to meet him in the harem's antechamber, swaying in a transparent fall of pleated white linen. The gown was caught below her pretty round breasts by a green ribbon studded with wrought-gold flowers, appealing in its simplicity. She offered him a cup of cool wine, took his arm as they strolled out into the gathering night. It had been a long day of hearing petitions, deciding on an endless stream of matters that seemed so small and insignificant to Thutmose. What did it matter which noble house would inherit the property left by some deceased merchant who had no heir? What did it matter how great a percentage of the emmer harvest should be set aside against famine the following year? What did it matter that the House of Hirkhepshef sought the blessing of the throne on the marriage of a daughter to some Ankh-Tawy lord? Nothing mattered at all, when set beside the empty wombs of Thutmose's wife and every one of his concubines. In the face of his dark fear, Henuttawy's soft, gentle bearing and easy smile were a welcome light – even if she did cast little sneers of triumph at the women who had not been quick enough to greet their king.

A purple dimness fell over the harem garden, softening the edges of the flower beds, soothing away the fierce heat of daytime. Bats emerged from their hiding places, dipping and weaving across the grounds. Thutmose lost himself in the peace of watching them, allowed his eyes to become pleasantly fooled by the crossing of their paths. Henuttawy's melodious voice lulled him, talking of some quiet nicety – a music lesson she had taken, the harp, the flute. As if in response to her story, distant music rippled across the grounds from the direction of the House itself, a tinkling of electrum bells, the strings of a harp singing a smooth counterpoint to the rhythm.

She led him to a favorite place, a small clearing surrounded by a ring of sycamores. Hundreds of tiny white flowers bloomed among the short grass, little stars in a reversed, violet sky. Suddenly Henuttawy dropped her story mid-sentence and kissed him, lifted his hands to her firm breasts. "Here, my lord. Take me here."

"Here? Outside?"

"Ah, yes – the women will all stay away. I made sure of it. I told my servant where we would be."

"Why here?"

Henuttawy sank gracefully to her knees, her hands working now at her own soft breasts, shivering. "When a woman's skin touches the earth during the act of love, it increases her fertility tenfold. Didn't you know that, Majesty?"

He could not tell whether she was telling the truth, or whether she had invented the story just to be clever. Henuttawy was fond of clever little tales. But he reasoned that anything, at this point, was worth trying. He bent over her, kissed her long and deep while his hands loosened the ribbon beneath her breasts, an expert by now at a maneuver that had once confounded him. Henuttawy's flimsy gown fell into the grass, and she turned on her knees, pressed her face into a patch of the little star-flowers, moaning with anticipation. Thutmose hiked the hem of his kilt and went willingly toward his duty.

But before he could take the girl, a harsh scream cut through the night air. The music from the House of Women faltered abruptly.

"Gods," Henuttawy said, scrambling upright, clutching her gown about her. "What in the name of Sobek...?"

The scream came again, high, panicked, painful. Thutmose ran from the grove.

Women streamed from the pillared portico of the house, looking about in confusion. Meritamun, tall and slender and the most sensible woman in the harem, saw him and hurried toward him.

"What is it? Who is hurt?" he demanded.

"No one, Majesty – at least, no one that we can tell."

"Where did the scream come from? Some woman is in distress, clearly. I want to know who."

Meritamun shook her head, at a loss – and in the same moment, as if directed by the same unseen hand, she and Thutmose both looked toward the other building on the grounds: the little palace of the King's Daughter.

There it stood, so unassuming in the night-time, surrounded by the shadows of its shade trees. A single small fire burned at its apex, where Neferure kept her shrine to Hathor. A lamp flickered dimly somewhere just below, passing by a window on the second floor.

"Come," Thutmose said, and sprinted for the palace.

There were no guards on the door. There never were, for Neferure was strange and distant enough that the women of the harem feared her, though none would admit it. Thutmose shoved against the door, but it was blocked from the inside. He kicked at it desperately, and gained only an inch or two of space before it jammed.

"Set!" he swore, striking the cedarwood panels with a fist. The door would not give.

A cry came from the upper floor, weak and frightened. Thutmose left the door and circled the wall of the palace. A flock of women trailed after him, chittering in their agitation like unsettled geese on a pond. Yet more women hung back in the garden, their linen blurs of brightness in the twilight, too frightened to approach the dwelling of the Great Royal Wife.

"Here, Lord!" Meritamun appeared from around a corner, waving him on urgently. He came to her and looked where she pointed. The black eye of a narrow window opened above them, staring unseeing out into the garden. It was high up, but Thutmose thought he might just be able to make the leap.

He sprang into the air. His hands smacked against the stone still, clawing; his fingertips held him, though they shrieked in pain. He flailed his legs against the mudbrick wall, searching desperately for a toe-hold, and hands caught at his leg, braced him. Meritamun crouched beneath his foot and straightened, levering him upward with his foot braced on her shoulder. His chest cleared the sill.

Thutmose grunted, twisted himself sideways, reached one arm through the window, pulled himself halfway inside. The room was dark, unlit; couches and tables loomed in the blackness, four-footed and crouching like beasts waiting to spring. Thutmose heard a sob from the second floor, and a woman's voice pleading. He kicked, pulled, cursed – and he was through, toppling onto the thick rugs of Neferure's floor.

He held himself very still, waiting, but no alarmed cries came, and the heart-wrenching sobs continued unabated. He crept to the front door and dragged aside the chest that leaned against it, marveling that little Neferure had been strong enough to place it there. Then, bracing himself against the menacing dark, he groped his way to the staircase and climbed to the second floor.

The beautifully appointed sleeping chamber of the Great Royal Wife was on the second story, where the windows and wind-catchers might cool her rest during the worst heat of summer. A single lamp flickered on its three-legged stand, the warmth and merriment of its light a grotesque counterpoint to the scene unfolding before Thutmose's astonished eyes. Amidst the finery of the Great Lady's chambers, between a large standing chest of oiled cedarwood and the red silk couch that had been a wedding gift from Thutmose, the form of a woman huddled, pressed against the prettily painted wall, her arms thrown up over her face. She bled from a gash on her arm, an ugly wound that pulsed a dark flow onto the bright white tiles and puddled about her drawn-up feet.

Neferure stood before her, back turned to Thutmose, as tense and fierce as Sekhmet. She held a copper blade in her hand, its edge streaming with the other woman's blood.

"Tell me," Neferure said, her voice vibrant with triumph, thick with disgust.

"Please, Great Lady," the woman begged.

Neferure advanced toward her, raising the blade; although the woman did not look up, she cringed back from the sound of Neferure's sandals on the floor, another piteous scream rising from her throat, broken by hysterical sobbing.

"Stop; I will tell you," she cried, and a note of defeat wailed in her voice. "The steward is your father. Him – your nurse – Senenmut."

Neferure paused in her advance. Her shoulders relaxed, her head tilted as if considering something of no consequence – a child's song, a pretty stone. The only sound was the cowering woman's weeping.

"By all the gods, Neferure, what is this?"

She whirled at the sound of Thutmose's voice, and the woman pressed against the wall looked up from the poor shelter of her own arms. It was Batiret, Hatshepsut's fan-bearer. When she saw it was the Pharaoh who spoke, her tears began afresh, her face wrinkling with the sobs of her relief.

There was a crash from the lower floor, the door being flung open with force, and masculine shouts. Meritamun had summoned the harem guards. Neferure stared at Thutmose for one heartbeat, her eyes flashing with fury. Then she bent slowly, gracefully, and laid her knife upon the tiles. It gave one solitary ring, bright as a temple chime, when it connected with the floor.

Neferure smiled lightly, and, as the guards came up the stairway shouting for the Pharaoh, she held out her hands before her and went willingly, docilely, into Thutmose's custody.

Chapter Twenty-Seven

I T WAS LONG PAST MIDNIGHT. Khonsu had closed the white disc of his eye hours ago, draining the soft silver touch of moonlight from the world, leaving it bleak and bare. In perhaps two hours more Re would arise golden and glorious from the horizon, spreading his warmth and benevolence across the Two Lands. But for now, the sky was emptied of divinity, and Ahmose felt terribly alone.

She had not been asleep when the Pharaoh's messengers found her. She woke after only a short time in her bed, and, knowing she would not get back to her dreams any time soon, she had dressed without waking her body servant and made her way to the portico of her estate, elevated on a little bluff that overlooked the river. She had not really wanted sleep tonight, anyway. Her dreams had been unsettling mazes, full of bright colors that confused the heart and burned the eye, full of voices speaking in strange tongues, repeating with the image of blood spilling from the rim of a bowl, running over the knuckles of an unfamiliar hand. Ahmose sat patiently, her eyes on the river, until the sails appeared, moving quickly from the direction of Waset.

Thutmose's men had been surprised to find her waiting at her little quay, alert and ready, but they bowed to her and handed her aboard without even taking the time to tie their lines.

"Trouble at the palace, Great Lady," one had said. "The Pharaoh wishes your counsel."

And now she rode in a litter through the sleeping streets of Waset, the curtains drawn tight against the bleakness of the night sky. The litter tilted, making its way up the final rise before the palace wall. Her eyes blinked as a brief, denser darkness settled over her – the passage through the great pylons into the palace's outer court. When she stepped from her litter into the pre-dawn courtyard, Ahmose shivered.

She was conducted at once to Thutmose's chambers. A double guard was on duty, standing still as statues in their blue-and-white kilts. In the hall outside a young man paced, his kilt rumpled and stained with spots of wine, his hands twisting into knots. She recognized him: Senenmut's assistant, the brilliant scribe. Kynebu – ah, that was his name. She had no time to greet him; her eyes met his, and she stumbled one step backward at the force of helplessness and anger burning in his eyes. Then the Pharaoh's doors swung wide, and Ahmose was called in.

She saw Neferure first, small and still on one of Thutmose's great couches. The girl sat with her hands folded primly in her lap, her eyes downcast, mild, looking at the floor without emotion, bearing the force of the anger that filled the room. Two great hulking guards stood to either side of the Great Royal Wife.

Thutmose stalked between Neferure and a stool in the corner, where young Batiret, Hatshepsut's fan-bearer, sat shivering and whimpering, a pair of the Pharaoh's women fussing over her, speaking to her in low, soothing tones. A length of linen bound one arm just below the shoulder. Ahmose could plainly see the red stain seeping through the bandage. Batiret's lip was split, too, and a small cut stood out above one eyebrow, clotted with dark blood.

"What is it?" Ahmose said slowly, sick realization growing in her stomach.

"What indeed!" Thutmose clenched his fists, unclenched them, rounded on her with a stark rage on his face that Ahmose had never seen before.

"You put these ideas into her heart, Ahmose. You!"

Ahmose glanced at Neferure. The girl did not look up, did not respond to Thutmose's shouts. She only remained quietly in her place, her eyes fixed on nothing, peaceful as a cow in a field.

"I don't know what you mean, Majesty. I beg enlightenment."

"I cut her," Neferure said, her voice light as a pipe. "I found out."

"Found out what?" Ahmose felt her hands go cold, her face go hot.

"That Senenmut is my father. That I am a product of filth and adultery." She said it easily, without rancor, a statement of plain fact.

Ahmose sucked in a chilled breath.

"It's why I am the way I am, isn't it, Grandmother?"

Ahmose said nothing. Her mouth was stopped by sudden fear.

"Amun spurns me – the gods will not enter me, because my very beginnings are a vile offense to them. No wonder I have never been able to reach them, as you can do. Now it makes sense."

"I did not put these thoughts into her heart," Ahmose said quietly, urgently, as Thutmose paced. "I did not counsel her to abuse a servant."

"She used a knife on the poor woman! Look at her!"

Batiret cringed under their stares, and the women tending her huddled close in defense.

"I..." Ahmose tried to form some response, but she could see only the vision from her terrible dreams, the blood spinning in the bowl, dropping over its rim to fall upon hot, smoking coals.

"Neferure must be confined," Thutmose said, loudly, a command to the soldiers – to everyone present. "She will remain under strict guard until Hatshepsut returns. No one will see her but one servant of my choosing – and myself, should I have any need to speak to her further." He glared at the girl, and Neferure went on blinking into the near distance, unconcerned. "Make it so," Thutmose said to one guardsman. The man saluted with a fist across his chest, then sped away to prepare a confinement chamber.

"If I may, husband," Neferure said. "I would ask for one of my shrines to Hathor to be placed in my room, if it pleases you. And a harp, so that I may play hymns."

Thutmose looked uneasily at Ahmose, searching for some reason to object. But Ahmose could think of none, and reluctantly, she raised her chin.

"Very well. Now get her out of my sight."

The girl went unresisting from the chamber. When she was gone, Thutmose knelt beside Batiret, who shivered on her stool. "Sweet lady," he said, "loyal woman. I cannot make this right for you. I cannot undo what my wife did. You have always been a good servant to the Pharaoh – to my mother, and to me. You will be compensated. And you will be protected; I will see to it. What would you have? Would you be released from service?"

"No, Majesty," Batiret said quietly. "I would continue to serve Maatkare. I would ask only – there is a certain scribe, Kynebu." Batiret's eyes flooded with tears once more, and she dashed them away with the back of her hand. "I would see him if I may, Majesty."

"I believe the lad is outside now," Ahmose said. "Shall I send him in?"

Batiret fell into Kynebu's arms, keening, and he led her gently away, kissing her hand, tucking her trembling shoulders under his arm. The women who had tended her followed, with instruction from Thutmose to communicate with Hesyre in the morning. He wished to know how Batiret fared, and would send her gifts to make some small amends for the abuse she had suffered.

When the lot of them were gone, the young king dropped all his careful self-possession as a child drops a stone into the water. The Pharaoh's majesty and anger fell away from him with an undignified plunk. He rounded on Ahmose, a terrible plea in his eyes.

"Gods, Ahmose, help me. I don't know what to do, how to

handle this."

She drew a deep breath, seeking steadiness that would not quite come. Her legs trembled, and she sank onto the end of the couch, far from where Neferure had perched. "We haven't much choice but to await Hatshepsut's return. And her judgment. The matter concerns her, after all. And she is the senior king."

Thutmose snatched the wig from his head, hurled it against the wall. He pressed the heels of his hands against his eyes, let out a long breath that hissed through his tight-pressed lips. When he had marshalled his emotions, he watched Ahmose steadily for a moment, and she felt pinioned by his stare.

"Is it true?"

She nodded.

Thutmose sighed. "And what of the throne – of our house's safety? How long has this been going on, right beneath the gods' noses, and what kind of punishment can we expect? Gods, Ahmose – none of my women are with child – not a one of them, and not for lack of trying! Is this the price we will all pay? Or will it be something else, something yet to come? You are god-chosen: tell me!"

"Thutmose," she said, and her voice sounded weak even in her own ears, "Majesty, even the god-chosen do not know what the gods intend all the time. I cannot see the end of this. They show me nothing. I am sorry."

He sank onto the couch opposite her, slumped, his shoulders trembling.

"We all must live with the uncertainty," Ahmose said quietly, "until the gods choose to make their judgment known."

CHAPTER TWENTY-EIGHT

THE PHARAOH RETURNED TO WASET in triumph nearly a month later. She stood straight and regal beneath a sun-shade, surrounded by her servants and a chosen cadre of noble ladies who stared with wide eyes from behind their fans as the ships were unloaded. Noble men ranked themselves well back from the quay, heads bobbing like storks as they watched the treasure of Punt come ashore, as they discussed the new wealth, its exotic nature, the obvious bravery and cleverness of Maatkare, her obvious favor with the gods. Basket upon basket came ashore, mounded high, the mounds secured with sturdy, coarse linen, holding the goods tight against the rocking of the ships and the stumbling of the expedition's donkeys through the sands of the Red Land. The cages were borne down the ramps with their baboons huddled close inside. Ivory, silver, obsidian, agate, cloth dyed the intense sun-yellow that Queen Ati had favored – all the fine goods made their way to shore as Hatshepsut looked on in approval, then gave the signal for the litters and chariots and servants to do their part. She stepped aboard her own fine litter, uncurtained so the city might look upon their Pharaoh's victorious face, and made her way to the great palace at the head of the parade.

Her family was waiting to greet her when she was lowered into the courtyard. Thutmose stood in his red and white double crown, arms folded across his chest, eyes distant and troubled in his mask of careful paint. Despite his obvious distress, she smiled to see him. She had been gone only a few months, but it seemed in that time he had grown yet more, become more of a man, and her heart was constricted by the strength of her love for him. *Little Tut*, she said to herself, longing to hold him in her arms again as a tiny babe.

Ahmose waited a step behind the young Pharaoh. The long strands of an ornately braided wig fell over her shoulders to the middle of her chest, framing a face that seemed far more deeply lined than Hatshepsut had remembered. There was something of worry in the look Ahmose turned on her daughter, something of regret and shame – something of fear.

As the parade of goods made its way into the courtyard behind her, accompanied by raucous cheers and the singing of palace servants, the excited chattering of the courtiers, Hatshepsut looked round for Neferure. At first she thought the girl absent. Then she spotted her, standing sedately between two very large palace guards. The size of them made Neferure look as tiny and fragile as a child's doll, and Hatshepsut was overwhelmed by a surge of warmth for the girl, a gladness in her presence that she seldom felt. She stepped toward her daughter, her hands just moving, just beginning to outstretch for a mother's embrace – and stopped short, blinking. Neferure wore the vulture crown upon her head, the golden visage of the goddess Nekhbet rearing from the smooth, pale brow to stare into Hatshepsut's eyes, the wings of lapis and carnelian, malachite and gold falling to either side of the demure little face.

It was the crown of the Great Royal Wife.

There was no time to ask questions. Hatshepsut swept past Thutmose and her mother, led the whole lot through the wide promenade flanked by its rows of sandstone columns, into the Great Hall where her throne awaited her. The parade followed behind, chanting her name, and Hatshepsut could feel joy at none of it, for an unseen dagger as cold as the spray of the cataracts twisted inside her gut. She flowed down the length of the Great Hall like a cataract herself, noisy and wild, her golden sandals slapping against the polished malachite floor, and climbed the steps of the royal dais to all but throw herself upon her throne. Thutmose took his throne with careful ceremony, staring out across the hall, avoiding Hatshepsut's eyes.

Her subjects filled the whole length of the hall, lining the walls to a depth of five or six men, decked in celebratory bright colors, the perfumed wax cones of festival attached to many of their wigs and filling the vast space with a riot of sweet scents. Hatshepsut raised a hand, and the presentation of the goods commenced. The baboons leapt and twisted on their leashes, baring their sharp teeth, snorting at the crowd, glad to be free of their cages at last. The bolts of yellow cloth were unrolled and carried in the many hands of a long rank of servants, past the front rows of the crowds to the left and the right, that they might touch the fine fabric and wonder at its spectacular dye. Senenmut and Ineni led in a contingent of basket-bearers, their shoulders well browned from the desert sun. They tipped the baskets out at the foot of the dais: nuggets of silver ore, sawn rounds of ivory, and whole tusks, too, longer than a man was tall.

Nehesi approached the throne, his great arms wrapped around the breadth of one of the heaped baskets covered with linen. Two dozen more men paraded behind him, each with a basket of his own. Nehesi tore the cover from his burden and upturned it at the foot of the dais. The translucent pieces of resin rattled as they poured onto the gleaming green floor, resins of amber and pale green, deep green and golden-grey, and resins of blood red – all of them crucial in the making of the ceremonial incense that so pleased Egypt's gods. Nehesi's men upended their baskets atop the pile, and it grew in height and breadth, spreading, raising until it was as tall as Nehesi, while the court first gasped, then murmured, and finally raised a cry of *Maatkare! Maatkare!* The cheer shook the very pillars of the Great Hall.

And last, the true prize entered to parade the Pharaoh's victory before her subjects. Teams of men bore poles upon their shoulders, and between the poles swung the saplings –

the precious myrrh trees for Amun's garden, roots bound in sturdy cloth, suspended from the poles like prized birds on a hunter's string. The court exclaimed as one over the sight. It was as fine a good as any trading mission had procured, for now Egypt could harvest its own myrrh in great quantities, and Amun, the lord of all the gods, would never lack for its scent.

When the ripple of voices died away, Hatshepsut called out in a voice that all could hear: "Chancellor Nehesi. Lord Ineni. Great Steward Senenmut. Stand forth."

They did, stepping to the foot of the dais with bowed heads.

The silent Thutmose looked away.

"For your good work in this expedition, I present you with this, before all the court." And she lifted her hand, motioned to her servants. They came at once with the gifts she had decreed, fine collars, necklaces, cuffs and armlets of gold and electrum. Bowls of silver, platters of ebony wood, ivory to make knife handles and drinking cups. Her men accepted the gifts humbly, and when she dismissed them to their places, Hatshepsut felt Thutmose shift on his throne with an irritated twitch.

Hatshepsut was well pleased to return to the comfort of her fine apartments after so long sleeping in gritty tents in the suffocating heat of the desert. But she had no time for the leisurely bath and massage she wished for. She sent at once for Thutmose, and he arrived so quickly that she knew he had been waiting for her summons.

The double crown was gone from his head, but he wore the cloth wings of the Nemes crown affixed to its golden circlet, and Hatshepsut was uncomfortably aware that she wore only a wig. She squinted at him, at his air of defensive swagger. He came through her double doors and halted, folding his arms tightly across his chest, jaw set, saying nothing.

"And where," Hatshepsut said, "is your Great Royal Wife?"

Thutmose scowled. "In confinement, where she belongs. I would have left her there for your return processional, if I'd thought I could have done so without arousing the court's suspicion."

"What right do you suppose you had, to take my heir and make her your wife?"

Thutmose took one menacing step toward her, and she was suddenly aware of his strength and size, of the advantage his very sex gave him. But she did not shrink back from him, did not call her guards.

"This right," he said, tugging at one wing of his Nemes crown. "I am as much Pharaoh as you, Mother, and I am not insensate to the troubles our house faces. I am not unaware of your reasons for going to Punt. After all, you and *Senenmut* took great pains to teach me."

Hatshepsut's mouth tightened at the venom in his voice when he spoke Senenmut's name.

"Imagine our security if I could have had an heir growing in my wife's belly when you returned with all your riches. Anyone who plotted against you – against us – would have been thoroughly undone."

"Why Neferure, my heir? Why not some other woman – any other woman?"

"Because she is four times royal. Or so I thought."

Four times royal. It was an idea that would have come from only one source. "Ahmose."

"She is not to be punished for this. It was a good plan – better than yours – and it would have worked, if not for you angering the gods."

"Be careful what you say, boy."

"I am no boy. I am the Lord of the Two Lands."

"As am I."

"Then behave as if you are, and not like some rekhet slut rutting in an alley."

She crossed to him in two quick steps, and her slap across

his face cracked loudly against the walls of the Pharaoh's chamber. The circlet slipped on his brow, and the Nemes crown hung askew.

"How dare you?" Hatshepsut grated.

Thutmose pressed one hand to his reddened cheek, then dropped it to his side. "How dare *you*?"

Hatshepsut forced herself to walk calmly away from him, sat lightly upon a couch. After a moment, Thutmose, eying her warily, joined her across the empty table.

"Explain this mess to me," she said.

"Neferure has been wild to learn why she can't speak to the gods for years. You would have known that, if you ever paid any attention to the girl, instead of trotting her out for ceremony and then putting her away again like a trinket in a box."

"Speak to me civilly, or you will not speak to me at all."

Thutmose gave one quick, jerking nod of his head, and made an obvious effort to rein in his rage. "With you away, she felt free to search for a reason for her affliction. She found your fan-bearer, lured her into her own palace, and tortured the poor woman with a knife until she told everything she knew."

Hatshepsut pressed her palms together. Her hands shook, and were cold as a dead fish. "Batiret."

"She is well enough. I found her in Neferure's palace and stopped it before any real damage could be done. But she'll have scars; that is certain."

Thutmose fell silent. He blinked rapidly, unwilling to allow tears into his dark eyes. Hatshepsut watched him, fearful of his words, of what he might choose to do now that he knew her secret. She savored the silence, aware it was her last refuge of safety, and might be broken when Thutmose spoke again. But he maintained his silence, and Hatshepsut marshalled enough courage to speak on.

"So, then, what shall we do?"

Thutmose met her eyes, and in his own she saw his ambition, his pride, his love for the throne. She saw his love for her, too, reluctant though it was, and clouded by anger. She knew in a sudden rush that the balance between them had shifted, and now hung poised on a fragile fulcrum – knew that there was no senior king now, but rather two who stood shoulder to shoulder on shifting footing, equally matched in pride, equally matched in desperation to retain their respective power. The change struck her like a blow. She rocked back under its impact, and felt both regret and relief wash across her, throb with her rapid pulse beneath her skin.

He has power now – real power. If I meet him in compromise, he may yet preserve me.

"You know what you must do," Thutmose said slowly.

Hatshepsut's heart cried out, wailing against the blackness inside her chest. But when she spoke her voice was calm, the controlled, regal voice of a king.

"Yes."

PART FOUR

THE GOD'S
JUDGMENT

1466 B.C.E.

Chapter Twenty-Nine

T HE BLACK BULL SNORTED IN the dust of its own churning hooves, a repetitive roar that sounded in time with Hatshepsut's own ragged breaths. It tossed its head to avoid her, rolling its peevish eye toward the gold-plated goad in her hand. Spittle flew from its muzzle, spattered in the dust, and was trampled beneath the bull's blue-painted hooves. The sun-disc tied between its horns shimmered in the sun; the twin plumes rising from the disc thrashed against the sky as the bull bellowed and lunged toward her.

Hatshepsut danced aside. The tail affixed to her belt swung heavy against her legs and stung when it slapped her skin. It was the tail of a bull who had been as black as this one that now reeled around her, calling its anger to the distant crowd.

The people stood well back, watching breathlessly beneath a forest of sun-shades. The ceremonial circuit outside Waset's walls was wide and dusty, hot as an oven in the mid-day sun. Hatshepsut was thirsty, her mouth sticky and dry, her nostrils crusted with dirt. She watched the bull carefully, waited for it to turn, lunged with her goad and dealt it a stinging blow along its flank. It bleated an undignified moo and lumbered in the correct direction – toward the two granite pillars at the far end of the circuit, where the priests of Hapi-Ankh stood waiting. The bull picked up its pace, and Hatshepsut ran after it, the black tail streaming behind her.

The snorting creature saw the two lines of priests fanning out from the pillars, and slowed its progress just enough for Hatshepsut to overtake it. For the final spans they ran together, woman and bull, king and god, she near enough that the heat of the sun reflected from the glossy black hide and beat against her skin. When they passed between the granite pillars raised in celebration of her own glory, she laid a hand on the bull's withers, and felt its answering bellow shiver through her bones. The great ring of watchers – all the population of Waset, noble and rekhet, priest and royal – shouted in acclaim.

The Hapi-Ankh priests slowed the bull with familiar gestures, calmed it with the soothing words it had learned as a calf. Hatshepsut approached with the garland in her arms, and draped it round the bull's neck.

"Renewal!" she shouted, raising one fist to the sky, and the crowd echoed her word.

Nehesi came to her, bearing a skin of cool water, which she received gratefully. It took several long swallows to slake her thirst. She tossed it back to her guard half-empty, and he grinned at her before leading her back to the large dais that had been erected to overlook the circuit.

It was the Feast of the Tail, Hatshepsut's Sed-festival, the jubilee to renew her strength on the throne, to ensure her ongoing glory. Pipers took up an old soldiers' victory tune as Hatshepsut climbed the steps to her shaded throne, and the people, drunk on celebration and on strong beer, clapped and danced.

Hatshepsut fell gratefully onto her seat. The golden plating of her throne was cool beneath the canopy, a pleasure against her sweaty back. The bull's tail stuck out between her knees as she slumped, catching her breath.

Beside her on his throne, Thutmose smiled. "You did well," he said, and she was pleased to note that there was nothing grudging in his voice. Much of the anger he had felt over Neferure's origins had dissipated over the past months as their house continued strong on their thrones, though there was still a vague uneasiness between them. Perhaps there always would be. How could Hatshepsut yield her former power, once so complete and unchallenged, without some conflicted emotion? But Thutmose was gracious in his strength, careful of her pride, quick to share both duty and power equally.

He had no interest, though, in sharing her Sed-festival. It was a celebration typically reserved for a king's thirtieth year of rule, and Thutmose was made uneasy by any breach of tradition. Hatshepsut, recalling that her father Thutmose the First had died before he could celebrate a Sed-festival of his own, suggested the rite on behalf of their entire house. "Not just for me," she had told her co-king, "but for you, and your grandfather, may he live. He sat the throne fifteen years, and I fifteen more. Taken together, the time is right."

But the time was not right according to Thutmose, who had glanced sidelong at Neferure and refused to take part in the ceremonies himself, refused to share in this rite as they had so often shared rites before. Indeed, it was not until Neferure herself had warned that the gods would be displeased by such a breach of tradition that Thutmose agreed to allow the Sed-festival. Despite the girl's warning and Thutmose's superstitious fears, his loathing for his sister-wife was stronger than his dread. He approved the Feast of the Tail in Hatshepsut's fifteenth year chiefly because Neferure opposed it.

Perhaps, too, Thutmose felt a little sorry for Hatshepsut, and wished to appease her or comfort her in some way. She had done what was required of her and sent Senenmut out of Waset, confining him to his estates. Her bed and her heart had both been empty for months, but she still filled her throne, and that, she considered, toying with the long hairs at the end of the bull's tail, was enough for now.

Batiret offered cool, sweet melon and honey cakes on a tray, and Hatshepsut ate hungrily, laughing with her mouth full at the drunken dancing in the circuit below. Batiret laughed along with her mistress, and plied her ostrich-feather fan happily, waving the dust of hundreds of dancing feet away from Hatshepsut's face. Her most loyal and trusted servant had taken some time to recover from the shock of Neferure's mistreatment, but she had steadfastly refused to retire from service in the Good God's personal chamber. After so many years of service she had become more friend than servant, and now, without Senenmut for company, Hatshepsut found herself turning more and more to Batiret for the things she lacked: laughter, comfort, reassurance, joy. For her part, Batiret had not only her loyalty to her mistress as motivation to stay on. With Senenmut gone from Waset, Hatshepsut had been in need of a new Great Steward, and was quick to appoint Kynebu to the position. She suspected her fan-bearer and her steward might soon be wed, and the thought brought her the pain of envy along with genuine happiness. In moments when pensiveness overtook her, Hatshepsut wondered whether Senenmut kept any women at his estate, whether he had filled his bed and his heart with someone else.

In due time, the priests raised their rattles, shaking them hard and long, but it took many long moments before silence spread throughout the drunken crowd and attention returned to the dais. As rested and refreshed as she was ever likely to be, Hatshepsut rose to bless the crowd, which brought about their cheers once more, then she descended with Nehesi to run the circuit – the final rite of renewal she must perform before the Feast of the Tail could truly begin.

Four pillars had been raised, roughly delineating a great rectangle in the flat, dusty earth. The crowd retreated, exposing the grounds of the circuit once more, and as Hatshepsut stepped from beneath her canopy the force of the sun fell upon her, unrelenting in its glare. A faint pain twinged in her hip; she rubbed it away, shook out her legs one at a time, limbering for her last feat of strength. A troupe of musicians struck up a marching tune, and, pausing first before the High Priest Hapuseneb to receive his blessing, Hatshepsut began her run.

At once the sweat sprang up on her body, and it cooled her somewhat in the breeze of her own motion. Soon enough, though, the heat in the air, in her own muscles, became oppressive. She gasped as she rounded the second pillar. Before she was halfway to the third, her throat began to burn. She completed the first of four circuits and loped into her second lap. The faces of the crowd blurred as she passed, stretching into one long swath of brown skin and black wigs, white fans, the flash of canopy poles flitting past her vision. Hands raised as she went, pale palms seeming to slap at her sight. She fell into a steady rhythm of breaths, each one dry as it entered her throat, burning hot as it left. She passed the starting pillar for a second time, swung into her third lap with a wheeze, her breasts painful from the bouncing, her knees protesting, her ankles swollen and stiff. Hatshepsut pushed on. Sweat ran past her temples, onto her chin, her neck. The furrow of her spine was like a river. As she was nearing the final pillar of her third lap, her eyes suddenly caught and held on something in the crowd – a half-familiar face, leaping out amidst the blur of all the other faces, there and gone. She could not stop, but ran on, and several flagging paces more her heart processed the sudden vision, and she recognized the face.

As her final lap came to a blessed close, Hatshepsut turned to look into the crowd in the place where he had been. Senenmut stared back at her, his eyes locking with hers, his mouth forming some word she could not read before she passed him by. Mut's wings snatched up her feet like a hawk snatches up a mouse, sudden and unexpected, and Hatshepsut fairly flew the last stretch of her race.

When Nehesi helped her back to her shade canopy, pressing another skin of water into her hands, Hatshepsut fell into her chair gasping with grateful laughter, tears running down her cheeks to mingle with her sweat.

"It seems you enjoyed that run," Thutmose said, chuckling.

"Oh, ah," she replied, "never have I felt so renewed."

When Thutmose turned his attention to the roasted duck his servants brought him, Hatshepsut slipped her arm around Batiret's shoulders, pulled her close, stopped the girl's hands in their busy-work of toweling the sweat from the Pharaoh's body. "Send me Kynebu," Hatshepsut whispered. "I have a message for him to carry to someone in the crowd."

Batiret saw the pleasure sparkling in her mistress's eye. "Ah, Great Lady. As you wish."

Chapter Thirty

THE MORNING AFTER THE FEAST of the Tail dawned too bright and sharp for Thutmose's aching head. He had managed to conduct himself with seemly restraint throughout Hatshepsut's rites in the circuit, and had kept himself in check for most of the feast. But when the throne of the Great Royal Wife remained empty beside him and he realized at last that Neferure would not present herself at the festival she opposed, Thutmose had sunk sullenly into his cups.

The girl disturbed him when he recalled with a pang of impotent fear the way she had calmly set upon Hatshepsut's servant with that copper knife. He did not know quite what to do with her. He couldn't keep her indefinitely in her confinement cell, only drawing her out to set on display when festival or court made it necessary. Had he not accused Hatshepsut of the very same misdeed? And yet he could not keep her as wife, either. He knew now that he despised Neferure, her unfeeling coldness, her abnormal preoccupation with the divine. He could never again bring himself to lie with her, and so she was useless as a Great Royal Wife. But to set her aside, and leave her free to marry? She would be snapped up by a noble house faster than any former harem girl, and his and Hatshepsut's fears for their security would be redoubled. He might expose the secret of her parentage to the court, but only at great cost to Hatshepsut, the only mother he had ever known.

Thutmose shifted the problem of Neferure this way and

that inside his heart while the Feast of the Tail went on raucously around him, a seething crowd of revelers, acrobats, dancers, servants, laughing and shrieking in the expanse of the Great Hall. And Hatshepsut had sat triumphant and glowing upon her throne, accepting the happy acclaim of her court with a confidence she had not shown in years. She was renewed in truth. Thutmose could not deny it.

Before he had realized just how many cups of wine he'd consumed, Thutmose was well and truly drunk. He barely remembered Hesyre leading him back to his chambers, giving quiet orders to the soldier who guided Thutmose on his strong arm. Now, in the stark light of morning, Neferure returned to his thoughts to plague him like the ache in his head.

He gave himself a long time to collect and order this thoughts, soaking in a warm bath, breathing deep of the bracing, invigorating oils Hesyre selected for his massage, allowing the pleasure of one of a servant woman's kneading hands to soak into his bones. At last, as prepared as he could be, Thutmose slid the Nemes crown onto his brow and stood eying his own reflection in his dressing-room mirror.

"We must go to her – Hatshepsut and I," he said to his own image. "We must decide her fate, and do it today."

And so he met with his co-Pharaoh late in the morning, accompanied as she always was by Nehesi and her new steward Kynebu. Thutmose nodded a silent greeting to her in the courtyard that lay between their two separate apartments. He did not fail to note the somber expression on her face, braced and accepting. She knew, too: the time to sort the tangle of Neferure had come at last.

They walked without word to the confinement chamber, a small, isolated affair set in a wing of the palace mostly filled with the locked doors of storage rooms and disused servants' quarters. Thutmose had been inside a time or two, hoping to pry some explanation from his sister, some remorse, some affection. It was a small room with an even smaller privy and a cold, unadorned bath. A narrow, hard bed stood against one wall, and opposite, a small table with a single stool where Neferure took her meals. The remainder of that wall was dominated by the platform of her Hathor shrine, where seven carved and painted figures stood, each representing one of the Lady's aspects, each staring at Thutmose with hard black eyes. Above the shrine, the wall and ceiling were dark with the residue of countless offerings of incense and charred meat, for Neferure prayed almost constantly. A single door gave admittance to a very confined and none too cheery garden. Thutmose had ordered the single scraggly tree in the garden cut down, the vines cleared from the stones so that Neferure might have no opportunity for climbing. A guard stood atop the roof above her chamber day and night, watching for any sign that the Great Royal Wife might attempt to scale the slick stone of the garden wall, ready to call for reinforcement should she make any bid for freedom.

But Neferure seemed accepting of her captivity. She made no complaints, only made occasional requests via the one woman who tended to her needs for more incense, and oil for her baths.

Thutmose and Hatshepsut drew up outside Neferure's door; Thutmose accepted the salute of the guard on duty with a distracted grunt.

"Well," Hatshepsut said quietly.

"Open the door," was Thutmose's command.

He knew something was amiss the moment the door swung wide. It took him a few heartbeats, hesitating on the threshold, to discern why. The smell of incense was stale and old. Neferure had burned no recent offerings to her seven-faced goddess. Clutched by sudden dread, Thutmose rushed into the room, Hatshepsut and her men on his heels. A tray of half-eaten food lay on the neatly made bed. In the doorless bath, the recessed tub, tiled in old, cracked faience, stood overfull, the water puddling on the floor. He pressed on through the doorway and out into the garden. The light stabbed into his head.

"Gods," Hatshepsut swore. "Where is the girl?"

The garden was a flat expanse of half-dried grass, ringed by weedy flower beds. There was not so much as a bush where Neferure might conceal herself. Thutmose raised his eyes to the roof, caught the salute of the guard on duty there, turned away with a growl.

"She's nowhere – gone!"

"How...?"

Thutmose flashed a sharp eye toward Nehesi; the man at once apprehended the guard on the door, and called down the man on the roof. Both men groveled at the feet of the Pharaohs, clearly as shocked by the disappearance of the Great Royal Wife as the kings. After careful questioning, Thutmose had no choice but to let the men go, dismissing them from service.

Thutmose at last turned to Hatshepsut, his palms up in a show of weak desperation, a gesture he hated and cursed within his heart even as he made it.

"She'll go straight for Iunet," Hatshepsut said. "For the Temple of Hathor."

"Right."

"Nehesi, summon your best men – the men you trust the most. And Kynebu, go – use my seal to secure the fastest boats available; I don't care who owns them; they are mine now. Get to Iunet with all haste. She will be there."

The men sprinted from Neferure's chamber to do Hatshepsut's bidding, and Thutmose turned away from her eyes. In the small room there was nowhere to rest his own gaze but on his wife's shrine. The bronze offering bowl was greasy and black with char on the inner surface, but its outer side was smooth and clean, well-worn from Neferure's near-constant handling. It surface reflected his own image back at him, bent, distorted by the curve of the bowl, a blur that could hardly be said to resemble a man. Around the reflection, the seven Hathors stood tall and perfectly formed, a pretty mockery of his weakness.

The Iteru overspilled its banks, yielding to the endless cycle of time, filling the fields with muddy water and the life-giving silt that would blacken the earth anew when the river receded. There was no hesitation to the flood, not so much as a day's delay: nothing to indicate that the gods were displeased. The reassurance of the flood, its familiar wet odor hanging heavy on the air, should have bolstered Hatshepsut's kas. But weeks had passed without word of Neferure. There was no hint of her whereabouts. Messengers from Iunet and further afield streamed constantly into the palace, as Hatshepsut had commanded, but all of them carried the same news. The Great Royal Wife had not been found.

Other messengers, though, did bring novel word. It was word she would rather not have heard. At the remote borders of the northeastern reach of the kingdom, the Heqa-Khasewet were raiding, sweeping down upon Egyptian outposts and villages, burning and pillaging, making captives of children, raping. The number of Heqa-Khasewet offenses increased with each breathless messenger who fell on his knees before the throne. It was a clear bid for war.

"They must be stopped," she said wearily when she was alone with Kynebu and Nehesi, trying to concentrate on her supper. But Hatshepsut knew she had no stomach left for battle. She was not the youth she once was, and as time had diminished the strength of her body, her worry over Neferure diminished what little taste she may have mustered for bloodshed.

"May I suggest, Majesty," Kynebu said carefully, "that you send the young Pharaoh to deal with the Heqa-Khasewet? Menkheperre is spoiling for action. He is as troubled as you are, I think, over the loss of the Great Royal Wife. Perhaps even more so. A young man sunk so deep in his troubles often finds relief on the battlefield."

And so Hatshepsut summoned Thutmose to her chambers

that very night to put the proposition to him directly. For whatever Kynebu evidently thought, Hatshepsut no longer held the absolute authority of months gone by. She no longer could *send* Thutmose anywhere the king did not wish to go.

Thutmose stood in her doorway, his broad shoulders nearly filling it. He had grown so heavily muscled that she could no longer recall the image of him as a fat, giggling baby, could barely feel the weight of him sitting on her knee as a little boy, still naked and wearing his side-lock. He watched her, wordless, casually attentive for her leave to enter her private rooms, her invitation to sit and drink her wine. She allowed him to stand a moment longer, feeling protective of this territory, the senior king's apartments, the only place where her rule was still absolute.

Thutmose cracked the knuckles of one hand. He seemed content to wait forever, if she should decide to make it so. He was still a youth, brimming with strength and rage. She was a woman falling ever faster toward the middle of her life, and after that....

She jerked her head, her braids swinging across her shoulders, admitting him. Thutmose stepped inside and nodded a dry greeting.

"You have heard of the raids in the northeast," she said.

"Ah, of course."

"We have already proven, you and I, that we can keep this country sailing straight on its keel with one of us on the throne and the other away."

Thutmose, lounging against the backrest of Hatshepsut's couch, sat suddenly forward, his eyes keen. *Kynebu had the right of it.*

"If you think it wise," she said carefully, loathing the deference that prudence forced into her voice, "if you agree, I suggest that you lead the army against the Heqa-Khasewet, while I remain here, overseeing the court."

The air of resentment dissipated from him. He nearly smiled, and his eyes flashed with eagerness. "It is a good plan," he said, his voice low, deep. It had never been high and childlike, surely – she had never heard him call to her across the garden, *Mawat, I've made a palace out of mud, come and see!*

"Good," she said, and her throat constricted unexpectedly on the word. She opened her mouth to say more, then closed it. There was nothing more to say.

Thutmose gazed down at the floor a moment, a furrow appearing between his dark brows. "Neferure..."

"Will be found. I will keep up the search. She is out there somewhere, and I will bring her back."

"I only meant," Thutmose said, stammering a little, suddenly uncertain. The unexpected waver in his manly façade clutched at Hatshepsut's kas, piqued her as a leopard is made keen by the scent of blood. She watched him with pursed lips and said nothing, waiting.

"I only meant, what of the marriage – our marriage? My marriage to Neferure?"

That damned marriage. Had she been a leopard, or the seshep her soldiers had once thought her to be, Hatshepsut would have flexed her claws. The boy had undone her work – he and Ahmose together – removed her heir, loosened Hatshepsut's grip on her own throne. Thutmose saw the stark anger on her face. He glowered, and the return of his petulance only heated her rage all the more.

"Your marriage was no marriage at all," she spat, her weeks of resentment over the issue boiling out of her carefully tended pot all at once, before she could think to stir the heat away.

"It was. It *is* – we said the words before the Priests of Amun."

"She was my heir first – part of my plans. You had no right to undo what I did, and well do you know it."

Her arrow struck true. Thutmose blanched; she drove her point home.

"Now you have endangered us all, Thutmose, and left me to clean up the mess you made. What a child you can be, for all your man's strength."

With careful dignity, his emotions under cold control,

Thutmose stood, smoothed the folds of his kilt. "It is not I who have endangered our house. It is not I who conceived a child in sin, and set her in the temple as God's Wife to offend Amun – even set her on the throne as heir."

Hatshepsut did not reply, but stared at him darkly until he turned away with the smallest smile of triumph.

"Get out of my sight, boy," Hatshepsut said, her words as low as a leopard's call. "You have a war to win. Do not come back to Waset without victory."

Chapter Thirty-One

SENENMUT STOOD ON THE LOWER terrace of Djeser-Djeseru in the blue shadow of a seshep. He watched a white sail furl as the king's ship rounded the bend of the canal. The eye of Horus painted on the sail crumpled, sagged, fell toward the deck. Dozens of oars ran out from the red hull, their caps flashing with electrum in the afternoon sunlight, and the great barque backed against its own momentum, slowing, turning, pointing its nose toward the quay beside the temple road. Along that road the myrrh trees they had fetched from Punt were thriving. They stretched away beneath Senenmut's vantage, an orderly row, tidy, well maintained, even and neat as nothing else in this life was. The ship drew nearer, playing the shadow of its bulk across the line of trees. Senenmut watched the leaves dancing, darkening as the king's barque passed, brightening again in the steady sun. Then he turned and walked from the terrace, deep into the heart of the temple he had made for her, so he would not be seen by any of his lady's servants.

Inside, he dropped his bag of scrolls and tools – the disguise he wore, his excuse for coming to this place. He waited in the appointed location, a private sanctuary not far from the main door. He struck oil alight in a small brazier. The walls came to life around him. They were scenes of Hatshepsut in worship, carrying a shrine before Amun and his holy family, the mother, the father, the child. His lady wore a placid smile, a look of contentment Senenmut had not seen on her face for months – not since Punt – before Punt, in truth. She had been troubled by her own power for many years. *The poor girl.* He recalled her as she had been, flushed, sure of herself, grinning her gap-toothed grin, a woman barely more than a child in her garden, bright beads around her neck. Where had that Hatshepsut gone? And had this Hatshepsut – the one of the carvings, striding bold and unafraid – ever been? Senenmut was sure she had. *She must have been.*

Behind the image of Hatshepsut making her offering, the straight, perfectly proper figure of Neferure stood, stretching forth her hands in a display of worship that was all too familiar. Senenmut ached for his child. He knew – Kynebu had told him – that there had been no word of her whereabouts.

The distant sound of shouts reached him through the temple door, an airy drift of voices rising, falling away, no louder than a gnat's hum. The sailors were casting on their lines. His lady would be here soon.

They had made it their habit to meet at Djeser-Djeseru as often as court would allow. Senenmut stayed well away from Waset, as Hatshepsut had ordered him, keeping to the fine estate he had not seen in years. But Djeser-Djeseru was no part of Waset, and Senenmut had responded eagerly, with pounding heart and singing ka, to the summons Kynebu brought him the night of the Feast of the Tail. He had risked much by returning for her Sed festival. But he could not countenance missing it. It had been worth the danger to see her renewed, dancing with the black bull, goading it, running beside it like the dream of a god, strong, lean, her body brown as the earth, glistening and golden. It had been worth the risk, to watch her lap the four pillars, sweating, her face rigid with concentration, the crowd cheering her – cheering his lady, his king, the sister of his heart. And when their eyes had met in the flight of her passing, Senenmut's blood had burned as hot as it ever had before when he had held her, feeling the urgency of her movements, tasting the sweat of her skin.

Each time they met at Djeser-Djeseru it was the same: the

declaration of their passion, each tripping over the words of the other, the urgency of their kisses, Hatshepsut's tears at the necessity of separation, Senenmut's pain at parting.

Now he heard the familiar tread of her sandals on the stone ramp, a soft scuff, a whisper like an indrawn breath. His arms tingled with the desire to hold her. But his heart tightened with the pain of Neferure's loss, and he could not go to his lady eagerly and sweep her up in his arms. He waited for her to come to him instead.

"Senenmut," she said when she found him, her voice a sad melody.

"Great Lady."

They kissed. The feel of her lips was so familiar. It was a thing he had always felt – a thing his ka had felt before his body was even made.

"You are so quiet," she said. "So melancholy."

"It's Neferure. I have heard – there is still no word of her."

"I'm sorry." She took his hand in both of her own, squeezed him gently. "I worry for her, too."

"Do you?" he whispered.

Outside the temple a flock of geese passed overhead, drawn to the bright water of the canal. Their wings beat the air like horses' hooves in the sand. Senenmut recalled how Hatshepsut had climbed into her chariot, there beside the canal that cut the valley below them, lifted the myrrh branch above her head and declared victory. He remembered the scent of the sap on her palm. Is this what their victory came to? Senenmut banished, their only child disappeared, Hatshepsut a pale, frightened shadow of the king she had been?

She let his hand fall. "I love Neferure as much as I love anyone. Or I have tried to love her so. She has not made it easy for me."

She is only a girl. She had only ever been a girl, he wanted to protest. *You put too much weight upon her. No girl could bear that much responsibility – no girl but you, the girl you once were. And even that girl has cracked and faltered under the strain.*

But he did not wish to upset her, to spoil what little time they had to enjoy one another in the fading afternoon. So he held his tongue and kissed her again.

Their kisses grew more ardent, and soon the door to the sanctuary was closed, shutting out the eye of the sun. Their lamp was the only light. It darkened the grooves that delineated the gods, outlined Hatshepsut as she had been, fearless and bold. Senenmut lifted her, amazed his aging body could still hold her up. He braced her back against the wall. She turned her face away from him, eyes shut tight with an insistent kind of ecstasy, her cheek pressed against the carvings. Senenmut closed his eyes, too, so he could not see the gods watching.

Later they sat catching their breath in a corner, both their backs against the wall now. She leaned toward him almost shyly and rested her head on his shoulder like a virgin girl. He kissed her brow.

"Why do we still do this?" he said. "Why the risk? The gods – why do we chance their anger?"

Her hand crept round his arm. "Because I love you, steward."

"You love Egypt more. You love maat more."

"Clearly I do not." There was a hint of laughter in her voice, the old spirit of arrogant mischief reviving for one pale flicker, dying away again. Then she said soberly, "It makes no difference. The gods will do as they will do, and men can influence them little, if at all."

"Even Pharaohs?"

Hatshepsut said nothing.

"Don't you ever fear this? What it might mean for us in the end – in the afterlife?"

She sat up. "No. Not anymore. Well – sometimes I do. There are times when I remember Punt, and the blood falling on the coals."

Senenmut shook his head, lost, but Hatshepsut ignored his confusion and spoke on.

"You were right, Senenmut, that night in Punt. In the

field, under the moon – do you remember?"

"I am not like to forget it."

"You said that my name and my image are everywhere. I am graven into the very bones of Egypt. Whatever the Field of Reeds may hold for me, I will still live, here." She touched the wall beside her face, let her fingers trace deep into the score-marks of a carving. "It is the best kind of magic, the truest, to have one's name and one's image carved into stone. Stone will never fall away – not for millions of years. My kas will dwell wherever my image stands. And it stands everywhere."

Yet she still seemed sad, for all her brave words. Senenmut pulled her hand gently from the wall, kissed her fingertips.

Hatshesput struggled to her feet, pressing one hand into her hip, cursing the ache she felt there. "Senenmut – I've only just thought of it."

"What is it, Lady?"

"Get your bag – the tools."

He went out into the temple proper to fetch them, and she spilled out after him, a laugh rising up in her chest, the sweetest music Senenmut could ask to hear. She snatched the leather bag eagerly from his hands like a child greedy for sweets, and reached inside to rummage among the tools. She pulled a chisel and mallet free of the mess she had made of his papyrus scrolls, and crouched behind the temple door with the chisel raised.

"Here – what are you doing? You'll ruin my beautiful temple!"

Hatshepsut grimaced at the clumsiness of her own hands, the awkward feel of holding a tool to the vertical wall, so different, as Senenmut well knew, from holding a reed pen above a flat sheet of papyrus. "You will have to help me."

He crouched beside her, put his arms around her body to guide her wrists with his own hands. "What would you carve?"

"Your name," she said simply.

Senenmut rocked back on his heels. "Gods, Hatet. I am not worthy of such a thing. My name in your temple..."

"It is your temple, my love. You made it."

"I made it for you." And unbidden, unexpected, tears sprang to Senenmut's eyes. He wanted to tell her all the words that thudded at once in his heart, crowded on this tongue. That her body was his temple, her kas his offering fire, that no matter how the years and the strain of power fell upon her, lining her sharp, unlovely face, she was always the girl in the garden to him, the one who pressed the scarab bracelet into his hands. He wanted to tell her that she was a light like the stars, arcing across an eternal sky, bright, unending. But faced with her smile, he could not speak. He drew a breath to steady himself, and took her wrists once more, and guided her as she tapped her magic into the stone.

"There," she said when it was done. "And now you will live forever."

With her, Senenmut pleaded silently to the gods – to whatever god still deigned to look upon the two of them with any shred of favor. *Please let it be.*

Chapter Thirty-Two

THE FLOOD RECEDED, THE CROPS were sown, the gods remained content. Hatshepsut went on with her duties, tending to maat attentively between her lone visits to Djeser-Djeseru. The visits grew fewer as Thutmose's campaign intensified in the northeast, and Hatshepsut was required to spend longer hours at court, receiving the steady stream of messengers who brought her news of how the army fared against the Heqa-Khasewet. There were a daunting two weeks when the news was rather dark – a good portion of the Egyptian army destroyed by clever ambushes, and another lot of men lost to the common diseases that plague the camps of campaigns. In spite of their ill parting, she fretted for Thutmose, longed for his safe return. She went each night to Ipet-Isut to leave her offerings and her earnest, almost desperate prayers at every shrine in turn. Every shrine but Hathor's. Hathor's shrine was the territory of Neferure, and Hatshepsut was seized by a superstitious fear when she contemplated going inside. If she did it – if she showed her despised face to the goddess she had spurned – Neferure would never be returned to her, and she would lose Thutmose, too. She knew it with a certainty she had never felt before, not in the fields of Kush, not as her obelisks were raised, not in Iset's arms, or Senenmut's. And so she quietly passed by Hathor's shrine, ducking her head in her Nemes crown so the goddess would not notice her fear.

At last, half a year after he'd departed, a messenger boat

arrived at Waset's quay, the Hapi-Ankh priest onboard sounding a great bronze gong from its stern. "Victory," the man called in a high, nasal voice. "Victory against the Heqa-Khasewet!"

Hatshepsut prepared a festival for Thutmose's return, and when his great, swift war ship moored, the entirety of the city was turned out to greet him. The moment his flashing silver sandals touched the stone of the quay, Waset came to life with cheers. Hatshepsut welcomed him into her two-seated litter, and he kissed her cheeks before the watching crowd, greeting her as a long-gone son greets his mother, lifting her hand with his own above their two crowns.

The litter carried them up the main road thronged with celebrants. Rekhet crowded the rooftops, waving their arms; families of the higher classes leaned from their windows to salute the returning king. The smell of thousands of flowers, flung before the feet of the royal litter-bearers, made the city's usually rather fetid air sweet as a garden in the season of emergence.

Hatshepsut leaned close to his ear and called above the shouts of the city, "You seem content."

He patted her knee, a brusque, happy endearment, and replied only, "I am glad to see you again."

They passed through the gates of the palace followed by Thutmose's entourage – a fine-looking crowd of nobles and ladies, many of them wearing the muted colors and longer wigs popular in the tjatis of Lower Egypt, the northern reach of the kingdom. Hatshepsut stood regally still to receive their bows, then looked round for Thutmose. He was engaged in quiet, almost urgent conversation with a lady in a pale red robe, who nodded attentively, her delicately painted eyes keen on his face. Hatshepsut was loath to interrupt him, and was somewhat tired by the morning's spectacle. She indicated to Kynebu that he should make arrangements for Thutmose's entourage, and made her way to the Great Hall unescorted for the triumphant king's formal reception.

The hall was nearly empty when she reached it, its broad,

gleaming, dark-veined malachite floor faintly echoing with the hurried steps of the staff who went about their last-minute preparations. Lamps as wide as shields burned between the massive painted pillars, their reflective discs glowing like a line of banked stars. Vases as wide as two men standing hip to hip were scattered here and there, and they overflowed with flowers, bright and sweet. A long line of musicians rushed into the hall as Hatshepsut made her way down its impossible length. Her eyes were on the two thrones on the elevated dais, small beneath the towering figures of Amun and Waser on the rear wall of the chamber, but no less imposing, no less obvious in their power. The musicians began to play as she climbed to her throne. She turned slowly to face out into the lovely green length of the Great Hall. It spilled out before her, a river beneath her feet, a current carrying her as it had carried so many kings before.

Kynebu pushed the double doors wide. They were small from this distance, Kynebu a toy of a man clutching the staff of his stewardship. It looked like a reed from the height of her throne.

The steward called above the music. "The Good God, Menkheperre Thutmose, the third of his name."

Thutmose entered with his entourage ranked behind him. He came to the foot of the dais, and to the credit of his followers, most of whom had likely never seen a palace as large as the Great Hall, let alone the hall itself, they kept their eyes appropriately downcast in the presence of their kings.

"Welcome home," Hatshepsut said, "formally, officially. Welcome."

"Is this all?" Thutmose said, a teasing note in his voice. "I expected a feast."

"You shall have one, but not until night falls. Egypt is well pleased with her king, and she will show it." Hatshepsut glanced beyond Thutmose's shoulder at the northern courtiers gathered behind him, a signal that she wished to be introduced.

"Erm," Thutmose said, suddenly tense with anxiety.

Hatshepsut raised her brows, and the tight band of her double crown pinched at her forehead.

The girl in the light red robe stepped forward. She made a deep and humble bow, showing her palms to the throne and holding the pose gracefully, uncomplaining, until Hatshepsut ordered her to rise.

"This is my lady, Meryet-Hatshepsut, daughter of the house of Senedj of Ankh-Tawy." Thutmose paused awkwardly. "She is my Great Royal Wife."

Hatshepsut swallowed hard. Despite her firm hold on the arms of her throne, the Great Hall seemed to spin around her for a moment, whirling away Thutmose's words as he went on introducing the various members of the house of Senedj. He had taken a new woman as his wife, and named her the chief of all his women. There was nothing so unusual in that. Was he not the king? But in doing so, he had clearly repudiated Neferure – cast her out of his own house, divorced her before the gods. He must have, in some temple or other, probably in Ankh-Tawy with Senedj and his brood looking on. Else, how could he have taken this slip of a girl, this little unknown chit who dared to wear Hatshepsut's own name, as his Great Royal Wife?

Then she drew in a slow, deep breath, calming her frantic thoughts, and she smiled at the girl. Meryet-Hatshepsut returned the smile fractionally, testing the Pharaoh's mood. Her eyes shone with intelligence, with the habit of careful consideration, a rare trait in a woman of her age. She could not have been older than fifteen. And Meryet-Hatshepsut – *beloved of Hatshepsut*, the name meant. She must have been born sometime around the end of Hatshepsut's first year of reign. The house of Senedj had meant to send a clear message of support by naming a daughter thus. Hatshepsut felt herself softening toward the northern family, though not by much. For all the flattery of the girl's name, she had still displaced Neferure who, though unaccounted for, was Hatshepsut's own daughter, her own blood.

As the evening fell, Hatshepsut welcomed Thutmose and

his new Great Royal Wife into her chambers, led them out into the garden which was glowing in the last red light of sunset, the blossoms on the hedges like clusters of fire. They made their way to the shore of the lake, Hatshepsut drawing the girl into conversation, probing carefully at her limits, gently assessing. The girl was young, of course, but especially astute. She was as keen-eyed and quick as the best palace stewards, as careful as a seasoned diplomat.

"I should be pleased," the girl said, her voice low but soft, "if your majesty would call me simply Meryet. My whole name is rather long, don't you think? And the latter part sits better upon you, Majesty, than I."

Artfully done. Yes, this Meryet might do very well as a Great Royal Wife. Hatshepsut had to concede that the girl was more collected than Neferure, and more outwardly turned – more concerned, as was proper for a woman of her new station, with the affairs of state, and not just with temples and goddesses. At length their conversation grew thin, and Hatshepsut glanced at Thutmose, who strolled contentedly at his lady's side. Meryet caught the subtle shift of Hatshepsut's eyes, and with a smooth bow she excused herself to some distance away, affecting an interest in the fish leaping from the lake to take the evening flies, pocking and marring its silverine surface.

"Well," Hatshepsut said.

"You're angry," Thutmose replied. He was decked in a lovely, fine kilt of the formal length, brushing his sandals and falling from his golden sash in a spill of sharp pleats like the rays of a sun-disc. An eye-of-Horus pectoral hung upon his chest, enhancing the broadness of his shoulders. His wig was the Nubian style plaited vertically, banded horizontally, short to his chin. He looked so fine a man that Hatshepsut nearly fluttered her hands at the sight of him like an addle-headed old nurse.

"I'm not. Truly. I was at first – not angry, but surprised. But she is a good choice. You chose well."

"Senedj has a powerful house," Thutmose said. "Good

connections, and loyal, as you can see. He has influence over many other houses in his region. He holds them quite tightly. I made sure of it first. I was careful to be sure."

"I am sure you were."

"And Meryet is an intelligent woman – you can tell that for yourself." He seemed anxious that she should agree with him, concerned that perhaps Hatshepsut had not noticed.

She laid a hand on his arm. "She is. A very fine young woman."

"Through her house, we have more sway than ever before in Ankh-Tawy. It's an important city, an important alliance..."

Hatshepsut cut his words short. "And you love her."

He looked down, suddenly abashed, and gave a self-deprecating little laugh. "Yes. And I love her."

"I'm glad, Thutmose."

He drew her close, pulling her tight to his strong young body with one arm about her shoulders. Distantly, from the direction of the Great Hall, the din of voices raised – the nobles of Waset gathering for the feast. "There is more," Thutmose said quietly. "She is already with child."

"Ah," Hatshepsut sighed. "Amun's eyes, but that is good news."

"An heir." Thutmose turned, gazed at his Meryet, who stood with one hand clutching the neck of her robe, her eyes patient on the fish. "The gods are content, I think, Mawat."

"Yes, child. Yes, my Little Tut. The gods are content." Hatshepsut raised her voice. "Meryet, my little daughter, Great Royal Wife. If you have had your fill of the fish, we have a feast to attend. Your husband is home victorious, and Egypt waits to celebrate him."

They walked to the Great Hall together, Hatshepsut's arm linked with Meryet's. The memory of Neferure was a distant pain, distant enough that Hatshepsut found the strength to push it well away.

Chapter Thirty-Three

WALK, THE VOICE CALLED. IT woke Ahmose from a fitful sleep.

"Mut?"

The goddess did not answer.

Ahmose pushed herself carefully up from her bed. Her arms shook with tremors these days, which even honeyed wine could not quite control, and a weakness had overtaken her day by day until she could scarcely walk on her own anymore. She went about her estate with a servant close by at all times, in case she should have need of a younger woman's shoulder, a strong arm.

Walk.

"I am trying," Ahmose muttered. She took a few hesitant steps away from the safety of her bed, and to her surprise, her legs held steady. *It is about time they did what I want them to do.* She had passed her fiftieth New Year – her fiftieth year of life. She was old, she knew, but not so old that her body should refuse to obey. Whatever plagued her had crept up on her faster than it overtook other old women. There were men twenty years her senior still working in the palace – even in the bakeries and forges, the weaving mills of Waset. Not many, but some.

The weakness made her peevish and short with her servants, a fact she regretted, but in the face of these new limitations she could never seem to hold her temper in check for long. It wasn't fair. But justice was a thing for men to fret over, not the gods.

Moonlight streamed through the door to her garden. It made one great bar of silver upon the floor, and Ahmose moved toward it as if drawn upon a string. She stepped into the glow, felt the brush of minute grains of sparkling dust against her cheeks, the motes dancing on the indiscernibly slight rise in temperature within the moonbeam. Eyes closed, her body unshaken and strong again, a memory flooded her heart. She remembered sitting up in a bed, a fine bed with blood-red linens, and reaching out a hand to her husband. Thutmose's face was half moonlight, half shadow, vital and filled with wonder. The bar of light falling over his form split him in two, man and god, and she saw his other guise, the arm and shoulder blue as lapis. She smelled again the perfume of myrrh. She breathed again the breath of life.

"You foolish old thing," Ahmose chided, and opened her eyes.

The garden beckoned her, all shadow and moon-glint. She stepped barefoot into the grass, and when the cool, yielding blades touched her skin, she heard laughter among the flower beds. Ahmose turned her head. Out beyond her low wall, a single dark raft moved with the current of the river, a chip in a flood, tiny, drifting ever away. The laughter sounded again, and she checked herself from running. Ahmose walked with the dignity befitting a lady of the court, a regent, a Great Royal Wife. And yes, God's Wife of Amun, too. She turned a bend in the grassy path. A shape moved from one clump of lilies to the next, glowing white in the moonlight, the gown trailing, a wisp of silk ruffled by movement. The pretty young face was turned just away from her, so she could not be sure of the features, but she heard a voice say, low and rich, "I believe you were right, little sister. He is suitable."

"Mutnofret?"

"Sisters, first and always," Mutnofret whispered, and laughed, her laugh receding into the garden.

She hurried after the white glow, tears burning her eyes, nearly running. She ached with the need to hold Mutnofret in her arms, to press her cheek against her sister's, to let their tears mingle in the immeasurably thin space that separated them, a space of so little consequence that only the salt of their weeping could find its way between. But when she rounded another bend in the path, Mutnofret was gone.

Walk, the voice called.

Ahmose stood still.

She thought, suddenly and absurdly, of Meryet. The girl's belly had grown big, and soon another life would enter the world, another squalling babe, another child running naked through the garden, her wet-nurse cursing her, catching her up, Ahmose's husband laughing at the spectacle, laughing and drawing Ahmose in close beside him. *Let's ride in the chariot*, she whispered, and the child squealed and laughed from somewhere in the garden's depths, and evaded her nurse again.

Meryet will bear an heir for the king. Neferure is gone – poor child, we will never see her again. If only you would have taken pity on her, Mut, Amun, and spoken to the girl. It was none of her doing, none of her fault. She could never help who her father was.

And Hatshepsut – she could not help who she loved, for Ahmose knew as well as any woman that the heart seeks what it will seek, and finds what it will find.

Walk, said the voice. And Ahmose, her mouth bitter with sorrow for Hatshepsut, for Neferure, for kind and good Senenmut, even for herself, found defiance at last. Fifty years she had been the faithful servant of the gods, always turning to their goad, tame as a steer. Now her legs were strong. She could stand on them unshaking.

"No," she shouted at the sky.

Ahmose braced, shocked at her impiety, terrified for one wild heartbeat that in her anger she had undone everything. But the night insects went on singing their mindless chant. The moon moved slowly, shyly behind the branches of a sycamore. And Ahmose whispered, her heart hot with a secret and welcome fire, "I will not."

She smiled.

She heard a rustle in the doorway, one of her women come to check on her, no doubt roused by her shout. Ahmose turned to call to the girl, a good one, no doubt, as they all were. She turned, and opened her mouth to tell her she was all right, was only a foolish old woman enchanted by the moon. But the wrong words came from her lips – words she did not intend to say, words she could not quite understand.

"Lady?" the girl said, a note of panic in her voice.

Ahmose raised a hand to comfort her, felt it raise but saw it hanging limp and useless at her side.

"Oh," she said faintly, "Amun."

Her legs gave way. She fell weak as water into the grass.

Her women brought a guest as dawn broke over the garden wall. Ahmose had indicated, with the last of her strength, her words halting and half of them wrong, that she wanted to lie out there, in the garden among the flowers, so she could watch Re rise full of hope and forgiveness in the morning sky. She did not want any guests, but she no longer had the power of speech, and so she turned her face slowly, with great effort, to see who came to her garden.

He fell onto his knees beside her bed, and his sorrowing face hung close in her clouding vision. He was older, of course, as was she. The lines were so deep around his eyes, and Ahmose feared, gazing at him in wonder and gratitude, that there were more lines of sorrow than of laughter.

I would have made it otherwise, if I'd been able, she said. She said it with her heart, not her throat, for her heart's voice was the only voice left to her.

But whatever the nature of the age that marked him, his look was still gentle, still a little shy, but fulsome and bright with love.

Ineni pulled something from his belt. He held it up to the rising sun. The rays lit it, and it glowed from within: a piece of myrrh, pure as clear water, golden-green, Amun's favorite.

"I kept it for you," he whispered, "from Punt. The best piece in all the god's land."

Her lips twitched, and he smiled back at her.

"Ahmose," he said, and said nothing more. The name was enough, laden with long years of regret, with the pain of loss she herself had felt time and again, with joy and peace and love.

Ineni held the myrrh to her nose. She breathed deep. The odor was sweet: the odor of all the good things in her life. Hatshepsut's soft head as a babe at her breast, the feel of the regent's throne against her back, Mutnofret giggling in the harem, a girl, an adoring sister. The smoke of incense in the temple. The sweetness of Amun's kiss, and Tut's, and Ineni's.

He placed the bit of myrrh into her cold, stiff hand, helped her close her fingers around it.

"To give to your husband, when you see him," Ineni said. "A gift for the lord of the gods."

CHAPTER THIRTY-FOUR

THUTMOSE FOUND HIS WIFE IN the garden, lying on a blanket in the shade of the great sycamore's spreading, fragrant branches. Her ladies were gathered about, spinning quietly or gossiping in whispers, one of them mending a linen gown spread across her lap, the needle she plied glinting in the sun. Meryet did not see him at first, and he hung well back on the path, content to simply watch her, savoring this rare moment of peace.

Motherhood became Meryet as all things became her. She took to it with the same natural grace, the same quiet, thoughtful pride she showed in handling a foreign emissary, presiding over a feast, or sitting the throne of the Great Royal Wife. She lay on her stomach, lifting her soft, pale shoulders with propped elbows. Her collar of jewels swung like a curtain in a breeze, hiding from his sight her sweet breasts, already regaining their shape after her pregnancy, after she had turned the prince over to a wet-nurse to feed. Her neck was slender, graceful, bending gently over the squirming baby. The braids of her wig fell away from her nape as she leaned down to kiss the boy, and she cooed softly, her voice low and soothing.

The prince caught one of his mother's braids in his little fist. She pried his fingers away, laughing, the wet-nurse looking on with a fond, plump smile. Amunhotep, the second of his name, grew quickly. He had been a small thing, even for a newborn, when he had arrived in the world. But he was ringed all about by soft folds of fat now, and Thutmose loved to watch the way the boy's eyes would focus suddenly on a face he recognized, and the little red mouth would open in an early approximation of a smile.

He approached delicately, faintly regretful to disturb the idyll. Thutmose nodded to the women who bowed to him, murmured *Majesty*; he greeted Meryet with a kiss on her brow.

"He can nearly roll over," she told him. "Watch." And she blew on the boy's cheek, making his eyelids flutter, until he turned his face toward her and arched his back, squawking like a baby bird.

"Nearly," Thutmose agreed. He caught the babe's little warm foot in his hand. It was so tiny, so carefully made.

Amunhotep. Meryet had suggested the name, for she was keenly observant even in the hours after giving birth. She saw how Ahmose's sudden death pained Thutmose, for she had been the only grandmother he had ever known.

The death pained both the Pharaohs. Hatshepsut had withdrawn into her chambers and seldom emerged when duty did not demand her presence. She never had made amends with Ahmose over the Neferure mess – had never recalled her mother to court, had not, so far as Thutmose knew, spoken a word to her since Neferure disappeared. "A grudge only wounds the one who carries it," Meryet had said softly when Thutmose tried to explain the state of his family to his new wife. Hatshepsut was surely wounded now, bereft of her mother, made to place Ahmose in her tomb with so many words between them unsaid.

And so Meryet had named their child Amunhotep, the name of Ahmose's father, with the hope that the babe would remind Hatshepsut – would remind them all – of the unbreakable bond of blood and the redemption of renewal.

But it was more than a family name to Thutmose. *Amun is satisfied*, it meant. And surely this child was proof of the god's appeasement. More of Thutmose's women were pregnant now; more children on the way, his house increasing. The succession was secure, the northern sepats well within his control through Meryet's house. The throne was his, and would remain his. Hatshepsut could rest easy. The god was satisfied, in spite of her sins.

Thutmose scooped the boy up. Never had his hands seemed large to him before, but now, holding his tiny son, they were as broad as paddles. Gingerly, he tucked Amunhotep against his shoulder and rocked him, smiling into Meryet's eyes. *Would that this moment could go on forever*, he pleaded in his heart. *Would that I never had to hear another petition, judge another man, fight another battle.*

But Meryet's eyes slipped from his, slid beyond his shoulder and the baby to the depth of the garden. The smile left her face abruptly. Thutmose heard the pounding of sandals on the pathway, and a breathless call.

"Majesty!"

Thutmose sighed, handed the child back to its mother, who tucked Amunhotep protectively against her breast. The baby fussed at the interruption.

It was Kynebu who came running, Hatshepsut's chief steward. The man was usually the very image of calm control, but his face was terrible with worry, a mask of twisted grief.

Hatshepsut. Thutmose was on his feet before he realized he had moved. "What is it, man? Speak!"

Kynebu, forgetting himself, clutched Thutmose's arm, as raw a gesture as if they had been brothers alone in their father's house. "Majesty...a...a good and loyal servant to the throne is dead."

Not Hatshepsut, then. Thutmose drew a deep breath of relief. "Who?"

Kynebu's head dropped suddenly into his hands, and he gave voice to a low wail of pain. "Senenmut, my lord."

Thutmose's immediate reaction was anger. He had not thought of the steward's name in nearly two years, not since he had made Hatshepsut send the man away. Then his thoughts were all for Hatshepsut, his mawat, already grieving the death of her mother and the disappearance of her daughter.

"Does Hatshepsut know?"

"Not yet," Kynebu said. "I thought it better to tell you first. I thought...I thought it best to show you."

"Show me?"

"How he died, lord." The quiet chill in Kynebu's voice gripped Thutmose's heart with a fist hard as stone.

Senenmut's estates were not far to the north of Waset. Thutmose, tailed by ten of his personal guard, covered the ground quickly in his chariot, Kynebu clinging grimly to the rail beside him, weeping silent tears. They crossed the long causeway that passed above Senenmut's fields, drew rein in his courtyard – fine and well maintained, Thutmose noted, even through the urgent worry gnawing at him. Grooms appeared from the great house to hold the horses' reins, their faces red with weeping.

"Take me to him," Thutmose said, and Kynebu, ducking his head in obedience, led the way.

They passed from an outer portico through a room – quaint by Thutmose's standards – set for isolated living: a solitary couch, a lone table, a single tall harp in the corner, dust clinging to its strings. A niche in the wall held a few statues of gods, but the offering bowl was clean and bright, seldom used. Kynebu hesitated on the threshold of another door. Thutmose could see beyond his guide a plain, serviceable bed, a dressing chest that lacked ornate carving. And the rank stench of blood hit him with a terrible force.

"Here," Kynebu whispered.

Thutmose stepped past him.

The floor of the chamber was bright with blood, a lake of it, dark and congealing around its edges. A great cloud of flies circled above, singing their unceasing, sickening tune. The man lay sprawled face-down in the pool. His kilt was soaked red; it clung to the backs of his legs.

"Majesty," a low voice muttered.

Thutmose whirled. Nehesi stood, his dark face rather blanched, his eyes dull with sorrow.

"I have stood vigil ever since Kynebu told me. I have allowed no one to touch the body."

"Why?"

A strange question – Thutmose knew it sounded both strange and childish the moment it left his lips.

"I wanted you to see it first. To see the manner of his death."

Thutmose did not need to roll Senenmut's corpse over to see the manner of his death. He had spent enough time on the battlefield to know. Only the vein that tracked up the side of the throat would bleed so profusely, forcefully enough to create a lake of blood.

"His throat was cut."

"Ah, Majesty. By a knife."

A chill fell into his ka so intense that Thutmose's legs tremored. He stare around the room, and noted a line of bloody prints leading out into the garden. The footprints were small – so small only a child could have made them, or a very small woman.

"Neferure," he said.

Nehesi nodded.

"Very well." Thutmose gripped his self-possession desperately, grateful his voice did not shake. "Kynebu, tell one of my guards to take you back to the palace. The Great Royal Wife and my son are to be placed in secure chambers, with my personal guard to watch them at all times. *At all times.* Am I understood?"

"Ah, Majesty." Kynebu fled the house, obviously grateful to be gone, grateful for work to which he could turn his mind.

If only I could shut out this horror as easily as he, Thutmose thought.

"Summon the poor man's servants, Nehesi. They must take his body to the palace enbalmers. I will pay the cost myself. He will have all the funeral rites of a noble – of one who was loyal to the king."

Nehesi's jaw tightened. His eyes closed briefly – his only concession to grief. "We went to Punt together," the man said at last. "He was my brother – my brother in service to our lady."

Thutmose laid a hand on his arm, the only comfort he could think to offer. "I know."

"Who will tell her?" Nehesi asked.

"I suppose I must, though it pains me to think of it."

"If you will allow it, Majesty, I will come, too. This is a burden one man should not carry on his own. Not even a king."

CHAPTER THIRTY-FIVE

HATSHEPSUT TOOK THREE WITH HER to Djeser-Djeseru, and no one else.

Batiret, her scarred arm strong beneath Hatshepsut's quaking hands.

Meryet, pretty and fine, young and worthy, still untempted by life, unmarked by sin.

Sitre-In, hobbling on a staff of ebony wood, most of her teeth gone, a little sack of myrrh swinging from her hand.

They sat silent around Hatshepsut beneath the canopy of her boat, folding their bodies around her, shielding her from the eyes of the people and the gods. They touched her with gentle hands, they whispered to her in sympathy, in love, but she and her kas were far distant, beyond their reach, drifting.

Batiret guided her ashore, and Hatshepsut stood on the quay, gazing at her temple with dull eyes.

This is all that is left of him, she thought. *It is all that is left of me.*

They walked with her down the long avenue, the paving stones bright in the unforgiving sun. She went at a dawdling pace, absently trailing her hand along the base of a seshep statue, then the rough bark of a myrrh tree, the stone of a statue, the hot dryness of a tree. She remembered the soldiers crying *Seshep!* in a long-lost place, a place that had never been, shouting the name to a woman who had never been, and never would be. That woman was rent by the lion-claws of grief – a lifetime of it, piled one loss upon another, one duty upon another, one sin upon another. When she pressed

313

her hand to her face to rub at her tears it smelled sweetly of the trees' sap. *Like our salvation,* her heart whispered to Senenmut. She saw him smiling at her beneath Khonsu's white eye, heard the whisper of millions of dark leaves. And his laugh turned into the call of a hunting cat, the black of his eyes to smoke rising on a fire in Punt.

Hatshepsut climbed the ramp to her temple's terrace, where her own face smiled at her from countless seshep. She had never looked so at peace, so strong. She turned in the midst of the statues, bewildered, circling to take in the sight of her own self. She was stone – hard and unchangeable, and yet she was changed.

She had meant to go with her ladies into Amun's dark sanctuary, to throw herself down in the god's presence and admit defeat, weep in abasement, beg for mercy. But she passed the door, and her ears caught the sound of a chisel, light and far away, a happy ring. She sank to her knees behind the door and found with her fingers his name, traced it in the cold, pale stone.

Senenmut.

A wail ripped from Hatshepsut's throat. She screamed her hurt, screamed her losses, one long, ragged, wounded cry that went on and on into eternity, until she drew a burning breath and screamed again, rocking. She fell against the wall, let her tears run into the symbols of his name, and she sobbed against the stone, "Live."

But he did not live. Nor did Iset, lolling on her bed, sparkling in chains and cuffs of silver, more beautiful than any woman had ever been. Nor did Ahmose, leaning over Hatshepsut in her bed, scowling at the wound across her groin. Neferure did not live. Neferure, still wet with her birth water, held close in Senenmut's arms. Her brother Thutmose, riding with her in the Feast of Opet. Her father, holding her upon the rail of a ship while the pyramids slid by, dark in a red, red sky.

Senenmut did not live. Senenmut, holding her up against the wall of the sanctuary as he entered her, his face earnest and guilty with passion. Holding the black braid in his palm in the darkness of a starlit garden. *We catch falcons.*

Hathor had won – had exacted a payment from Hatshepsut too weighty to bear. Hathor had punished her for her pride, her singular focus on the throne. And Amun – Amun had spurned her, leaving her to grope in doubt.

Why, Father? she demanded of Amun, one last flicker of pride giving her strength to ask, a dying ember in her heart. She stared about her, searching for an answer, stared out into the terrace where the sunlight was impossibly bright. When she closed her eyes tight, crumpling under the blow of Amun's silence, the terrace light echoed against her lids as green as resurrection fire.

Her ladies drew close about her, bending to offer their comfort, their voices, their hands.

She shrank against the temple wall, clinging to it, clawing it, knowing it was the only afterlife she would have. For her kas would be damned when she went to the Field of Reeds. Damned for her pride, and damned for her love.

And so Hatshepsut pressed herself against the stone, until her skin burned with its rough grit, until it scraped her raw and she bled. She pressed, seeking in vain to push herself into the blocks themselves, where she might find Senenmut dwelling, moving like water in the tracks of his carvings, waiting in the stone of his creation.

Truly my heart turns this way and that, when I consider what the rekhet will think and say - people who will see my monument years later, who will speak of what I have made. ... As long as my father Amun refreshes me with the breath of life, it must be said that I have worn the white crown, and I shine in the red crown. I have ruled the Two Lands like Horus. I am strong like the son of Nut. Re sets in the boat of night and rises in the boat of morning. As long as the sky is there and Re's work is steady, I shall be forever like the star that does not end. I shall reign in the afterlife, bright as Aten.

-Inscription from the obelisk at Ipet-Isut by Hatshepsut, fifth king of the Eighteenth Dynasty

HISTORICAL NOTES

I write this note with more than a little trepidation.

For both The Sekhmet Bed and The Crook and Flail, I've received lovely feedback from readers praising my accurate working of real history into these fictional portrayals of the Thutmoside Dynasty. Well, as I worked on Sovereign of Stars, let us just say that "my heart turned this way and that" nearly as much as good old Hatshepsut's. I'm afraid I played much faster and looser with history in this book than I am used to doing, and I feel I must make amends for it here by setting the record straight.

I confess to freely reorganizing events in Hatshepsut's reign to suit the particulars of my story. The golden-crowned obelisks were not commissioned until the fifteenth year of Hatshepsut's kingship, and finished in the sixteenth. This is clearly indicated on the obelisks themselves, so I plead no contest to messing with reality here. I moved the event forward in Hatshepsut's reign to about the seventh year, simply because it was just the thing I needed to shape the characters' development, to set them up for the denouement of the novel. As Hatshepsut's approximately twenty-two years on the Horus Throne were characterized by a wealth of monuments, temples, and restoration projects on a scale unseen in the reigns of most other Pharaohs before and after, I figured she was likely to have built something interesting and grand in her seventh year. It just wasn't anything fancy enough to replace the less impressive pylon gates of her half-brother Thutmose II.

(If you are wondering, by the way, whether it gives an author of historical fiction a certain thrill to rejigger actual events from world history in order to suit her own creation, well, I plead no contest on that count, too.)

I also changed the date and circumstances of the expedition to Punt, moving it forward in time by about four years. It actually occurred around her tenth year on the throne, and while it was considered a momentous enough achievement to become one of the featured stories depicted on the walls of Djeser-Djeseru, Hatshepsut almost certainly did not visit Punt herself. She sent her representatives, Nehesi, Ineni, and Senenmut. However, I wanted my fictional Hatshepsut to experience Punt for herself, and particularly to meet the strange and mysterious Queen Ati, and so I contrived an excuse to send her there. I think the real Hatshepsut would have wished to go, to see the fabled God's Land for herself. Why not?

The exact location of Punt remains a total mystery, but that it was a real place, visited now and then by the ancient Egyptians for purposes of trade, is not in dispute. In fact, the expedition scene in Hatshepsut's temple is one of the key pieces of evidence for Punt's factuality. The carvings of the exotic fish in the water below her expedition's boats are so specific and so accurate that scientists have been able to identify them down to the species name – and have used this information to place Punt somewhere along the Red Sea, or at least accessible via the Red Sea. That is about all that's known of its location, though, and less is known of its culture. Most of what we do know – the type of housing, the fashions, the trade goods – comes again from Hatshepsut's temple.

And let us discuss for a moment poor Neferure. It's here I feel I have the most special pleading to do, waving my artistic license frantically in the air.

Hatshepsut's daughter – her only child, depending on which Egyptologist you ask – is another mystery of the 18th Dynasty. Not much is known about her roles or her fate. She appeared very prominently in inscriptions and art throughout Hatshepsut's reign, up until approximately year 17. At that point, she disappeared entirely from the record. It was never clear whether she was married to Thutmose III or not, and there is much speculation amongst professional and armchair Egyptologists whether she was Hatshepsut's heir, and whether Hatshepsut intended the throne to pass from herself down a new line of female Pharaohs. We will never know the truth of it. The only clear certainty about Neferure's place in the historical record is that she served as God's Wife of Amun, that, like all God's Wives, she played a prominent role in religious ceremony, and that she disappeared when she was still very young – presumably dying in her late teens, though even that is uncertain, as her tomb has never been found, nor has any inscription that seems to reference either her death or her continued life amongst Hatshepsut's or Thutmose III's court. She simply vanishes without further mention, though later in Thutmose III's reign some monuments show where Neferure's name has been carved over with the name of one of his confirmed wives, Satiah.

It has been popular in Egyptian fiction to portray Hatshepsut as the usurper of Thutmose III's rightful throne, and Thutmose III as a wronged man biding his time until he could rescue his kingdom from the clutches of his wicked stepmother. It's a dramatic tale, but has been known not to be the truth for a long time. Hatshepsut and Thutmose III ruled jointly for about twenty-two years, until Hatshepsut's death from natural causes. The pair evidently worked well together and were mutually content to share power. Otherwise, one would have killed the other early on and had done with it. Rather than going with the popular depiction of Hatsheput as usurper and Thutmose as vengeful victim, I did my best to tell a story that was nearer to historical fact – in this respect, if in no other. I think the reality of the two Pharaohs' peaceful co-rule provides a much richer opportunity for drama and poignancy than the familiar myth of the quintessential wicked stepmother.

I hope you agree.

-Libbie Hawker
Seattle, WA, 2013

Notes on the Language Used

This novel is set in historical Egypt, about 1500 years before the Common Era and roughly 1200 years before Alexander the Great conquered the Nile. With the dawning of the Greek period, a shift in the old Egyptian language began. Proper nouns (and, we can assume, other parts of the language) took on a decidedly Greek bent, which today most historians use when referring to ancient Egyptians and their world.

This presents a bit of a tangle for a historical novelist like myself. Culturally, we are familiar with Greek-influenced names like Thebes, Rameses, and Isis. In fact, even the name Egypt is not Egyptian; it has a long chain of derivations through Greek, Latin, and French. However, the historic people in my novel would have scratched their heads over such foreign words for their various places, people, and gods. And linguistically, the modern English-speaking reader will probably have a difficult time wrapping her head and tongue around such tricky names as Djhtms – an authentic and very common man's name for the time and place where Sovereign of Stars is set (rather the equivalent of a Mike or Tom or Jim).

On the balance, cultural authenticity is important to me, and so I've reverted to ancient Egyptian versions of various proper nouns and other words in the majority of cases. A glossary of ancient Egyptian words used in this book, and their more familiar Greco-English translations, follows.

In some cases, to avoid headaches and to preserve (I hope) the flow of the narrative, I have kept modernized versions of certain words in spite of their inauthentic nature. Notably, I use Egypt rather than the authentic Kmet. It is a word that instantly evokes the reader's own romantic perceptions of the land and time, whatever those may be, and its presence in the story can only aid my own attempts at world-building. I have opted for the fairly Greeky, English-friendly name Thutmose in place of Djhtms, which is simply a tongue-twister; and the word Pharaoh, which is French in origin (the French have always been enthusiastic Egyptologists) rather than the Egyptian pra'a, simply because Pharaoh is such a familiar word in the mind of a contemporary reader. Wherever possible, I have used "Pharaoh" sparingly, only to avoid repetitiveness, and have instead opted for the simple translation of "king." I've also decided, after much flip-flopping, to use the familiar Greek name Horus for the falcon-headed god, rather than the authentic name Horu. The two are close, but in every case reading Horu in my sentences interrupted the flow and tripped me up. Horus flies more smoothly on his falcon wings; ditto for Hathor, who should properly be called Hawet-Hor, but seems to prefer her modernized name.

As always, I hope the reader appreciates these concessions to historical accuracy and to comfort.

GLOSSARY

ankh – the breath of life; the animating spirit that makes humans live

Ankh-Tawy – Memphis

Anupu – Anubis

deby – hippopotamus

Djeser-Djeseru – "Holiest of Holies," the name of Hatshepsut's mortuary temple, known today as Dier-el Bahri.

Hapi-Ankh – Apis, the bull god worshiped in Ankh-Tawy (Memphis).
Heqa-Khasewet – Hyksos

Ipet-Isut – "Holy House"; the temple complex at Karnak

Iset – Isis

Iteru – Nile

Iunet – Dendera

ka – not quite in line with the Western concept of a "soul" or "spirit," a ka was an individual's vital essence, that which made him or her live.

Kush – Nubia

maat – A concept difficult for modern Westerners to accurately define: something like righteousness, something like divine order, something like justice. It is to a sense of "God is in His Heaven and all is right with the world" as the native Hawai'ian word *aloha* is to an overall feeling of affection, pleasure, well-being, and joyful anticipation. It is also the name of the goddess of the concept – the goddess of "what is right."

mawat – mother; also used to refer to mother-figures such as nurses

Medjay – An Egyptian citizen of Nubian descent

rekhet – people of the common class; peasants

sepat – nome, or district

seshep – sphinx

sesheshet – sistrum; ceremonial rattle

tjati – vizier; governor of a sepat or district

Waser – Osiris, god of the afterlife, the underworld, and the dead. Also used as a prefix when referring to a deceased king.

Waset – Thebes

Acknowledgments

I owe big thanks to Rebecca Lochlann and Richard Coady, two historical novelists whose work I admire very much. I was fortunate to receive advance critiques of this book from Rebecca and Ric, and the book (and my writing in general) is much better for it.

Whenever I finish an Egyptian historical novel, I feel I ought to thank Joyce Tyldesley and Barbara Mertz. These two Egyptologists have written the best and most readable nonfiction works pertaining to ancient Egypt I've ever read. I turn to their books constantly while researching and writing my own.

A heap of thanks to my readers, whose great enthusiasm for the first two books in this series kept me working away happily on this one as well as the fourth and final book in this series. It is a very gratifying experience to receive emails asking when the next books are expected, and to read about readers' enjoyment and anticipation in reviews. I appreciate it so much. And thanks, readers, for your understanding when I pushed the release date back so I could get married.

Speaking of which, my biggest thanks of all go to my husband, Paul Harnden. I couldn't do any of this without his big goofy smile for motivation. Every story I write is for him.

About the Author

Libbie Hawker joined the independent literature movement after her first novel, *The Sekhmet Bed*, was thoroughly rejected by every publisher on Planet Earth. Since then, *The Sekhmet Bed* and its sequel, *The Crook and Flail*, have enjoyed three years of steady presence on Top 100 lists in the largest bookstore in the world, and Hawker has become a leading voice in the genre of historical fiction, where she strives to recreate the drama and humanity of the past with literary style and authentic atmosphere.

When she is not writing, she's painting, hiking through the mountains of the Pacific Northwest, or canning in her kitchen, which is much too small for canning.

Find out more on her web site: LibbieHawker.com

Made in the USA
Columbia, SC
17 March 2018